FIRST

CUT

...

Also by
Leah Ruth Robinson

BLOOD RUN

FIRST CUT

...

Leah Ruth Robinson

AVON BOOKS NEW YORK

FIRST CUT is an original publication of Avon Books. This work is a novel and has never before appeared in book form. Any similarity to actual persons or events is purely coincidental.

AVON BOOKS
A division of
The Hearst Corporation
1350 Avenue of the Americas
New York, New York 10019

Copyright © 1997 by Leah Ruth Robinson
Interior design by Kellan Peck
Published by arrangement with the author
Library of Congress Catalog Card Number: 96-28358
ISBN: 0-380-97458-4

Library of Congress Cataloging in Publication Data:

Robinson, Leah Ruth.
    First cut / by Leah Ruth Robinson.
        p.   cm.
    I. Title.
PS3568.0297F57   1997   96-28358
813'.54—dc20   CIP

First Avon Books Hardcover Printing: April 1997

AVON TRADEMARK REG. U.S. PAT. OFF. AND IN OTHER COUNTRIES, MARCA REGISTRADA, HECHO EN U.S.A.

Printed in the U.S.A.

FIRST EDITION

QPM   10   9   8   7   6   5   4   3   2   1

For my husband, John Rousmaniere
With love

In memory of Bruce King

And with special thanks to my "first readers": Maureen Baron; Dr. Douglas Bernon, a psychologist and psychoanalyst practicing in Newport, Rhode Island; Dr. Geraldine Yarnal Dawson, physician and dear friend; Dr. Edwin G. Fischer, associate professor of surgery and neurosurgery at Harvard Medical School and New England Deaconess Hospital, who I hope someday will write his own novel; my agent Barney Karpfinger, who has stuck with me through thick and thin; and Trish Lande Grader, my editor at Avon Books.

CHAPTER 1

AFTER it happened, I tried to shake it off.

This was New York, after all. Citizens got pushed in front of subways by crazy people, thirteen-year-olds shot one another in Harlem; you name it, it happened. That summer we even had rumors of a new serial killer, a guy who had raped and bludgeoned two women since June, each time leaving a child's babydoll at the scene of the crime. You couldn't pick up the paper anymore without being screamed at by headlines: GRIM FORECAST WAS RIGHT: LAWMEN PREDICTED BABYDOLL KILLER WOULD RAPE AGAIN or HOW THE MANIAC STRIKES: COPS HUNT ELUSIVE FOE.

So when I was walking up the hill from Riverside Drive on my way to the hospital at 6 A.M. and somebody hit me from behind and sent me flying, the first thing I thought was, Jesus, it's the Babydoll Killer. I tried to get up and he barked, "Stay down!" and before I could recover my wits, he was yanking the tails of my Brooks Brothers button-down shirt out of my chinos and pulling it over my head. Oh my God, oh my God, I thought, panic closing my throat, this is it, this is it—

1

He's going to rape me.

But he didn't rape me. He pulled my shirt over my head so I couldn't see him.

Then he ran away.

By the time I got myself untangled from my shirt, he was twenty yards off, running flat-out, an athletic-looking man in a T-shirt and running shorts, wearing a backpack. I thought maybe he had seen someone and had been scared off, but when I looked around for a would-be savior, I saw no one. Of course, the moment I took my eyes off my assailant, he disappeared.

Finally the adrenaline kicked in and I was in a familiar mode: Dr. Evelyn Farley Sutcliffe to the rescue; start the theme music, roll the credits. PAN CAMERA across a busy New York City hospital emergency room. ANGLE ON a tall, slender woman: me. Light brown hair cut in a modified wedge, hazel eyes, tortoiseshell eyeglass frames. Mid-thirties; I went to medical school late. I carry all the accoutrements of Welcome-to-the-Big-Time-Medicine. The white coat. The hospital badge with my photo and name in big letters. The stethoscope slung casually around my neck, the tourniquet for drawing blood tied through the belt loop of my chinos, the penlight, the otoscope for looking in people's ears and the ophthalmoscope for looking in their eyes. I have endured medical school, internship, a year of residency with four to go, little sleep, bad hospital food, and patients' vomiting on my shoes. All this shows in my face: eyes and mouth full of exhaustion and concern, mascara smudged, lipstick slightly askew.

But I am usually ready for anything, and I have seen a lot worse in the ER than a woman who has been knocked down and had her shirt pulled over her head. Let's keep everything in perspective, I told myself. At least it wasn't the Babydoll Killer. I assessed the patient: me. Nothing seemed broken. I didn't find any blood. My glasses were a little loose at the hinges, but I had an optician's repair kit in my locker at the hospital. I started to get to my feet, but on second thought sat right back down again, on the front steps of a brownstone. I didn't trust my vestibular responses to keep me upright just yet. Besides, before I went any-where I wanted to collect a few brain cells and formulate a mental picture of what the guy looked like.

Unfortunately, I hadn't seen much. A glimpse of him after he knocked me down, but I couldn't tell you what color hair he had or what color eyes. I had the impression he had light eyes and hair, but I couldn't swear to it. Running away from me, he seemed athletic. Well-muscled thighs and calves. But he didn't seem like a *big* guy. Not bigger than I was, at least. I was six feet tall with my shoes on. I sighed. I could just see myself reporting this: "Well, officer, he was six feet tall and had really *nice* legs."

Nonetheless, I looked at my watch and noted the time. Six-oh-seven A.M. I noted the weather, too: dull, overcast sky, so humid you could take the air and wring it out like a wet washcloth. The regionwide steam bath was expected to intensify, too, with ominous predictions that it would reach the highest humidity ever recorded in these latitudes. It was hot already and would be very hot later if it didn't rain. Nothing like August in New York City.

Finally, I got to my feet—slowly, dusted myself off, and tucked my shirt back in my chinos. If I didn't hustle, I wouldn't have time for breakfast before rounds. I wasn't hungry, but I knew from experience I'd pass out at the least convenient moment possible if I didn't eat breakfast, especially if there was a code and I wound up in a room with five or six doctors and nurses but only three people's worth of air. I also never knew whether I'd get a chance for lunch or not; breakfast might be the only thing I'd eat until well into the evening.

I started up the hill again toward Broadway, trying to psych myself up for food of any kind.

I was just about mentally prepared for a mozzarella-and-basil sandwich on a nice French roll from Sami's Café when I noticed the right sleeve of my shirt felt wet. It was wet, all right: with blood. I rolled my sleeve up, but I couldn't see at first where it was coming from. After a second I deduced my elbow was bleeding on precisely that point I couldn't see no matter which way I twisted my arm. Guess I smacked it when I fell.

But wait a minute—hadn't I fallen forward? How could I have hit my elbow?

Because you were turning toward him when he hit you. You heard him coming up on you from behind, running, and you were turning to look when he hit you.

He knocked you on your back.

I realized with a sudden chill that there had been something familiar about my assailant. Something familiar—but *what*? I racked my brain all the way to the hospital, but I couldn't put my finger on it. Not even after five minutes of staring into space and concentrating hard while I wolfed down that mozzarella-and-basil roll at Sami's, my favorite breakfast, and knocked back a double espresso.

Not for lovin' nor money.

As Dr. Michael Healy might say.

When I got to the hospital and bumped into him in the corridor outside the doctors' locker room, that wasn't what he said.

He said, "Kee-*rist*, Ev, are you out of your mind, letting a patient bleed on you like that?"

"What are you talking about?" I said. "That's not a lot of blood. Besides, it's mine." After such a tantalizing lead-in, of course, I then had to tell him what had just happened to me.

Having been born in the old country, Healy retained certain fanciful notions about women. Despite his relative youth (he was thirty-seven), he pitched headlong into a froth of chivalry not seen since the days of Camelot. "Gooot Lard, wummin!" he cried. Excitement always accentuated his charming Scots-Irish lilt—an accent peculiar to County Donegal—sometimes to an utterly imcomprehensible, full-blown brogue. "Are ye owl right?" He threw his big arms around me, clutching me to him with an urgency that took my breath away. He had just showered. His hair was still wet and he smelled of a delicate citrus aftershave, and baby powder.

The baby powder somehow accentuated the rawness of his sexuality.

I disentangled myself from his embrace before I swooned in it.

"Let's have a look," he insisted, hauling me into the doctors' locker room and rolling up my sleeve. He rummaged in his pockets, fished out a couple of alcohol wipes, and gently swabbed my elbow.

"Mick, I really don't think I need the attention of the assistant chief of neurosurgery for a boo-boo."

He ignored me, and I gave in. Might as well take the opportunity to admire him close up. This was a man you could feast your eyes on. Sandy-colored hair falling rakishly into cornflower-blue eyes. Nose broken in some long-ago street fight. The two scars from the accident three and a half years ago—one across his forehead like a second right eyebrow, the other a perfect half-moon on his right cheek—lent his face a romantic cast. Lips—

I swallowed. Now, now, Sutcliffe, I chided myself.

"Hmm," Mick said. As he calmed down, his accent leveled out to its baseline lilt. "Couple of butterflies should do it."

"You can't patch me up with butterflies," I protested. "I'll have limited range of movement. Do me a favor, just wrap it."

"Might bleed."

"Let it."

Meanwhile, having extracted myself from his embrace not sixty seconds earlier, I was trying to think up some way to get back in it. Mick had that effect on women, and not all of it was lust. I wanted to take him in my arms, banish his sorrows. Three and a half years was a long time for a man still to be in mourning.

Then again, not many people had been through what he'd been through. He had awakened in the midst of a great commotion, people shouting and crying, to find two of his four brothers bending over him, their faces streaked with shock and tears. They were lifting him onto a stretcher. He remembered the accident, the car flying up the front steps of Corpus Christi Church as he and his family were coming out after midnight mass—but where was his wife? Where were his kids? No one would tell him anything. When he tried to get off his stretcher to go look for them, the medics tied him down. Finally, in the emergency room, Healy's father arrived with the horrifying news: Cathy, Mick's wife of eleven years, and Brendon and Michael James, Jr., his twin nine-year-old sons, had died at the scene. A drunk driver, Mick's father said bitterly. Drank a fifth of bourbon at the office Christmas party, got behind the wheel of his car, and drove the fucker seventy miles an hour up the steps of a *church*, can you believe it? On *Christmas Eve*. Right through the front doors and into the vestibule. Murdered six people, not just Cathy and the boys, but Monsignor, too, and Monsignor's elderly parents visiting from Chicago. Another fourteen people, Mick included, had been hospitalized.

At thirty-three years of age, Healy suddenly found himself a childless widower. After he got out of the hospital, he did the macho thing and drank. He was never drunk in surgery to anyone's knowledge, but people said he often staggered in hung over, alarming the residents and interns who had to operate with him. Finally one of his brothers asked him: Was he going to kill himself with booze just like that guy had killed Cathy and the boys with booze? Mick wised up and dried out, and took up jogging. He now ran every day—winter, summer, spring, or fall—regardless of the weather. He ran for his sanity, and from his bitterness and anger and grief.

Healy straightened up, accidentally brushing his nose against the side of my face. My eyes crossed.

"Ahem," he said, clearing his throat. "I'll fetch some gauze."

"Thanks."

The door to the locker room banged open. "Ev?"

"Here," I called.

Lisa Chiu, one of the medical students, came around the bank of lockers. She glanced from me to Healy and back again, undoubtedly assessing the humid atmosphere. I was amused to see Healy flush. You'd think we had been stumbled upon in flagrante.

"What a lovely scarf, Lisa," he said quickly.

"My latest disguise, dahling," Lisa breathed in a throaty voice, striking a pose and showcasing her brightly colored Hermès head-scarf and huge Lamy sunglasses.

"What are you, the reincarnation of Jackie O?" I smiled.

Lisa threw back her head and laughed. "Can you see the *National Enquirer* headlines? 'JACKIE O LIVES AS ABORTION MILL MURDERER!'" She took off the scarf and sunglasses, shaking loose her black, shoulder-length hair. "Look what they did to me yesterday," she said, cocking her head. "Is that a black eye, or is that a black eye?"

Lisa didn't have to say who *They* were. Everyone who worked at University Hospital knew who Lisa's *They* were.

When people asked Lisa what kind of medicine she wanted to specialize in, she usually said OB-GYN. Obstetrics and gynecology. A handy answer for cocktail parties, or for formal situations where she had to be polite. Although, once in a while, if she was feeling provocative, she might say instead that she thought she would specialize in "pregnancy-related services." Which of course raised eyebrows among people who knew what she was talking about.

If she was feeling particularly defiant, she would come right out with it: She was going to become an abortion provider.

"Are you out of your mind?" most people responded. "They'll follow you everywhere, fire-bomb your house and your car, chase your friends and relatives, waving pictures of bloody fetuses. *You know what your girlfriend does? She kills babies.*"

"Oh," Lisa would say, waving a hand dismissively, her dark eyes twinkling, "it'll be character-building. People can always use a little character building."

"But they might shoot you. A couple of abortion doctors have been shot dead right in front of their clinics."

"I'll get a bulletproof vest." She'd shrug. "Aren't you pro-choice?"

Almost always the answer was "Yes. Of course I'm pro-choice. Yes, of course."

"Pro-choice means trench warfare," she'd say. "I am going into the trenches."

Of course, as a fourth-year med student, Lisa first had to finish med school, then internship, then a residency in OB-GYN. But she was chomping at the bit to enter the fray of pro-choice warfare. In addition to her duties as an extern in the ER—"extern" was what you called a fourth-year med student on rotation—Lisa worked as a volunteer orderly down at the Westside Women's Health Center, or "WW," as it was informally known. Some wags called it "Double Your Trouble." It had certainly doubled the trouble in Lisa Chiu's life. The relentless *They* left hate messages on her home answering machine. *They* stood in front of the Doctors' Residence where most of the house staff lived—including me— and prayed for her death, loudly and ostentatiously. *They* had recently begun picketing the Doctors' Residence day in and day out with large "Wanted" posters with Lisa's photo, name and phone number. If Lisa went out of the building, *They* shouted, "Lisa, Lisa, don't do any killing today! Shame on you! Repent!"

I thought Mick Healy would fall all over himself at the prospect of rescuing *two* damsels in distress, but he merely clucked "Tch, Lisa, what a shame," and went off in search of gauze to wrap my arm. Lisa watched him leave. "He's in love with you," she said.

"No, he's not." I smiled. "He knows I have Phil."

Lisa looked down her nose at me playfully. "Well, Mick's thoroughly unreconstructed, anyway," she said. "All those cops."

"Who, his brothers?"

"Father, brothers, sister. The whole family are cops except for Mick." She tapped the side of her head. "Cop mentality. Mom, apple pie, save the world, chivalry. It's the chivalry I could do without. Chivalry puts women in their place." Then her manner changed. "I showed you mine. Now you show me yours."

"It's nothing," I said quickly.

"You fell?"

"I got knocked down."

"I see. By whom?"

"I don't know."

"Ah." She waited. Lisa had a seductive way of waiting that transcended all barriers: race, sex, age, your reluctance to tell her whatever. I was twelve years older than she was, but she worked her magic. I took a deep breath and described my encounter with my strange assailant.

"Why don't you want to talk about this?" she asked.

I shrugged.

"Ev, it's not like you. You're usually so bold."

I looked pointedly at her black eye. "So, someone socked you?"

"One of the 'sidewalk counselors' in front of WW. He interfered a little more physically than usual. It's the same old same old. Don't change the subject."

I changed it anyway. "Listen, you were asking if you could use my locker," I said. "I wrote the combination down for you. It's in my wallet. I don't think anyone will mind."

She grinned, her expression a mixture of exasperation and indulgence. "Ev, we can talk about your locker later. I mean, I appreciate the fact that you're letting me use it, but—"

"No, let me give you the combo while I'm thinking of it." I awkwardly managed with my left hand to extract my wallet from my right back pants pocket and fished out the card I'd written the combination on. "Here."

Lisa made a face, but pocketed the card. "Is this guy who knocked you down someone you know?" she asked.

"No," I said.

"Did you tell the cops?"

"No. Did you?" I asked.

"Oh, yes. I had him arrested for assault and battery. He'll be right back out there tomorrow, but I went through the motions. You should, too."

I gave her a long look.

"She's right, you know," said Healy, coming back with the gauze. "Take it from someone whose entire family is on the Job."

I didn't say anything. I held out my arm to Healy for him to wrap.

The emergency room at University Hospital was pretty much the same as any other New York City emergency room, or any inner-city emergency room anywhere in the country, for that matter. At 7 A.M., phones were ringing, stretchers were caroming by, people were raising their voices, and patients were staggering around, wanting the bathroom, or their doctors, or their breakfasts. The usual bedlam. The word "bedlam," in fact, originated with a hospital: London's Bethlehem. "Bedlam" was how you pronounced "Bethlehem" with phlegm.

Adding to this morning's general commotion was Lisa Chiu, who pursued me like a noisome terrier yapping at my heels.

"Ev, your judgment is skewed. A guy knocks you down, pulls your shirt over your head and bares your breasts in public, injures you—and you stop off at Sami's for breakfast? You don't think there's something a little odd about that?"

"Why are you making such a big deal about this?" I asked. "Julio, do you have Kareem Johnson's blood chemistries and urine tox?"

The clerk handed over a sheaf of lab results and I scanned them. Just as I thought: the kid was zonkaroo on benzodiazepines and marijuana. It was a wonder he could walk and talk.

"You need to call the cops," Lisa said for the nth time.

"Why? So I can make more paperwork for them? Lisa, listen. The guy knocked me down and pulled my shirt over my head. Big fucking deal. Even if they found the guy—which is unlikely, since I didn't really see him—what are they going to charge him with, harassment?"

"But—"

I cut her off. "Lisa, I am very short-tempered this morning. Please drop it."

The EMS batphone rang, and we cocked our heads while the clerk answered. "Stand by for a twenty-year-old female in traumatic shock," he announced over the PA system. "ALS has been initiated. She's A-plus-oh-times-one, lapsing in and out of consciousness. ETA two-to-three minutes."

"You're shaken up and *embarrassed*," pronounced Lisa.

I threw my arms up in the air and stomped over to the ambulance-bay doors to wait for the ambulance. I was becoming sorrier by the minute that I hadn't just told her I'd fallen and left it at that. Moreover, I had yet to tell Phil, who would be his usual concerned, kind, sensitive self—and ask me fifty minutes' worth of shrink questions about my thoughts and feelings. My boyfriend, the psychiatric attending.

The siren wailed around the corner of Amsterdam Avenue. Lisa Chiu came to stand next to me, along with the charge nurse and the ER paramedic, Brian Linhardt. We took up our stations, poised on the balls of our feet. I pulled on gloves and tensed as if for the starter's pistol. When we heard the beep-beep-beep of the EMS van backing into the ambulance bay, we threw open the doors and surged out onto the dock en masse, just as the EMS crew and a uniformed cop opened the doors of the van and surged toward us. Surfing on the roiling sea of these two waves crashing upon each other was the gurney with the patient.

When I got a look, I saw this: a face completely swathed in bandages except for one bruised eye blinking fretfully, and a bruised and bloodied mouth, missing teeth. An oxygen line snaked out of her nose, and one medic held an IV bag aloft. They had "collared and boarded" her—strapped her head-to-foot to a long wooden board to immobilize her in case she had spinal injuries. With her bandages and head straps and one winking eye she looked like King Tut newly exhumed, unraveling.

She gurgled, and one of the medics suctioned blood out of her mouth.

"Son of a bitch beat her with a pipe, looks like," said the cop, a tall, gawky woman with red hair. "Found her in an alley. She was supposed to start work at six A.M. We found her at six-forty."

We pulled the gurney into the emergency room and positioned ourselves for the heave-ho, quickly transferring the patient to one of our own stretchers, board and all; the patient would stay immobilized to the board until after she'd had cervical-spine X rays. "No, no, no," whimpered the patient feebly as we moved into the emergency room's OR One.

I leaned over the patient, angling myself into her field of vision so she could see me with her one eye. "Hi, can you tell us your name?" I asked.

She said something that sounded like "Derez Kah" and made waving motions, as if to ward me off. I looked questioningly at the cop.

"Theresa," she said. "Theresa Kahr. She's a German national."

Beside me, Lisa gasped.

"Theresa, can you tell us what happened to you?"

"No, no!" she cried.

"She's still fighting the guy," said the cop. "When I found her, she was waving like that."

"You get him?" Brian asked.

"No."

With my mind's eye I saw the well-muscled thighs and calves of my own assailant. I shook my head to clear it. "What's her blood pressure?" I asked.

"Eighty palp. Pulse about a hundred, respirations twenty-eight and shallow."

"She tell you anything?"

"She said, 'Bad back,' " relayed one of the medics. "I checked her back, but I'm not sure what she meant."

"Theresa, does your back hurt?"

She had no response to this, but continued to bat weakly at me. I put my hand on her arm. The skin was cold and clammy. Bending over her bandaged face, I shone my penlight in her good eye. The pupil contracted, but sluggishly. I stuffed the earpieces of my stethoscope in my ears. "I'm going to listen to your heart and lungs," I said, baring Theresa's breasts very gently. Her pulse was fast, and her breathing continued rapid and shallow. Quickly, I palpated her abdomen. When I covered her up again, she put her hand over mine. "We'll take care of you," I assured her. I started barking orders. "ABG, CBC, Chem-twenty, cross-match, stat! Two units of packed RBCs! Julio, I need a neurosurgeon down here right away—get Dr. Healy if you can. Call CT and book a slot, then get X Ray in here for skull- and C-spine films. Brian, start a large-bore."

"You got it."

"Theresa, do you know where you are?" I asked gently.

She blinked at me. Then, to her credit, she made an effort to look around. When her eye fell on Brian, she let out a small shriek.

"She's afraid of men," said the medic. I looked up. She mouthed the word "rape." Glancing around, I noticed for the first time that the medics were both women, and that a second cop, the only male in the EMS party, hovered in the background, careful to stay out of the patient's line of vision. Brian Linhardt noticed as well, and signaled Lisa to take over from him.

Lisa leaned into the patient's field of vision and said loudly, "Theresa, it's Lisa Chiu. You're at University Hospital, and this is Dr. Sutcliffe." With very steady hands Chiu slid the large-bore IV needle into the patient's arm, drawing blood, and hooking up the IV. But I saw her face was pinched with anger, and she was blinking back tears. I too found myself struggling with emotion; my early-morning terror returned full-force. He was yanking my shirt out of my pants and pulling it over my head—

"Ev?" Lisa Chiu was holding out to me the heparinized syringe for the arterial blood gas. I thrust the needle under the skin of Theresa's wrist into the radial artery and carefully advanced it, watching as if transfixed as the blood filled the syringe. *That could be me there,* I kept thinking. *That could be my blood.*

With that thought, the boundaries between me and the patient dissolved irrevocably. "How did you find her?" I heard myself ask the cop.

"She was in the alley behind the bakery," she said. "You know, the Good Earth? When I'm on nights, I always stop by the back on my way to the station house. When I go off shift. They're not open yet, but they give me a muffin."

My head snapped up. "This is the German girl from the Good Earth?"

"Yes," the cop said. "You know her?"

I stared at the patient in horror. "I buy my bread there. She makes my bread. I didn't know her name."

"I know her, too," said Lisa, her voice catching. "We're friends."

"I'm sorry," said the cop. Her manner changed subtly. "I found her in the alley. She was all tangled up in her shirt, I guess the guy pulled her shirt over her head. She was moving her feet, trying to get away—"

Just then, the neurosurgeon arrived, in the form of Mick Healy. "What have you got?" he asked, shouldering his way through the throng around the stretcher. Observing that the patient was boarded and collared and could not turn her head, Mick did just as I had done earlier: He angled himself over the patient so he was right in her line of vision.

For a split second, they stared at each other.

He blanched.

And she began to scream.

CHAPTER 2

YOU have to be something of an adrenaline junkie to want to work in an emergency room.

Most people who work in emergency rooms will not come right out and admit it. They'll tell you all kinds of other things like they love people, or they want to "help," or they don't *mind* working in the ER, so why not? Some people tell poignant, involved stories about how they were chronically ill as children, or grew up with parents or siblings who were chronically ill, and they spent a lot of time in emergency rooms, and now they're paying their debt to medicine by working in the ER and aiding others. Then you get the more eccentric motives. One nurse I know says, in a melodramatic basso profundo, "Honey, I work here because I want to create order out of chaos." Another theorizes she volunteered for the ER because she secretly desired control over her own life, which eluded her, but the ER offered her the opportunity to gain control over *other* people's lives—of course, she didn't know this at the time, but she realizes it now after reading *Women Who Love Too Much* and attending Adult Children of Alcoholics meetings for five years. You'd think after five years of excruciating introspection in a twelve-step program, she'd also realize she's an adrenaline junkie.

Like all the others.

Like me.

For years I told people I went into medicine for the need to know. When I was in graduate school working toward a Ph.D. in English literature, my dad suffered a debilitating heart attack requiring quadruple bypass surgery. I didn't understand anything the doctors were saying to me—when I could get them to talk to me, that is. Dad enjoyed the mixed blessing of treatment at a suburban New Jersey medical center where he was an attending pediatric neurologist and where my mother, the All-August, All-Competent Joan Berman, R.N., M.S., Ph.D., was Vice President of the Hospital and Director of Nursing. The doctors wouldn't talk to anyone but her, not even her children. And she was too stressed out and in too much denial to reduce their medicalese to common layperson's terms. With one of my brothers hysterical and the other huffing and puffing in a fit of steady-as-a-rock-in-the-face-of-crisis machismo, I was left to my own devices to deal with my father's hospitalization. I did what I knew how to do: I hit the books. I sat in the visitors' room outside the Cardiac Care Unit, waiting for my once-an-hour five-minute visit with Dad, reading a book by a heart surgeon in Houston that intelligently explained every heart ailment known to modern man and woman. From there I progressed to Cecil's *Textbook of Modern Medicine*. Eventually I discovered, much to my amazement, that medicine was more gripping than English literature.

All my life I had resisted such a discovery. The child of a doctor and nurse, I had naturally been subjected to pressure to elect medicine as my own career. "No, of course we want you to choose your own profession," my parents protested when I complained. "We just want you to keep your options open." To keep my options open, I took a double major in college in biology and English. When Dad had his cardiac bypass, I was halfway through my Ph.D. dissertation in English literature (*Men Playing Women Dressed as Men: Androgyny in the Plays of William Shakespeare*). I had landed a good job teaching at a prestigious women's college.

But something was missing.

English lit was interesting. On good days, it was fascinating.

But it wasn't *gripping*.

It wasn't life and death.

Voilà. A would-be physician was born. They let Dad out of the hospital after lecturing him on the merits of losing weight, watching his blood pressure, quitting smoking, and cutting down on booze. And they let me into the hospital as a newly declared premed volunteer orderly.

That's when I found out I was an adrenaline junkie.

At first, I wasn't able to articulate it. A woman jumped out a fifth-floor window and landed on a cast-iron fence, impaling herself through the chest on one of the spikes. The Emergency Service cops cut away the part of the fence she was impaled on and brought her to the ER with the fence still sticking out of her like grotesque, evil ribs. Anyone could see she was impaled right through the heart. In fact, the medics were doing CPR *on the fence*. I was struck dumb with horror. As the ER filled up with cops, I saw *they* were struck dumb with horror. (You know it's bad when the cops are shocked.) Even the Director of the Emergency Department was quiet, moving quickly and deliberately but giving orders in a very low voice. There was none of the usual hollering or black ER humor.

I thought, this is the center of the world. This is Mount Olympus, the temple of the gods. The *sanctum sanctorum*, where God reaches down from the heavens with a finger pointing at Adam and says, "Stay," or "Come." I was horrified. I was thrilled. I was horrified to be thrilled. I felt privileged to be there, and guilty to feel privileged and alive, alive, alive when that woman was so clearly dead, dead, dead.

Of course she was dead. Two hours after they had pronounced her and people had recovered their wits, everyone was going around saying, Why'd they even bring her in? They couldn't see that the fence was right through her fucking *heart?* Why didn't they pronounce her at the scene?

Because they were adrenaline junkies, and they had to do something with their adrenaline. They couldn't just stand there looking at the woman impaled on the fence. They had to give her their best shot. So they got the Emergency Service cops to come cut her down like the crucified Jesus from the cross, and they bore her off to the holy of holies to be commended into the hands of God. When they came into the ER with the stretcher, you could practically hear the adrenaline squooshing in their shoes.

Not long after The Woman With the Fence, as she came to be known in ER lore, I began to collect evaluations to submit with my medical school applications. There were all kinds of interesting euphemisms: I was "calm under pressure." I was "quick-thinking." I was "unemotional." I "combined intellectual with practical skills" and exhibited "psychological maturity." (Read: I was as good as a man.) What all this boiled down to was, adrenaline had a calming effect on me. I tolerated it well. I didn't suffer debilitating side effects from it. I couldn't drink coffee except with meals because it upset my stomach and played havoc with my blood sugar, but I could take adrenaline.

Unfortunately, like caffeine, adrenaline is addicting. And like any drug, it has three actions: the one you want, the one you don't want, and the one you don't know about.

When adrenaline flowed, it tripped an inner switch in me.

It turned my emotions off.

They were off now.

Which I suppose was just as well, because on the morning of Thursday, August 3, I had to talk to Detective First Grade Richard Ost, NYPD. Ost was interested in a clear-headed, unemotional rendition of the Who-What-Where-Why-and-How of my having been knocked down by a man who may or may not have been running from the battery and rape of Theresa Kahr.

I like police. To me, they are doing the same job I'm doing, which is helping people in crisis. Only they do it with a little more bluster, a lot more sentiment, and a whopping load more suspicion. Cops have amazing problem-solving skills, and minds that can go in forty different directions at once. But they do have their quirks. There's an old medical maxim: When you hear hoofbeats, look for a horse, not a zebra. The police version of this seems to be: Never mind the horse, find the fucking zebra.

Or at least it seemed to me. I had a long working history with police officers and detectives—among them Detective Ost—who came into the ER on a routine basis to question patients who had been stabbed, shot, assaulted, or injured in some way that drew the attention of the authorities.

Ost and I had gone over the whole spiel of my "knockdown." We had rehashed the business with the shirt. Theresa Kahr's guy had pulled her shirt over her head; my guy had pulled my shirt over my head. Theresa had complained to the medics of a "bad back"; I suggested she might have been trying to say *backpack*, and my guy had been wearing a backpack. Possibly, I said to the police, because he wanted to have a change of clothing; he could easily have changed out of his bloody clothes after beating and raping his victim, and left the scene in a pristine pair of jogging shorts and a T-shirt, which was what my guy had been wearing. Perhaps he had discarded his bloody clothes, I suggested, or had carried them from the scene of the crime for disposal at a more clandestine location.

"Just a suggestion," I repeated.

Ost nodded and wrote in his notebook. A kind man in his early forties with graying hair and Everyman features, Ost was in his work mode: he seemed to be moving and thinking at a snail's pace, and his face betrayed nothing. Mentally pursuing his zebra of choice, no doubt, when I had just handed him a perfectly good horse.

"Okay, Doc," he said noncommittally. "Now you said you thought there might be something familiar about this guy who knocked you down. You think you know him?"

"Well," I sighed, "I'm not sure. I can't put my finger on anything, and although I thought at the time that there might be something familiar, I can't recall what it was."

"You got any other thoughts?"

I hesitated. I did have other thoughts, and I was going to make a couple of strategic phone calls, when I got a minute. "Only that I have no idea why he knocked me down," I said after a moment.

"Come again?"

"Why would he want to do that and call attention to himself? He was dressed for running. If he had just run past me, I wouldn't have noticed him at all. And then, after he knocks me down, he has to go through the business of pulling my shirt over my head so I won't see him."

"Unless you know him," Ost pointed out.

"I don't know him. I've gone over this in my mind."

"A few minutes ago, you weren't so sure."

"I said I thought there was something familiar about him," I said. "I didn't say I thought I knew him."

Ost gave me a long look. "Maybe he knows *you*, Doc. Let's say the guy's coming up on you, he sees you and recognizes you, and he's got some reason to believe you might recognize him and place him near the scene. So he knocks you down and pulls your shirt over your head. Like he did with the girl."

A chill went through me. "This is the Babydoll Killer we're talking about here, isn't it?" I asked.

He sighed. "Doc, we got an awful lot of media hype here—"

"Did you find—"

"No comment. Now I need you to think about this. Maybe you do know him. Try that old trick of thinking about it before you go to sleep, and again as soon as you wake up in the morning. In the meantime, let's run through your impressions again. He's about six feet tall?"

I nodded. My wonderful breakfast at Sami's was beginning to disagree with me. "About my height."

"Age?"

"I don't know."

"A big guy, skinny, what?"

"I'm not being much help, Ozzie. Medium build. I dunno."

"Twenties? Thirties?"

"I really can't say."

"Color hair, eyes?"

I lifted my hands helplessly. "I think he had light hair and eyes, but I'm really guessing."

"Anything else?"

Amazed that I still had a sense of humor, I heard myself say, "He had great legs."

Ost lifted an eyebrow. "What to you is great legs?" he asked, keeping a straight face.

"Runner's legs. Well-developed muscles in the thighs and calves." I paused. "Like yours."

"I have runner's legs?"

"Ozzie, you have *great* legs."

Ost struggled to maintain decorum, gave up, and laughed with pleasure. "When have you ever seen my legs?"

"Oh, but I've thought about them."

"I see."

"I have a very good imagination."

"I could show them to you and you wouldn't have to imagine."

The clerk stuck his head in the doctors' lounge. "Dr. Sutcliffe? You have a phone call. One-eight-one-five."

"Thank you, Julio. I was just about to get myself in a lot of trouble." I stood, and picked up the phone. "Dr. Sutcliffe."

"Dr. Sutcliffe, my name is Jennifer Garland. I'm calling for Wendell Sisk, the film director?"

There was a long moment while my mouth fell open and I shut it again. *"Excuse me?"* I said finally, not quite getting a grip on my astonishment. "Windy Sisk, the *director?"*

"Yes. We have your name from Kennedy Bartlett, who, as you may know, has worked with us from time to time."

"Uh," I said.

"You do know Kennedy Bartlett."

"Oh, yes, yes." I cleared my throat. "Ken Bartlett is a good friend of mine. Yes."

"You may have heard about Mr. Sisk's new project, which we're filming now. We're about to do some scenes involving a character who's in the hospital, and we need some technical medical advice on the set. We would be quite happy to pay you your normal daily rate."

A sense of disconnectedness with reality washed over me. One minute I'm talking to Ost about Theresa Kahr's assailant, the next I'm cracking wise about his legs, and now I'm listening to a famous movie director's assistant tell me he wants to meet me.

"Our estimate right now is two or three days of work, if you could manage that," Garland went on.

Was this a joke?

"I'm certain you're extremely busy with your own professional obligations, Doctor. Mr. Sisk thought—"

"If you're sure you want me," I interrupted. "I mean—"

"Mr. Bartlett recommended you very highly," Garland said smoothly. She had an educated, almost British-sounding accent, and a perfect assistant's manner, velly, velly dignified. "Besides," she went on, "what we have in mind is an emergency room scene, something with a little more action than a routine visit to the doctor. Something exciting, something that moves the story forward. Mr. Sisk would like your input."

"You'll have to excuse me if I seem a little flabbergasted," I said finally.

"Not at all. Will you come for a meeting? Mr. Bartlett thought it might be convenient for you to work with us on Saturday or Sunday, given your own obligations."

I put my hand over the mouthpiece. "What day is it?" I asked Ost.

"Thursday. The third."

"Ms. Garland," I said, speaking into the phone again, "I'm free on Saturday."

"Excellent."

We agreed that she would call my home phone and leave the details on my answering machine. As I hung up, I was surprised that Ken hadn't said anything. What if Mr. Sisk didn't like me? Only yesterday I'd read in the *News* that he'd fired the actress contracted for the leading role. A big-name actress, too.

"Just another minute," I said to Ost, as I dialed Ken Bartlett's number. "You could have at least told me you were giving my name to Windy Sisk," I said to his machine, "but of course I said yes. Thanks for the referral."

"Friends in high places, Doc," Ost said admiringly before he put his work-face back on. "Now. You know this German girl, right?"

"Wait," I said. Garland's upper-class accent was ringing in my ears. British-sounding. I snapped my fingers. "He had an Irish accent. The guy who knocked me down. He said, 'Stee doon.' "

" 'Stee doon?' "

" 'Stay down.' When he knocked me down, he said 'Stee doon.' "

"Now we're cookin' with gas," said Ost.

I tried to think of anyone I might know who spoke with a brogue.

Other than Mick Healy, of course.

CHAPTER
3

"**Ev,** you're out of shape," Lisa Chiu said. "You need to take up jogging or something."

"It's almost a hundred degrees out," I gasped defensively, trotting to keep up with her. "I'm already diaphoretic, I'm hyperventilating practically to the point of respiratory distress, my heart rate is probably one hundred and twenty-five—and you want me to *jog*? It's bad enough being a doctor in the emergency room, I don't want to wind up there as a patient."

"C'mon—you want to know what happened as much as I do," she complained. But she stopped.

"Thank you." I rested a moment by bending over, my hands on my knees. Sweat dripped from my face to the pavement. My tailored shirt, crisp from the Chinese laundry that very morning— admittedly a long time ago—was as damp and gritty as a filthy dishrag. Even my chinos were clammy.

Having escaped from the hospital in a timely manner at six-thirty, we were halfway across the University campus, on our way to the Good Earth. Lisa had got it into her head that the bakers might not have told the police everything they "knew" about Theresa Kahr's assault, and might be willing to talk to us instead. Lisa based this supposition on the fact that almost all the bakers at the Good Earth were foreigners. "Suspicious of authority," she pronounced. I didn't disagree. I had always suspected that the bakers, many of whom seemed to be students at the university, did not possess the type of visa required to work. But why they would want to spill their guts to *us* I didn't quite understand; to me, doctors seemed as much a part of the authority establishment as police.

When I caught my breath, I said, "Look. I know you do T'ai chi and yoga. I know you jog—"

"Not much," said Lisa. Although she glistened with sweat, it looked sexy on her, as if she had just stepped out of an ad for Nike running shoes or Evian water. "Only about a mile a day."

A mile—not much. Ha. "But just because you're so virtuous doesn't mean I can be so virtuous."

"Maybe you can be virtuous in other ways," suggested Lisa. "While we're standing here, maybe you could tell me what you found out this afternoon about Theresa's attack."

"Mm." I straightened up and scrutinized her. She had insisted on being present for Theresa Kahr's forensic exam and the collection of evidentiary material, and ever since had seemed unduly distant and subdued. I knew that look: horrified, thrilled, privileged, and guilty. For a moment I wanted to say, Welcome to Mount Olympus. You take cream and sugar with your adrenaline, or you drink it black?

Except that I knew that Theresa's evidentiary exam had been even worse than the standard gruesome evidentiary exam.

During the exam, the cops had quietly played the card they'd been holding close to their vests all morning: In all likelihood, Theresa had been assaulted by the man the newspapers were calling the Babydoll Killer.

In hushed tones, the news disseminated throughout the emergency room. Nobody was surprised; rumors had been circulating almost since the moment Theresa came through the doors of the ambulance bay. But the shock of confirmation was a cheap thrill. Many of us had seen the tabloid reports after the killer's second assault, or watched the breathless, trembling-voiced TV reporters recount the lurid details. Two young women had been brutally battered and raped, the first in June, the second in July. Both had succumbed to severe head injuries, dying in the hospital shortly after arrival. Each time, a doll had been found at the scene of the assault, and after the July killing, we learned from "sources close to police" that the doll had been posed between the legs of the second victim.

Still, nothing had prepared us for the raw reality.

Theresa had been found with the doll's feet stuffed up her vagina, as if she were still in the process of birthing it.

"A plain rubber doll, naked baby," Dr. Janusz Androfski, the OB-GYN who had conducted the exam, confided to me afterward. The shock and disgust in his Polish-accented voice rang in my ears. "Unfortunately, the rapist insert the feet with some force," he sputtered indignantly. "Some tearing of the gentle tissues."

The phrase jelled in my brain. *Some tearing of the gentle tissues*. Androfski meant "genital," of course; he misspoke. But his slip seemed to underscore the violence of the rape somehow, and spun my mind off into gyrations of free association. Gentle. Vulnerable. Suddenly, anything could happen. No one was safe. *I* wasn't safe. As we walked, I looked across the university campus at all the long-legged young women, some lounging on the vast steps of the library, chatting with girlfriends; others sprawled on the lawns with boyfriends, or reading books. *They* weren't safe.

The late-afternoon sunshine slanted through the shimmering haze, softly bathing the columns and porticoes of the classic Greek architecture in pink-and-gold light. I often paused in the middle of the campus to revel in it; *this is as nice as Paris*, I would think. Or *this is as nice as Rome*. The still, hot air lent an aura of travel to exotic places. Summertime, and the livin' is easy. Lulling. Transporting.

But not today. I asked the question that sometimes came to mind after a particularly distressing day in the ER: which is the real world, this or the emergency room?

This or Theresa Kahr?

I hadn't actually known Theresa's name before this morning. I knew her as the German girl at the Good Earth. When I'd go into the bread shop, we'd exchange pleasantries. I'd ask what bread they had. She'd tell me. I'd buy some. She had a very heavy German accent, so thick it might have been the parody of a German accent, like you might hear in a "Saturday Night Live" skit.

She was cute and boyish. Big brown eyes, dark hair cut short and floppy.

She was young.

Just recently turned twenty.

Just like all these kids here, lounging on the university campus . . .

Not safe.

Going with Lisa to the Good Earth to find out what we could about Theresa's assault began to take on the dark coloration of fear and self-defense.

I said loudly, "Lisa, you're too calm. I know Theresa's evidentiary exam upset you."

She snorted. "Look who's talking. Pot calling the kettle black, don't you think? This morning you were so fucking calm after the guy knocked you down, you stopped and had breakfast at Sami's with your elbow dripping blood all over his floor, but when I tried to get *you* to talk about it, oh no! 'Lisa, I'm very short-tempered this morning,' " she went on, mimicking me. "'Please drop it.' "

"That was then, this is now," I sputtered, feeling the color flash hot in my cheeks. "You wanted me to call the cops, and—"

"Yeah, and you didn't want to make a scene. You gained some perspective on it real fast when they brought Theresa in. And you gained even more when you found out it was the Babydoll Killer."

"Okay, so I woke up a little. But you can give me a wake-up

call, and I can't give *you* a wake-up call? You can come to me in the locker room and say, 'Gee, Ev, why don't you want to talk about this?' but I can't say the same thing to you?''

Lisa's face was red, and not from the heat. But, like me, she wasn't willing to admit she was wrong. ''Here's what I don't like,'' she snapped. ''You're trying to tell me I should be more *emotional* because I'm her friend. *You* get to be numb and shocked and guarded, but I have to be *emotional?*''

''Okay,'' I said slowly, ''I'll show you mine, then you show me yours.'' I took a deep breath. ''Yes, it was shocking. Yes, it was enormously distressing. Yes, I was distracted most of the day, thinking about her. And yes, I probably transferred all of my feelings about getting knocked down onto Theresa, and parked those feelings in the Intensive Care Unit along with her and her stretcher. So, I'm probably in deep denial.'' Pause. ''Now you.''

Lisa tossed her head, and her damp black hair flew out around her shoulders. She had a round face and button nose, and gorgeous golden skin. The daughter of a Hawaiian mother and Chinese father, she liked to joke that she ''checked all the boxes'' when asked her race, or sometimes sketched in her own box, which she labeled ''chameleon.'' Today she looked Amazonian, back from the wars, athletic and sweaty. Her almond eyes flashed with defiance and machismo.

And anger. ''You know, Androfski and I had to dig the glass out of her,'' Lisa said.

''I know.''

''Her shoulders, her ass, the back of her legs. Not only did the guy beat her and rape her, he raped her in a pile of broken glass.''

I put my arm around Lisa's shoulders and squeezed. Her body heat rose up like a cloud around her, as did mine, and for a moment steamed us together. She patted the back of my waist, then slipped away.

''Let's keep walking,'' she said, taking off at a brisk pace again. ''I just can't get this out of my mind—we had to pick each little piece of glass out with tweezers, one piece at a time. I just—I just—do you know we had to comb her pubic hair with a special little comb? And then pluck out hairs, preferably with the root still attached to each hair? It was like black magic or voodoo or something; what are we going to do with these hairs? I mean, I *knew* we were going to send them to the lab, but . . .'' She trailed off, at a loss for words. Then she shot me a look sideways in the confused way people do when they've forgotten entirely what they were talking about.

"It's pretty grim," I agreed. I waited for her to bring up the doll.

"Vaginal swabbings, oral swabbings, anal swabbings," Lisa recited, pumping her arms as she walked, flailing the air. She laughed mirthlessly. "Christ, we took something called a 'nasal mucus sample.' In case she had cum up her nose!"

"The cops have to cover all the bases," I said, as kindly as possible. "Especially since she was unconscious and couldn't tell us anything."

"Yeah, well, thank God she was unconscious. I can't believe they put conscious rape victims through this. If I ever get raped and have to undergo these procedures, promise me you'll put me out with a whopping dose of Versed so I don't remember anything."

"*Kayn aynhoreh*," I said. "No evil eye."

"What is that, Yiddish?"

"Yeah, my grandmother was from the old country. Russia."

"You're Jewish? With a name like Sutcliffe?"

"My father was killed in a car accident before I was born," I explained. "That was Sutcliffe. My mom is Jewish, and so is my stepfather—I think of him as my real dad. His name is Berman, which is why my brothers have a different name than I do. So yes, we're Jewish. But we're pretty Reform. We go to shul on Yom Kippur and that's about it. Although I was bat-mitzvahed."

"Huh," said Lisa. "You never told me. My mother says she's part Russian."

"Your mother says she's part everything. Would you please slow down?"

"*This* is too fast?" Lisa reined herself in as one might rein in a thoroughbred racehorse. "Ev, you're how old now? Thirty-six? What are you going to do when you're sixty?"

I laughed.

"Okay, okay, I'll lay off. And we'll walk slower. But I want to know what you found out."

"I really didn't find out much that was new," I said. "Most of it was just confirmation of the rumors in the papers."

Lisa groaned and shot me a you-think-I'm-dense? look. "Hey," she said, "I was at the same wedding, remember? James and Bobbi Strathearn. The last weekend in July. All the doctors standing around with champagne and canapés, talking about— what else? Their patients! Ben Eisen from Jewish Memorial saying he'd treated the woman the papers were making such a big fuss about, what with the doll posed between her legs and all, and Cat Schyler from St. Jude's saying, 'Wait a minute, *you* treated the second one? I had the first one!' "

I nodded. "Right, they only found out with Eisen's patient that there might actually be a serial killer—"

"—so after we brought Theresa Kahr up to the ICU, you put in calls to Eisen and Schyler," Lisa said. "What did they tell you?"

I looked away. For a reason I could not fathom—except perhaps motherly protectiveness which grew out of our mentor-student relationship—I did not really want to discuss this with Lisa. "How do you know I called them?" I asked.

"Because *I* called them. They told me to talk to you."

I smiled briefly, feeling that mixed thrill of affection and indignation a parent sometimes feels when a child insists on trumping her parent, or a student her teacher.

Then I sank into my own thoughts. Cat Schyler's patient, a young Hispanic woman who had worked as a cash-register clerk at a famous Upper West Side Jewish deli, had been raped in an outside stairwell on Eighty-second Street near Broadway. She was discovered by a passerby who heard her moaning about 4 A.M. Severely beaten about the head, with a shattered left orbit, she had died of shock twelve hours after being brought into the emergency room at St. Jude's Hospital. Nobody I knew remembered hearing anything about it at the time, except, of course, Cat Schyler, who ran the Intensive Care Unit down at St. Jude's.

Ben Eisen's patient was the media-sensation kickoff. An aspiring young actress who worked as a waitress at a restaurant across Columbus Avenue from the Museum of Natural History, she had been raped in Riverside Park near the Soldiers and Sailors Monument at Eighty-ninth Street. She was found by a jogger and was believed to have been assaulted between 4 and 5:30 A.M. Taken to the emergency room at Jewish Memorial Hospital, she died on the third hospital day, of swelling of the brain due to extensive head injuries. It was Eisen's patient who had been left with the doll between her legs, as if she had just given birth.

The murder of a white, pretty blonde who did bit parts on "As the World Turns" and "General Hospital" would have been news even on a big-news day, and the bizarre twist of the posed doll rocketed the story into front-page headlines and top-of-the-hour sound bites and video clips. When word leaked that cops remembered a doll at the scene of a murder four weeks previously, the media went wild.

"You have any more info on that doll?" I asked Cat Schyler when I got her on the phone.

"Yeah, one of the cops kicked it down the stairs," Schyler said, laughing wryly. "Now he's kicking himself for not having bagged it as evidence." Schyler, it turned out, had had a brief hot affair with one of the detectives who brought the first victim in to the hospital, so she'd called him and got the details. "Apparently the doll was near her, but not near enough for them to think it had anything to do with anything. It's long since gone—nobody has a clue what happened to it."

"What did it look like?" I asked.

"Your ordinary, basic babydoll, from what I can make out.

Nothing remarkable. Rubber, I guess. Naked. My hot little detective did remember it was naked—he would."

I didn't want to get into the details of Cat Schyler's provocative sex life. "Thanks," I said, hanging up and dialing Ben Eisen.

"A regular rubber babydoll, naked," Eisen said. "Didn't walk or talk or do tricks."

"Did you see it yourself?" I asked.

"No, overheard the medics talking about it. Listen, gotta go. Incoming."

Next I called Dr. Rebecca Bayard down at the Medical Examiner's Office. After telling her about Theresa Kahr and engaging in a brief discussion of the injuries sustained by the other two victims, I asked, "Beck, you see any others?"

"I didn't think you were calling for the anatomic," she observed dryly. "No, we haven't. At least not in Manhattan. Striking wounds like this are definitely discussed in our three-thirty meeting, and we'd all know if there was a repeat."

"Can you tell me anything else?"

"He beats them first, looks like with a lead pipe, then he rapes them. You do rape kit?"

"Yeah."

"We find sperm, it goes to our DNA lab. If the guy ever shows up, we'll have a match—and the conviction will be short and sweet."

"Hope so," I said. I steeled myself. "Think he's escalating?"

"You betcha. First he leaves the doll near the victim, then he poses the doll between the victim's legs, and with your patient he forces the doll's feet up her. What's next—cesarean section?"

Lisa and I exited the University campus onto Broadway and turned north toward the Good Earth.

"You're not telling me something," said Lisa. Taking a deep, jagged breath, she burst into tears.

"Oh, honey," I said. "Come over here and sit down for a moment." Sliding my hand under her arm, I led her to a low wall in front of the women's college. We sat. Lisa cried quietly for a while, her chin ducked on her chest. I handed out Kleenex and thought, this is the first time I've seen you like this. You're always so crusty and competent.

"I think I'm okay now," Lisa announced eventually. "Sorry. Let's go."

"Feel better?" I asked.

"No. Now I feel dumber." But she laughed, albeit wryly.

"Tell me about Theresa," I said, as we continued up Broadway.

"Well, let's see." Lisa's face softened with affection. "You know she's from Germany."

"Anybody who talks to her knows that," I said. "She's got an accent thicker than Colonel Klink."

"And she's Green Party. Very, very aware. Wears only natural fibers—undyed cotton, that kind of thing. Washes her hair only with stuff that won't ruin the environment. Uses some kind of natural Egyptian kohl for eye makeup. I think it makes her look like a raccoon, personally. But she likes it. Let's see, what else . . . She's not like a lot of fanatics who have no sense of humor. She says her English isn't good enough for her to make jokes, but she likes other people's jokes. Unfortunately, you tell her a joke, and half the time she doesn't get it. So you ruin it by going through this long explanation. She loves to party—she can really put away the beer." Lisa laughed. "You should have seen the time she tried to order radishes with her beer. At the West End Gate, can you imagine?" The West End was a popular hangout for University students. "Oh, and she's a lesbian. Or so she says."

"So she says?"

"Well, there's some guy who keeps coming in the shop and asking her out. She hasn't said yes, but she keeps talking about him."

"Really?" My antennae went up.

Lisa shrugged. "I didn't know what to say. 'What do you mean, some guy—I thought you were gay'? Her sex life is her business."

"Well, but don't you think—"

She cut me off. "No. Serial killers don't ask you for a date first."

I shot a look sideways. Lisa's face was pinched. "Maybe this one does. What did they talk about, did you know?"

"Ev, she didn't tell me, okay?"

"Do you know what he looks like?"

"No."

I didn't know what to make of Lisa's vehemence. "Are you feeling guilty this happened to her?" I asked.

Lisa stopped and turned on me. "Will you knock it off?" she shouted. "Why are you so touchy-feely all of a sudden?"

"Sorry," I mumbled, taken aback.

"Don't be sorry. Just stop."

"Lis——"

"*Es genugt,*" she barked. That's enough.

"Since when do *you* know Yiddish?" I asked, stung. "I suppose now you're going to tell me your mother says she's Jewish, too."

"I didn't learn it from her. I heard it from Jeff Cantor."

Jeff Cantor was the doctor whose apartment Lisa was subletting. He was in Bosnia with Doctors Without Borders for the summer, and Lisa was cat-sitting his Maine coon cat, Fat Face. "Ah," I said. "How is Jeff, anyway?"

Lisa relayed the details of her latest communiqué from Cantor. There was no electricity in Sarajevo again, and they were boiling water on big cook fires to sterilize the—

I stopped listening. Lisa had hurt my feelings. Still in a funk when we reached the Good Earth a few minutes later, I became downright cranky when I saw the gates were down in front of the shop. Great. We had walked all this way for nothing. They were closed.

Lisa stopped talking and looked around. Yellow crime-scene tape stretched across the width of the storefront. On the sidewalk in front of the shop, flowers, cards, and mementos had already begun to appear. A teddy bear held a card that said, "Theresa, we pray for you." Someone had even lit a votive candle in a large red jar; it flickered in the lengthening twilight.

"God," said Lisa. "You'd think she was already dead." Then, raising her voice,"Khalid! It's Lisa Chiu!"

"Back door!" came the muffled reply.

Lisa and I exchanged a look.

"Brace yourself," I said. Suddenly, I wasn't so sure I wanted to see the place where Theresa was assaulted.

Next to the Good Earth was a liquor store, on the corner. We went around behind it to the alley.

Actually it was more than an alley. A high wrought-iron fence stood between us, on the sidewalk, and a warren of yards that stretched the length of the block between the buildings that fronted on Broadway and those that fronted on Claremont Avenue. A gate in the fence stood open, although it, too, was criss-crossed with yellow crime-scene tape. Steep concrete stairs led down half a story from the sidewalk level into the cement "back-yard" shared by the liquor store and the Good Earth. A slightly built man with Semitic features looked up. He had just poured a bucket of soapy water on the ground, and swept it with a broom toward a drain.

He was weeping.

Lisa raised her hand to her mouth.

I found myself hoping, fervently, that the flood gates would open. That I'd react with tears. Screams. Anything . . .

But as I stood in the shimmering heat and gazed down upon the soapy concrete, I felt nothing.

My eyes were open and seeing, but my heart was hard.

CHAPTER
4

"WATCH the paint cans," Dr. Philip Carchiollo warned when I walked into his apartment. He wiped his hands on a dish towel, pushed his longish blond hair out of his grape-green eyes, and planted a salty kiss on my lips. "The painters are a little mañana-mañana—they'll finish tomorrow. Come in here and tell me what you think."

I followed Phil into the empty living room, where three or four industrial fans pushed the hot air around. He had chosen a soft, off-white shade of paint with just a hint of pink, but in the glare of bare lightbulbs, it was harsh and dazzling. "I need my sunglasses," I said.

"Yeah, kind of gives you snow blindness, doesn't it?"

"It'll be fine with your regular lamps. They did a really good job, Phil. It doesn't look like they got any paint on the floor."

"Damn straight, they didn't." He grinned. "I put the fear of God into them. I told them my father and brothers were in the construction business. They cogitated on that for a while: Italian last name, construction business . . . *mafia*. I could almost see the lightbulbs going on in their heads. Paint on the floor, I busta you kneecaps. Worse: *cement shoes.*''

I laughed.

''C'mere—wait'll you see this,'' he said, tugging on my elbow and pulling me through the French doors into the dining room, where it was blessedly air-conditioned. He shut the doors behind us to keep the cool air in. ''Joe and Sal brought Mama's dining-room furniture today. Ta-*da*!''

''Oh, Phil, it's gorgeous.'' I ran my hand over the black-walnut table. Old stuff, good stuff. Solid. Immediately I began to twitch. The old ploy again: Isn't this a nice table? Wouldn't you like to move in here? This can be *your* table, too!

''And Dad sent Mama's good china and crystal.'' He started opening boxes, unpacking plates and saucers.

Oy vay. *China and crystal.* China and crystal were what you got when you got married.

Concealing my panic, I did my best to admire Mama Carchiollo's dishes and make all the appropriate noises. Actually, the pattern was quite nice; classic and understated, off-white with blue-and-red trim. I picked up a salad plate and turned it upside down. Lenox. Not bad. As the dining room quickly filled with crumpled newspaper, and plates and saucers and teacups were stacked up on the lovely walnut table, I forced myself to smile. C'mon, Sutcliffe. This is a lot of fun for him. Join in.

''Oh, Ev, look at this,'' Phil exclaimed, ''the champagne glasses! We'll have to have champagne. I'll get a bottle tomorrow.''

I took off my glasses and pinched the bridge of my nose.

Phil *would* have to move out of the doctors' residence. He couldn't leave well enough alone. Christ, why should we live together? I had my apartment exactly the way I wanted it, he had his apartment exactly the way he wanted it, and all we had to do to see each other was walk up or down two flights of stairs. Now we had to walk nine blocks. I couldn't figure out what the logic was supposed to be here. Was he rebelling because he thought I was taking him for granted? Was I supposed to appreciate him more if I had to walk nine blocks to see him? Was the new apartment supposed to force me to make a decision—fish or cut bait? Or was this *reverse* logic: You don't want to move in with me? Fuck you, I'll get a place of my own that's *farther away.*

Maybe he thought his nest in the doctors' residence wasn't big enough or grand enough to entice me; he'd buy a palazzo on the tenth floor of a pre-war Riverside Drive building and see if maybe *that* got my attention. Two large, airy bedrooms; two full baths, one with both a claw-footed bathtub and a separate shower stall; a living room with a functional fireplace, huge windows with a river view; formal dining room; an eat-in kitchen with a breakfast nook; and a professional consultation suite with an office and waiting room, constructed by Phil's helpful brothers out of the former servants' quarters so that Phil would have an office in which to see his analytic patients outside the hospital. The place was utterly fantastic—every New Yorker's dream. It irritated me to the point of teeth-gritting that I liked it so much. Moreover, I appreciated the operative biological theory inherent in the situation, which made me even crankier. Phil and I had both learned in pre-med biology how male red-winged blackbirds seduced the mate of choice: they procured the best piece of the swamp. And the future Mrs. red-winged blackbird hopped right over and settled down.

Usually I was able to muster *some* reason and humor when I suffered an attack of the marriage jitters—I did almost always remind myself that maybe Phil's new apartment wasn't about winning me at all, and that I was reading into things—but tonight I felt depleted of my usual coping mechanisms. I pulled one of Mama Carchiollo's black-walnut chairs out from the table and sank down onto it.

Phil looked at me with concern. "I'm sorry," he said. "I'm rattling on, and here you've had this terrible day. How's your arm?"

"Hurts a little," I admitted. Twice during the day I'd had to ask Lisa to change the dressing because the damn thing had started to bleed again, just as Mick Healy had warned. But I couldn't work with an immobilized elbow.

"You're worried about the German girl."

"Mm." Actually, I was tired of talking about her.

Phil and I had already been through Phase One in the emergency room, the are-you-all-right drama with the hugs and kisses, much to my embarrassment. (Lisa Chiu had prevailed upon me until I called Phil and told him I'd been attacked on the way to work, and he had come right over to the hospital to be comforting.) By the end of the day, after two gunshot wounds, a cardiac arrest, a woman whose baby I had to deliver in the elevator on the way to the maternity ward, the usual two dozen patients suffering through some extremity of AIDS-related crisis, the asthma-exacerbated-by-heats, the emphysema-exacerbated-by-heats, the four firefighters who got pelted with bottles and rocks by an angry crowd when they tried to close an illegally opened hydrant, the hardhat from the hospital's new Storrs Pavilion construction site who fell out of an elevator hoistway, and the ten other patients I had already forgotten, and after my trip with Lisa Chiu to the Good Earth, the sun of Theresa Kahr's ascendancy was dipping into the horizon of my mind.

"Well, what would you like?" Phil asked. "A drink? A shower?" He smiled suggestively to let me know what we could do after the shower. All the while he assessed me with what I had come to call his "shrink eye," an intense and steady gaze that let me know I had his complete and undivided attention—and behind which his mind whirred and buzzed relentlessly.

"Oh, honey, I don't know what I want," I sighed. "Maybe a drink and some quiet time while you shower, and then I'll shower by myself, if you don't mind."

I knew what I *didn't* want: I didn't want to be shrunk. I didn't want to talk anymore about having been knocked down, or about Theresa Kahr.

And I didn't want to get married, or move in with him.

*   *   *

"So what's the prognosis?" Phil persisted, when we had set-tled ourselves in the kitchen for dinner. The kitchen, dining room, and master bedroom were the only air-conditioned parts of the apartment at the moment; the rest was open to air out the paint fumes. "Think she'll make it?"

I sighed and scrutinized the wallpaper, which I had helped pick out, under duress. It had a pattern of tiny red-and-blue de-signs commemorating the bicentennial of the French Revolution. Revoltingly chic, but I had to admit, it *did* look nice. The kitchen was the one room in the apartment that wasn't in a stage of uproar and redecoration, having been gutted and reconstructed by Phil's brothers weeks ago. New cabinets, new everything. It now resem-bled an English cabinetmaker's showcase. A gorgeous new flag-stone floor was cool under my bare feet. I was expecting the photographers from *Metropolitan Home* any minute.

Phil was going to discuss Theresa Kahr whether I wanted to or not. Well, he was curious. I'd be curious too.

"Iffy," I said, giving in. "After screaming at Healy she lapsed into unconsciousness. We made some headway stabilizing her and I had her admitted to the Intensive Care Unit, but by the time I signed out this evening, she still hadn't regained consciousness. She's in critical condition with multiple skull fractures, her one orbit is utterly shattered, and her jaw is broken. I called Mick and he said that her injuries were very similar to those sustained by the Central Park jogger, and at first all the jogger's docs had been sure she would die, so he wasn't going to make any predictions. It's out of my hands." As an emergency room physician, I was the starting pitcher. After I did my job, the relief pitcher took over— in this case, Mick Healy—and I went back to the dugout.

"God, that poor woman," said Phil. "And poor Mick, having her scream at him like that."

"Yeah, I know. All the other men were standing back—the male cop especially was making a big effort to stay out of her line of vision—but we didn't have time to tell Mick that she was afraid of men. He barged in and leaned over her with his face right in hers and she went berserk. He was quite rattled."

"I'm sure he was." Phil opened the bag of takeout that had just been delivered from the Greek restaurant. In the wake of any catastrophe, Phil, true to his Italian heritage, insisted one should *eat*. If possible, one's favorite food. Cooked by someone other than oneself. And don't forget a cocktail before dinner, and a nice wine with dinner. "Mangia, mangia." Having heard "Iss, iss, mein Kind" throughout my entire childhood from my mother and Bubbeh Hazel (my Russian grandmother), I agreed wholeheartedly.

"I didn't know whether you wanted tzatziki or taramosalata," he said. "I got tzatziki. And the lamb stew. And for dessert, rizogalo."

"Did you get some olives?"

"Of course I got some olives." Phil kissed his fingertips. "For you, bella mia, *anything*."

Phil poured each of us an inch of ouzo, a Greek aperitif, over ice. "Here's to you," he said, raising his glass.

"Here's to both of us," I gushed recklessly. I was rapidly coasting into Phase Two, the elation of guess-what-happened-to-me-today. Winston Churchill once said, "Nothing in life is so exhilarating as to be shot at without result." No modern psychotherapist would accept such a declaration at face value—but who cared? So I was in deep denial. It wasn't as if the rapist had actually raped me. He had only knocked me down.

We clinked glasses and Phil beamed. Too late, I realized I was feeding his marriage mania again. But hell. My mood had changed; I was becoming expansive. And you never knew; one day I might actually marry him, if he stopped pressuring me to do it. I certainly loved him enough.

At least most days I thought so. But I was never really confident. Phil and I had a shared checkered past that tended to cloud the issue of commitment and marriage. When we first got involved, it was casually, as platonic friends who just happened to fall into bed one night. At the time, Phil had another "platonic" friend he was sleeping with, a woman named Beth, who worked as a production assistant for a major news network and who was rarely in New York more than four or five days a month. *She* had another lover named Nicko, who lived in London. This chummy ménage had been going on for years, everybody apparently happy and non-threatened, and it seemed like the ne plus ultra of New York cosmopolitan-sophisticated-intellectual chic when I joined the club. At the time I thought my brothers, Craig and Alan, were insufferably provincial for objecting, and I waved off their concerns about AIDS with a bored insouciance I now found embarrassing in retrospect. We were wise enough to use condoms, but not wise enough to consider the psychological harm we were doing ourselves with our cavalier attitude toward sex.

I often wondered whether Phil and I were still paying the piper.

Things first began to change when I fell in love with Phil, and Beth decided to marry Nicko, and Phil decided he loved me after all, despite the fact that I had a one-night stand with an intern the very same weekend Beth told Phil she was marrying Nicko. Phil and I became monogamous. But had things changed enough for Phil and me to marry? Beth and Nicko were already divorced. It all seemed too complicated for words, and straight out of a John Updike novel, or some short story in *The New Yorker*. Or—worse—an episode of "Melrose Place"—which I would never admit to watching.

Some of the complications seemed inherited. Take, for example, the saga of my two fathers: My mother was engaged to marry Sandy Berman, ran off with Evan Sutcliffe, and decided Berman was her true love only after Sutcliffe ran his car into a bridge support during a thunderstorm and killed himself before I was born. Berman forgave her and took her back with great fanfare, they married, and I got a wonderful new dad, one gracious enough to adopt me while insisting that I bear Sutcliffe's last name as a memorial to him, since he was dead. And I got two neat brothers, Alan and Craig. But something never jelled for my mother, and by the time I was twelve or thirteen, Mom was sleeping around among the husbands of her friends with scandalous regularity. Dad was the prototype enabler; he tried to pretend nothing was going on, and ate until his weight doubled. Finally he suffered the first of a series of heart attacks, and my mother got her behavior under control.

They now seemed happily married, entering their golden years contentedly together.

But I was a cynic for life. I was afraid that deep down I was as cavalier as my mother, or as vulnerable to the same seductions, and I didn't want to tempt fate by marrying.

My mood, so expansive a few minutes earlier, slid back into the familiar groove of skepticism. Love, yes. Marriage, no.

Even though he was a fabulous catch.

"I'll put the stew in the oven while we eat the appetizers," Phil said, moving fluidly to the stove.

I gazed at him and contentedly sipped my drink. He still carried himself with the grace of the high school gymnast he had been twenty years before. Sleek and slender, he seemed even more so in the summer months, with his tanned and freckled face and arms, his blondish hair highlighted red by the sun. I thought the highlights set off his grape-green eyes especially nicely.

"You and Lisa Chiu stop by the Good Earth?" he asked, sitting down at the table again.

"Oh, Phil, they were so upset. I mean, who wouldn't be? The Arab kid was hosing down the back alley when we got there, and I thought the kid with the dreadlocks was going to plotz. The media had rattled them and had only just gone away, and they had finally received permission from the cops to open up again. There was blood everywhere—the cops tracked it in with their shoes. It was all over the floor of the kitchen. You could even smell it."

"How many employees do they have there now?"

"I don't know—a dozen, maybe."

"All foreigners?"

"Foreigners from the University, yeah. Kids with student visas. Except the kid with the dreadlocks. I'm sure he's American."

"Hmm," said Phil. He slathered some tzatziki onto a piece of bread and munched thoughtfully. "What do we know about Theresa Kahr?"

"She's from Berlin, her parents are dead, and she's in this country on some kind of German orphans' scholarship. She's brushing up her English and studying political science at the University. She's a lesbian feminist and a Green Party fanatic. Very anti-nukes. Lisa knows her. They were co-organizers of that bus trip to an abortion-rights march in Washington last year, and Theresa used to be an escort at Westside Women's."

"Used to be?"

"She quit. I'm not sure why. Lisa was a little vague."

"Did Theresa and Lisa have some kind of falling-out?"

Trust Phil to zoom right to the heart of the matter. "I don't know," I mused. "But it's a possibility."

"You think Theresa made a pass at her?"

"That would hardly be enough reason for Lisa to fall out with her. Lisa gets lots of passes, from both men and women, from what I hear."

"Ah," said Phil. "Is she bi?"

"No, she's straight—if you really must know—and I think she's got something hot going with somebody. But she's very secretive."

"How do you know it's a man?"

"She's on the pill."

"In this day and age? She must be serious about her partner if they've progressed from the condoms stage of the relationship. Well, that clinches it, I suppose." Phil ate some more tzatziki and ruminated on Lisa Chiu's sex life. He was really an incurable gossip about people who were not his patients. "How do you know she's on the pill?"

"For God's sake, Phil." I laughed. "We were fixing our lipstick in the ladies room at the Philharmonic, and I saw them in her purse, okay?"

"So who do you think she's sleeping with?"

"I have no idea."

"Well, if anyone would know, it would be you," Phil said. "How are her financial problems, by the way?"

"The hospital's making arrangements to hire Lisa as a needle-sticker and at the same time give her credit for her ER externship, but it's very hush-hush because it's so irregular." I sighed. "She's not even sure the arrangements will go through. Apparently they're asking a patron to pay her salary, and there's a tax issue for him, plus an insurance problem for the hospital, among other things." Lisa also had some kind of agreement with a small medical practice to help computerize the patient records, but I didn't really want to get off on a sidetrack about Lisa Chiu's complicated finances. Draining my glass, I poured another inch of ouzo and watched the liquor turn from clear to milky white as it hit the ice. Drinking ouzo always transported me to the tavernas of Crete, where I had spent a magical vacation during graduate school.

I wished I were in Crete now.

I realized I had left out the part about the Babydoll Killer. So I told him. "And then, with Theresa, he stuffs it up her—" I took off my glasses and rubbed my eyes. I was seriously beginning to consider getting drunk.

"Oh, God, Ev," Phil said. He got up and came around the table, knelt next to my chair, and put his arms around my waist. "God, honey. Are you all right?"

"I'm okay."

"But this makes what happened to you worse. What if he hadn't found her first? He might have chosen *you*."

"I know."

He laid his head on my breast and I stroked his hair. I knew he needed me to need him. He needed me to unburden myself to him, and he needed to comfort me. But to need him, I had to have access to my emotions. And they hadn't turned back on yet.

"Well," he said, after a few minutes had passed and I showed no signs of collapsing into his embrace. "Maybe we should eat." He got up and took the stew out of the oven. If I didn't respond to caressing, I might respond to food. He'd unlock me yet. After all, that's what he did for a living. I always did think he should hang out a shingle that read "Philip Carchiollo, M.D. Attending Physician and Assistant Clinical Professor of Psychiatry. Locksmith, Safecracker, and Can Opener. By Appointment."

"So," he said invitingly, sitting down and folding his napkin primly in his lap.

"Phil, I really do love you." I smiled.

"Good."

"And thank you for the dinner."

"You're welcome."

"It's very comforting."

"I'm glad." He ate some stew. "But I think you should talk it out."

"Well, I'll take a stab at it—but there's a power failure, you know? The electricity's off."

"I know, honey."

I pushed some stew around my plate. "What would make someone do something like this?" I asked. "Beat a woman's face in and then rape her?"

"Well, I've been thinking about it," Phil said musingly, "ever since Ben Eisen's patient." He put his fork down and picked up his wineglass, holding it in both hands, elbows on the table. "I'm not a forensic psychologist, but this business of beating the woman about the head—she literally loses face. He makes it impossible for her to face him, or for him to face her, for that matter—nobody can face anybody in this thing. And bashing in the two highest orifices, the eyes—that achieves humiliation and blinding. Penetration of the head. Head-fucking. It's wonderfully oedipal; you remember the play *Equus*? 'The eyes have it.' Then there's this amazing business with the babydoll; that has a real psychotic flavor. He really has to be in La-La Land—or what you and I would know as La-La Land. He fucks her, then he completely compresses the gestation time to a couple of seconds, and voilà—the child is born immediately. Only it's nonhuman. Which says that *he's* nonhuman—all he can produce are plastic effigies. A small, unfeeling, unknowing, unmoving, unliving baby—leaning against a mother that cannot give because she's comatose or dead. So he's replaying his own experience. He's that baby. He feels dead. But the question is, who's he killing? We don't really know who the person is in his mind that he's killing."

I ate some stew. Suddenly I found myself ravenous, and began to eat in earnest. Phil continued talking, but my mind drifted off to a place where it was quiet and there were no thoughts. Eventually I realized all my food was gone and my wineglass was empty, and for a split second I suffered a strange hallucination. I didn't know where I was. Or who had eaten my dinner and drunk my wine.

"Ev. Honey, are you all right?"

"Phil, I have to go out for some air. Please don't take it personally."

"I'll come with you."

"No, please. I think I just need to walk it off."

"I wish you wouldn't."

I racked my brain for a peace offering that would take away the sting of my not needing to be with him in this my hour of desperation. "Phil, I need to be by myself tonight, but tomorrow let's get out and go down the Village for dinner at Volare's." Ristorante Volare was our special romantic restaurant. "Tomorrow I'll be better company."

He assessed me.

"I'm not drunk," I said. "I had two inches of ouzo and one glass of wine."

"It's been a very traumatic day," he protested.

"I've been through worse." Which I had.

He sighed. But above all, Phil was a man who prided himself

on being reasonable and considerate of the feelings of others. He swallowed his disappointment and kissed me good night.

"Don't walk home by way of where you were attacked this morning," he warned, tapping me on the nose with a school-marm's finger.

Of course, after he shut the door on me, that's precisely what I did.

The night was close and still. Around lunchtime we had had brief thunderstorms and, weirdly, *hail*, but the heat had broken only for a half hour or so. It was now oppressively hot and more sultry than ever. Across the street from Phil's apartment, not a leaf stirred in the park. Still, as I turned south on Riverside Drive, I felt as liberated as if I had stepped naked into the dripping torpor of a tropical rain forest. I took a deep breath of the steamy air and thought, finally.

For the first time all day, I could have a private thought in the quiet of my own head, away from the bedlam of the ER.

And away from Phil's hovering concern.

I turned up the hill toward the hospital.

Nothing happened.

I began to argue with myself. Well, what did you think was going to happen? You think the guy's standing here, waiting to see if you'll walk up the street again so he can knock you down a second time?

I looked around. On one side of the street were row houses, among them the white brick residences where a community of nuns lived; on the other side several buildings comprised the University's School of Social Work. In the side streets between Broadway and Riverside Drive it could get very, very quiet from time to time, especially late at night. It was quiet now. I was alone with my thoughts.

What I wanted was to have a reaction and get it over with. All day I'd had the uneasy feeling you get when you're lying in bed feeling nauseous, waiting to see if you really will have to get up and go vomit. Hoping the nausea will pass.

I was becoming extremely exasperated with myself. So, Sutcliffe, you wanna walk up and down this street until you have an emotion, or what? Go home, have a drink, and go to bed! Sleep it off. You'll be better tomorrow, the whole thing will fade in your mind.

I found the brownstone steps I'd sat on that morning and I sat down again.

Nothing happened.

The street remained quiet. Two doors down, where the nuns lived, the windows were dark except for one on the top floor, where a small lamp shone cozily. Some sister burning the midnight oil, I guessed.

I looked at my watch: almost midnight.

Air conditioners whirred in the night.

I waited for a thought.

Nothing happened.

Or an emotion.

Nothing.

Still I lingered. I began to think about Theresa Kahr, about the man who had been going into the bakery and asking her for a date. That bothered me, and it clearly bothered Lisa Chiu. But Lisa had brushed it off.

Serial killers don't ask you for a date first.

But what if they did? Or, more specifically, what if this one did?

I sighed and got to my feet. If I'd expected an epiphany that would reveal to me all my most-hidden inner thoughts and feelings about the day's rude brush with violence, it clearly wasn't going to happen.

Again I wondered what I expected to feel and think.

In my imagination, I heard running footsteps coming up on me from behind. The hair rose up on the back of my neck.

I realized the footsteps were not in my imagination.

I turned.

A man running. Jesus Christ, *it was him!*

A startled cry escaped my throat. Then he was upon me, reaching for me—a man with sandy-colored hair, in a white T-shirt and blue running shorts—

It was Mick Healy.

"Ev, what is it?" he asked, his arm coming around my shoulders. He was breathing hard from his jog. "What's the matter, darling?"

"Don't do that," I snapped. I put a hand on his chest. His shirt was soaked with sweat, and clouds of heat and steam rose from him.

I began to cry.

I can't reconstruct precisely what happened next. Mick's exactly my height and, with my hand on his chest and his arm around me, I guess our mouths were too close. After having been bottled up all day, I found myself in sudden extremity, in the arms of a sweaty, panting man, who, I dimly realized, had waited a very, very long time to kiss me.

CHAPTER
5

AT 6:30 A.M., I was standing in the middle of the emergency room, writing an order in Joshua Waterman's chart.

And praying to God for less excitable colleagues.

The ER clerk appeared at my elbow. "Dr. Sutcliffe?"

"With you in a minute, Julio," I said.

"Have you seen Lisa Chiu this morning?"

"Not yet. Why?"

"Dr. Murkland was asking for her."

I sighed and continued writing. "Let's try not to encourage Dr. Murkland vis-à-vis Lisa Chiu, shall we?"

"Um . . . Dr. Sutcliffe?"

"Yes, Julio."

"Linhardt is yelling at Dr. Shehadeh again."

"I hear him."

That morning there were two bedlams taking place. The usual ER bedlam, and the bedlam inside my head. My thoughts clamored like an Asian gong concert. Theresa Kahr's coma had deepened. Detective Ost's temper had peaked. *Jesus Christ, Doc, the last*

*thing I need is sixteen docs gossiping among themselves about the simi-
larities of the cases. You think I can't make phone calls? You think I
can't call the detectives on those other cases, just like you called the docs?
You never heard of 'Loose lips sink ships?'*

And Mick Healy's passion had—

Christ, he very nearly made love to me right there on the
street. I had a great deal of trouble convincing him we were losing
our heads and that I couldn't possibly sleep with him because I
already had a boyfriend. I had even more trouble convincing myself. In fact, the conversation seemed to consist almost entirely of
my moaning "I can't do this," and his groaning "I know, I know,"
while we continued to devour each other whole, having by this
time stumbled down two or three steps into the well of a brownstone, where we could grope each other in comparative privacy.
How I extracted myself finally and wound up alone in my own
bed, I'm not quite sure.

It was just as well, too, because Phil let himself into my apartment at 5:30 A.M. to bring me tulips and freesia from the all-night
Korean greenmarket. My favorite bouquet.

I swiped the arm of my white coat across my forehead. The
air in the ER was close and heavy, fetid with the odors of feces,
urine, blood, and vomit. The air-conditioning was malfunctioning
again. The heat was expected to break in the New York region by
midnight, with a cool front from Canada bringing rain and tem-
peratures in the eighties, but midnight seemed very far away. And
the temperature already was above ninety degrees—at 6:30 A.M.
I felt as if I were working in the sewers, or in a jungle. At least in
the jungle, I thought, I'd be outside.

God, it was hot.

With half an ear I listened to the pitched voice of Brian Linhardt. At this hour, you'd think people wouldn't have the energy
to get riled up like that. Maybe the early hour didn't bother Linhardt because he used to be in the Army. On the other hand,
Linhardt, a Ranger-trained paramedic, was always "on." Six-
thirty A.M., and he was going great guns.

"Dr. Sutcliffe?"

"Yes, Julio."

Too late. The new intern, Dr. Guy Shehadeh, crashed into me, hotly pursued by Brian Linhardt, the ER paramedic. "He has nuchal rigidity, inappropriate affect, a temperature of a hundred and three, and a white blood cell count of twenty-two thousand," Brian was hollering. "What does that tell you?"

I wanted to say to Linhardt, "Shehadeh is red in the face and near tears, what does that tell *you*?" Instead I put an arm out in front of Linhardt like the bar coming down at the train crossing. "Brian, don't yell at the interns in the middle of the ER," I said.

"Aw, Jesus, Ev!" Brian exploded. "He doesn't know what he's fucking doing!"

"Lower your voice. He'll learn. You're undermining his authority, yelling at him in front of the patients like this."

Not that the patients we had this morning were paying any attention. It had been a surprisingly quiet night given the exceptionally sultry heat, and the few patients we did have were parked on their stretchers, helter-skelter up and down the corridors of the ER, most in the drug-induced stupor of their choice. Heroin was making a big comeback in New York.

"No, he won't learn, not if—"

I cut him off. "Brian, didn't they ever tell you in the Army 'not in front of the men'? You're the sergeant here yelling at the lieutenant. If you have something to say to an intern, you take him or her aside and you say it quietly, with respect."

"Yes, ma'am!" barked Linhardt, leaping into an exaggerated salute. He stomped off.

I rolled my eyes and went back to Waterman's chart.

"Dr. Sutcliffe?"

"Yes, Julio."

"The students are ready to round." Julio cleared his throat significantly.

I sighed. What he meant was: The students are ready to round and Dr. Shehadeh is probably in the bathroom with his head in a sinkful of cold water. Which was where Shehadeh seemed to be spending a lot of his time these days—and not just because of the record heat.

I finished my note and handed Julio the chart. "I'll go get him."

This was not what I had in mind when I went to medical school, I thought as I made my way through the utility room and doctors' lounge, out the back of the ER and down the corridor to the doctors' locker room. Four years of school, a grueling internship, a year of residency—and for what?

I was an exalted den mother.

"Guy, come out of there right now," I said, banging on the door of the bathroom.

I opened the door and, sure enough, there he was with his head in the sink. Shirt off, dazzling me with his magnificent body, his big hands splayed on the sides of the sink, the muscles of his back and arms rippling with tension.

He had to come up for air sometime. I waited.

The Linhardt-Shehadeh game was now, by my reckoning, in its thirty-fourth inning, if you counted one inning per day since Guy Shehadeh showed up to begin his internship in the emergency room at University Hospital. Thirty-four innings and no end in sight.

Defending for the home team, ladies and gentlemen, Brian Linhardt. Thirty-six years of age, five feet ten, short blond hair in a conservative cut, nice blue eyes. Modestly handsome in his own way, especially given his physique, which he fanatically maintained in top-notch condition.

Batting for the visiting team, Guy Shehadeh. Twenty-five, six feet one, copper-colored hair falling into his drop-dead, gorgeous hazel eyes, long and limber, the whole package straight out of a Ralph Lauren ad.

Brian Linhardt, fluent in Spanish—several dialects, in fact—had also mastered the patois of Haitian and Dominican French. He was in great demand as a translator. Add that to his clinical skills, and the fact that he could take a flawless patient history without help from a physician, was greatly appreciated by the rest of the ER staff, especially now that the hospital was downgrading and replacing nurses with paramedics and EMTs.

Guy Shehadeh, who knew maybe twenty words of Arabic from his parents—a language not much in demand at University Hospital—was lucky if he could stumble through a patient history in his mother tongue, English. And, invariably, he forgot to ask the patient the one key piece of information necessary for the diagnosis.

Brian had been filing applications to twenty or thirty medical schools every single year for the past ten years, and had failed to be accepted by any of them. Like many fine EMTs and paramedics, he learned best hands-on, but did poorly in an academic setting. The fact that he could name every single beta-blocker on the market, along with side effects and contraindications, did not offset a C average in pre-med physics, biology, and organic chemistry.

Guy, who had the coveted "Dr." in front of his name, probably knew less "real" medicine than Brian did, but he'd done well at a decent college and had bumbled and fumbled his way through medical school. He was great if called upon to answer questions about the tetralogy of Fallot, but relatively clueless when asked to devise a treatment plan for the homeless, TB-racked multi-drug abuser with cellulitis and osteomyelitis.

Who knows what lurks in the hearts of men, where all the competitive macho bullshit really gets started?

They hated each other.

When Shehadeh finally surfaced, gasping and dripping, I said, "You can't let Linhardt get your goat like this. What are you going to do—spend your whole intern year with your head in the sink? You do that and I'll tell you right now, I'll put it in your evaluation." I threw a towel at him. "This is *not* professional behavior."

"Oh, and I suppose Linhardt's is," he snapped. "Why don't you talk to Linhardt about his attitude problem, instead of yelling at me for throwing a little water on my face so I don't just haul off and slug him right in the middle of the ER? How about giving me a little credit for not doing that, huh? Or maybe you'd rather I just belted him one."

What did I tell you? An exalted den mother. "Let me spell this out for you," I said slowly. "You are in trouble. You don't know your place in the pecking order. You don't know how to stand up to Linhardt, and you don't know how to address me, your resident, in an appropriate manner."

He looked at me sullenly. Beads of water ran down his face.

"And," I said, "your work is sloppy. We have to supervise you more closely than we should. God forbid, Guy, that you should ever kill a patient, because it's going to be your ass, not mine. Now you have three seconds to get out there and round with those students."

That cut him and he flushed. "Okay, okay," he sputtered, tugging on his shirt and white coat, striding next to me as I barged back to the ER. Both the unbuttoned shirt and coat flapped in the breeze, making him look like Superman routed out of his telephone booth on a day he forgot to put his costume on under his civvies. "But it's not just me Linhardt razzes. He gives shit to all the interns, and he really heaps it on the med students. You should have heard him yesterday beating up on Lisa Chiu—"

"Lisa knows how to take it. You don't."

"Does that make it right? Doesn't it bother you, the temper he has? And God only knows what he did down in Central America with the Rangers, all that clandestine stuff he says he can't talk about. He was probably down there shooting people for the CIA. You think I'm gonna kill one of the patients, you should worry about him killing one of the staff."

"Don't be so flip. If you aren't petrified every single moment of the day that you're going to kill one of the patients, and if you aren't utterly terrified of assuming greater responsibilities next year, when you're a junior resident, you are not taking your job seriously enough. Which is my point."

We burst into the emergency room, both of us red-faced and panting, Guy in a fine state of dishabille.

One of the nurses whistled.

"Nice pecs," commented another.

"Phat!" said a third.

Guy buttoned his shirt and then unzipped his fly and stuffed his shirttails into his pants, starting a small commotion and scandalizing Dr. Harold Murkland, one of the attendings from the Pediatrics ER.

"Somebody told me Shehadeh can't keep it in his pants," Murkland commented sourly, giving me a look over his reading glasses that said, Can't you control your people?

I smiled wearily and clapped him on the back. Murkland and I went way back. He had been my resident during my third-year clerkship on the Pediatrics service, when we had developed a warm friendship and collegiality.

"What can I do for you, Hal?"

"Well, I just thought I'd wander over and see Joshua Waterman, look in and say hello." He wiped his neck with a handkerchief and squinted around the ER. "Christ, it's hot in here. Lisa Chiu here yet?"

"No." Ever since Chiu had rotated from the Pediatrics ER to the adult ER for the second half of her summer clerkship, Murkland had been "wandering over" to the adult ER several times a day, ostensibly to "look in on" former patients of his who had reached the age of sixteen and had graduated from Peds to the adult ER. Normally, he had a sense of humor about his "mid-life-crisis crush" on Chiu, as he called it, but I didn't think this was the morning to tease him about it. Something flickered behind his gray eyes.

"You look tired," I said, sliding my arm through his. His face was puffy, and he hadn't shaved.

"Mmm." He was noncommittal.

Then I noticed the gashes. "What did you do to your face?"

"Don't ask." He tried a small laugh that didn't quite work. "I cut myself with a dull razor yesterday. That's why I haven't shaved today."

"You did this shaving? What in God's name were you shaving with, an ax?"

"Ev, please. Could I just get Waterman's chart?"

"Hal, are these *sutures?* You cut yourself with a razor and you needed *sutures?*"

"It's a long story." Murkland sighed. He spotted Waterman's chart in the rack behind the nurses' station, leaned over the counter and scooped it up. "Julio, I'm taking Waterman's X rays," he called to the clerk, collecting those as well.

"Hal—"

"I'll handle Denny," he said firmly.

Dr. Denise Aubuchon was Murkland's partner, and had inherited Joshua Waterman from Murkland once Waterman turned sixteen. Hal did Peds, Denny did adults, and they fought over the adolescents. Ostensibly the two had gone into practice together on a grant to study maternal-childhood AIDS infections, but many of us were coming to the conclusion that the real raison d'être of their partnership was quarreling and one-upmanship. To make matters worse, Denny had hired Joshua after he finished high school to help with computerization of Hal's and Denny's office records, and she had developed a warm mother-son relationship with the boy, further exacerbating Hal's jealousy.

"Oh, I get it," I said. "Denny got fed up once and for all with your wandering over here to look in on her patients, and she attacked your face with an ice pick to get your attention."

"Very funny. If you must know, I went to a bachelor's party last night."

"You did? You hate bachelor's parties."

"It was my cousin Robert. I couldn't get out of it." He flipped the chart open. "We were toasting him, and this guy was standing on a chair and he fell on me. I was raising my glass for the toast and it broke on my face—"

I tried to imagine Hal Murkland at any party boisterous enough for people to fall off chairs.

"—and I bled like a stuck pig all over her bedroom. So, what's the story, pneumothorax?'' he asked, moving toward the emergency room's OR One as he read.

"Yes. What do you mean, 'her' bedroom?''

"The bride's.''

"You were toasting the groom in the bride's bedroom?''

"Why do you think I never go to bachelor's parties? They get worse and worse. You have a chance to look at these?'' He held the chest X ray up to the ceiling light.

"Yeah, they show the left upper lobe has collapsed—see this here?'' I pointed to the air shadow between the lung and the chest wall. "We've been seeing this a lot with the aerosolized pentamidine—it doesn't seem to reach the upper lobes of the lung very effectively. Pneumocystis sets in and the lobe collapses.''

"Maybe he should be on dapsone instead. Is Denny still prescribing the AZT?''

"No, DDC. Hal, why are you looking over Denny's shoulder like this? Let her handle it.''

Murkland put the X rays back in their envelope and continued toward OR One. "Someone coming down to put in a chest tube?''

"McCabe, as soon as he's out of the OR. Who sutured your face?''

"I did.''

"You sutured your own face? Were you drunk?''

"Very.'' He coughed.

We flattened ourselves against the wall so a stretcher could go past; the ER was a perpetual logjam. Standing there, I thought about Pick Day, the day fourth-year medical students find out which hospitals they'll be going to for their internships. After I found out I'd be going to University Hospital, I called Hal and we went out for a couple of drinks to celebrate. He drank too much and afterward I had to half-carry him back to his apartment. Unfortunately I also drank too much and stayed there with him. Which was the one and only time Hal and I had sex.

It was a surprising experience. Working together with Hal I'd gotten used to his quirky personality and nerdy awkwardness; I'd even gotten used to his conservative, Republican opinions. He was one of those guys women never looked at twice—until they got to know him and discovered how nice he was. Then you would see them staring at him fixedly, and you could practically read their minds: gee, he's really *nice*, and he's not bad-looking, especially without his glasses . . . But he's such a nerd—how is he ever going to find someone to sleep with? Which was what I had thought back then, myself.

Then I fell into his bed quite by accident and discovered he had hidden talents, one of which was, startlingly, wanton abandonment. Unfortunately, even wanton abandonment in bed did not make up for the fact that here was a guy who was known among his medical students as "Turkey Murky." I am ashamed to say that early the next morning when I awoke, I did something I had never done before and which I have not done since—I sneaked out of a man's bed without waking him to say good-bye.

I followed Murkland into the ER's OR One, where a subdued and guarded Joshua Waterman lay listlessly on his gurney. Delicate and small-boned when in the best of health, he now seemed reduced to a pile of twigs. His glazed chestnut eyes swiveled in the hollows of his eye sockets over protruding cheekbones as he looked up at Hal and me. Doctors had a word for patients who looked like this: *sick*.

"Not too perky, huh?" said Hal empathetically. He took Waterman's hand and held it briefly before slipping his fingers to the wrist for the pulse. "Sorry you have to hang out here. I know it's Calcutta, and even more so than usual with the air-conditioning not working. We're just waiting for the chest guy to come down and put in a chest tube for you."

"Thanks," croaked Waterman. He seemed embarrassed to see Hal, and averted his eyes. As Denny's and Hal's receptionist, he probably got an earful of their patient rivalries, and I imagined that he was quite uncomfortable to find himself the possible fodder for yet another quarrel. But, like the dutiful child caught between two warring parents, Josh made the best of it. "Dr.

Sutcliffe's taking good care of me in the meantime," he said, smiling bravely. Josh used to have a smile so dazzling you thought the sun was cresting the eastern sky; now it was like the waning moon. AIDS did that to people.

Joshua Waterman was barely nineteen years old, and he was declining like an old man.

"So what's the story?" Hal asked when he finished watching Waterman's chest rise and fall, counting the breaths per minute.

"Well, you know the Bactrim made me sick," Josh began, glancing at me. I'd already been through all this with him, but working for doctors he knew that as soon as another doctor walked in the room, you told your story all over again, from the beginning. "For the pneumocystis? I was nauseous the whole time and had these really bad headaches, and I could hardly get out of bed. And after ten days I didn't think I could stand it anymore, so a friend of mine's mother in New Jersey said, 'Come over here and let me feed you some mom food and take care of you.' So I went. They live out in the country, and I got to lie on the porch all day and look at the cows and horses in the back field, and breathe fresh air. After five days of this I began to feel *much* better. Then I got up from the couch yesterday and this pain kind of stabbed me"—he fluttered a birdlike hand over his upper left chest—"and I thought it would go away, but it didn't. It got really worse and I thought I was having a heart attack. So my friend's mom drove me here."

"Wise choice," Hal said. "Sit up for me now?" He put his big arms under Waterman's emaciated rib cage and helped lift him into a sitting position. Josh grimaced in pain. "Deep breath."

Waterman drew a jagged breath. "Hal, you know your Medicaid bills . . . ?"

"Not now, Josh. Plenty of time to worry about that when you're well. We've got Lisa Chiu filling in for you. Deep breath. Good, good. Another."

Afterward, Murkland and I conferred in the utilities room.

"Amazing kid," said Hal. "His lung collapses and he's worried about the work on his desk back at the office."

"You put an awful burden on him, fighting over him like this," I pointed out.

Murkland bristled. "*I* don't put a burden on him, *Denny* puts a burden on him. The kid fucking worships her, and she takes him for all he's worth."

I put my hands up. "Hal, consider your professional behavior. Behave professionally. That's all I'm asking."

"It's none of your business," he snapped, pulling off his gloves.

"It *is* my business. Waterman's my patient, too—and this is my ER. *You* do not belong here. Go back to Peds."

"Pardon me, Miss Manners." He stomped off, flinging Waterman's chart and X rays onto the nurses'-station counter as he went by.

"Dr. Sutcliffe?"

"Yes, Julio." I made a face at Murkland's retreating back. Couldn't anybody this morning get along with anybody else?

"Can you sign these pharmacy slips, Doctor?"

I signed. "Julio, what's the status of that patient who came in earlier, the guy who was confused and febrile?"

"I think Dr. Shehadeh's sending him upstairs for a CAT scan. That is, if he and Linhardt ever stop arguing about whether the guy needs a CAT scan."

"I'll look in." By now I could hear Linhardt's and Shehadeh's pitched voices wafting out of OR Two like an operatic duet. I went in, smiled at the patient—who blinked at me lethargically—and said, "Gentleman, may I see you in the corridor, please?"

There is no privacy in the ER, except the kind you get from football-type huddles. Huddling, however, tended to make Linhardt start behaving like a rat in a corner, and I never drew him into it if he was mad. So I took the two men out of the ER and around the corner by the nurses' locker room. "What is this about?" I demanded.

Shehadeh, glaring at Linhardt, took a deep breath. "This is a fifty-one year old professor from the University," he began, launching into a full-blown, formal patient presentation. Guy couldn't collect his thoughts unless he presented the patient formally, and there was no use in my butting in to cut to the chase— it would only confuse him. I put my hands on my hips and gritted my teeth.

Next to me, Linhardt crossed his arms over his chest and smirked.

The patient had become restless and developed chills during the night, which had awakened his wife, who found him feverish and confused. The wife brought him to the emergency room. Shehadeh ticked off details on his fingers: His temperature was 103, his blood pressure 150 over 100, pulse 95 (rapid), respiratory rate 26 (a little high), and he had a stiff neck ("nuchal rigidity"). He perfunctorily reeled off the rest of his physical findings, then plunged into the history: The patient had not lost consciousness, he had no psychiatric problems, and nothing like this had ever happened before, according to the wife; he was not diabetic, he took no medications, he didn't drink or do drugs. Before he went to bed the previous night, his wife said, he had complained of a headache.

Shehadeh looked at me meaningfully.

"So he was fine until last night but now he's lethargic and moaning and febrile," I said. "Is he hypertensive?"

"No."

"Does he smoke?"

"No."

"Overweight?"

"No."

"Family history of stroke?"

Shehadeh flushed. He'd forgotten to ask.

"Any focal findings?"

"There's the rub," said Linhardt softly.

"He has no focal signs?" I looked from Shehadeh to Linhardt and back again. Focal signs were neurological clues that something was wrong with the brain; for example, a dilated or constricted pupil on one side but not the other; a drooping eyelid; weakness of the left hand but not the right. The presence of focal findings helped confirm the diagnosis of stroke; the absence of them helped rule it out. "Any papilledema?" Swelling of the optic nerve, which is one of the things the doctor is looking for when he or she examines your eyes with the ophthalmoscope. Another sign of stroke.

"Dr. Know-It-All here hasn't mastered the ophthalmoscope," taunted Linhardt.

"Shut up," Shehadeh said.

I gave Guy a long look. Red-faced, he averted his gaze.

I knew that Shehadeh, in addition to not having mastered the ophthalmoscope, had not mastered the delicate art of the spinal tap. Which was what this patient needed. In fact, I strongly suspected Shehadeh was sending the patient upstairs for a CAT scan so he wouldn't have to ask me to watch him tap the guy.

"First off," I said, "you have no business sending this patient to CAT scan without consulting me or the attending. Now how bad was this headache?"

"Bad," Shehadeh said in a defensive tone of voice that somehow suggested that the headache had actually been mild and nonthrobbing.

"Vomiting?"

"Yes. He's got papilledema—"

"How do *you* know?" scoffed Linhardt.

"—nuchal rigidity, he's confused and restless—"

"Any convulsions?" I asked.

"He didn't ask," Linhardt shot in. "Ev, he didn't even check for the fucking focal signs. *I* checked. There are no focal signs. He just doesn't want to tap the guy—"

"I am *not* going to tap the guy when he has signs of hemorrhagic stroke—"

"*What* signs of hemorrhagic stroke? He has *no focal*—"

"Shut up, both of you," I said loudly. "It's too fucking hot for this kind of bullshit." I turned to Shehadeh, who still would not meet my eye. I saw he was blinking back tears. "Guy, I appreciate your concerns, but you can't afford to send this patient upstairs for a CAT scan to rule out stroke. That's an hour or two before you get him back downstairs again. He has meningitis and you have to do a spinal tap and start antibiotics immediately—"

"What did I tell you?" Linhardt cried gleefully.

"Brian, *shut up*," I snapped.

"But—" protested Guy.

"Because if you delay the tap and antibiotics, he could die before you get him back from CAT scan," I said as gently as possible.

"Ev, if he had a bleed in his brain or an abscess and increased pressure, I would have killed him if I tapped him—"

"You're right. You would have sucked his brain right out the bottom of his skull. It's valid to rule out hemorrhagic stroke and abscess before you do a spinal tap. All I'm saying is, you don't need a CAT scan. You rule it out with a good eye exam and by checking for focal findings. Which is what Brian did. And if the patient is non-focal, then it's fine to tap him."

Shehadeh opened his mouth to say something but his voice caught. Reflexively, I patted him on the back in motherly fashion.

"Oh, give me a fucking break," said Linhardt. "He almost kills the patient, and you pat him on the back." He turned on his heel.

Shehadeh shot out an arm and grabbed Linhardt by the collar of his shirt. The next thing I knew, Guy was flat on his back on the floor and Linhardt was standing over him with his fists balled up. It happened so fast I hadn't even seen what Linhardt did to him.

"Brian," I said, "if you don't step back, I'll haul your ass before your union for disciplinary measures."

Shehadeh sprang to his feet and lunged at Linhardt, who threw him a second time. Effortlessly. "Yeah? Who's assaulting whom here, Ev? Why don't you haul *his* ass before the Doctors' Council?" Linhardt snorted derisively. He stomped off.

Shehadeh got to his feet, more slowly this time. He was so thoroughly humiliated, and I was so disgusted with him—not for misdiagnosing the patient, which was an honest mistake, but for pigheadedly failing to consult me and even more pigheadedly getting into a row with Brian Linhardt—that I couldn't think of anything to say. I left him standing there.

Back at the nurses' station I checked the board to see who my next patient was. A carpenter from the construction site for the new hospital wing, laceration of the hand.

"How come this guy with the lacerated hand isn't being seen in the Boo-Boo Room?" I asked the clerk.

"They think he seized."

"Oh, well, that would explain it." I reached for the patient's chart just as the batphone rang.

Julio answered, listened, and spoke into his PA microphone. "Stand by for a gunshot wound to the chest, ETA six minutes."

"What have you got, Julio?" I asked.

Then I saw the look on his face.

"They shot Dr. Lamartine over at the Westside Women's Health Center," he said.

He didn't have to say who *They* were.

Lisa Chiu's *They*.

"Jesus," I said. I looked at my watch; it was nearly 7 A.M.

I couldn't remember whether Lisa was working this morning down at Westside Women's, or whether she was supposed to be here in the ER.

That was when I started to worry about her.

CHAPTER
6

"I was *wearing* the goddamned bulletproof vest," Dr. Jean-Jacques Lamartine complained in his lilting West Indian baritone. "Son of a bitch got me through the armhole." He raised his left arm over his head so I could see the tiny, not even dime-sized hole in his armpit. Maybe a tablespoon of bloody fluid oozed from the wound, but not more.

"What'd they shoot him with?" I asked the nearest cop, who smelled of adrenaline and sweat, as we pulled Lamartine's gurney into the emergency room's OR Two.

"You're not gonna like this, Doc. It's a twenty-two long-rifle rimfire."

I looked up. "Is there something I should know about this besides the caliber?"

"It's called a 'devastator'—you know, like Hinckley shot Reagan with." He put his arm up and wiped the sleeve of his shirt across his forehead. "Damn. It's just as hot in here as it is outside."

I groaned. "An explosive bullet? So what's the story? It didn't explode on impact, so it's a dud, or it can go off any minute now?"

"Worst-case scenario, it's gone off already. You'll know if you find lots of black residue in the wound channel—you'll get fragments of copper and lead, too. But if it hasn't blown up by now it probably won't. These exploding bullets are mostly ineffective, which is why you don't see them so much anymore."

"I hope you at least got the guy," I said to the cop.

"No, but we will." His face hardened. "Fucking fanatic. All we need in the fucking heat, too, is shit like this."

"I didn't even know I was shot," Lamartine said. "I mean, I saw the guy shooting *at* me—"

"You shot anywhere else, Jock?"

"I don't think so. I didn't think he hit me at all, I thought I was short of breath from the excitement and maybe that pain in my ribs was the bullet bouncing off the vest, maybe I was bruised—"

"Pain in the ribs where?"

"Here," he said. He placed his hand gingerly over his lower left rib cage.

I turned to the EMTs. "You guys vital him in the bus?"

"BP one forty over ninety, pulse one hundred and ten, respirations twenty-eight. You wanna transfer him?"

We positioned ourselves for the heave-ho. Lamartine was a big man, and heavy, but with the help of the two burly EMTs, the nurse and I were able to transfer him from the ambulance gurney to the ER stretcher without too much difficulty. The EMTs finished their report, said "Ciao," and left.

Lamartine had been stripped to the waist by the ambulance crew and we removed the rest of his clothes now. There was nothing to see on his glistening mahogany skin, no bruising, no discoloration. "Let's roll him," I said to Marie Sook and Helen Yannis, the nurses. Gently but quickly, we rolled Lamartine onto his side and I looked for wounds on his back. Satisfied that he hadn't been shot anywhere else, Marie started Lamartine on oxygen and Helen slapped a BP cuff on his arm as I got out my stethoscope. "All right, Jock, let's have a listen." I auscultated both sides of his chest. His breathing was rapid and shallow, and I heard no lung sounds on the left side; the left lung had probably collapsed. Heart sounded normal so far.

Still, with a wound of this kind you never knew exactly what was going on, exploding bullet or no exploding bullet. We would have to work fast to prevent him from going into shock. And we'd need to get him up to the OR chop-chop to see what damage had been done and to have the bullet removed. Christ, I hoped the damned thing wouldn't blow up. "You might have a little pneumothorax," I said.

"Yeah, I figured. Can somebody call my wife?"

"Yes, in a few minutes." I palpated his abdomen. He was in a cold sweat, too, despite the hot day.

"You're short of breath."

"Yeah."

"Getting worse?"

"Yeah."

"Any chest pain?"

In response to this question, Lamartine asked, "Tell me I'm not having an MI." By MI, he meant myocardial infarction, or heart attack.

"You're having chest pain? Cardiac or pleuritic?"

"Ev, I can't tell—I've got mid-sternal pain but it's not radiating anywhere, and pain on inspiration—"

"We'll get an EKG." Gingerly I felt the spot where Jock had complained his ribs hurt. No swelling. "That hurt?"

Jock winced.

"BP one forty over ninety, pulse one twenty, respirations thirty-two," said the nurse.

"Julio!" I yelled out to the nurses' station. "Put the OR on standby for an emergency thoracotomy and get me a thoracic surgeon down here, *right now!*"

"Yes, Doctor."

"I'll need X Ray, too!"

"Okay."

"Where's Brian Linhardt?" I asked Marie.

"Helping Guy Shehadeh and the attending with that spinal tap," she said. "You want bloods?"

"Yeah. CBC, Chem-twenty. Get me an ABG syringe, too, will you? And we'll want type and cross-match. Set up for a chest insertion. And we need to push some fluids. Hang a bag of Ringer's. Julio, call the blood lab and get us a couple of units of O-neg. Anybody seen Lisa Chiu this morning?"

"I thought today she was here with you guys," said Lamartine.

"We thought she was with *you*, Jock," Helen said.

"No, that's Saturdays."

I had a sudden vision of Lisa Chiu lying on the sidewalk in front of the Westside Women's Center, in a pool of her own blood. "Was anyone else hurt?" I asked the two cops, dreading the answer.

They shook their heads. "No one else."

The thoracic surgical resident, Dr. Alexander McCabe, arrived at that moment and did a double take when he recognized Lamartine on the stretcher. "What'd you do to yourself, mon?"

Lamartine raised an arm and the two black doctors exchanged a muted "my man" handshake. "They shot me," said Lamartine.

McCabe didn't ask who. "Where?"

Helen got the IV running while McCabe did a quick listen, then Marie started slapping cardiac leads for the EKG. McCabe was senior to me; now that he was here, he would give the orders, make the decisions. Which was just as well. My hands were on Lamartine but my mind was on Lisa Chiu. She should have arrived in the ER by now, and I was becoming uneasy. I hoped she wasn't off somewhere investigating Theresa Kahr's assault. It would be just like Lisa to go out sleuthing at 5:30 A.M. because that was the time Theresa Kahr normally traveled to work. Well, I consoled myself, if Lisa decided to canvass the neighborhood for someone who might have been on his or her way to work the previous morning at the time of Theresa's assault, she'd only run into cops doing the same thing. Which couldn't be too dangerous.

I hoped.

I was startled out of my reverie by the arrival of the X-ray technician and his lumbering portable X-ray machine. As the machine began to click, whir, and beep, we all exited the room briefly to avoid irradiation.

"So, Sutcliffe," McCabe said, "what *is* the problem with the AC down here?"

"Gimme a break," I snapped. "You think I don't know how hot it is in here?"

"Your temper's hot, too," he noted cheerfully. "In a lighter vein, you moving into Carchiollo's new apartment yet?"

I groaned.

"What, no wedding bells?"

"Don't talk to me about wedding bells," I retorted. "You were only in love with Moulin Ma for two whole years before you even asked her out to dinner."

"She was married."

"No, she was separated."

"To me, that's married."

"Um-hum." I pushed my glasses up on my nose. I was sweating so much, I was lucky they didn't slide right off my face. "She hadn't even *seen* her husband in two years; he'd gone back to Brazil. You want to call Lamartine's wife, or should I?"

"Why don't you let me," McCabe said. "I see them socially and I know her." He looked at his watch. "I should be able to catch her before she goes to work."

I noticed Julio groping distractedly to hang up the ER phone. He stood with a hand over his mouth, his body hunched as if from a blow.

I put a hand on McCabe's arm.

"Now what?" McCabe asked. "Julio, one of these days someone around here is going to shoot the messenger."

"Lisa Chiu's been stabbed," said Julio.

"*Stabbed?*"

"In the abdomen." And then, in a rush: "They found her in

the hall outside her apartment in the doctors' residence—she's in traumatic shock and she's not oriented at all—lapsing in and out of consciousness. They just called for a stretcher."

"Who's with her?"

"Dr. Aubuchon and Dr. Carchiollo."

"I'll go," I said.

"Where the *fuck* have you been?" Dr. Denise Aubuchon yelled when the elevator doors opened on the twelfth floor of the doctors' residence. I had commandeered Brian Linhardt and one of the two EMTs who had brought Lamartine to the ER, and we spilled out of the elevator into the stifling hallway with a gurney laden with crash-cart gear, oxygen, suction, bags of IV fluid, and a Lifepak portable monitor and defibrillator.

My brother Craig the movie buff once said that Dr. Aubuchon on a good day looked like Sigourney Weaver before she hardened herself to play Lieutenant Ripley in *Alien*, and on a bad day like Sigourney Weaver *after* she'd hardened herself to play Lieutenant Ripley in *Alien*. He should only see Denny now. The veins in her temples pulsed. Anger radiated from her like lightning bolts issuing from the brow of Zeus. Her auburn hair, usually a mass of soft, undulating waves, practically stood on end like Medusa's snakes. The effect was all the more heightened by her bare feet and the striped cotton bathrobe she was wearing, which made her look downright biblical. "It's been four fucking minutes!" she roared.

"What were we supposed to do, carry the gurney up twelve flights?" I yelled back. "Why didn't you send someone down to the basement with the elevator?"

"You put the OR on standby?"

"Yes."

"Surgeon in the ER?"

"Yes."

"Respiratory?"

"Denny, the whole fucking hospital is on standby, now where is she?"

Aubuchon scooped up the blood-pressure cuff from the gurney, grabbed my stethoscope from around my neck, and took off down the hall. Not a woman of wasted word or action.

I steeled myself before I looked to where Lisa lay on the floor. She was as still as Denny was animated. They had turned her on her side to prevent her from drowning in her own stomach contents; beside her head was a glistening pool and her hair was streaked with blood and vomitus. Phil knelt beside her suctioning her with my Thanksgiving turkey baster. A few feet away, Rita Firenze, wife of Dr. Anthony Firenze and Lisa's next-door neighbor, fretfully clutched her violin case to her bosom and watched the action, glassy-eyed and openmouthed and green around the gills.

Rita looked the way I felt. I almost envied her her horror and shock and queasiness; she had the luxury of indulging those feelings; I didn't. *Snap out of it, snap out of it.* My heart was in my throat, but I swallowed it.

"C'mon, Lisa," said Aubuchon, pumping up the BP cuff. "Gimme a pressure. You gotta help me!"

"She's completely unresponsive," Phil told me in a low voice when I knelt down next to him. "I don't get any pulse anywhere except the carotid and that's thready at best. And watch this." He handed me the turkey baster, peeled back one of Lisa's eyelids, and beamed his penlight directly into the eye, quickly repeating this process with the other eye. Her pupils were blown—widely dilated and fixed—an ominous finding.

"Shit," I said under my breath. "Head injury? Drugs?"

"Have to be considered. But first things first. She's barely breathing—we'll need to bag her." More loudly, he said, "Lisa, Ev Sutcliffe and Brian Linhardt are here with an EMT."

"We're going to take you to the ER," I said, just as loudly, handing Phil the suction wand. The adrenaline kicked in and I detached; *Mission Control, we have lift-off.* I began to watch myself from about three feet behind my head, my vision, hearing, smell and touch becoming more and more acute in reverse proportion to my receding emotions and sensibilities. Phil and Denny had already cut away Lisa's bloody scrub shirt, and she lay naked except for a pair of bikini briefs that had once been baby blue but were now soaked red. A first-aid kit had been upended on the floor, and scissors, rolls of hospital tape, and the aluminum wrappers of occlusive dressing littered the hallway. Lisa's abdomen was a welter of tape and bandage from the rib cage to the pubic bone. I rapidly counted the patches: nine. It looked as if she had sustained stab wounds to the stomach, liver, bowel, and possibly the bladder. As I leaned over her I caught a whiff of fecal matter and urine. "Oh, baby," I said, and lay my hand on the side of her head. It was impossible to evaluate her temperature; the air was body temperature, and she was as sweaty as I was, no more, no less.

I noticed the door to Lisa's apartment was propped open with a surgery textbook. "Do you know what happened?"

"No," said Phil tersely. "Rita found her here. Half in and half out of the door. Rita came out and literally tripped over her, and started hollering for help. I was coming up the stairs to see Denny on a consult and we heard Rita. I've got a book in the door so the cops can get in."

"You called them?"

"They're coming."

"Christ," said Denny. "Sixty. You call that a pressure? Lisa, you are *not* fucking helping!"

Swiftly, Brian and I rolled Lisa gently onto her back and set up the cardiac monitor. Meanwhile Phil coordinated suctioning with the EMT, who hooked up the oxygen apparatus and the bag-valve mask, which is attached to a balloon that looks like an inflatable football. You squeeze and unsqueeze the football and this inflates and deflates the patient's lungs.

"Ready when you are," the EMT said.

I took my stethoscope back from Denny Aubuchon and

quickly auscultated Lisa's chest. Brian handed me the monitor paddles and I slid one under Lisa's left breast and plunked the other down on her sternum. Brian set the monitor to quick-look without my asking him—that's what I liked about Brian, he could read my mind—and everyone turned to watch the oscillograph on the small TV-like screen.

"She's still in sinus," observed Brian.

That was good news but there was no way of telling how long it would hold. I now began to work entirely without thinking. The *whoosh-plop-whoosh* of the bag-valve mask as the EMT squeezed the football became a kind of mantra sound track. I got a large-bore IV going in one of Lisa's arms and started running in fluid. *Whoosh-plop-whoosh*. Brian drew blood from the other arm and got an IV going there as well.

Whoosh-plop-whoosh.

"We bring any pressors?" Brian wanted to know.

"Right here." I gave an amp of epinephrine, IV push.

"Where's the endotrach kit?" Denny asked. She had calmed herself somewhat and no longer had lightning bolts coming out her forehead.

"We couldn't find one," Brian said. "They're calling Respiratory and they'll have a tray set up when we come down."

A few minutes earlier Rita Firenze had gone downstairs to let the police in and she arrived back now with two uniformed officers and a Batman-and-Robin team—a jaded, I-seen-it-all detective with a beer belly shepherding a younger man whose gold shield was so new it radiated like the sun from its leather holder. As we sounded off in a bizarre roll call so Batman could take down our names, we collapsed the gurney down to the floor and lifted Lisa onto it. Her head lolled lifelessly. Oh, sweetheart, I thought. Tucking a sheet around her, we left Phil and Rita Firenze to talk to the cops, and lurched into the elevator with the gurney and our gear. When the elevator doors cranked open at basement level, we lurched out again. Below street level there's a tunnel that connects the doctors' residence with the hospital. We took off down the tunnel, running pell-mell, four people and a gurney, holding IV bags aloft. At the far end there was a steel fire door which, due to some long-forgotten spasm of architectural humor, opened onto the vestibule of the morgue. One of the pathology techs had propped the door open for us and stood holding the morgue elevator with his foot. "This is a first," he said, stepping aside as we caromed past and into the elevator. "A patient making the trip *from* the morgue *to* the ER."

A chilling moment. One that later became a freeze-frame in my mind.

The path tech saying, "This is a first."

Denny's head snapping up in horror.

And Denny making that spitting noise—phtt phtt phtt—to ward off bad luck and evil spirits.

She was too late.

We couldn't even get Lisa's gurney out of the elevator. When the elevator doors opened on the vestibule of the ambulance bay, it was jammed with plainclothes cops, uniformed cops, doctors, nurses, paramedics and—I did a double take a mile wide—*the mayor of New York City*. "Everything is under control," the mayor was saying firmly. Amazingly, he looked cool and crisp. "We are not going to let religious fanatics take over New York City. This is not Pensacola, Florida. I'll be making a statement shortly. Please clear the area."

"Stretcher coming through!" yelled Denny. "Stand aside, stand aside!"

Instead, several agitated people crowded *into* the morgue elevator, to let another stretcher come through the vestibule from the ambulance bay.

"What's going on?" Brian asked.

"A bomb went off in front of an OB-GYN's office on Columbus Avenue; the doctor was conducting clinical trials with RU-486 and the Right-to-Lifers went after him."

I groaned. What was this, National Anti-Abortion Day? "How many hurt?"

"About eight. It was right by a bus stop."

I could hear the beeping of a second ambulance as it backed into the bay. Somewhere—outside on the ambulance dock, it sounded like—a woman was wailing. Flashbulbs were popping. Hizzoner began snapping his fingers and waving and pointing. "Get the media out. *Out,*" he ordered. Big guys in suits surged forward. "We're closed! We're closed!" a voice yelled above the din. Probably the associate medical director of the ER, whose duty it was to put the ER "on diversion" when we reached a saturation point. There were only three ORs in the emergency room and we could handle only so many critical-care cases.

"Stand aside! Coming through!" Denny was barking in her best I'm-the-doctor-here voice. Nobody paid one whit of attention. It didn't help matters that her bathrobe had come untied, revealing the red silk slip underneath—which was all she apparently had on. You don't project a whole hell of a lot of authority in your underwear.

"I'll go get what we need," I said. "See if you can push her into Holding."

"Get Respiratory! Get a surgeon!"

My heart began to pound. With this kind of commotion, we could give up on Respiratory. I'd be lucky if I could get my hands on an endotrach kit without having to scour the hospital—which I didn't have time for, not with Lisa spiraling downward into life-threatening shock. Desperately I shouldered my way past the mayor and the cops and the press, who had somehow managed to storm the ER. If I could just get my hands on an endotrach kit—

I came into the ER proper and even I—jaded trauma junkie that I am—gawked at the carnage. A man lay on a stretcher, his face and hands bloodied. He was being coded and physicians and nurses swarmed the stretcher like bees. On another stretcher, a large, beefy man lay weeping quietly with pain. He, too, commanded the attention of half a dozen medical personnel, and as I squeezed by I saw he had lost both feet in the explosion. In OR One, there was another code going on. They were shocking the patient's heart and the patient's body was arching off the stretcher. In OR Two, yet another blast catastrophe. The ER clerk, Julio, was shouting into the phone at the blood bank, ordering what sounded like every last unit of packed red blood cells in the hospital. He had mobilized all the clerks from Admitting and they were shouting into the other phones. Pre-med volunteers in their distinctive blue coats cradled trays of blood samples in their arms and clamored to be allowed to pass so they could get to the labs on their blood runs. Adding to the din were the shouting members of Hizzoner's entourage, and shouting surgeons trying to be heard above all.

I grabbed the first person I could get my hands on who didn't seem to have his or her hands on a patient. "Guy," I said, "we have Lisa Chiu in the morgue elevator. We can't get by all these people. I need an endotrach kit, *right now!*"

Shehadeh looked at me blankly.

"Lisa Chiu's been stabbed and we've got her on a stretcher in the morgue elevator. We're trying to move her to Holding. I need an endotrach kit!"

He almost dropped his vial of spinal fluid but caught it just in time against his chest. *"What?"*

But he'd heard and understood. After one or two jagged breaths to steady himself, he handed his spinal fluid to a frenzied clerk, got her attention, gave his orders in a succinct, commanding voice, and said, "You look in OR One and I'll check Two and Three. What else do we need?"

This was not the Guy Shehadeh I knew and scorned. God bless him, he was rising to the occasion. Quickly, I reeled off what supplies we would need to render care to Lisa in Holding—even if her heart stopped beating and we had to code her—God forbid.

We could intubate her ourselves without Respiratory if we had to, but we needed a ventilator, as well as the endotrach kit. And we still needed a surgeon to assess Lisa's stab wounds.

First things first. I charged into OR One, shouldered my way around a team working frantically on the patient on the stretcher, and started opening the supply cabinets that lined the far wall. I scooped up an ABG syringe for the blood gas, a handful of syringes and blood tubes, a bag of crystalloid IV solution, a box of IV tubing, a pair of patient slippers for Denny, who was still in her bare feet, and—

There was no endotrach kit.

Cursing, I ran out of OR One and smack into Guy Shehadeh. "I've got one, I've got one!" he cried. I saw he was blinking back tears. Demented, we galloped around the corner and almost knocked down Hizzoner, who took no offense and graciously snapped orders to his people to let us by. Yet another ambulance was backing into the ambulance bay, beep-beep-beep.

"Took you long enough," Denny said grimly as we charged into the cubicle in Holding where she and Brian had established a kind of M.A.S.H.-unit trauma room. Overhead, Lisa's heart rhythm blipped across the screen of a cardiac monitor, the brady-cardia no better, no worse than it had been upstairs in the hall outside Lisa's apartment. Miracle of miracles, a brand-new, state-of-the-art ventilator stood parked in the corner, hooked up to the wall oxygen and ready to go.

"How is she?" I asked.

An anguished cry escaped Shehadeh. "What happened to her? Who did this?" he choked, leaning over Lisa's still form and batting helplessly at her upper arms and shoulders, as if he suddenly didn't know how to touch her. "Lisa. *Lisa*." He began slapping her on the breastbone with his fingertips. "Oh God, oh God."

"Don't wuss out on me, Shehadeh," barked Denny. "Get a grip." To me she said, "She has no reflexes and her pressure's bottoming out. We need to get her intubated, we need blood—and I don't care how many bombing victims are stacking up in the ER—and we need to push volume." She turned to Brian. "Linhardt, you go down to the blood bank and if they won't give you four units of un-cross-matched O-neg, shoot the fuckers."

Brian scornfully eyed Shehadeh, who was unpacking the endotrach kit on a tray and weeping openly, wiping his nose on the sleeve of his white coat. "I think I should intubate her," Linhardt said.

"No," said Denny. "Go."

"But—"

"Shehadeh can't go, I need *you* to go."

When Brian still didn't leave, Denny snapped, *"Look at him."* She tossed her head toward Shehadeh. "You think he can get blood for me what with all those bomb patients out there? *You go.*"

Brian saw her point. I took over the Ambubag from him and he left.

In all fairness, the one thing Shehadeh probably did just as well as Linhardt was intubate patients, and he now quickly and efficiently intubated Lisa, lifting her jaw and gently sliding the endotrach tube down her throat and into her windpipe. The ventilator would now do the job we had been doing with the ambubag, and get oxygen into Lisa's lungs.

"Tidal volume of seven hundred, rate of twelve," I said, talking more to myself than to Denny and Guy as I punched the settings in. "F-I-oh-two, one hundred percent."

"That should help," Denny said, as the ventilator began to thump and hiss. "Now all we need is the O-neg; her blood looks like Kool-Aid." We could give Lisa all the oxygen in the world, but if she didn't have enough red blood cells to transport it around her body, that oxygen would not reach her brain.

"Come on, Linhardt," Denny muttered under her breath. She started a third IV line in Lisa's left femoral artery and hooked it up to a second bag of crystalloid.

"Her color's not very good at all," I said, frowning. I put my stethoscope in my ears and leaned over to check Lisa's breathing.

Things happened rather quickly then.

I heard no breath sounds in the left lung.

Brian triumphantly returned with four units of O-negative blood.

I heard no breath sounds in the right lung.

The ventilator was going great guns. When you hook a patient up to a ventilator, chest rise is quite dramatic as the air is going in; it's the same kind of breath you take when the doctor says, "Breathe deeply."

But it wasn't Lisa's chest that was rising.

"Guy," I said. "You intubated *the esophagus*."

"Oh, Christ," said Denny. "She's bradying down."

I glanced at the overhead cardiac monitor and saw the line on the screen deteriorating into wide complexes, almost like sine waves. "Agonal rhythm!"

Lisa's heart had stopped functioning.

"Lisa!" Denny yelled. "Don't give up on me!"

If we had been working at a concentrated pitch before, we now went into hyperdrive. While Linhardt ripped out the endotrach tube and reinserted it correctly—checking with his stethoscope afterward to make sure the air was going into the lungs, not the stomach—I handed Denny little pre-dose syringes of epinephrine and atropine and Denny shot them into the IVs.

"She's bleeding out," Denny said. "What about cracking her chest or doing a left thoracotomy to cross-clamp the aorta?"

I froze. "Who—you?"

"Aw, man," said Brian as he climbed up on a riser. Lacing his fingers together, he began chest compressions. "Unless it's a heart wound, you don't save people by doing that maneuver—"

"She's young, we have to give it every shot!" This from Guy, who had given up trying to be a doctor and was standing stock-still, staring at Lisa with tears rolling down his face.

"Anybody done one?" Brian asked quietly.

"Not me," I said. I handed Denny another amp of epi. "And I've only seen two. Denny, it's futile unless it's chest trauma."

Denny's lips twisted and her nostrils flared with suppressed rage. She often worked in a rage; Denny generally seemed mad at the world, and took every downward turn of every patient as a personal challenge and insult. She was not only mad at whoever did this to Lisa, she was mad at *Lisa*—for not "helping." I had once seen Denny ball up her fist and punch a patient in the chest because he had coded on her and died—she wound up like a baseball pitcher and threw so hard I think her feet actually left the floor.

"What's the BP, Brian?" I asked quietly, staring at the cardiac monitor as I dialed the lab for the results on the bloods we had sent up earlier.

"Fifty."

I groaned. My throat began to close down on me and I felt my jaws convulse. "We've got to get her up to surgery," I said. "She's bleeding out internally."

"And do what with her—park her in the hall outside the surgical suites? There are no surgeons, Ev."

"Denny, we've got three drips going and the blood pressure is *falling*. We need someone to assess these wounds." Which could only be done by a surgeon, in surgery.

"Whaddya wanna do, code her in the fucking hall?"

"She's *bleeding out*."

Behind me, Guy Shehadeh slid to his knees. Stifling his sobs, he bit his lips until the blood ran down his chin. Every now and again he gasped and tried to catch his breath.

The center of this small universe, Lisa lay motionless on her stretcher, her head thrown back, and heaved great sighs on the ventilator. Brian's hands went up and down on her chest. A large quiet suddenly loomed, punctuated only by Lisa's ventilator breaths and Guy's jagged ones. I had a sudden vision of Romeo with his vial of poison in Juliet's tomb—"Arms, take your last embrace"—and turned to look at Guy Shehadeh with new eyes.

"Stop a minute, Brian," I said. Wild-eyed, we all looked to the cardiac monitor.

Flatline.

"Oh, God," I breathed.

Unlike on TV—where the docs seemed to shock any and every patient with an abnormal rhythm, and when that didn't work cracked their chests—shocking and cracking the chest were not universal options. With a closed chest and trauma, it was unlikely to be helpful to shock. Or to crack the chest.

"Give me another amp of epi," said Denny.

I handed over a syringe of epi, and another of atropine.

Still flatline. While Brian did compressions, the monitor showed cardiac rhythm. But when he stopped, nothing.

I shouldered Brian aside and took over the compressions. Behind me, Guy Shehadeh had assumed a position as if he were praying to Allah. Kneeling, his head bent toward the floor, he rocked back and forth and keened.

But despite our efforts, after an hour of chest compressions, epinephrine, atropine, and a couple of other meds we desperately injected into Lisa's bloodstream, the cardiac monitor still read flatline. By the time Denny said, "That's it," I had long since imagined Lisa's soul drifting out of her body, floating up toward the ceiling, and turning for a last look before traveling on to the beyond.

Now we had Guy Shehadeh to deal with. He was pounding his forehead on the floor, crying, "I killed her. Oh, God, I killed her."

CHAPTER
7

I floated in serene detachment. Not only were my emotions off, my thoughts were off. Only my senses seemed to be on. I was aware that my heart was beating wildly against my breastbone. Banally, my mind began to fill up with lines from Shakespeare again: *Death lies on her like an untimely frost / upon the sweetest flower of all the field.* And, as I turned off the respirator and disconnected the line from the plastic airway in Lisa's mouth, *Thy lips are warm.*

Suddenly leaping around Lisa's stretcher, Brian Linhardt yanked Guy Shehadeh to his feet and slugged him full in the face. Guy staggered back, sending my meds tray flying, and collapsed at my feet. Glancing down, I stepped over him. I had things to do. Things for Lisa. Shehadeh gagged and snorted and spat blood, but I ignored him. In the corner of my vision, Linhardt paced back and forth, his nostrils flaring like a Spanish bull as he breathed deep breaths through his nose. I ignored him, too.

"Son of a *bitch*," muttered Denny Aubuchon. She snapped off her gloves and angrily threw them down like some kind of gauntlets after the fact. I knew what she was thinking: How dare Lisa die on her. She stomped off. I let her. After a moment, Linhardt disappeared as well.

All of Lisa's IV lines had to remain in place for the medical examiner. Systematically, I began to snip them off, about six inches from the body, tying the loose ends in overhand knots to prevent fluids from leaking out. Shehadeh dragged himself to a chair, climbed onto it, and sat hunched with his head between his knees, pinching the bridge of his nose. His blood, as it dripped to the floor, made tiny *pat-pat* sounds. Nose probably broken. I paid no attention, going about my business, cognizant of the fact that I had already begun to think of Lisa's body as "it." There is nothing deader than a dead body. Hearing myself think these thoughts, I became aware of the level of shock and denial I was in, and shame swept over me. "Lisa," I said out loud, but under my breath. "I'll take care of you, honey."

Shehadeh found he was able to stand, and slunk off.

I clipped off the leads to the cardiac monitor, leaving the sensors taped in place on Lisa's chest and under her breasts.

Gently, I tied her wrists with Kerlix gauze wrap, crossing them over her chest like a mummy's.

Then I swathed her face and head.

I prepared two mortuary tags with her name, age, sex, and race. I left "religion" blank. I tied one tag to her right forefinger, and the second to her great left toe.

I called the medical examiner's office. "I have just received the body of a person who died by violence," I heard my own voice say, remotely, from another planet, "and I was unable to resuscitate." I despised the formula announcement even more than usual. The ME responded with his half of the formula, saying, "Here's your number," which I wrote down, and "under my authority I accept this case."

I prepared a chart with all the details, transferring the information I had noted on a crash-cart checklist while we ran the code, repeated the necessary details on the death notice, and called the hospital morgue.

I left a message on Denny's answering machine, reminding her that she had to sign the notice.

When Detective Ost came looking for me, he found me sitting on a riser, forearms around my knees, hands clasped, staring into space.

My mind was blank. I had no idea how long I'd been sitting there. When I put a hand to my face, it was wet with tears.

The morgue boys had come and gone.

Without my seeing them.

I hadn't even said my final farewell.

"Full moon *and* high tide," Ost said, handing me a Styrofoam cup of iced caffè latte from Sami's. "They come crawling out of the woodwork, I swear to God. Shoot the abortion doc at Westside Women's, blow up a bus stop in front of an obstetrician's office, stab a Chinese medical student. Drink this or I'll hold your nose and pour it down your throat."

I smiled wanly. My adrenaline was wearing off; Ost was still flushed with his: the thrill of the chase. "Take your time," he suggested expansively. Then, realizing his mood was inappropriate: "I know this is hard for you."

I mopped my face with an alcohol wipe and blew my nose. My elbow ached. Turning my arm around, I saw that the dressing was spotted with blood. Have to get Lisa to change it again, I thought, before I remembered that she was dead. The memory was like a grenade going off. My God—was this what mourning was going to be like—Bouncing Betties and claymore mines? I took a small sip of coffee. Ost, God bless him, had remembered that I took only half a packet of sugar. Holding the cup under my nose, I inhaled the scent of cinnamon gratefully. I couldn't enjoy it very long, of course. Almost immediately, I was assailed by guilt. It was always the same: I was alive, alive, alive and the patient was dead, dead, dead. Only now the patient was Lisa.

After a moment I said dully, "I was her mentor. I'm not married, you know. I don't have any children."

Ost nodded sympathetically as if he understood this non sequitur perfectly. He got out his notebook.

I was sitting at a desk in Holding; he sat on a chair nearby. For some reason, Holding was quiet and empty this morning. The cubicles were dark, and the sole light spilled into the windowless nurses' station from one of those old-fashioned, metal-shaded lamps that throw illumination down but not up. Lighting for the Twilight Zone, a perfect metaphor for Holding. Usually it was full of all the people not sick enough to be admitted but whom we couldn't send home because they had no home to go to—or if they did have a home, no one to care for them when they got there. So we stuck them in Holding and waited for them to get well enough to leave or sick enough to be admitted.

It seemed a little cooler—perhaps maintenance had got the air-conditioning to work a bit better—although Ost, who had just come in from outside, looked wilted in his bulletproof vest. He had once told me that a BPV in summer was hotter than three Irish sweaters, and soaked up an entire family-size canister of talcum powder a week.

The injured from the bus-stop explosion had been rushed upstairs to surgery, including the man who had suffered traumatic amputation of the lower extremities. Two victims had been declared dead in the ER. Dr. Jean-Jacques Lamartine was also in surgery, undergoing an emergency thoracotomy to remove a bullet that might blow up.

My boss, Dr. Christopher Cabot, the director of the Emergency Department, would have his hands full with the press conference. ABORTION CLINIC SHOOT-OUT and DOCTOR'S OFFICE BOMBING. I could almost see the CNN graphics.

Lisa Chiu so far had come to no one's attention except ours and that of the police.

And Ost was determined to keep it that way as long as possible.

The coffee was a ploy, I realized belatedly. Ost wanted my complicity in keeping Lisa's death quiet.

Ost took out a handkerchief and wiped his face. "Listen to me,

Doc," he said earnestly. "I don't gotta tell you, we have a fucking media case on our hands. My life is going to be very, very difficult until we solve this thing. It's very hard to work with the reporters breathing down your neck and making all kinds of inflammatory and way-out-of-line observations on the six-o'clock news. And of course as soon as the media get involved, the police brass start leaning on everyone and demanding reports every goddamn five minutes. I don't think I gotta explain politics to you. I'm sure you got politics here at the hospital, and certain higher-up docs you gotta pussyfoot around."

"What are you asking me, Ozzie?" I said warily.

"I'm asking you to keep a lid on it. I'm asking you to not go blabbing to the other docs, or calling up Doctor X at Hospital Y and asking did he have a patient six months ago who had her head beat in and died."

I stared. "Head beat in? What—Are you saying that you think *Babydoll* killed Lisa?"

"Look—why don't you handle the patients and let me worry about who did what."

"But Lisa's injuries were entirely different. For one thing, she wasn't beat about the head like Theresa and the other victims were—"

Ost put his hand up. "Time out. You gotta calm down. You can't keep raising all these questions. Trust me—I know how a snowball rolls down a hill. And my job isn't just finding the guy and nailing him. I gotta find the guy, build a case that will stand up in court, nail him, *and then take the case to the end zone*. Think of it this way: You open your mouth, anything you say can prejudice potential jurors. Anything you say can hand the whole fucking case to the defense on a platter. *I need you to keep your mouth shut.*"

"But—"

"You hear anything I just said to you?"

My mind went off in sixteen different directions at once. "Loose lips sink ships," I said distractedly.

"Good. I'm making a dent. Now I need to know what you know and when you knew it, and what happened with Lisa Chiu when you guys went to the Good Earth yesterday. He-said-she-said. The whole spiel. But first run by me with what happened this morning when Chiu died."

I made a mental checklist and filed it: people to call, questions to ask. Then I took a deep breath and launched into the Who-What-Where-Why-and-How of Lisa's transport and care. With great effort, I concentrated on the clinical details. I had already cried once this morning, and I was determined not to start up again, especially not in front of Detective Ost.

Just a routine rundown of one of the many patients I saw in a given month who had been stabbed, shot, assaulted, or whatever and now required the attentions of a police officer in addition to those of a physician.

Routine.

When I had finished, Ost asked, "Can you be a little more specific about how she died from these injuries?"

"Cause of death due to advanced shock, secondary to multiple penetrating sharp-instrument wounds," I intoned formally. God. I sounded so cold. "I suspect that the knife—or whatever it was—nicked the thoracic aorta or some other major blood vessel and she bled out. There wasn't a lot of blood externally, but you can lose your entire blood volume bleeding into your belly."

"So you never saw her conscious."

"I didn't, no."

"She didn't say anything in your hearing."

"No."

"You physician of record?"

"No. Dr. Denise Aubuchon ran the code. She's an attending."

"I understand you prepared the body."

"Yes."

"Don't the orderlies usually do that?"

"Yes."

He glanced up, then decided not to pursue it. "When did you last see her alive?"

"Yesterday."

"When you both went to the Good Earth."

"Who told you that, Dr. Carchiollo?"

"Pretend nobody told me. Pretend you're my very first witness."

I sighed and told him everything.

"Did the bakers have any theories about who attacked Theresa Kahr?" Ost asked.

"No. We asked. But Lisa did say something that struck me. God, I'm kicking myself now because I didn't press her about it. She said that Theresa had mentioned to her that there was some guy who had been coming into the shop and asking her out. Theresa hadn't said yes, but Lisa said that Theresa kept talking about him to her. Now this is a little odd—but Lisa didn't seem to want to talk about this guy. She seemed irritated that Theresa—who had told her friends she was gay—showed interest in a man who was asking her for a date. Immediately my antennae went up—I mean, this could be Babydoll! And I said as much to Lisa. But she said, 'Serial killers don't ask you for a date first.' She insisted that Theresa hadn't told her what she and the guy talked about, she hadn't told her what he looked like—Lisa was very dismissive. And that struck me."

Ost had put down his pen and was watching me very carefully, hanging on my every word as if I were the Oracle of Delphi.

"So when Lisa and I were at the Good Earth," I went on, "I brought it up with the bakers. Khalid and the guy with the rasta hair were the bakers we talked to. The shop was closed and no one else was there. And my asking made Lisa all antsy again—I had a very strong impression that she felt guilty about something. But the bakers didn't remember any guy asking Theresa for a date, or coming in and flirting with her."

"Lisa say anything else about this guy?" Ost asked.

I shook my head.

"What kind of work he does?"

"Nothing."

"You think Lisa knew this guy?"

"I have no idea. She didn't say." But I was immediately struck by lightning: *Jesus Christ, she knew him. And suspected him. And Ost thinks so, too.* "Ozzie, you're not thinking Babydoll came after Lisa because she went around asking pressing questions, are you?"

"You and Lisa do any other sleuthing I oughta know about, Doc?"

"No. I mean, not together. I have no idea where she went or what she did after I left her. Look, I just don't understand how you're accounting for the difference in the MO. Theresa and the other two victims were beaten about the head—Lisa wasn't. Lisa was stabbed—the others weren't. Plus, the other victims were assaulted outside, on the street or in a park. Lisa was assaulted in her apartment, right?"

"You and Lisa tell anyone what you'd found out at the Good Earth?"

"I told Phil . . . Dr. Carchiollo."

"Anyone else?"

"No."

"And at what time did you last see Lisa Chiu alive?"

"Ozzie, did this guy break into Lisa's apartment, or did she let him in?"

He brought his eyes up from his notebook and rested them on my face without expression.

Suddenly, the hair rose up on the back of my neck. "She let him in, didn't she?" I said slowly. "Because she knew him. The MO is different because he wasn't there to rape her, he was there to kill her—to shut her up."

"Do me a favor. Don't take the ball and run with it."

"How are you sure she knew him? Did she give him a drink? Did you find two wineglasses or something like that?"

Ost smiled faintly. "You been watching too much 'Murder,

She Wrote.' C'mon. You *know* I can't answer these questions. What time did you last see her?"

"No, I want to know," I said. "You're telling me the guy who killed Lisa may be the same guy who assaulted Theresa Kahr. Who may be the same guy who knocked me down. Who might have knocked me down because he was afraid I might recognize him. Whom Lisa might have let into her apartment because she *did* recognize him. And who presumably killed Lisa because she was snooping and about to find out something that would allow her to put two and two together and implicate him. And who might now come after *me* because I was snooping with her!"

"What time did you last see Lisa Chiu yesterday evening?" Ost persisted maddeningly.

I rocked back in my chair and threw my hands up in the air. "I don't remember. We left the hospital at six-thirty and walked over to the Good Earth. Which would have got us there maybe twenty-five minutes later. And then I guess we were there a half hour or so. I didn't walk back to the doctors' residence with Lisa because I went directly to Phil's."

"Dr. Carchiollo's."

"Yes."

"On Riverside Drive."

"Yes."

"And you got there what time?"

"Ah! Exactly at seven-thirty. The church bells rang the half-hour just as I was coming around the corner at Phil's—I remember that now."

Ost nodded. "So, you left Lisa Chiu a few minutes before."

"Right."

"And you were at Dr. Carchiollo's until when?"

"A little before midnight."

"At which time you walked back to the doctors' residence."

"Yes."

"Arriving in your own apartment at approximately what time?"

I blinked. "Are you—Jesus Christ, Ozzie, you want to establish my *alibi?*"

"Answer the question, please, Doc."

I was so flabbergasted I laughed. Then it suddenly dawned on me that I might be required to account for the time I had spent passionately groping Mick Healy down in the well of that brownstone. I put my hand over my mouth, a gesture Ost noted immediately. Nothing escaped his eagle eye. Letting my hand fall as naturally as possible into my lap, I lied, "I dunno. Twelve-fifteen, maybe."

It had been closer to one A.M.

"Did you meet anyone on your way?" Ost asked.

"No."

"When you were coming along your street, see anyone?"

I pondered this. "I don't remember. There are always kids from the University on the street at all hours. I just can't recall." Of course, I had been in such a state of hysterical arousal at the time, it would have been amazing if I had noticed *anything*. Even now, just thinking about Mick Healy's body pressed against mine, I squirmed in my chair.

Ost seemed to be watching me very carefully. "And when you came in the building? See anyone then?"

"I saw Guy Shehadeh taking out the garbage in the courtyard."

"At about twelve-fifteen."

"Well, uh, I think—" I stammered. "Maybe it was more like one A.M."

"One A.M.," repeated Ost.

There was a brief silence.

"You revising the time you left Carchiollo's?"

"No," I said miserably. "I met someone on the way."

"I see."

"We spent a few minutes talking on One Hundred Thirteenth Street."

"Talking."

"On the steps of a brownstone. We sat down for a few minutes."

"On One Hundred Thirteenth Street."

"Yes."

"You mind me asking who you met?"

"Dr. Michael Healy." I cleared my throat. "The assistant chief of neurosurgery. He was out jogging."

Ost coughed delicately into his fist. "Ah, Dr. Healy with you when you come home, Doc?"

"No."

"He walk you to the door?"

"No." I drained the last bit of coffee from my cup.

"So you come home, you walk in the front door of the building about one A.M., and you see Dr. Shehadeh taking out the garbage in the courtyard. You speak to him?"

"No, I don't think he saw me. I saw him going into the courtyard."

"Doctors in the habit of taking out the garbage at one A.M.?"

"It's not unusual. We all suffer from sleep disturbance. Since the Libby Zion rules went into effect, we're only supposed to work an eight-hour shift, but by the time you get done with sign-out and the paperwork, it's more like twelve hours, and sometimes you get off work and you're too tired to sleep. So you clean the house or bake muffins or whatever. Then there's night float, when you have to work the night shift, and that throws your circadian rhythm off. People behave a little strangely from the sleep disruption."

"Shehadeh on call Thursday night?"

"There's no 'on call' in the ER; there's only night float. But he's not doing that this week." Where in the world was Ost going with this questioning? I wondered.

"You meet Healy on purpose on One Hundred Thirteenth Street?"

"No. I told you. He was out jogging."

"You're not in cahoots with him to investigate the scene of

the crime? Look over where you got knocked down, maybe come up with some theories?"

"I think I can safely say that Healy and I are not in cahoots to do anything," I said dryly.

"You didn't discuss with him the details of getting knocked down by this guy *right on this very spot,* the guy who probably raped and beat Theresa Kahr?"

"I did tell Healy earlier in the day what had happened to me. I had split my elbow open falling, and Healy gave me some first aid. And of course he knows all about Theresa Kahr—he's her neurosurgeon."

"You describe the doll to him?"

"I never saw the doll."

"Answer the question, please, Doc."

"No, wait. I talked to Healy in the morning about getting knocked down. Then I presented the case to him of Theresa Kahr before he took her to surgery. That's all we talked, okay? *Then* Lisa and I went to the Good Earth. And when I met him jogging—"

I stopped. I realized I was talking very defensively about Mick Healy.

And that I had nowhere to go with what I was saying, because when I met him jogging, we didn't *talk.*

"—ah, when I met him jogging, we didn't talk shop."

Ost, who has probably heard every last damn story on earth, did not so much as blink or raise an eyebrow. "You and Dr. Healy had a conversation of a personal nature," he suggested diplomatically.

"Yes."

"You did not discuss with him your earlier conversation with Lisa Chiu, or what you found out about Theresa Kahr at the Good Earth."

"No."

"And you talked to Healy about a half hour and then went on home."

"Yes."

"Arriving there about one A.M."

"Yes."

"When you saw Dr. Shehadeh taking out the garbage, but didn't speak to him."

"Right."

"You went directly upstairs to your apartment?"

"Yes. Well, I got my mail and went upstairs."

"And went to bed?"

"I had a glass of wine and went to bed, yes."

"About what time was that?"

"One-thirty, maybe."

"And which apartment you in?"

"I'm in 8A."

"The same line as Dr. Cantor's apartment, where the deceased was living."

"Right. That apartment is 12A, and I'm directly underneath, four floors down."

"Who lives above you?"

"Hal and Carol Murkland."

"That would be 9A?"

"Yes." I shifted in my chair.

"All these A-line apartments exactly alike?"

"Yes."

"Two bedrooms, a foyer, living room, and kitchen?"

"Right."

"Who lives in 10A?"

"I don't know. Why are you asking all this? Did the killer leave by the fire escape?"

"Moving right along," Ost drawled elaborately, "did you sleep last night with the air conditioner on, or with the windows open?"

"With the air conditioner."

"You have curtains, drapes?"

"Yes."

"They closed all night?"

"Yes."

"Ah, Dr. Carchiollo joined you at your apartment at some time. When was that?"

"He came in at five-thirty. My alarm goes off at five twenty-five and I was just getting into the shower when he came in."

Ost nodded, as if he had pursued a line of reasoning to its logical conclusion. But then he dogged on: "Now, without jumping to several fascinating conclusions, did you hear anything on the fire escape or in the courtyard during the night?"

"No."

"You a sound sleeper, Doc?"

"No, I'm a light sleeper, actually. But I hear less when the air conditioner is running. It makes a kind of white noise. It even—"

I was about to say that the air conditioner even drowned out the frequent sounds of Hal Murkland fighting with his wife.

Ost looked up from his notebook. "You were saying?"

"It even drowns out the cats screwing in the courtyard," I said.

"I see. So there were no cats screwing last night, or if there were, you didn't hear them."

"Right."

"All right," said Ost. He perused his notes.

"Lisa had no defense wounds," I said. "How come she didn't fight back?"

Ost ignored me once again. "Tell me about Dr. Guy Shehadeh's statement this morning: 'I killed her.' "

"He didn't kill her. He was putting an endotrach tube down Lisa's throat for oxygen, and instead of getting it into her trachea, he missed and the tube went into her esophagus. This doesn't help you get oxygen, obviously. But this kind of mistake happens a lot; you're supposed to check by listening with your stethoscope to make sure the air is going into the lungs and not the stomach, but Guy was rattled because it was Lisa and he didn't check. About a minute later maybe—I'm sure it wasn't more than a minute—I noticed the error and Brian Linhardt, the medic, reinserted the tube correctly."

"I understand there was some dispute about this?"

"Yes. Linhardt punched Shehadeh in the nose."

"This normal behavior in the ER, one member of the staff punching another?"

"Of course not." I sighed. "Linhardt is a hothead and She-hadeh is . . . Well, let's just say Shehadeh is an emotional type and he's a little overwhelmed. He just graduated from medical school. We were all a bit overwrought because we knew the pa-tient, and we were working shorthanded, without a nurse, and then, well, when she died . . ." I trailed off.

"So you lay this down to emotion of the moment. This 'I killed her' business."

"Yes."

"He didn't kill her."

"No."

"Can he be accused of killing her?"

"He could be brought under peer review, yes. But in my opin-ion there was no negligence."

"You Shehadeh's regular supervisor?"

"Yes and no. I'm the third-year resident and I run a team, and he's one of the interns under me. But the attending is the real supervisor. And in this case that would be Dr. Aubuchon, since she's privileged to practice in the emergency department, al-though she generally doesn't."

"How would it happen, a peer review?"

"The case would be brought before the Quality Assurance Committee, and the committee would make a recommendation to the chief of service, if the committee felt some kind of action should be taken. Ozzie, you're driving all over the road. You going to tell me where you're trying to go?"

Ost graced me with a huge, shit-eating grin. Then immediately he was deadpan again. "Just one or two more questions, Doc, then

I'll let you go . . . What can you tell me about her employment situation?"

I wondered if Ost relished throwing questions from left field. "Well, it's complicated," I said. "Lisa's parents suffered some financial setbacks recently, and told her they wouldn't be able to pay her fees for medical school anymore, and said she'd have to come up with the money herself. So she arranged with Hal Murkland—"

"This Dr. Harold Murkland, from the Pediatrics ER?"

"Yes. Hal—Dr. Murkland—and his partner, Dr. Denise Aubuchon, went on-line computer last summer, and Hal hired Lisa to help computerize their medical records. This summer she was scheduled to do a clinical clerkship in the ER, which is unpaid, but then the shit hit the fan with her father's investments, so Dr. Cabot—the director of the Emergency Department—was trying to finesse some complicated arrangement for her to get paid as a needle-sticker and at the same time receive academic credit for her clerkship. Plus I believe she asked Dr. Lamartine at Westside Women's if there were some way she could receive a stipend for her work there, and he's also trying to work something out for her."

"So she was working three jobs? With Dr. Murkland, with Dr. Lamartine, and here at the hospital?"

"Right."

My beeper went off. I looked at the digital readout to see who was calling and debated whether to take the call.

"This Linhardt, he in love with her?" Ost asked.

"*Linhardt?* You gotta be kidding. He's a Right-to-Lifer, he doesn't like minorities, and he thinks women are stealing all the good jobs from red-blooded, all-American males—by which he means *white* males. Shehadeh, maybe. Linhardt, no.

"She sleeping with anyone?"

I quickly repeated the business about seeing birth-control pills in Lisa's purse. "But I don't know who she was sleeping with. She was very secretive about it."

"What about this Dr. Jeffrey Cantor she was living with?"

"She wasn't living with him. She was looking after his cat and house-sitting his apartment. He's in Bosnia for the summer with Doctors Without Borders. Besides, he's gay."

"If you had to guess, there a doctor here she might've been sleeping with? Affair with a married guy, maybe? I don't gotta tell the guy's wife necessarily."

"My guess is Shehadeh." I mulishly did not mention Hal Murkland, although I would be hard-pressed to explain why not. "Ozzie, at least tell me if there was a doll at the scene."

He let exasperation play across his face. "Doc, I am not in any position to trade you tit for tat," he said. "Please. That's not the deal here: you tell me who the deceased was sleeping with and I tell you whether there was a doll at the scene. I gotta proceed according to the rules. Which means not commenting on certain stuff. Now, you have any other ideas who she might've been sleeping with, besides Shehadeh?"

I turned my back on Ost and picked up the phone, punching in the code for my waiting call. "Dr. Sutcliffe," I said.

"Ev, Mick here."

"Hi." Thank God, other doctors never thought you were being abrupt; they just naturally assumed you were busy. It would never occur to Mick, calling me at work, that I might be tongue-tied because his phone call increased my heart rate and dilated all the capillaries in my face.

But then he said, "Brace yourself, darling. Theresa Kahr just died."

"Oh, Jeez."

"Thought you'd like to know. I know it's doubly horrible coming on top of Lisa's death. I'm so sorry, Ev."

"Yes. Thank you."

"Buy you a drink later?"

"I'm with Detective Ost," I said, as neutrally as possible. "I'll tell him.'' I gently replaced the receiver in its cradle.

I wondered what Lisa had known, and how Babydoll had known she knew it.

And if he thought I knew it, too.

CHAPTER
8

"YOU'RE not *listening*," I said when I could get a word in edgewise.

A loud, noisy sigh came over the phone line. "You always think I'm not listening when I disagree with you," Dr. Harold Murkland complained in his maddening, deadpan voice. "What— you think there's no room for two opinions here, yours and everybody else's?"

I held the phone against my chest for a moment and counted to five.

Sitting next to me at the doctors' desk in the nurses' station, in the middle of the ER, Denny Aubuchon rolled her eyes. "I had this conversation with Hal already this afternoon, Ev. I didn't get anywhere with him."

"—not going to talk to the cops," Hal was saying when I listened again.

"Yes, you *are* going to talk to the cops, Hal," I said as patiently as possible. "And you're going to come clean about that glass. Now what exactly happened there? Did Lisa break it and attack you with it? What were you *doing* to her?"

"Look. I did not kill her, okay?"

"Nobody's saying you killed her, Hal. I'm talking about the cuts on your face. Now would you please give up this cock-and-bull about some guy falling on you while you were drinking champagne at a bachelor's party—and tell me what really happened?"

Next to me, Denny mouthed something. I shook my head, not understanding her.

"All right," said Hal. "I had a glass in my hand, and I tried to kiss her, and she slapped me. The glass got in the way and it broke on my face."

"She slapped you?" I found this hard to believe. What year was this, 1952? "For a *kiss?*"

"Oh, Jesus Christ," said Denny. She wrote me a note. It said *Wild sex—fell off bed on glass.*

"And now the cops are going to think I killed her in a jealous rage," Hal went on. "Because she wouldn't have sex with me, or because I was in love with her and I found out she didn't love me back."

I stared at Denny's note. "Hal, nobody knows who killed her. There's even some possibility it was Babydoll. The cops have to talk to all the people who knew Lisa, all her friends and colleagues. Just a minute." I cupped a hand over the receiver. "*What?*" I said to Denny.

"He and Lisa were having wild sex and the champagne glass was on the floor next to the bed, and Hal fell off the bed and landed on the glass," said Denny. "They were drinking champagne in the first place because Hal finally decided to leave his wife for Lisa, and they were celebrating. There was a lot of blood; they mopped it up with her scrub shirt. What is he telling you?"

"That he tried to kiss her and she slapped him and the glass broke on his face."

Denny threw her hands up in the air and made a face. "Not what he told me, sweetheart."

"He told you they had wild sex?"

"Uh-huh. *Hot.*"

"And that he's leaving his *wife?*"

"About time, don't you think?"

"Has he told her?"

"Who knows?" Denny lifted her shoulders in an exaggerated shrug. "He hadn't told her by dinnertime last night, because I was there for dinner and Carol was her usual wifey self—grilling the perfect heart-saver meal out on the fire-escape, fussing over him like she always does, 'Not too much salt, lover.' Although now I think of it, he did seem a little nervous, and he was drinking an awful lot—"

I cut her off with a wave of my hand. "Hal," I said, "you bullshit the cops, and you are going to be in a lot of trouble. *Don't do it.*"

"Is someone there with you?" he asked suddenly.

"Yes, there's someone here with me—I'm in the ER."

"Denny's there, isn't she? What is she telling you?"

"What do you think?"

"Do me a favor—don't listen to her. Ev, I need your help. Don't say anything in front of her. What do you know about computers?"

"Computers?" I repeated, confused.

"Christ, Ev, not in front of her, okay? Can you show me how the computer in my office works?"

"Hal, are you out of your mind? Lisa's dead, you haven't talked to the cops yet, you don't even have your story straight—and you're asking me about your computer?"

"Is he talking about the computer again?" Denny asked.

"Great. That's just fucking great," said Hal.

"He's embarrassed he hasn't learned how to work it yet," Denny explained.

"Just stop, both of you," I said. "Hal?"

I realized he was weeping. "Oh, God, Ev," he choked. "I was so in love with her, what am I gonna do?"

My heart softened. "Talk to the cops, Hal. Tell the truth. You'll feel better knowing you're helping the police find the guy who did this to her."

But he had put the phone down.

"Who sutured Hal's face?" I asked Denny. "You?"

She snorted. "I offered. He insisted on suturing his *own* face, can you believe it?"

The clerk was at my elbow. "Dr. Sutcliffe?"

"Yes, Julio."

"Dr. Weber's on the phone. He wants to know why you ordered a patch for Mrs. Broadbent, broken hip? He says her blood pressure's only a hundred forty over seventy."

"I didn't order a patch for her. Why would she need a patch with a BP of a hundred forty over seventy?"

"You wanna talk to him?"

"No. Is he reading the right chart? Tell him I'll talk to him after he reads the chart."

"I don't know why Hal keeps going on about that computer," Denny said. "I keep saying, 'Hal, just give the info to Josh and let him punch it in. You don't understand computers, you've never understood computers, and you're not going to understand computers. Just give up. You can review the bills if you like after Josh prints them out.' " She picked up the phone and dialed. "Edward? Denise Aubuchon. An FBI sting hit your pharmacy yesterday morning, and I need to talk to you about your prescriptions. Is this a good time for you, or are you with a client?"

La-La Land, I thought. We're all in La-La Land. Lisa Chiu and Theresa Kahr are dead, but Hal's talking about computers, Denny's on the phone to patients, and I'm writing orders in charts— as if nothing had happened. Two young women, yesterday alive, today dead. And so far I hadn't done a single thing about it. I hadn't made a condolence call to Lisa's parents. I hadn't mourned. I wasn't sure what I meant by "mourning," but whatever it was, I hadn't done it. I was drowning in guilt. Although I understood intellectually that I'd done what I could medically speaking for both young women, emotionally I was beating up on myself for

"letting" them die. They died on my watch. It was my fault. Moreover, Lisa was my dear, dear friend. What was I going to say to
her *mother*?

"Dr. Sutcliffe?"

"Yes, Julio."

"There's a patient with an avulsed leg in the Boo-Boo Room
asking for you."

I turned in my swivel chair. "I'm not doing boo-boos today,"
I said. "Dr. Weinstein's doing boo-boos."

"I think it's Dr. Healy's brother."

Denny, always the unrepentant eavesdropper, cupped her
hand over the phone receiver. "Dr. Healy has four brothers," she
said. "Which one?"

"Um," said Julio.

"Oh, *that* one," said Denny. "Go get'm, Tiger." She resumed
talking to Edward.

I made a face at her, stood, took the chart from Julio, and set
off down the hall, tugging my white coat around myself. Hospital
maintenance had fixed the air-conditioning so well that the ER
now seemed colder than the inside of a meat locker. This was
worrisome. The air-conditioning system was so old, we were all
sure it could not maintain this kind of cold, and would blow up
any minute now from the stress and strain. The hospital would
come crashing down around our ears like the federal building in
Oklahoma City, and we would all be buried alive for days until
the disaster workers dug us out.

My mind was buzzing. But my ER resident's mind routinely
buzzed with several things at once. Why should today be any
different, I thought bitterly, just because a medical student died?
The polydrug overdose in OR One, the pulmonary embolism in
OR Two, the multiple-gunshot wound coming through the swinging doors of the ambulance bay, the nurses, the med students, the
other residents, the labs, the X rays, the procedures, the consults,
the family and loved ones—you name it, my mind buzzed with
it. Might as well bone up for the Emergency Medicine Board orals,

even though they were several years down the road. At the orals I'd be expected to manage three simulated ER crises simultaneously, sustaining life without confusing Patient A with Patient B with Patient C. Of course, the Emergency Medicine Board orals were unlikely to present me with the death of a friend, near seduction by a fellow physician, and the task of devising an appropriate treatment plan for the avulsed leg of that physician's brother. Not to mention the imminent explosion of the air-conditioning unit. Oh, and Hal—let's not forget Hal: the grief of a pediatrician. Grief that was, moreover, having an adverse effect on the pediatrician's judgment. And why shouldn't that be *my* worry, too? Buzz, buzz.

Flipping open Donal Healy's chart, I scanned the triage notes. Twenty-six years old, 113th Street address, next of kin Dr. Michael Healy (brother) UNIVERSITY HOUSE STAFF. (Triage always typed UNIVERSITY HOUSE STAFF in caps when it was staff family, to make sure we knew whom we were dealing with.) Let's see, no third-party medical insurance. Denny was right—Oh, *that* one. *Pt states fell down subway steps. Avulsion anterior lower left leg approx 10 cm. Pt denies loss of consciousness, dizziness, drugs, ETOH* . . . ETOH was alcohol. I looked at my watch; 4:35 P.M. A little early in the evening to be falling-down drunk. Then again, this was Mick Healy's black-sheep brother we were dealing with here.

Mick was the eldest of six children, and, as Phil liked to say, the only kid in the family who didn't grow up to be a professional superego. The whole family except Mick were cops. Cops with troubles. The father, a captain, had been relieved of his command when his Bronx precinct capsized in a storm of scandal, and although he had been exonerated and reinstated (he now worked in some capacity at One Police Plaza), he was a broken and bitter man. One brother—Matthew, I think, or was it Simon?—had been caught up in the "Dirty Thirty" sweep in Washington Heights; although not indicted, he languished at desk duty while the department decided what to do with him. Donal, formerly undercover with some kind of Times Square anti-crime team, had been brought up on charges of abusing and robbing penny-ante drug dealers and prostitutes the previous summer. He and five other "rogue cops"—as the *Daily News* so aptly called them, in headlines splashed across the front page for weeks on end—were summarily drummed out of the police department altogether. Donal was also summarily drummed out of the Healy family, anguishing Mick, who felt called upon to negotiate rapprochement. Judging from Donal's chart, Mick also felt called upon to house him; Donal had given the triage nurse Mick's address as his own.

I'd met him before. I'd met all of Mick's brothers, and their sister Bernadette as well, at a party Mick threw for Bernadette when she made detective first grade. Donal, of all the brothers the most gorgeous, was also the most unruly, especially when drunk. He lacked Mick's subtlety and gentlemanly manners, and his charming Scots-Irish lilt waxed but mostly waned, interchangeable with a guttural Brooklynese cop talk larded with police jargon; Donal, unlike Mick, had been born in this country. Still, he had flair. Even drunk and unruly, he was flirtatious, witty, roué, and very, very sexy. In fact, I was glad I'd been summoned to evaluate him in the Boo-Boo Room, where patients did not need to disrobe for treatment. Which meant I wouldn't have to deal with Mick's sexy younger brother naked.

I barged into the Boo-Boo Room and looked around. As usual, the place was full of bicycle messengers waiting for someone to evaluate their C-spine X rays or the various sundry wrist injuries sustained during headlong flight over the handlebars. And as usual, elderly but spry Dr. Esther Weinstein, her slip showing two inches below her skirt, was lecturing one of them. Her voice still bore traces of her native Vienna, even after fifty years in this country. "Ze first autopsy I attended as a medical student vas a *bicycle messenger*," she was saying. "He vent under a bus. And you, my friend, are going to go under a bus too, *if you don't get into a different line of vork.*"

"It's only a matter of time," I said to the bicycle messenger, a Hispanic kid who looked about sixteen years old and who was staring at Weinstein with wide eyes. On both wrists he sported Ace bandages.

Dr. Weinstein smiled; I was stealing her lines. "Dr. Sutcliffe knows," she said. "If you von't listen to me, *listen to her.*"

"No, listen to Dr. Weinstein," I told the patient. "She's been in this business a long time. The patient she's talking about was a brownshirt on a motorbike who went under a trolley in pre-war Vienna."

"What's a brownshirt?" the kid wanted to know.

But my attention was drawn away. "Over here, Doc," said a voice from a corner.

He was even more gorgeous than I remembered. All the Healy brothers looked alike; all had inherited the same sandy-colored hair and cornflower-blue eyes. But it was as if Mother Nature, experimenting with a series of prototypes while producing the elder brothers, had achieved her *Meisterstück* only with the last and youngest. The tight running shorts and sleeveless T-shirt, plus the wolfish grin with which he greeted me showed he knew it, too.

"Mr. Healy," I said, extending my hand. "Evelyn Sutcliffe."

He stood and we shook. He held my hand for too long, and an electric current shot up my arm. "I know you," he said, somehow managing to imply that he knew me in the carnal sense. "We've met."

"Yes, we have," I said, blinking. "At your sister's party. But, ah, maybe you're confusing me with someone else." The man had an extremely disconcerting gaze. I tore my eyes from his, and, bending, pulled on a pair of gloves as I looked at his legs. The right knee was loosely bandaged with gauze. A flap of skin about the size of a tea saucer hung down over his left shin midway between knee and ankle, exposing the tissue beneath. "How did you do this?"

"I fell up the subway steps about an hour ago. When I got home, I noticed blood on my jeans and took them off, and saw this."

"What about this bandage on your knee?"

"I dropped a crystal bowl on the kitchen floor and it shattered, and I crawled in some of the pieces while I was trying to clean it up."

"Let's see," I said.

He obligingly unwrapped his knee. Cuts and bruises.

I straightened up, snapping off my gloves. "I'll get someone to clean the wound for you," I said. "Then the surgeon's assistant will sew you up. You clean these cuts on your knee yourself?"

"No, Mick did. He even insisted on opening one of those packages, you know, with all the stuff for suturing. I said I didn't want sutures."

I smiled. "I fell on the sidewalk yesterday and Mick patched up my elbow. He wanted to put butterflies on it."

"Yeah?" said Donal. "Not surprising. He's always been the squad leader. I don't imagine it's any different here than it is at home. You work under him?"

The double entendre nailed me before I could duck, and I found myself laughing. "No," I said. "Any loss of consciousness?"

"No."

"Dizziness?"

He shook his head.

By now I really was beginning to wonder if he had me confused with someone else. He was leering at me with an open-mouthed, knowing grin, his chin tilted up flirtatiously, undressing me with his eyes as if he had already undressed me in reality on some previous occasion I was bound to remember any minute now if I just put my mind to it. As if any woman could forget having been to bed with him. "Take any medications?"

"Nope. So, you like my brother?"

So that was it. Suddenly irritated, I snapped the chart shut and recapped my pen. "You'll need suturing," I said. "I'll call the surgeon's assistant." Had Mick told Donal about last night? Did he go home and brag to his brother about wowing me with his prowess? I mouthed the usual pleasantries to Donal and excused myself, stomping off to call the surgeon's assistant. I had no intention of carrying on an affair with Mick, yet the idea that he would tell his brother—whatever he had told him—was nonetheless unsettling.

I slid back into my chair in the nurses' station and reached for another chart, scowling. Denny was still schmoozing Edward on the phone, or perhaps another of her patients. Denny was an internal-medicine doc, specializing in infectious diseases—which these days meant AIDS. Most of her patients had AIDS. Lisa Chiu was dead. Hal Murkland was in a state of extremity. I decided Donal Healy was not worth getting exercised about, and I resolved to concentrate on my work.

A little while later, I had four more charts to go and I could sign out of the hospital for the evening. Normally I liked chart work. It gave me a chance to order my thoughts about patients, make suggestions for their continued care, and let off steam if a patient had been particularly self-abusive or noncompliant. After seeing patients, chart time was often a welcome moment of sanity. But not tonight. Despite my earlier resolution—or perhaps because of it—I had spleen to vent. Who *cared* if Patient X resolutely ignored all medical advice and routinely guzzled a gallon of vodka a day while taking anti-seizure medication? And so *what* if Patient Y wanted to shoot heroin into his IV line when he thought his doctors weren't looking? Let them all kill themselves. Sez I.

I'd never told Lisa how much I liked her. How she seemed like me at that age, only so much better. More mature. More sure of herself. When I was twenty-four, I was a wreck. No self-confidence, didn't know how to say no, not really sure of what I wanted to do in life. Lisa had a vision and she pursued it aggressively.

I never told her how much I admired her.

And now I would never get the chance.

I wished I had someone to yell at, and for a moment I envied Denny Aubuchon acutely. Denny, whose primary mode of self-expression often seemed to be an explosive mixture of passion and rage, had spent most of the day venting *her* spleen at FBI agents, petty bureaucrats in the Justice Department, and policy wonks at the Food and Drug Administration. The day before, Federal officials had arrested more than one hundred pharmacists and other health-care workers in fifty cities nationwide for prescription-drug fraud, including sixty-nine in the metropolitan New York area. Two large pharmacies within walking distance of University Hospital had been plastered with FBI notices and trussed up with yellow police tape to bar entry. The pharmacists were carted off in handcuffs in police vans. Denny's patients, after milling around on the sidewalk with other bewildered customers trying to figure out what was going on, had begun to put in panicked calls to her office.

Denny actually lived for moments like that. Her skin glowed as if she had spent the day at a health spa. She positively radiated power and might. A lithe and athletic person by nature, she metamorphosed with a little rage into Mother Conqueror. "The doctors charge the Medicaid patients for full workups and all these tests, when all they've really done is write a prescription," Denny explained huskily into the phone, her voice a medley of sentiment, righteous indignation and we-have-a-problem-here-but-we-can-solve-it practicality. "Then the patient takes a prescription to a pharmacy and gets it filled. But it's a scam prescription and the patient sells the meds to a middleman and uses the money to buy crack. The middleman sells the meds to a central distributor, who sells them to *another* pharmacy for forty percent below wholesale. *That* pharmacist repackages the drugs to disguise where he got them. But I'm probably telling you way more than you want to know. To make a long story short, the FBI has arrested your pharmacist. Now, I want to direct you to a pharmacist who was *not* arrested"—little joke here—"whom I've made arrangements with to have your prescriptions filled."

I imagined Denny's patient, utterly dazzled by her can-do aggressiveness, thanking her profusely for calling and keeping him abreast of developments in the arena of Medicaid fraud. Right now he was probably telling Denny what a wonderful doctor she was, and how lucky he was to have her. Edward had it wrong; it was the other way around. *Denny* was lucky to have *him*. A name partner in an award-winning architectural firm that designed and built airports and municipal buildings all over the world, Edward Zoller sent Denny postcards from exotic places when he was away and wined her and dined her when he was home, regaling her all the while with stories of cross-cultural misunderstandings and jet-set faux pas. He was smart, well-read, handsome, funny, gracious and charming.

I should be so lucky. I scowled at the chart I had in front of me. The junkie with the methadone overdose—and whatever else he'd swallowed. We must have pumped a dozen liters of water into him for the stomach lavage before we were sure we'd recovered most of the tablets. The nurse was giving him activated charcoal. I ordered IV naloxone and dextrose, and penned a cautionary note: "Pt is known to staff as a repeat offender and prone to violence. On previous occasions pt has unlocked handcuffs with homemade keys that he has secreted upon his person despite body searches by hospital personnel and police officers. Under no circumstances approach without police escort."

Denny finally hung up the phone. "Long day, huh?" She wrapped her arms around herself and tucked her hands into her armpits. "Think they'll ever fix the air-conditioning in here so that it's *cool,* not hot or cold?"

"They need to completely overhaul the entire ventilation system before we all get TB," I said sourly. My mood was worsening.

Denny shot me a sidelong look. "Christ, this business with Lisa."

"Yeah. You talk to her parents?"

"I talked to Lisa's cousin," Denny said. She took her hands out of her armpits and kneaded her knuckles. "The one who's the Episcopal priest. Lisa's parents weren't taking phone calls. Apparently when the cops came to Lisa's mother's office with the news, Lisa's mother flew over backward and landed flat on her back on the floor and afterward had to be sedated. It was only luck that the cousin happened to be visiting at the time."

"Oh, God," I said.

"She was their only child."

"I know." I reached over and took Denny's hand; she, too, had lost her only child.

Denny gave my hand a quick squeeze, then tucked her hands back into her armpits. She didn't like to dwell on it. "Think Hal did it?" she asked.

I snorted. "C'mon."

"Crime of passion?" She smiled provocatively.

"Yeah, nine stab wounds. Don't even joke about it." I finished another chart and tossed it in the pile. "I find it hard to believe he was actually sleeping with her. That's so unprofessional."

"Why, because she worked in our office?"

"Not only that—he had to evaluate her for her work in the Peds ER."

"That was last semester. He wrote that a long time ago."

"Still."

"Well, I'm not surprised one bit," Denny said. "Carol Murkland has it coming. She may be the perfect *Frau Doktor* and take care of his food and house and dry-cleaning, but I've never been convinced—not for a *minute*—that she's in love with him. Even Hal had to wake up one morning and realize his wife wasn't in love with him."

I sighed. It was true—Carol Murkland didn't love her husband and probably never had. Once a penniless graduate student working by day as an administrative assistant in the University's Dean of Students Office, and burning the midnight oil toward her Ph.D. in anthropology, Carol had jumped at the chance to marry the nice, lumbering lunk she'd met at the big University fund-raiser. In her eyes, marriage to Hal was clearly a convenient arrangement. She ran Hal's personal life and household with the same efficiency with which she'd run the dean's professional life and office. Suddenly Hal's clothes were clean, his shirts were impeccably ironed, his apartment was tastefully decorated and spotlessly tidy, and his colleagues were welcome for deliciously cooked meals composed of healthful ingredients and plenty of fresh fruits and vegetables. Carol never complained about Hal's long work hours or the fact that he could take very little vacation. On the contrary, his long hours gave her plenty of time for her anthropology studies. Moreover, Hal paid for those studies and supported her in a style appropriate for a rising young doctor's wife.

But she didn't love him. She seemed fond of him.

My theory was, Hal was so grateful anyone would marry him, the fact that *he* adored *her* was enough to keep him going for a while. But they'd been married two years now and, as Denny said, even Hal had to wake up one morning and realize his wife wasn't in love with him. And lately Hal and Carol had begun to quarrel, often late at night in their bedroom, directly over my own bedroom in the doctors' residence. Their voices were never loud enough for me actually to hear what was being said, but the angry tones were unmistakable. I'd begun to wonder if they were arguing about sex. I realized I hadn't heard their bed creaking and Hal's exuberant cries of passion for some time now.

"Yeah, but I don't think Lisa was in love with him either," I said. "Do you?"

But Denny had progressed to her next thought. "Those fucking Right-to-Lifers," she said with sudden vehemence. " 'You wanna cut babies outta people? We'll cut one *into* you!' What I want to know is, how come there's no feminist vigilante revenge squad? You know, some big, muscle-bound lesbians in leather and bandoleros, lined up in front of the abortion clinics, mowing down the Right-to-Lifers with high-tech automatic-weapons fire?"

I laughed. "You can't be serious."

"I *am* serious. That guy who shot Lamartine this morning, wouldn't you like to stand him up in front of a firing squad? He probably *hates* homosexuals—he certainly hates women. Wouldn't you like to see a band of female Arnold Schwarzenegger look-alikes just mow him down? I would."

"It's a nice thought, but no. What do you mean, 'You wanna cut babies out of people, we'll cut one into you?' "

"I mean the guy just sliced her open, Ev. It was like a Pfannenstiehl incision. And there she is clutching this doll."

I drew a sharp breath. "Oh, God, Denny, are you saying—"

Denny mimed a cesarean section, drawing an imaginary scalpel across her lower abdomen.

"—Jesus, I didn't notice. You and Phil had already bandaged her."

"Well, we did the best we could. She really needed a surgeon. Christ, I have to tell you, though, I got chills when I saw that doll. When we got there, she was still holding it against herself—I dunno, maybe to tamponade the wound." Soak up the blood and stop the bleeding. "You know, one of those cloth dolls. Like Raggedy Ann. I had the wit to ask Rita Firenze to put on a pair of gloves and bag it for the cops."

I struggled against the emotions rising up in me. "Tamponade the wound? She knew her anatomy better than that—I mean, the veins are deep in the pelvic bowl—"

"So maybe she was trying to hold the edges of the wound together," Denny snapped. "Or trying to keep the skin from bleeding. Or—or—"

I turned my head aside and bit my lip. *Or maybe she was trying to keep from looking at it.*

"Yeah," said Denny. "Me too. Now you tell me if you wouldn't like to shoot the fucker." She picked up the phone again and started dialing.

A big wave had crashed over my head, knocking my feet out from under me. I fought to get my head above water. "Wait," I said. "Denny, why would your mind jump immediately to the anti-abortionists, when there's a guy out there killing women and leaving babydolls at the scene? Is there some piece of logic here I'm missing?"

"Ev, don't you read the papers? Look at the pictures of the anti-abortionists picketing the clinics. They're all standing there waving signs and *babydolls*. You run the gauntlet to get into the clinic, and they're yelling, 'Mommy, Mommy, don't kill me, Mommy'—and they stick this doll in your face. Theodore? Denise Aubuchon. An FBI sting hit your pharmacy yesterday morning, and I need to talk to you about your prescriptions. Is this a good time for you, or are you with a client?"

I clenched my teeth. Did all Denny's patients have clients? And was she going to schmooze every single one of them with this pharmacy-scam song and dance? Well, I could make phone calls, too. I picked up the phone and dialed Rita and Tony Firenze, Lisa's next-door neighbors.

Their answering machine picked up.

"Ev Sutcliffe," I said, after the beep. "Call me. I need to touch base. By the way, has anyone seen Jeff's cat? Someone's feeding him, I hope. If you need volunteers to help with cat care, let me know."

Next I dialed Hal Murkland's office. I hoped he had calmed down a little.

"Dr. Murkland."

"Hal—don't hang up. I have to ask you something else. Did Lisa ever talk to you about her friend Theresa Kahr? The woman who was raped and beaten early yesterday?"

"Jeez, Ev," Hal exploded. "I know who Theresa Kahr is. Why is everyone talking to me in this patronizing tone of voice?"

"Sorry."

"You're forgiven. The German girl. Yeah, what do you want to know?"

Next to me, Denny was schmoozing Theodore. I put a finger in my ear. "Well, for starters, do you know of any disagreement they might have had lately?"

"Let me think." A literalist, Hal then proceeded to do so.

I waited.

"They had an argument about nuclear disarmament," he said finally. "Something about when the French Green Party fired on the nuclear cruiser . . . No, wait, was it the German Green Party and a French nuclear cruiser? Whatever. In any case, Theresa stormed off in a huff. Lisa said that Theresa basically thought the end justified the means. I remember this because she was really mad and rolling her eyes."

"Who, Theresa?"

"No, *Lisa* was mad and rolling her eyes. She said she had no patience with people who think the end justifies the means. We were all at the West End Gate, the three of us. Theresa was trying to order radishes. So they didn't have radishes and Lisa disagreed about nuclear disarmament and Theresa stormed out." His voice caught, and he put the phone down. I heard him blowing his nose.

A dispute about nuclear disarmament wasn't exactly what I'd had in mind. "I see," I said when Hal came back on. "When was this?"

"End of the school year. May something. All these asshole jocks from the University were there, celebrating the end of exams and getting drunk and vomiting in the men's room."

"Did Theresa say anything about a guy bothering her at the Good Earth, or following her?"

"No, that was later. Ev, I can't talk about this right now. My patients are backing up. I'm two hours behind as it is."

"Hal—*Don't hang up*. Just tell me this—have you told the police?"

"Of course I told the police. You think I'm an idiot? Theresa called here and said she was nervous because she thought she saw the guy following her home one night, and Lisa said, 'Don't do anything—let me find out if he's who I think he is.' But that's the last I heard of it. Now I'm kicking myself I didn't ask her who she thought it was." He put a hand over the phone and I overheard a muffled conversation. "Ev. *I gotta go*." He hung up on me.

I put my forehead down on the desk and closed my eyes.

Lisa thought she recognized Theresa's assailant.

It was possible that Theresa's assailant—if it was the same guy who knocked me down—recognized me.

The Babydoll Killer knew who I was.

Denny had finished talking to Theodore and was flipping through her appointment book, undoubtedly choosing her next schmooz-ee. "We know anything from Phil?" she asked. "About what happened when the cops came?"

I shook my head. "I talked to him briefly around lunchtime," I said distractedly. "He said he managed to insinuate himself into the crime-scene investigation by convincing the cops that they needed his psychological analysis of who would do such a thing."

"Yeah? What *is* his psychological analysis?"

"It's complicated. Let me get him to run it by me again, so I can repeat it to you."

"Yeah, keep me posted—I'd like to know. You guys eating out?"

"Favorite restaurant. I hope he isn't going to ask me to marry him again." I took a deep breath. "Den, I just can't believe she's dead. One minute I'm thinking, I'd better co-sign her charts or collect her for rounds, and the next it hits me—wham!—she's dead. But then I just go on working like it's a normal day here, like she's *not* dead—"

"I know," Denny said. "I know."

"Well, what did you do—I mean, how long . . . ?"

"When Gray died?" Denny's mouth twisted sadly. Gray was her son. He had been killed in a car accident when he was five years old, along with his father. "I was in utter, total shock for about two months, but I had those injuries," Denny said. "I've often thought, looking back, that I was glad for the physical pain, because it gave me some kind of pain to have instead of the emotional pain. Plus, when it got too bad for me, I just popped another painkiller or another sleeping pill or another Valium."

We all knew the Story of Gray. From time to time Denny told it, always exactly the same way, as if reciting a liturgy about a death that had occurred two thousand years ago. First came the Prom Date From Hell, who seemed like such a nice guy and had such gorgeous green eyes and looked *so* handsome in his tux that Denny allowed him to talk her into drinking half a bottle of vodka.

Eight and a half months later, a beautiful little boy was born, whom Denny named Gray because nothing was ever as black and white as the nuns made it out to be. Mother and baby moved in with Denny's sister and brother-in-law. Gray's father was half in the picture, half out—Denny was always a little vague on the details at this juncture of the story—and he was inclined to violence when he drank. He showed up one night, drunk and raging, having heard that Gray's nursery-school teacher had been to see Denny to warn her that Gray showed signs of "homosexual tendencies"—whatever *that* meant—and he beat Denny so severely, he concussed her and broke both her forearms. Then he kidnapped Gray and took the child away in his pickup truck. The truck was found by the state police the following morning, upended in a ravine not very far from Denny's sister's house. Both Gray and his father were dead.

"When did you feel like you had assimilated what happened?" I asked, grateful for her willingness to share this painful intimacy. Her hand was warm on mine. Around us, the clang and clamor of the emergency room receded for a moment, as if we had magically cocooned ourselves.

"You mean, when did I feel myself again? I don't know. It came and went. About six or seven months later I thought I was okay, but then, on the anniversary of his death, I fell apart worse than I had in the first place. Finally I went to nursing school and I began to take care of sick people. I think that's when I began to feel like I was climbing out of it, back into real life. And then eventually I went on to medical school, and I thought, This is for Gray."

"Oh," I said. I thought about Patient X guzzling vodka while taking anti-seizure medication, and Patient Y shooting heroin into his IV line. Somehow, caring for them didn't seem to be alleviating my shock over Lisa's death, and Denny's "This-Bud's-for-you" approach seemed a little facile. But maybe caring for a person I liked might help me tap into my emotions for Lisa.

"Thanks," I said. Again, I squeezed Denny's hand.

The emergency room reasserted itself; my beeper went off. I sat up and tilted it, squinting at the digital readout. Mick Healy. I was immediately transported to the well of the brownstone, devouring Mick whole. Smelling his sweat and feeling it on my cheek and neck. (So what if Donal Healy had been watching.) Irreverently, I thought, now sex with Mick—that might help me get back in touch with myself. I picked up the phone and dialed Healy's extension.

"Dr. Healy."

"Ev Sutcliffe."

"Hullo, darling. Just ringing to see how you're doing. Thought I'd offer to buy you a drink, if you're up for it. We could tell each other Lisa stories."

I looked at my watch. It was 5:30 P.M. Two and a half hours before I had to meet Phil downtown. I needed at least forty minutes to get to the restaurant, plus I should go home and shower . . . That left an hour and a half free. I wavered. No. "That's sweet, Mick, but I really can't," I said. "I've got a dinner engagement."

"Ah." His hesitation came down the line. "Okay if I ring you later?"

"Mm. Might be awkward."

"Of course. Forgive me."

A silence ensued, then lengthened. I racked my brain for something to say, something neither discouraging nor encouraging. C'mere-c'mere-c'mere-getaway-getaway-getaway, as Bill Cosby once said. Finally I realized I hadn't told Mick about his brother's injury. I opened my mouth, but before I could say anything, Mick dropped the phone.

"Good Lord," he said. In the background, I heard loud voices. When Mick picked up again, he sounded breathless. "The bloody cops are here."

I had to think for a moment where "here" might be. Then I remembered that Healy had offices with a couple of other neurosurgeons on Schiff Two. (The Schiff Medical Suites comprised the lower five floors of the doctors' residence, with a separate entrance on Amsterdam Avenue.) Hal's and Denny's offices were also on Schiff Two.

"I think they're arresting Hal Murkland," Mick said.

CHAPTER 9

I climbed the stairs out of the subway at Ninety-sixth Street and Broadway like Eurydice ascending from hell. The temperature topside was probably in the mid-eighties, but even the mid-eighties was cooler than on the subway platform. I gasped for air and plucked at the red silk blouse I was wearing. Both the blouse and navy linen trousers had been fresh from the dry cleaner's when I'd put them on twenty minutes ago. Already they were a sopping, wrinkled mess. I didn't know why I'd even bothered to go home from the hospital, shower and change.

I was in a foul, overheated mood, talking to myself in my head. Ranting might be more like it.

I ranted at Mick Healy, for having had the lack of good grace to kiss me on the street the night before.

Then I ranted at myself, for letting my defenses down so far that I'd been vulnerable to his taking advantage of me. You should have better control of yourself, Sutcliffe, I chided myself, so you can't be tempted like that. Christ, I was a fucking mess.

I stopped at the Korean market to pick up a few items for

Kennedy Bartlett. By the time I reached the checkout counter, I had exhausted myself with ranting. Nonetheless, I suspiciously watched the checkout girl ring up my purchases, lest she make a mistake and give me the opportunity to rant at *her*.

I was emotionally, physically, and mentally exhausted.

I needed a drink.

Which I was going to have just as soon as I finished walking Maxie, Kennedy Bartlett's aging black poodle.

"Why should I go back into the hospital?" Bartlett was saying into the telephone when I let myself into his apartment on Eighty-ninth Street with my key. "They hook you up to every machine imaginable and then dare you to die—is that any way to live?" Bartlett waved at me from his bed, a futon piled high with brightly colored pillows from his many travels through North Africa, Turkey, and the Middle East. He was wearing one of his old dance leotards and was speaking into a new portable phone. The combination of the phone and outfit made him look like Dr. McCoy on "Star Trek" talking into his communicator. "Can you imagine La Traviata gasping out her last aria on a respirator?" he went on, rolling his eyes. "No thank you. Besides, it upsets poor Maxie when I spend all that time in the hospital, and for what? So I can live ten minutes longer?"

Maxie, the dog, looked from me to his master and back again, as if to say, Can you believe he's still talking about this? He heaved himself up on his spindly legs and wobbled over to greet me, thrusting his snout between my knees.

I patted the dog and went through the dining room into the kitchen, where I began unpacking the groceries I'd bought. Ken's apartment consisted of the parlor floor of an old town house: the living room, dining room, and kitchen of a grand bourgeois household at the turn of the century. The kitchen had been subdivided into a kitchen and bathroom, so the layout was rather odd: You entered the apartment via the living room, which opened onto the dining room, which in turn had two doors: one to the kitchen, and one to the bathroom. Ken had furnished the dining room with floor-to-ceiling bookcases, a long table that had come from some shipping magnate's private library, and an assortment of chairs. None of the chairs matched, but all were wonderfully comfortable. Which they needed to be, because Bartlett did all his entertaining in the dining room. There was no furniture in the living room except the futon bed, rolled out on the floor like a monk's pallet. Along one wall ran floor-to-ceiling mirrors with a ballet barre at waist height. On the opposite wall, mementos from Bartlett's long career with the New York City Ballet hung chock-a-block: framed programs and photos; toe shoes under glass with dried bouquets of flowers; a poster showing Ken executing a tour jeté; inscribed photos of Balanchine, Nureyev, and Barishnikov. With the futon pushed against the wall, the living room doubled as a studio where Bartlett could teach his dance students. He retained a small clientele, and taught them from his bed, where he reclined like an aging Russian prima donna, waving a white handkerchief and calling out critiques.

At sixty-seven years of age, Kennedy Bartlett was dying of AIDS. Six months earlier he'd been diagnosed with AIDS-related lymphoma. He'd had two bouts of chemotherapy and there was some discussion of a third, which he was thinking of refusing. He'd had a long, successful career as a ballet dancer and as a private teacher of ballet, and he intended to die in his own bed, no regrets, with his beloved dog Maxie by his side. He had already made the arrangements to be cremated. Since he had no living family, he had designated me his next of kin; I even had power of attorney. My instructions were to send his ashes to be interred in the Bartlett family crypt in "New England's cemetery of choice," as Ken called it: Mt. Auburn Cemetery in Cambridge, Massachusetts. There was to be no funeral or memorial service. Instead, I was to notify a small group of his closest friends, some of whom were big-name celebrities, to come to a "going-away" party in his honor (Bartlett had already made arrangements with a caterer). And Maxie was to go live with a gay couple in upstate New York who had two dogs of their own.

That is, if Maxie didn't die first. He was almost eighteen years old, nearly blind, crippled with arthritis, and suffered from some kind of doggy skin disease that made his fur fall out in clumps. Some sections of his haunches were entirely bald, baring a gray, peach-fuzz skin. When I took him out, I had to carry him up and down the front steps of the house. He didn't need a leash because he couldn't walk faster than I could. As he staggered along with his head down to smell where he was going, with me one or two paces behind, passersby would look at me with incredulity. Once, one woman came right out with it: "It's a crime not to have that animal put down and out of his misery," she sniffed.

"He and his owner want to die together," I said. She looked at me as if I were nuts.

Ken's voice wafted in from the living room. "Don't believe the media," he was saying. "His wife left *him* for the ambassador. And there's absolutely nothing going on with the daughter's nanny. The nanny is a divinity student from Scotland and she has integrity coming out her ears. Take my word for it." Pause. "No, the nanny was with him at the horse show because the daughter was *riding* in the horse show." Pause. "The rumor about Barbra Streisand is utterly false. She's been at his house *once*."

Smiling, I opened the refrigerator, putting away what I'd brought him: three cartons of peach yogurt, two bottles of Pellegrino water, a couple of bananas, and some vanilla Häagen-Dazs ice cream. Ken and I were old, comfortable friends, well-versed in each other's quirks. Ten years earlier, on the recommendation of a mutual friend, I had consulted Ken about undertaking some kind of exercise regimen for my back so I didn't keep throwing it out all the time. Over a period of three or four weeks, Ken guided me through the exercises until I could perform them satisfactorily on my own. Gregarious and interested in everybody and everything, and explaining that, as "an old bachelor," he liked to have "young people around" to make up for his lack of family, Ken added me to his wide circle of friends and students whom he liked to invite for cozy dinners in his apartment. When I proved too shy to socialize with his more famous acquaintances, he began inviting me for dinners "just the two of us, dear." He would talk about the ballet and theater; I would talk about Shakespeare and English literature. Then one evening around Christmastime he took me to see the *Nutcracker*, and impulsively introduced me to his friend the conductor as his "favorite niece." Eventually I became his "favorite niece, the doctor." When he developed full-blown AIDS, it seemed only natural that I be officially designated next of kin.

While I had the refrigerator open, I scanned Bartlett's prescription meds, neatly lined up on the second shelf in front of the food. I liked to keep abreast of what Denny Aubuchon was prescribing for him. Hearing the refrigerator door, Maxie lurched into the kitchen to see if I might want to feed him something. He still ate voraciously, putting away more food than a Saint Bernard half his age and three times his size. "No, baby," I said. "I'll feed you after you have your walk."

"I gotta go," said Bartlett. "Ev Sutcliffe is here." He made kissing noises, and I heard him click the phone shut. "Put that stuff away later," he yelled. "Come in here and help me make this earth-shattering decision."

Uh-oh, I thought. I shut the refrigerator and went into the living room, leaning over the bed and kissing him on his ear. I never kissed him on the mouth anymore; God only knew what kind of germs I might be bringing from the emergency room.

We took a moment to appraise each other.

"I know what *I* look like," Ken said. "I look like death warmed over. Do you know what *you* look like? What did you do to your elbow?"

I smiled sadly and plopped down on the bed, leaning back on the pillows. I debated telling Bartlett about Lisa Chiu's death and Hal Murkland's having been taken away by the police—I still had no idea whether Hal had been actually arrested or merely hauled off to the station house for questioning—but I thought better of it. "I slipped on the stairs at the hospital and split my elbow open," I said. "I need a vacation."

"You need more than a vacation, sweetheart, from the looks of it." He lisped the "sweetheart" like Bogart. He picked up his reading glasses, which hung on a rhinestone chain around his neck, put them on, and peered over the frames at me. Then he looked at his watch and wrote a note in his daybook. "Why don't you pour yourself a drink while I take care of a little business here?" he suggested.

"Oh, I dunno," I said. Now that I'd sat down, I was suddenly too tired to get up and fix a drink. "I think I'll just lie here and take a nap. Wake me when you're ready." I closed my eyes and listened to Bartlett's fountain pen scratching in his little book. Probably writing down a précis of his phone conversation. Last week he'd said to me, "I'm thinking about killing myself," and had taken extensive notes during the conversation we had about it. We'd discussed the pros and cons, and I'd voiced my reasons for his not doing it. He'd written them all down.

"You should have lived at the court of Louis Quatorze," I said. "You could have written your *Mémoires historiques*."

"I have news for you. I *am* writing my *Mémoires historiques*." I felt his hand on mine. "I heard on the radio this morning that more than a hundred people have died from the heat. You lose any?"

I shook my head. "That was in Chicago. Cook County Medical Examiner's Office is still counting the dead."

"Ah, right," said Ken. "Cattle dying too, I hear."

"Well, not in Chicago. In the Midwest, though."

"But it's been pretty hot here. Yesterday it was a hundred and two. The sidewalk was too hot for Maxie to walk on—it hurt his feet." Pause. "You haven't lost anyone?" he asked again, more gently.

I opened my eyes. Ken was scrutinizing me with a fair approximation of Phil's shrink eye. "Perhaps a timely phone call would ease your mind," he suggested.

I sat up and laughed ruefully. Ken handed me his portable phone, and I dialed Denny's cellular phone number.

"Denise Aubuchon," Denny barked in my ear.

"What's going on?"

"I don't believe this. The asshole's refusing an attorney. Hasn't done anything wrong, he says. Right now they're fingerprinting him."

"Where are you?"

"The Twenty-sixth Precinct in Harlem. On One Hundred Twenty-sixth Street, just over from Broadway."

"Is he under arrest?"

"I don't think so. I think—"

"Have they read him Miranda?"

"What? Oh, you mean 'You have the right to remain silent,' et cetera? I have no idea. Should they have?"

"Only if he's under arrest."

She snorted. "You should be here, Ev, not me. All I know is, two hours ago you couldn't get Hal to talk to the cops if you hit him with a baseball bat, and now he suddenly wants to blab all over the place and *prove his innocence.*" Her voice rose with exasperation. "Meanwhile, I'm on the edge of the bench here thinking, why do I have the sinking feeling this is Dr. Richard Kimble redux? And that it's going to fall to you and me to find the one-armed man?"

"Denny, let's not get melodramatic before it's called for. What you're saying is, so far as you know, Hal is not a suspect at this time."

"I guess not. But what do I know? They sure as hell aren't telling me anything. On the one hand, Hal has cuts all over his face, he admits to being in her apartment last night, having wild sex with her, and breaking glassware. He's fat, messy, middle-aged, and married, and she was young and beautiful. On the other hand, he's a pediatrician. Anyone can tell he's gentle as a lamb. Too bad we couldn't get a few of his patients in here as character witnesses. They could coo and drool on the detectives and let them know what a swell guy Hal is. Wait—here they come. Talk to you later."

"May the Force be with you," I said and hung up.

"I won't ask," Ken drawled. "I don't know how that medical practice survives the soap opera of their relationship. You'd think they were blood relatives, the way they squabble. Relatives should not be in business together." He put his little book down and lay back against the pillows.

On impulse, I leaned over and lay a hand on his neck. His skin was dry and warm despite the air-conditioning. "You feeling okay?"

"Maybe a drink of water," he murmured.

"I think so—a large glass of it, if you don't mind. You really need to force fluids. And I think I'll take your temperature. Where's the thermometer?"

"Bathroom."

I got up and fetched the thermometer, shook it down, and plunked it under Bartlett's tongue. Then I went into the kitchen and filled a large tumbler with Pellegrino water. When I put the water back in the fridge, I noticed a quart container of chicken soup from the International Poultry Store on the shelf. "How about if I heat up some of this soup for you?" I yelled out to Bartlett.

"Thank you," he called back.

I zapped the soup in the microwave and took it out to Bartlett on a tray with the glass of water. "Who brought you the soup?" I asked, taking the thermometer out of his mouth. "You've got a slight temperature. Ninety-nine."

"Dr. Aubuchon. I always have a slight temperature."

"Well, if it gets much worse, you should give Denny a ring."

"She stopped by this afternoon," he said, ignoring me. "Some problem with the pharmacy."

"Ken, are you listening to me?"

"No." He sat up, looked at the soup with resignation, and tucked in, grimacing. Open sores in his throat made it difficult for him to swallow. He made himself eat five spoonfuls, then stopped to rest.

"Ken, if you spike a temperature, call Dr. Aubuchon."

"All that pharmacy business doesn't really concern me," he went on, raising his voice as if I were the one who had developed selective deafness. "That office boy of hers makes all my pharmacy runs for me. God, I hate eating. I used to love to eat. He's a sharp kid. Handles all the paperwork, too. Fills out all the Blue Cross and Medicare forms, and straightens things out when there's a fuckup. What's his name . . ."

I gave up. "Joshua Waterman?"

"Dr. Aubuchon says his lung collapsed."

I nodded.

"His health hasn't been very good at all lately, and this mess with Blue Cross—well, they've got that medical student to help straighten things out, I suppose—"

"Ken," I said, "you're not thinking of killing yourself again, are you?"

"—and she certainly seems competent enough." He took a few more spoons of soup and began to breathe deeply and rhythmically to counteract the pain, and his voice went up an octave. "What's wrong with Joshua's parents, by the way? He told me he's been sexually active since he was twelve and that's how he got AIDS. It's a disgrace. With parents like that, he should be in foster care."

"Because I wish you wouldn't." I was so full of death I couldn't bear the thought of having to deal with his, too. At the same time I felt a pang of guilt—here he was thinking about killing himself, and all I could think was how it would hit *me*.

He ate five more spoonfuls of soup, slowly, then handed me the bowl, motioning for the water. He drank the glass down, one painful sip at a time. When he finished, his eyes were watering. "I've been thinking of asking Dr. Aubuchon to help me," he said, in a quavering, willowy voice.

I took a deep breath. "Ken, if you really must do it, you don't need to involve your physicians. You put them in a terrible position even asking. Have you discussed this with Denny, or with your oncologist?"

He shook his head. "Not yet. Ev, I don't want to die in the hospital. The time is going to come where they'll put me in the hospital to die, and I just don't want that. What about that book, *Final Exit?*"

"I've heard of it." Oh, God, I thought. He's picking the way to do it. "I haven't actually seen it."

"You put pills in applesauce or something."

"Yes, you can do that."

He smiled wryly. "I haven't picked the date yet, if that's what you're wondering."

"It's your decision, Ken." I cracked my knuckles, avoiding his gaze. The memory of Lisa's death that morning was seeping over me like an autumn frost; my very joints felt chilled. "I won't help you, but I'll certainly make myself available for you to discuss things with. You know that. I'm not sure I want to know ahead of time exactly when you're going to do it, though."

In my mind, I was looking up again toward the ceiling, imagining Lisa's soul departing her body.

"Cheer up, Ev. You're allowed to try to talk me out of it. Tell me again what you said the other day, about suicide being murder."

"Well, I think suicide *is* murder," I said slowly, still staring at my hands. "There are good reasons for not killing someone, including yourself. Secondly, while I am not a religious person, I do believe in God, and I do think God puts us all here to accomplish something—and that only he can decide when we've accomplished it."

"I'm not really very big on God." Bartlett sighed.

"But you're moral. You're very moral."

"That's true." He made a motion with his hand, and I gave him his soup bowl. "But is suicide immoral? Don't answer.

Enough about me. Did somebody else die you don't want to tell me about?"

So I told him. About being knocked down by the guy who pulled my shirt over my head. About Theresa Kahr's attack and death—possibly at the hands of the same guy who had knocked me down. About the Babydoll Killer, and his other victims. About sleuthing with Lisa Chiu, and about Lisa's death the very next morning. And my theory that Lisa had been killed because of what she knew. I skipped the megillah about Hal's detention by the police. I would tell Ken about that when I knew more, and in the meantime he could deduce the situation from what he had over-heard.

When I had finished, Bartlett handed back his soup bowl, now empty, and said, "And you let me ramble on about killing myself? Why didn't you tell me before that that nice Chinese girl had been murdered? Even I know when too much is too much." He held out his arms, and I lay across his chest carefully, so as not to crush his frail rib cage, my face turned away so as not to breathe on him. We hugged. "We're still here for each other," Bartlett said.

Kayn aynhoreh, I thought. No evil eye.

By the time I carried Maxie down the front steps of the house and set him down on the sidewalk, I was really morose.

I thought about the Ken I used to know.

If you were depressed, he would put on some tango music, sweep you into his arms, and dance around the room with you, whispering instructions in your ear—now, *dip*, now *turn*—until you were transformed into the hottest tango partner this side of Barcelona. If you were bored, he entertained you with the latest outrageous gossip of the rich and famous, which he invariably had "from the horse's mouth." If you were in pain—say your neck hurt, or your back—Ken would show you a few exercises you could do to relax the knotted muscles, and you would walk out of his apartment an hour later standing up straight for the first time in weeks.

He used to take me dancing at the Rainbow Room.

Now he was so weak, he could barely manage to get to the bathroom.

Oh, Ken, I thought. Please don't kill yourself.

Maxie decided to stagger toward Riverside Park. Normally he just pissed on the tree and crapped in the gutter in front of the house, but today he seemed eager to see a bit of the world before returning inside immediately. Or, in his case, smell a bit of the world. The sultry August weather certainly contributed to the smelliness of the environment; even I could smell the urine, both animal and human, and the dog shit and garbage. I wrinkled my nose and began to feel as if I might jump out of my skin.

I wondered what kind of funeral Lisa's parents would have for her, and where it would be. Her parents lived in the Washington, D.C., area. What if I couldn't get off work to go? Residents weren't allowed to take vacation during July or August, for fear that the unsupervised interns would kill the patients. That was a laugh. I wouldn't be surprised if some people thought Shehadeh had managed to kill the patient—Lisa—with me standing right there looking at him.

Well, not quite, Sutcliffe. Don't start getting hard on yourself. Shehadeh fucked up the intubation, but you caught his mistake right away and acted appropriately. And Lisa'd lost so much blood she would have died anyway.

For want of something better to do while Maxie sniffed at a doorstep, investigating at his inexorably slow pace, I took my glasses off to polish them on my handkerchief.

That was when I thought I saw him.

Mick Healy. Standing on the sidewalk at the end of the block, looking at me.

Hastily, I put my glasses back on and peered toward Riverside Drive. No one was there.

A car went by.

Your eyes are playing tricks on you, Sutcliffe, I thought. It's dusk; you're tired. You didn't have your glasses on. *No, that was*

Mick. A sinister premonition suddenly overtook me. My heart pounding, I sprinted the half-block to Riverside Drive. Blue shirt, green scrub pants. When I reached the corner, I looked north and south along the Drive, and across the street to the tiered plaza of the Soldiers and Sailors Monument.

Nothing. A black woman with a little white girl and a big golden retriever; a man in a business suit getting out of a car. A kid on Rollerblades sailed past.

"Excuse me," I said to the woman. "Did you see a guy in a blue shirt and green pants run past?"

She looked up. She was picking up after the dog, who had just taken a giant poop on the newspaper she'd slid under his ass. She folded the paper deftly and shoved the whole mess into a plastic garbage bag. "No, I'm sorry," she said, looking around as she knotted the bag. "Taylor, you see the man like the lady says?"

The little girl, who was maybe five, shot her arm up in the air and started jumping up and down, like a kid waiting to be called on by her teacher.

"Yes, Taylor?" I asked hopefully.

"He went that way," she said, pointing south toward the Chofetz Chaim Yeshiva, an old brick mansion on the National Register of Historic Places.

I looked. No one. Somehow I didn't think he'd run into the yeshiva—not while wearing running clothes, and not on a Friday evening near sunset and the start of the Sabbath. He must have gone around the corner of Eighty-eighth Street.

"An' it was Superman!"

"I see." I pondered this. "How do you know it was Superman?"

" 'Cause he had the 'S' on his chest. The 'S' for Superman."

"You can read?" I asked.

"Uh-hum. Mommy teached me. An' I was Supergirl on Halloween, so I can grow up and be whoever I want."

"Get'm while they're young," said the black woman. She was smiling.

I thought about telling the little girl that I'd had the same message from my own mother and now I was a doctor, but I'd left poor Maxie alone on the sidewalk and I had to get back to him before he staggered out on the street into the path of an oncoming car. "Taylor," I said, "you're a good scout, and very observant. I'll tell Superman when I see him." Then I turned on my heel and sprinted back to Maxie, wondering if Lisa was prodding me from the other side to take up jogging.

Maxie was waiting patiently at the bottom of the stairs in front of the house. I scooped him up, and he licked the sweat off my face.

"So whaddya think, Maxie?" I said, cuddling him against me. "You think Mick Healy's following me? Or you think he's just out for his jog?"

Maxie appeared to consider my question, peering up at me gravely. After a moment I carried him up the steps and set him down in front of the door. Then I sat down for a moment on the top step and cradled my head in my hands.

When I didn't open the door right away, he barked.

"Maybe you'd like to apply for a job as my guard dog," I said.

CHAPTER
10

"I don't think I'm up for dinner," I told Phil, shifting the phone from one ear to the other. I was standing on the street on the corner of Eighty-sixth Street and Broadway, and there was a homeless person shuffling around, whom I wanted to keep well within eyesight. "I'm twitchy and restless and my elbow itches."

"Well, what are you going to do instead of dinner?" Phil asked reasonably. "You have to eat, whether your elbow itches or not."

He spoke to me in his formal shrink voice: kind, attentive, wise. I suspected he was considering various psychological reasons my elbow might itch—perhaps I was suppressing feelings I might have about having been knocked down by the Babydoll Killer that I should make conscious—but he didn't voice them, and I quashed the sudden impulse to rant about the itchiness of hospital tape and gauze dressing in 85-degree heat. "Are you with someone?" I asked.

"Just coming through the door now," he replied smoothly.

I smiled. Phil and I went through a kind of charade on the phone when he was with a patient. He liked to give the patient the impression that he was talking to another patient; God forbid the patient should realize that he/she was overhearing a personal conversation of the psychiatrist's.

"I suggest that you keep your dinner date," Phil went on. "Ask your date to reschedule an hour later, and spend a little time doing something nice for yourself. Why not drop by that place in SoHo you like so much and buy yourself an ounce of exotic tea?"

"I guess," I said listlessly. A truck lumbered by; I stuck my finger in my free ear so I could hear.

"At times like this, you have to mother yourself. Imagine what the mother of your dreams would do for you right now, and do it for yourself. Or, if it takes a little bit of planning, start planning."

The homeless person held out a grimy hand. I fished in my pockets and gave him two quarters. He salaamed, flashed me a toothless grin, and shuffled off. Belatedly, I realized I had treated him in the ER a couple of weeks previously, and had given him a good talking-to for not taking his TB medication regularly. The guy was a walking incubator for drug-resistant tuberculosis.

"But I feel so guilty," I said. "Lisa's dead and—"

"That's a normal feeling. Let's plan to discuss that at our next meeting."

I laughed. "I love it when you talk to me like that," I said huskily. "I'll see you at the restaurant, an hour later, at nine. Thanks. Love you."

"Anytime." He hung up.

I stood on the street for a minute or two wondering what the mother of my dreams could possibly do for me at this given moment. My own mother would want to hear all the medical details of Lisa's death, and then would start quizzing me about what I thought I should have done instead, which was not the kind of motherly attention I needed just now.

Sighing, I picked up the phone again. I should have made all these calls before I left Ken Bartlett's—the street was not the optimum site to conduct business—but Ken was dozing off and I didn't want to disturb him.

First, I dialed my brother Craig, an assistant district attorney in the Manhattan DA's office. "Hi," I said when his machine picked up. "A colleague of mine has been taken in for questioning in the murder of a medical student this morning. They apparently haven't charged him with anything, but I'm wondering if maybe he needs an attorney. So far he says he doesn't want one. I'm going out with Phil for dinner, but I need your advice. Talk to my machine. Thanks. Bye."

Next I called Hal Murkland's machine. "Hal, it's Ev. I'm leaving you this message while you're at the station house. I just want to say I'm really sorry you're having to go through all this, and I'm sorry if I was short-tempered with you this afternoon. Call me ASAP."

Then I called the Firenzes, Lisa's neighbors on the twelfth floor of the doctors' residence.

"Oh, Ev, I'm just in shock," Rita said. "I even went to mass. I haven't been to mass in years. And we can't find Jeff's cat anywhere. The window was open in the bedroom and the screen was up—"

"Lisa's bedroom window?"

"—and I'm afraid he got out. Right. The bedroom window. I was going to put a bowl of food out on the fire escape for him, but Tony said we'd attract rats. So we left our window open a crack with a little catnip on the windowsill in case—"

"How do you know the window was open?" I asked.

"I went out on the fire escape to water my tomato plants. I saw her window was open and the screen was up. So I went and knocked on the door and told the cops they should shut it, because of the cat. But he must have already got out."

The killer escaped down the fire escape, I thought.

Or up, to the roof.

"Rita, do you have a key to Lisa's apartment?"

"Ev, you're not going in there—"

"What if the cat's still in there? What if he has a special hiding place only he knows about?"

She thought about this. "Okay, I'll make a deal with you. If the cat doesn't turn up by tomorrow morning, I'll let you in. But I'm not going in with you."

"Deal," I said. "Do you know how to reach Jeff?"

"I called Doctors Without Borders. They said they'd get a message to him, but it may take a day or two." Her voice took on a sing-song quality. "He might not be in Sarajevo, he could have gone to Gorazde; nobody knows; somebody will find out, maybe he'll get back to me, maybe not."

"Helpful."

"Yeah. Well, there's a war on."

Next I called Denise Aubuchon's cellular phone again. She was still at the station house. "Nothing's happening," she told me. "I'm waiting. The cops are talking to Hal in a room down the hall."

I asked her to call my machine as soon as she knew anything, and leave a message. (As a lowly resident, I had the kind of beeper that did not work outside the hospital; long-range beepers were for chiefs and attendings only.) "By the way, Den—is your office suite under Jeff Cantor's apartment?"

"Excuse me? You mean in the same line?"

"Yeah. Specifically, is it on the same fire escape?"

"Oh, you want to know"—she lowered her voice—"if Hal came down the fire escape from Lisa's apartment? Yeah, he did. Scared the fucking shit out of me, too. I thought it was a burglar."

"Hal came down the fire escape after he left Lisa?"

"Didn't I tell you this? He was bleeding like a stuck pig. He didn't want to go down to the street and walk around to the Amsterdam Avenue entrance to the offices—he'd have to explain to Security what happened to his face. And he certainly didn't want to go home and have Carol see him like that."

Only Hal, I thought. For anyone else, descending ten flights via the fire escape would be extreme behavior. "Guess he didn't have his story worked out yet about the guy falling on him at the bachelor's party," I said dryly. "What time was this?"

"About two A.M."

"You were in the office at that hour?"

"I was catching up on chart work. And here comes this guy in through the window. I thought I would have an MI."

I sighed. "Christ, is there anything else Hal did to incriminate himself?"

"I hope not. Cross your fingers, kid. I'll call you when I hear." She hung up.

I spend so much time on the phone I sometimes think I should get a headset. I dialed my own machine and listened to my messages.

Beep. "Dr. Sutcliffe, this is Jennifer Garland, Wendell Sisk's assistant? Mr. Sisk was delighted to hear that you'll join our team. Please call with your fax number or E-mail address. I have some papers for you to look over. I have tentatively scheduled you to meet with Mr. Sisk at ten A.M., Saturday, August fifth." She then gave directions to Wendell Sisk Productions, as promised.

I'd completely forgotten about Windy Sisk and his movie. Fax or E-mail? Give me a break. I was lucky if my answering machine worked.

Beep. "Ev? Chris Cabot." Dr. Christopher Cabot was my boss, the Director of the Emergency Department. "I'm really, really sorry about Lisa Chiu. I know how close you guys were, and if I can do anything, let me know. Ah, regarding your report on Linhardt and Shehadeh—first, thanks. Top-notch, you really covered all the bases. I don't think anyone will be able to argue with it. But, ah, regarding the adverse outcome, you and I need a ten-second survey with Dr. Aubuchon. Nothing to get upset about, just in case. I'll try you again later. I'm in and out. But we must talk before Monday morning. Ciao."

"Ten-second survey" was EMT talk for "Cover your ass."

Which probably meant that the Quality Assurance Committee—
the peer-review people—would meet to decide whether the standard of care had been met for Lisa Chiu. If not, Shehadeh and I
might receive sanctions, which at the very least would entail written reprimands in our "trending-and-tracking" files, the permanent records kept by the hospital of all physicians' on-the-job
performances. Shit.

Beep. "Evie, dear, this is your *mo*-therrrr." Mom doing a Jew-
ish-mother send-up. "I *wo*-rrrry. No, seriously, Daddy's birthday
is in three weeks. We'll come in. Shakespeare in the Park? Dinner? Talk to your brothers. Let me know."

Beep-beep-beep.

I hung up the phone and resisted the urge to call my mother.
Not in the mood I was in. Not for this. I knew what kind of conversation we would have and it wasn't the kind of conversation I
longed for and needed. My mother, the All-Competent Joan Berman, R.N., M.S., Ph.D., had been at fifty million more codes than
I. She'd *run* codes when there was no M.D. available except some
fuzz-faced intern shitting his pants. I could just hear her now: You
let an intern intubate, and you didn't auscultate to check? You let
a *medic* punch an *intern*? You should be calm enough in the emergency room that your own father comes in, in cardiac arrest, *and
you keep a clear head* (this was a favorite theme of hers: *your own
father . . . clear head*). No, I did not want to talk to my mother right
now.

Which left me with Phil's imaginary mother of my dreams.
The mother of my dreams, I supposed, would hug me and then
sit quietly with me and pat my hand. Maybe tell me a gentle little
story about how a close friend of hers had died, and how she
herself had weathered the mourning period.

The mother of my dreams would probably serve me a bracing
cup of tea.

A fleeting image of Denise Aubuchon talking on the phone
earlier crossed my mind, and I smiled. No wonder her patients all
called her "Doctor Mom." Denny could be caustic, tempestuous,

and bossier than a drill sergeant, but when she was in her mother mode you came away from her feeling as if you had been mothered by the mother of God. What I probably needed was a quiet evening with Denny, or maybe a drive up to West Point with her to visit her son's grave. We could talk about Gray and Lisa and loss and mourning . . .

But Denny was over at the station house with Hal Murkland, mothering him—since his wife was missing in action—and my job for the moment was to mother myself. As usual, Phil was right. Buying myself an ounce of exotic tea began to seem like just what the doctor ordered. Now that we'd set dinner back an hour, I had plenty of time to make the trip to SoHo, buy the tea, and enjoy a leisurely walk from there to the restaurant, which was in the West Village.

I cheered up a little.

Buying a newspaper at a nearby kiosk, I headed down into the subway, which smelled worse than the street in front of Kennedy Bartlett's house. I should bring Maxie down here sometime, I thought. He'd love it. The reek of male human urine went up my nose and filled my sinuses like a dank, musky cloud. Just once I'd like to go into the subway and smell female urine, which I associated with an elderly, incontinent aunt and found sweeter and considerably less offensive.

At the end of the subway platform, a family of baby rats played like young kittens, jumping on top of each other and having a grand old time. Their mother was probably down on the tracks, scrounging for something to eat. Ah, New York, New York. What a helluva town. Urine and rats.

I looked at the newspaper. The shooting at the abortion clinic and the bombing at the gynecologist's office would be tomorrow's news. What I was looking for was something on Theresa Kahr's rape and assault.

Her death would be tomorrow's news.

I found it on page five.

BABYDOLL STRIKES AGAIN
STUDENT RAPED AND BEATEN IN
MORNINGSIDE HEIGHTS

Another lone woman has been raped and beaten in the Big City.

This time, a college student on her way to work as a pastry chef was dragged into an alley early Thursday morning by an unknown assailant, who raped and beat her. Law-enforcement officials have confirmed that a child's babydoll has been recovered from the scene, making this the third known attack by the "babydoll killer" who is terrorizing the city's young women.

The rape was also the 300th this year in the area covered by the ten precincts making up Manhattan North, mocking the words of Deputy Inspector Jack Kirschbaum, the executive officer of the Fourth Division, which includes Manhattan North. In June, Kirschbaum called Morningside Heights "the safest place in the world—a college kid's dream."

In the latest attack, police believe the 19-year-old foreign-exchange student from Germany was walking to work between 5 and 6 A.M. when she was assaulted. Bleeding and severely beaten about the head, she was found semi-conscious by a foot-patrol officer in the alley behind the bakery where she worked, at about 6:30 A.M. She was rushed to University Hospital, where she remains in critical condition in the Intensive Care Unit with multiple fractures of the skull. Doctors caring for her say that she was unable to tell them anything about her attacker.

A witness who may have seen the rapist running from the scene gave police a description of a fair-haired white male with light-colored eyes, in his twenties or thirties, about 6 feet tall and of medium build. The suspect was described as having "runner's legs" and is believed to be someone who runs or jogs regularly.

The number of rapes this year . . .

"What?" I yelled as the train rumbled into the station. *"What?"* The doors opened. I stumbled on like an automaton and sank into the nearest seat with a thud.

I couldn't believe it! Why not just give the guy my name and address? Oh, attacker, yoo-hoo! Guess who saw you and gave a description of you to the police? You know that woman you knocked down and pulled her shirt over her head? Doctor *Evelyn Sutcliffe*? She saw you, babe. You better get her while the getting's good, before they put you in a lineup somewhere and bring her in to ID you.

He knows me, and Lisa knew him. Great. This was just great. I closed my eyes and did some breathing exercises to calm down. When I opened them again, I made myself read the rest of the article.

The number of rapes this year already tops last year's total . . .

Blah, blah. Why do they always have to roll out the statistics?

A woman walking alone at night carries a certain element of risk . . .

Great. Blame the victim.

In earlier attacks . . .

And a rundown of the killer's two previous victims. Nothing I didn't already know. I folded the paper up and tucked it into my bag.

In a daze, I caught the local and switched to the BMT at Forty-second Street. I almost missed my stop in SoHo, leaping out at the last possible moment as the doors were closing. Then, when I got above ground, I went off down Prince Street in the wrong direction and had to double back and got lost a second time, because I couldn't remember whether the T Salon was on Prince or Spring.

Finally, as I came around the corner of Mercer and Prince, I ran smack into a man standing on the sidewalk outside the T Salon.

It was Mick Healy.

Unexpectedly, I felt my eyes well with tears, and before I could stop myself I blurted out, "Mick, why are you following me?"

"Ev, darling, what in God's name—" First one arm came around my shoulders, then the other. He sounded flabbergasted enough, but if I'd been caught following someone I'd make damn sure I sounded flabbergasted, too. As he pressed me against him, I could almost hear the gears going around in his head. Thinking up something plausible to say. To explain why he was following me.

He said, "Ah, you're on your way to your dinner date, then."

I disentangled myself from his embrace, feeling utterly foolish. "Mick, this is so embarrassing," I said, fishing a handkerchief out of my pocket and dabbing gently at my lower eyelids so as not to spoil my eye makeup. "Every time you see me I'm hysterical. It's not like me—"

"Of course it isn't. But look what you've been through these last two days." He still had hold of my upper arm, as if I might fall down if he didn't prop me up. The look of concern on his face was almost comic: his brow furrowed; his cornflower-blue eyes bore into mine. "Will you let me buy you a cup of tea? Have you time?"

I smiled. "Mick, you're really from another time zone. A regular knight in shining armor on a white horse." I eased my arm out of his grasp. "Thank you, but no. I'm just buying some tea here. Then I really have to go on."

"I'll come in with you," he said.

We went down the cast-iron stairs to the entrance of the T Salon, which is in the lower level of the Guggenheim Museum SoHo. As we came through the front door, Mick tucked a slip of paper he'd been holding in his hand into his pocket, and I saw him sneak a look at his watch.

He has a date, I realized. Much to my astonishment, I was immediately jealous. "Are you meeting someone?" I asked.

"Not until eight-thirty. I have time." He squeezed my shoulders and kissed the side of my head.

I wished he would stop kissing me. I was sure that he was marking me, like a cat, with his citrus aftershave, and I didn't want Phil smelling him on me later.

I wished we weren't in public. Mick was wearing a slightly crumpled beige linen suit and a light blue button-down oxford. All I could think about was unbuttoning it and running my hand through his chest hair.

I wished I didn't have these feelings for him.

I wished I could indulge them.

"Where are you meeting this person?" I asked.

"Don't worry yourself. Really. I don't mind being late, not for a minute."

But he looked at his watch again immediately.

I flushed. The saleswoman at the tea counter was busy with another customer. I feigned fascination with a display of teapots, focusing in particular on one in the shape of a typewriter. I picked it up carefully and looked at it. *Damn* this man. What was he doing to me?

"I can't stop thinking about last night," Mick said in a low voice, eyeing the salesgirl in case she might be coming over. "But I know you couldn't possibly want to talk about that right now— forgive me for mentioning it all—it's just that . . . It's just that . . . Oh, God, what am I trying to say?" He laughed self-consciously, tossing his head back, rolling his eyes. "Wait—let me start over." Taking my hand in his and looking into my eyes as if he were about to propose marriage, he said, almost breathlessly, without a trace of his sometimes Scots-Irish lilt, "I'm really, really sorry about Lisa Chiu. I know how much you cared for her. I wish you were my lover—or at least that you weren't already committed to Phil—and that I could just sit quietly this evening with you and comfort you, just hold you."

My breath caught. When I found my voice, I said, "Mick— what an amazing speech. I don't know what to say."

He brought my hand to his lips and kissed it. Not the back of my hand. The palm. Then, straightening up, he cleared his throat. "What kind of tea do you want, darling?" he murmured, looking over my shoulder.

"May I help you?" the saleswoman chirped brightly.

I jumped. *Yes*, I felt like saying, *Bring us a bed*. "Two ounces of *gyokuro asahi*, please."

"Certainly." She hauled down one of the huge tea canisters, hefted it onto the counter, and took off the lid. With a small metal shovel, she scooped out a handful of tea and held it up for me to smell. I inhaled the delicate scent and nodded.

"Let me buy that for you," said Mick. "Since I can't be with you tonight."

"Oh, Mick, you're making my life so complicated."

"Buying you tea isn't complicated." He took the small package from the saleswoman and handed it to me.

Outside on the street, with nothing to distract us, we gave in to the heat and kissed. But this was not a darkened street at midnight with no passersby, and neither Mick nor I were unself-conscious enough to exhibit much passion on a busy public thoroughfare in broad daylight. The kiss was brief and awkward. "Ahem," said Mick afterward, and we broke apart, blushing.

Then he looked at his watch again.

"What?" I said.

He shook his head.

"No, tell me."

He straightened up and looked away, moving his shoulders inside his jacket, shooting his cuffs and pulling at his coat tails. Mentally, he left me. I could sense his departure.

I said, "Mick, was that you I saw jogging on Riverside Drive and Eighty-ninth Street a little while ago?"

"When?" He came slowly back. Wary now.

"About six-thirty. I was out walking Kennedy Bartlett's dog."

He shook his head. "Not me, love. I haven't run yet today." Then he frowned. "Why is that name ringing a bell with me? Kennedy Bartlett . . . Did he not once dance with the New York City Ballet?"

"Yes, but that was years ago. That wasn't you—"

"Is he a rather gaunt man in his sixties? And the dog is losing its fur?"

"Yes, that wasn't—"

"Patient of Denise Aubuchon's?"

"Yes, that—"

"Chatty bloke. I see him in the hall outside her office." He looked off down the street.

I finally got it out: "That wasn't you in the blue Superman shirt and green scrub pants?"

His head whipped around so fast I thought it would make a full 360-degree rotation like the girl's in *The Exorcist*. "*What?*" Then, getting a quick hold of himself, "No. Not me."

And suddenly he stood there looking at me placidly, his eyes steady, his nerves and thoughts utterly concealed. After a moment he pulled at his cuffs, again moving his shoulders inside his jacket.

What *was* that? I felt myself go very still. "Mick, have you been following me?"

He gave me a look that said, *I'm being very patient now.* "Ev, what are you talking about?"

"Last night, on One Hundred and Thirteenth Street—"

"I live on One Hundred and Thirteenth Street. You were the one walking by . . . I was just going home."

"Well, what about this afternoon at Eighty-ninth and River-side—"

"I wasn't anywhere near Eighty-ninth and Riverside."

"—wearing a blue Superman shirt and green scrub pants?"

"I don't own a Superman shirt. And why would I be jogging in scrubs?"

"What about here? Outside on the sidewalk—"

"*You* bumped into *me.*"

"I see," I said.

We stared at each other. Mick cleared his throat. "Only these three times?" he asked.

"Excuse me?"

"Only these three times I was following you?"

I blinked. "You tell me, Mick."

Something flickered behind his eyes. I could have sworn it was relief. "We're following each other," he suggested with a flirtatious smile. "It's fate."

I wavered, confused. Shifting my weight from one foot to the other, I looked off down the street. "So you don't own a Superman shirt."

"Darling, what's this about?" Mick said. "Are you so upset by Lisa's death you've become paranoid?" He took a deep breath. "Or is it me—you're so ambivalent about me, you see me as a predator?"

Talk about the felling blow, the knife struck home. All the capillaries in my face dilated.

He jammed his hands in his trouser pockets and looked away, his face a roiling mixture of conflicting emotion; I saw there hurt, anger, impatience, scorn. "Let me give you some advice," he said, fixing his gaze on the teapots in the window of the T Salon. "Go home and write Lisa's parents a letter. Don't call on the phone— it's utterly exhausting to receive condolence calls, take my word for it. Write them a letter. Say how wonderful their daughter was, what you enjoyed most about her, what you respected. Tell some funny stories. Recall your favorite memories. Don't dwell on the fact that you picked her up off the floor and carted her off to the hospital. *Certainly* don't say she was viciously savaged—I wouldn't touch upon the circumstances of her death at all—and don't say that you're feeling guilty as hell for not being able to save her."

"Mick—"

"And make up your bloody mind. I'm not a predator. I'm in love with you. I'll give up if you say give up, but I'll not be dallied with." He turned back to me and took my hands.

"I assure you," he vowed, gazing into my eyes, "that I do not own now, nor have I ever owned, a Superman shirt."

What can I tell you?

I believed him.

CHAPTER 11

"I don't like this," said Dr. Anthony Firenze, Lisa Chiu's next-door neighbor. "It's not right."

With a deft turn of the wrist, Tony unlocked the dead bolt on the door to Jeff Cantor's apartment. "I don't know why I'm letting you in," he went on.

"Because Lisa would want you to," Phil answered, while I cut through the yellow police tape with a scalpel blade. There was also a notice from someone called the Public Administrator plastered across the door, declaring the apartment sealed.

"Oh, please. Spare me the violins," groaned Tony.

"Okay, because the cat has to eat," I suggested.

"The cat's not *in* there, Ev. Take my word for it. Nobody has seen the cat since yesterday."

I refrained from rolling my eyes. "Because Lisa's death has eclipsed everything else in my life. Because this is something I have to do."

"At one o'clock in the morning? Yeah, you and 'Hard Copy.'"

"We give up, Tony," Phil said. "Why *are* you letting us in?"

"Because Lisa would want me to," he admitted grudgingly. "And because I'm a loyal next-door neighbor. When Jeff Cantor calls, I want to be able to tell him I made every effort to find that blasted cat. And because Lisa's death has eclipsed everything in my life, too." A short, squat man who carried himself on the balls of his feet, like a cougar about to spring, Firenze hitched up his scrub pants, tying the strings more tightly. We had got him out of bed, and the scrub pants were all he had on. In the sweltering hallway, his bald pate glistened with sweat. He wiped the back of his hand across his upper lip. "One more," he said, turning the key in the last of the three locks.

"Banzai," said Phil softly, as the door swung open, creaking lugubriously on its hinges.

The smell hit us full in the face. The police had closed all the windows and turned off the air conditioner, and the blood and vomit were ripe in the shut-up apartment. Phil took out a handkerchief and pressed it over his mouth and nose.

"Aw, Jesus," said Firenze. "They couldn't leave the windows open, for Chrissake? It's like a fuckin' oven in here."

"Maybe not," I said. The doctors' residence had been built in the 1930s, with casement windows that had no screens. "Maybe they were worried about flies."

"Fuck the flies, it's them or baked vomit. I'm opening the windows."

"Wait." I shouldered in front of him. Reaching inside the apartment, I flipped on the foyer light by the wall switch. Firenze crossed himself. We stepped across the threshold, the three of us crowding into the tiny foyer.

"Here's where Lisa dragged herself," said Phil in a tight voice. He pointed at the floor, where traces of blood were visible. "The cops think she was stabbed in the dining room and dragged herself to the front door."

"Was she raped?" I asked.

"Have to wait for the medical examiner to say. It's real confusing. When Denny and I arrived, she still had her panties on, and a scrub shirt. So you would think not. But then the cops found a pair of scrub pants under the dining-room table, so you have to wonder if he took them off her, but then for some reason didn't—" He gagged. "Firenze, you got any Vicks?"

It took Tony a moment to answer; he was staring at the blood on the floor. "Not on me," he said distractedly. "You want some? Bang on the door and ask Rita."

Phil went out.

I wished Tony would go out, too. I wanted to be alone in the apartment. I thought the apartment might tell me something. But not if Phil and Tony were there. Only if I were alone.

I stood in the foyer and looked into Jeff Cantor's living room and dining room, for the last month and a half Lisa Chiu's living room and dining room. And last night her dying rooms. It sounded like a bad novel: *The Dying Rooms*. I was breathing short little breaths through my mouth, half to avoid sucking in too much of the vomit smell, half because the adrenaline was kicking in. I could feel the hairs standing up on the back of my neck, my body sinking instinctively into a half-crouch. I made myself straighten up. Okay, Sutcliffe. Look. Think.

I crossed the living room to a table next to the couch and switched on the lamp.

The decor was straight out of the Door Store and Workbench and the like: overstuffed, oversized sofa in sea-green with white piping; two matching club chairs; faux mission oak coffee table and end tables; and black wrought-iron floor lamps with pastel-colored shades. Fake kilim rugs, bright colors. Jeff was one of those people who ordered everything from catalogs. "You think all gay men like to *shop?*" he once said when I commented on this. "Old, new, imitation, original—who cares? What's the difference?" There were no pictures. Nothing on the walls. Impersonal. No *stuff,* as Lisa would say. That would suit her fine, I guessed; Lisa had been a minimalist. The place was like a hotel suite. The cat seemed to have more possessions than Jeff and Lisa put together; on the rug next to the coffee table were a catnip mouse and a rubber ball.

I whistled through my teeth the way people do when they want to get a cat's attention. "Fat Face," I said in a gentle, little voice. "Pussy cat." Whistled again.

No response.

"He'd come out if he was here," Firenze said.

"I know." A big brown-and-black Maine coon cat, Fat Face liked visitors indiscriminately, and greeted everyone who came into the apartment by rolling on his back at their feet.

"I'll go open the closet doors," Tony said. "Someone may have shut him in by accident." He moved off toward the bedrooms and the study.

Feeling as if I were about to rob a grave, I looked around the living room. No blood on the rugs. Streaks of it here and there, smeared, on the pale-blond wood of the floor. I imagined Lisa dragging herself along the floor to the front door, and my heart lurched. I crossed to the small dining room—really only an eating area separated from the living room by iron railings like porch railings, a popular architectural design when the doctors' residence had been built, all the apartments had them—and looked at the floor. No rug here, and not much blood. A few smears under the French café table. Two wicker chairs pushed aside.

I imagined Lisa lying on the floor under the table.

I imagined her lying there a long time before starting her snail's creep toward the door.

Why didn't you call someone? I asked her in my head. Tony and Rita had keys; why didn't you call them to come help you? I looked around for the phone, didn't see one. Maybe the phone was in the bedroom or study, and the front door was closer after all.

I peered into the tiny kitchen. Neat and clean. Dishes in the drying rack next to the sink, including a big bowl that said "Tuna Breath." Before she died, Lisa had fed the cat and then washed his bowl. Spices on the spice rack over the sink. Lisa used to cook a big pot of something on Sunday afternoon and eat it until it was gone, maybe Wednesday or Thursday. Her favorite food was leftovers, she liked to say. Then she would eat out Friday and Saturday.

I wondered where she'd eaten the night she was killed.

I opened the fridge. Celery, carrots, butter, beer, milk, orange juice. A container of rice pudding from Zabar's. No medications. Unless the cops had taken them.

Then I opened all the cupboards, one at a time. Nothing unusual. Pots, pans. Dishes. No cat.

Phil reappeared. He reeked of Vicks VapoRub, which he had smeared over the entire lower half of his face. That and his hair, plastered to his forehead with sweat, gave him a translucent sheen; he looked like a sea nymph just surfaced from the glimmering depths. "We're going to have to get a cleaning service in here," he said. "The detectives were talking about one that specializes in post-traumatic cleanup after murders and suicides."

"You're kidding," I said. "They *specialize?*"

"It's a mom-and-pop outfit. They work out of the barrio. People call them Los Muertos. The cops gave me their phone number."

I pondered this astonishing enterprise. "How long will the apartment be sealed?"

"I don't know. I'll find out." Phil turned his attention to the kitchen. "Detectives took the garbage," he said, indicating the empty garbage pail. "Shards of broken glass in it. Took the dustpan and dust brush, too." Phil offered me the jar of Vicks but I shook my head. I might need my nose later on.

"Where was the bottle of champagne?" I asked.

"On the dining-room table. Two glasses. Took those, too."

"Two glasses?" I asked. Did Hal drink more champagne after he broke his own glass? That would be strange—with his face bleeding. Even stranger, however, was the idea that Lisa offered the killer a glass of champagne after Hal left.

Assuming of course that Hal himself wasn't the killer.

Maybe it was time for me to start thinking of Hal as a killer.

Except that it didn't make sense. Hal Murkland the Babydoll Killer? Running around Manhattan bludgeoning and raping women? Because it wasn't just Lisa. It was Theresa Kahr and the others, too.

"Run this by me again," I said to Phil.

He took a deep breath. "The cops think Lisa was stabbed here in the dining room," he said. "You can see there's blood here, under the table. There was an open champagne bottle, two empty glasses, and a cutting board on the table, with a half-peeled apple. But no knife. So the cops think Lisa was peeling an apple and having a glass of champagne with the killer, the two of them probably sitting at the table. He grabs the knife and stabs her."

I wondered why Lisa would sit at her dining-room table drinking champagne with a man she suspected of having assaulted Theresa Kahr.

Unless the man who killed her wasn't the person she suspected of assaulting Theresa Kahr.

But if she suspected someone else, why would he have to kill her?

"Whatever happened, at some point the killer goes into the bedroom and the study," Phil went on, "leaving Lisa lying on the floor." As he spoke, we moved from the dining room through the living room, back to the foyer, down the hall toward the bedroom and the study, where we bumped into Tony coming out of the bedroom.

"No cat," Tony said. "Let's go. It's hot as hell in here. Besides, the place is giving me the creeps, to say nothing of the stench."

"As you can see," said Phil, "the killer then proceeded to trash the bedroom and the study."

I looked past Phil into the bedroom and gasped. What had once been a pristine room—queen-size futon bed, two simple night tables, a dresser—now lay in shambles. Books, papers and medical journals had been flung about the room. Clothes had been dumped out of the dresser drawers and closet.

"The window was open and the air conditioner was on when the cops came in," Phil said. "So they think the guy went down the fire escape. Or up."

I nodded, stepping over a crocheted pillow that said, "Is There a Doctor in the House?!?" and went into the room. I picked up the phone on the bed table. Someone had unplugged it. In fact, someone had taken away the wire to connect it to the wall. "Where's the phone cord?" I asked.

"Gone," said Phil. "Answering machine in the living room, phone in here, and phone in the study all disconnected and the cords removed. Cops couldn't make head nor tail of it. My guess is, it was symbolic: 'Don't tell.' "

"Huh," I said. I put the phone down and noticed the bare futon mattress. "Cops take the sheets off the bed?"

"Yeah."

"They did?" Tony asked. "Why?"

"In case she had sex with someone. The killer or her boy-friend."

"I thought he was going to rape her under the dining-room table, but then didn't," Tony said. "Why would they take the sheets in here, if they thought he was going to rape her in there? Oh, I get it—"

"Tony, you know who she was sleeping with?" I asked.

He puffed his cheeks up with air and blew it out slowly. "Well, you could have fooled me, but it looks like she had something going with Hal Murkland," he said, staring at the mess. "And he was here the night she was killed."

"When?" I asked.

"Late. After midnight. Some yelling going on. The other side of this wall"—he pointed at the far wall of the room, against which the headboard of the bed rested—"is our living-room wall, and I was up late reading at my desk."

"Yelling? What kind of yelling?" I asked.

"Cursing. Hal yelling, 'Jesus fucking Christ, that bitch, I'll fucking kill her.' "

"Who?"

"His wife—who else?"

"Carol?"

Firenze made a face at me. "No, his other wife, Marilyn Monroe."

"Sorry," I said.

"Hal was in a froth all evening about something, okay? I think he was drunk, too. About ten o'clock I was in Mick Healy's office—Mick's helping me bone up for the boards—and we heard them coming out of his office—"

"Heard who?"

"Hal and Lisa."

"You heard Hal and Lisa coming out of Hal's office."

"Well, actually, now that I think of it, I don't think Hal was in the office; *she* was in the office, coming out; he was coming up in the elevator, and they met in the corridor. We couldn't help hearing it—the air-conditioning in Mick's office was off because of some system tie-in with the new hospital wing—so he had the door to the corridor propped open, trying to get a wee bit o' breeze"—Firenze mimicked Healy's Scots-Irish accent—"because it was so-o *bloody* hot—"

"They were having an argument earlier as well?" Phil asked. "Around ten? About what?"

"Same topic: Hal's wife," Firenze said. "Here's what happened: Mick and I are sitting in Mick's receptionist's office; he's at the desk, I'm on the couch, he's throwing questions at me. Door's open. First I hear a door, and a key in a lock. Nothing unusual. Then I hear the elevator open and close, and Hal's voice. So Hal says, 'What are you doing here?' Sounds like he's real pissed off. Mick and I look at each other; what's going on? And she says, "I forgot to download all my notes onto disc. I told you and Denny I was working on that article on the office computer.' And he starts yelling, 'Oh, sure, you think that'll fly? You're in there going through the office records. *Shit.*' But at the same time Hal's yelling, he's also laughing kind of sarcastically. Mick gives me a look, like, *huh*? It doesn't really make sense. Then there's a scuffle, and Mick and I both think, shit, Hal's grabbed her. So we both jump up. But then Lisa says, '*Hal. You're completely out of control*' and it sounds like she's laughing. So Mick and I sit back down. Then Hal says, 'You think it's so simple, don't you? My ass is fucking cooked if she finds out.' Then there's, ah, rustling. They're kissing out there. Mick and I look at each other—*whoa*! Hal Murkland's making it with Lisa Chiu! Lisa says, 'Hal, you've been drinking.' End of conversation. They get in the elevator."

"This may be a dumb question, Tony," I said, "but you're sure the woman was Lisa?"

"Oh, yeah. No question. Mick and I both recognized her voice."

"And the man was Hal."

"She said 'Hal' to him. And you know Hal's voice. *Everybody* knows that voice."

"Hal does have a rather distinct voice," Phil said.

I looked around the room, wondering if there was any point in my picking through any of this stuff, when the cops had surely been through it all with a fine-tooth comb. Out of curiosity, however, I did get down on my hands and knees and crawled all around the bed, sniffing at the rug and floor, patting carefully with my hands.

"What are you looking for?" Phil asked. "The cops vacuumed in here."

"Mm," I said. I kept crawling and looking.

Nothing.

When I had finished applying the sniff-and-pat test to the floor, we went into the study. Here were all Jeff's and Lisa's books, some still lying on the shelves of floor-to-ceiling built-in bookcases lining three walls of the room, the rest strewn about the floor. Against the fourth wall was the desk, a simple affair consisting of a door across the tops of two file cabinets. That too had been trashed, the contents of the drawers added to the files and books on the floor.

"Can we leave now?" Tony pleaded.

"There was blood on the computer," Phil said. "Also, it was on. They thought maybe she was doing some kind of work when the guy came in."

I quickly reviewed what I knew about computers, which wasn't much. I had heard of Cyberspace, of course, and the information superhighway, and I knew what the Internet and E-mail were. But that was about it, if you didn't count movies I'd seen, like *Ferris Bueller's WarGames,* or whatever that movie had been. Computers run amok and nuclear war imminent until Matthew Broderick types JOSHUA to disarm the program—or maybe you typed JOSHUA and got the name of the hacker who wrote the program and *he* disarmed it; I forget. I had mastered the few simple commands for the new on-line program at the hospital, to call up patients' test results, but those had been designed specifically with computer illiterates in mind: nothing complicated. And I was learning the program Phil had recently bought to computerize his patient records; I knew how to call up a file, enter data, and print. But that was about it.

I sighed and began to look through the books on the floor for Jeff's and Lisa's computer manuals. I immediately spotted *Mastering WordPerfect 5.1 for DOS* and something called *Fastback Plus,* which I had seen on Phil's desk. A backup program, if I recalled correctly. "Cops take any discs?" I asked.

"Yeah, a couple of boxes full."

"They think the killer took anything?"

"If he did, nobody knows what. Lisa's keys and wallet and checkbook were all here. Wallet had a hundred dollars in it."

"Then what was he looking for?" I asked. "Why trash the place, unless you're looking for something? Moreover, if there was blood on the computer, that means the killer came in here after he stabbed her. You think he was looking for information, records of some kind?"

"Good point," said Phil. "She keep a diary?"

"Not that I know of." I got down on my hands and knees and

went over the floor and rugs in this room as I had in the other. I did not find what I was looking for and got to my feet again, puzzled.

"What are you *doing?*" Firenze wanted to know.

I waved him off. After a moment I got down again and sniffed the rug under the desk and around the file cabinets. The spot, when I finally found it, was no longer wet. But the distinctive smell remained. Here, not the bedroom. I stood. "Tony, that shouting you heard when you were sitting at your desk last night—could that have come from this room?"

Tony thought. "Could have," he said. "I assumed they were yelling in the bedroom—"

"They were both yelling, or only Hal?"

"He was yelling, she was raising her voice. Saying things like, 'Hal, would you please calm down?' That kind of thing."

"But that argument could have been in this room," I said.

"Yeah," said Tony. "Both these rooms are against my living-room wall."

"Ev, what are you getting at?" This from Phil.

"And the yelling was at about two A.M.," I said.

"About that," said Tony. "Maybe a little earlier."

"Did they have sex?"

Tony snorted. "Christ, Ev, I don't know—"

"You'd know," I said. "Hal makes noise, Tony. I live downstairs from him and Carol, and I've heard him." I didn't say that I'd also heard him firsthand.

"Hal makes noise?"

"Hard to believe, isn't it?" Phil said dryly.

"Well," said Firenze, shaking his head, "maybe she likes 'em noisy. Hal must've had *some* attraction if she'd throw Guy Shehadeh over for him. Now, can we please leave?" He turned and moved toward the door.

"Guy Shehadeh?" Phil and I said in unison, following Tony down the hall.

"He was over here a lot the beginning of July," Tony said,

shrugging a shoulder and leering a little. "Nice looking dude, but, you know, not too bright." He tapped the side of his head.

Phil was staring at Tony, his mouth half open, his attention riveted. If he were a hunting dog, he would point. Gossip. Yum. "God," Phil said. "Who says we don't work at General Hospital?"

I slapped him on the arm. "C'mon, Phil. She's dead."

"What?" he said, turning. "You weren't just asking about whether she was sleeping with Hal?"

I sighed and went back into the bedroom, where I swiftly unlocked the fire-escape window and opened the window a few inches, just enough for the cat to get back in if he was outside on the fire escape or up on the roof. By the time the men followed me in there, I was pretending to look around as if gathering my thoughts.

Actually, I had far too many thoughts to gather.

I would come back later, when my head was quiet.

CHAPTER
12

THE phone rang at an excruciatingly inconvenient moment.

"Don't answer it," Phil gasped.

I had no intention of answering it. After necking in the elevator on the way down from Lisa Chiu's apartment, dry-humping each other in the hall while I fumbled for my apartment keys, and pulling off each other's clothing in the foyer and down the hall until we finally managed to stumble into the bedroom, Phil and I were in The Throes.

I didn't even miss a beat. During my intern year I had acquired the useful skill, when the phone interrupted me in flagrante, of adjusting my rhythm to that of the ringing. If people really wanted you, they always called back. Besides, the phone rang only three times before the answering machine—in the living room, where we couldn't hear it—picked up.

With a few impassioned profanities, Phil gave a final groan and collapsed on me. It wasn't until our breathing finally slowed that the faint conversational tones of Kennedy Bartlett's rasping voice became audible.

"There must be something wrong if he's calling so late," Phil said, rolling off and squinting at the bedside clock. "Christ, it's three A.M."

"You're right," I said. "Especially if he's still talking." I leaned over Phil and picked up.

"Thank God," Ken yelled.

"Where are you?" I asked. "What's the matter?"

"I'm in the emergency room. I know *you* like it here, but I sure don't. You couldn't put this stuff on TV, no one would believe it. This guy just walked in right off the street bleeding like a stuck pig—"

"Ken, why are you in the ER?"

"—shot in the *head* and he's waltzing in like—"

"Ken—"

"—John Wayne, I swear to God, straight out of *Sands of Iwo Jima*."

"Are you being admitted?" I asked.

"And of course he had to pitch forward right on top of Yours Truly, blood and all—I look like I just stepped off the set of *Friday the Thirteenth*. I'm dripping with the stuff."

I put my hand over the receiver. "He's hysterical," I said to Phil. "Watch your eyes. I'm turning on the light."

"That poor man," Phil murmured. He put his arm over his eyes to shield them from the light. "Maybe he's having premonitions."

"Ken, are you having premonitions?" I asked.

"I don't know what I'd do without you," Ken said. I noted that his breathing was becoming labored. "You're the only one who understands his routine. I called that AIDS group, the one that walks your dog if you're too weak, but they sent over this guy—"

"I'll feed him," I said firmly. "I know the drill. Never mind the guy who's bleeding and the dog. Let's talk about you. How long have you been in the ER?"

"Oh, God, Ev," he said. "I don't know. A couple of hours."

"Are you being admitted?"

"Yes." Small voice now.

"Are you having premonitions?"

"Yes." Even smaller. I almost couldn't hear him.

"I'll be right there," I said.

"No. You need your sleep."

"I'll be right there," I repeated.

But by the time I got up, dressed, made my way over to the hospital via the tunnel under the street, found someone in the ER who knew to what floor and bed Ken had been admitted, and arrived at bedside, Ken was fast asleep, snoring with his mouth wide open.

I went out to the nurses' station, asked for Ken's chart, and scanned the intern's admission notes, which included Denny Aubuchon's telephone instructions.

I penned a note of my own: "Patient is greatly concerned about well-being of dog Maxie. Evelyn Sutcliffe MD will care for dog during patient's hospital stay."

Then I flipped the chart shut and went home.

When I staggered into the kitchen Saturday morning, Phil was up, shaved, and dressed, wearing a pair of blue chambray chinos and a black T-shirt from the Matisse Exhibition at the Museum of Modern Art. He was waving the *New York Times* with one hand and talking animatedly into the phone with the other. "Did you see this about Dr. Guderian's husband? Jesus Christ, how could something like this *happen?*"

I squinted at the clock. Seven-thirty A.M.

"Who are you talking to?" I asked. Only Phil knew people who were capable of coherent conversation at seven-thirty Saturday morning. Everyone I knew was still sound asleep, or, if awake, groggy.

Phil crunched the phone between his ear and shoulder, freeing a hand to make pointing motions at the teakettle on the stove. He mouthed the word "hot," then "Gina." The water for my tea was hot and waiting for me. He was talking to Gina, another shrink he used to share offices with. Then he tossed the paper on the table and pointed at that. I picked it up and read the headline he had circled in red:

DISGRUNTLED HUSBAND TARGET OF INQUIRY
DOCTOR'S MEDICAL RECORDS MADE PUBLIC
AFTER HER DEATH

Since Phil was pointing so insistently—clearly the message was "Read *Now,* Do Not Pass Go, Do Not Collect $200, Do Not Make Your Cup of Tea First"—I scanned the article. A Dr. Anton Reichert in Caldwell, New Jersey, widower of Dr. Lucie-Maria Guderian, the distinguished child psychoanalyst, was under investigation for allegedly mailing his dead wife's session notes—some with devastating commentary—to former patients of hers, now adults. Moreover, he had sent copies of these records to their employers and business colleagues. One former patient, who between the ages of five and seven apparently set more than fifty small fires in her own home and the homes and garages of playmates' families, had been dismissed from her job as a buyer for a well-known New York City department store after a suspicious fire in the ladies' room of the store—because her employer had in hand therapy notes from thirty-five years ago documenting treatment for pyromania.

You believe this? Phil mouthed when I looked up. To Gina he said, "Has Anton completely flipped out, or what? Does anybody know what his grievance is?"

"Maybe Dr. Guderian made him read newspaper articles before he had his morning coffee," I said, loud enough for Gina to hear. Phil made a face at me. I stuck out my tongue.

It was too early for me to deal with facts, especially facts that did not concern me. I spent half my life getting up too early and waking up too fast and having to deal with facts too soon, and I was damned if I was going to do it on my day off. Besides, I needed a convenient excuse to avoid the headlines I knew were on the front page. Lisa's murder. Theresa Kahr's death. The Babydoll Killer this, the Babydoll Killer that. Jock Lamartine's shooting. The previous morning's bombing. Nobody should be required to deal with all that before tea or coffee.

I deserved to indulge in a little denial, I told myself. I put the paper down and shuffled over to the counter, where I picked up the small package of *gyokuro asahi* tea Mick Healy had bought me the previous evening.

I wondered whether Mick was a morning person or evening person. Probably morning; most surgeons had to train themselves to be morning persons whether they were or not.

I wondered what Mick was doing right that minute. I imagined him sound asleep, naked under crisp white sheets.

Or maybe not-so-crisp white sheets, if he'd brought his dinner date home with him the night before. And why not? After all, I'd been rather noncommittal about his declaration of love for me. And why should he spend the night any differently than I'd spent it?

I carefully tucked the packet of *gyokuro asahi* into my spice rack, too guilty to drink it in front of Phil. Instead I carefully measured two teaspoons of Russian O.P. Georgie into my teapot and poured water over it. Then I set the timer for four minutes and slumped into a chair at the kitchen table.

I wondered why I was wondering about Mick at all, and buried my nose in the comics pages of the *Daily News*.

"Wait, let me get this straight," Phil was saying. "Dr. Guderian humiliated him publicly and in front of the children, and your interpretation is, he never found a good way to really ruin *her* name, the way she 'ruined' his—'She who was so revered by her wonderful former patients'—is that what you're saying? So he decides to fuck up a few of her patients by saying, 'Here's what this wonderful loving person really thought of you.' That's very good; I think you're right."

Maybe I was wondering about Mick because I found it so irritating to listen to Phil going great guns at 7:30 A.M. Or maybe the irritating part was listening to Phil going great guns with Gina. How come when he picked up the newspaper and found this riveting article about Dr. Guderian's husband, Phil rushed right to the phone to call Gina? How come he hadn't come rushing into the bedroom to tell me? Because Gina could talk shrink talk and the two of them could hash out a plausible, Freudian-consistent theory for Anton Reichert's behavior? Because Gina knew Drs. Reichert and Guderian and I didn't?

I looked up from "Doonesbury."

"The key definitely is that she humiliated him," Phil said to Gina.

"Wait a minute," I said. "Didn't I meet Dr. Guderian at that party for Rob Whitten, when he joined the New York Psychoanalytical Institute? And Rob was complaining that she was very strict, very German—'more like a person from Hamburg than a Viennese,' he said—wasn't that Dr. Guderian?"

"Ev's up," Phil told Gina. "She met Dr. Guderian at Robert Whitten's party."

"You and Gina went to her funeral," I said petulantly.

My tea-timer went off and I got up to pour my tea. I know Dr. Guderian, I thought at Phil in my head. You could have rushed into the bedroom to tell me.

In fact, I remembered Dr. Guderian very well: an elegant woman well into her eighties, stylishly dressed, who when introduced to you put her hand out as if you would kiss it rather than shake it—and then smiled wryly when you shook. (I had wanted to retort, "Shaken, not stirred," but had held my tongue.) I remembered that Dr. Guderian moved easily among the party guests, like Queen Elizabeth among the guests at one of her famous Buckingham Palace lawn events where she met the Commoners. I remembered the husband, too, trailing in Dr. Guderian's wake like Prince Philip, gracious and smiling. Mr. Dr. Guderian— I hadn't caught his name, which I understood was not the same as hers. Well. Maybe that had been part of the problem. Maybe he chafed at being known as Mr. Dr. Guderian. Or as "Anton," as Phil called him—while continuing to call *her* "Dr. Guderian."

"Of course he waited until she was dead," Phil told Gina. "There must be a joke here somewhere, since he's a pathologist. But none of this would have happened if Dr. Guderian had disposed of her records in her will like she was supposed to. It's just like her to die intestate, isn't it? I'm sure she thought death was for other people, not for exalted beings like herself. But all that aside, can the patients do anything? It's not illegal for him to release these records, is it? Oh, of course." Turning to me, he said, "They can sue."

"That's nice," I said. I sat down with my tea and picked up the comics again, snapping the paper. Mike Doonesbury's wife was leaving him for the guy in the hat, and Cathy was fretting about her new, younger boyfriend.

Maybe I was fretting about a new boyfriend; maybe I just didn't know it yet.

Maybe six months from now I would be with Mick, and Phil would be with Gina.

Maybe Gina would adore Phil's new apartment as much as he did and would rush right over and move in.

I imagined Gina, dark-haired, doe-eyed, svelte, in a pair of madras shorts and a halter top, helping Phil unpack his mother's dishes, exclaiming joyfully over every coffee cup, stacking saucers up on the beautiful black walnut dining-room table and simultaneously hashing out Freudian theory as applicable to the obviously tortured relationship of Drs. Reichert and Guderian.

"Would you stop talking to Gina?" I asked plaintively.

Phil looked first at me, then at the clock. He started. "I gotta go," he told Gina. "Ev and I are catching the nine-thirty train out to Long Island to see my folks, and I have to run over to my apartment and get my stuff."

My heart stopped. I'd completely forgotten. I couldn't possibly go to Long Island—I needed to talk to Hal Murkland about his questioning at the station house, and I wanted to call around to a few people and see if anyone knew what Lisa was doing the night before she was killed between the time she left me and the time she met Hal, and—

Jesus. I had a 10 A.M. meeting with Windy Sisk, too.

And I had to feed the dog.

"What's the matter?" Phil asked.

"Oh, God, Phil, I'm so sorry," I said. "I completely forgot. Windy Sisk called, and I guess I was so dazzled—I'm really, really sorry. I told him I'd come to a meeting at ten o'clock."

"Today? You made other plans for *today?*"

"I'm sorry."

He stared at me.

"And I have to feed Maxie."

"Can't that factotum of Denny's—what's-his-name, Waterside—"

"Joshua Waterman."

"Can't he feed Maxie?"

"Waterman's in the hospital. The upper lobe of one of his lungs collapsed. Phil, I'm sorry."

For a moment he didn't say anything. I could see him working his jaw muscles. His disappointment was palpable. Then the anger came, like a blast of arctic air. "What's this really about?" he demanded, yanking a chair back from the table. "Every single time we make plans to go out there, you find some way to get out of it. Why don't you just come right out and say you don't want to go?" He slammed the chair around, straddling it, and glared at me. "You're so fucking passive-aggressive. Why can't you just learn to say no?"

"I'm working on it," I protested. "I'm much better at saying no than I used to be. I think I've made a lot of progress in the saying-no department."

"Not if you deliberately 'forget' we're going out to the Island— Ev, we're been planning this for *weeks*. Sylvia's making her special three-day lasagna for you."

I groaned. Sylvia was Phil's stepmother. A woman who always

seemed dressed for church even when she was cooking—nice
dress or slacks, stockings, heels, makeup, jewelry—Sylvia was a
potential mother-in-law right out of a television sitcom. She spent
three days lovingly preparing your favorite food, beamed at you
with motherly delight while you consumed it, and with each bite
you took you felt guiltier and guiltier that you hadn't married her
favorite stepson ten years ago and borne her and Phil's wonderful
dad four grandchildren already. Never mind that Sylvia already
had sixteen grandchildren. She had that look about her, like a
zealous female version of Uncle Sam in a recruiting poster: "I want
You! and *Your Babies!*"

"Tell them somebody died," I pleaded. "It's the truth. I
couldn't possibly spend the day socializing with them, anyway.
It's too much, Phil. I don't have the emotional energy. I'd just be
distracted and withdrawn and hurt their feelings."

"The girls especially were looking forward to seeing you," he
said reproachfully, speaking of his nieces, who were eleven and
fourteen. "You're such a good role model for them."

"Of course I'm a good role model for them," I snapped, completely losing control of my temper. In the back of my mind a little
voice explained patiently, Now don't take it out on him—you're
really mad at *yourself* for fucking up, and you're only mad at him
because he's made you feel guilty about it. Perversely, I ignored
the little voice. "I'm probably the only woman your nieces know
who works outside the home!" I yelled.

And they're off. He said, she said. A few sentences later I was
yelling what I always wound up yelling when we had this argument: "I walk in the fucking door and the whole goddamn clan
is standing there, just *waiting* for the announcement we're getting
married!" And Phil was yelling what he always wound up yelling,
"You're making this up! The real reason you won't go is you're a
snob, you disdain their working-class values!" To which my usual
rejoinder was, "Don't blame this on me—the reason you're so
upset about this is *you're* ambivalent yourself about their working-
class values. You're an urban-sophisticated New York City intel-

lectual and you don't have anything to talk to them about!'' Or, if I was *really* seething, ''What do you mean, outside the home? Outside the *kitchen*! I go there, and the guys are all in the living room, and the women are all in the kitchen—and I'm damned if I'm going to go in the kitchen and talk girl talk and help your sisters-in-law wait on your brothers hand and foot!'' Which was about when Phil started yelling, ''Fine! Fine!'' and stormed out. Since the Clinton presidency, Phil had come up with a new final parting shot as he slammed the door: ''Fine! You and Hillary Clinton!'' Which never gave me a chance to point out that Phil often said he'd rather Hillary were President than Bill. So after these arguments I always went around the rest of the day storming in my mind, Oh *yeah*? Well, you're the one who thinks *she* should be President; when are you going to get in touch with your *ambivalence?*

The apartment seemed very, very quiet after Phil left. I drank the rest of my tea, weeping with frustration and rage. Soon I sank into abject misery; I thought it was very unfair of Phil to beat up on me like this when Lisa had just died.

Minutes later I was sobbing like a refugee. Eventually I had to get into the shower and turn on the cold water to make myself stop.

When I got out, I made myself a cup of the Japanese tea Mick Healy had bought me. While I drank it, I thought about nuzzling the little dip behind his ear, easing him out of his shirt . . .

I lapsed into reverie. I tried to remember everything I knew about Mick Healy, conversations and interactions I'd had with him over the course of the two years I'd known him, things other people had said about him. Most of the ER stuff swirled together: Mick wielding an ophthalmoscope or reflex hammer; snapping X rays into the light box; talking on the phone in the nurses' station, holding the cord high for me to duck under as I brushed past him to go about my own duties. Mick had always seemed charming and playful, yet at the same time sad and grave, burdened by ''the accident''—which was what we always called it, in hushed tones, when speaking of the horrifying Christmas Eve his wife and boys had been killed by the drunk driver. How could anyone hope to understand a man who had been through such a calamity? He was like a Holocaust survivor, bearing the burden of choosing to live when others have died.

And then there were the added burdens of his family troubles. The embittered father, the brother caught up in the "Dirty Thirty" police corruption scandal at the Thirtieth Precinct, Donal Healy's humiliation as a "rogue cop," with his photo splashed across the cover of the *Daily News*. Mick bore it all, stalwartly, impressing most people, although not Phil, who worried about him. "Mick's like a golf ball wrapped up a little too tight," Phil had said after Donal's forced departure from the police department. "One slice of the cover and that sucker's going to unravel all over the place."

I wondered what Phil would say about Mick now. Mick had bottled up his feelings for me for some time, and was now letting those feelings out, suddenly. Would Phil interpret that as a form of unraveling?

I wondered if Mick wanted to remarry, or if he would be content to date a woman as independent as I was.

Then I wondered if I really wanted to swap Phil's relatives for Mick's relatives.

But I had things to do. Either I could read the newspaper, or I could go see Hal Murkland.

I decided to go see Hal.

CHAPTER
13

"I'M sick and tired of idealistic people," Dr. Harold Murkland sputtered. "Sharing a practice with Denny is like sharing the revolution with Che Guevara. She's a one-woman fucking communist government. Jesus Christ, how did I ever get myself into this?"

"So leave the practice," I said. "Go into practice with someone else. Start your own practice."

Hal started to say something, thought better of it, started to say something else, and thought better of that, too. He shut his mouth with a snap. Finally he said, "I can't. Okay? I can't."

I took in his disheveled appearance: hair uncombed and standing out from the sides of his head as if electrified, two-days' growth of beard, gray eyes bloodshot, face drawn and pale beneath his tan. The sutures stuck out of the bristle of his beard like little pieces of barbed wire. He wore a striped yellow Brooks-Brothers button-down stained on one shoulder with baby vomit, jeans that could stand a washing, and boating shoes encrusted with hospital gunk. He needed a shower and he was AOB—Alcohol On Breath.

At a momentary loss for words, I reached into the bag of breakfast goodies I'd brought from Sami's Café and handed Hal a container of caffè latte. He took it and stood aside so I could come through the door to the office suite he shared with Dr. Denise Aubuchon. It was eight-fifteen Saturday morning.

"And on top of everything else, we've got all this construction bullshit going on, you can't hear yourself think. Jackhammers and buzz saws and generators and God only knows what all—sometimes I think they're throwing metal girders around just because they like the noise, like a two-year-old with a spoon banging on a pot. To say nothing of the dirt."

A couple of weeks ago, workers at the new Storrs Pavilion that was rising next door had opened up the five lower floors of the doctors' residence—which comprised the Schiff Medical Suites, including Hal's and Denny's offices—to tie in steel to connect the two buildings. An enormous cloud of dust had blown into the medical suites, like a sandstorm from the Gobi Desert, and continued to blow in, daily. On a bad day, if you stood too long in the corridor waiting for the elevator, your hair turned white from it, and your shoes caked up.

"Next week they're going to start running in the mechanical systems," Hal complained, gesticulating wildly. "They're going to turn off the *electricity*, they're going to shut off the *plumbing*—do they think we're all shrinks here, we don't work in August?"

He turned on his heel and stomped off toward his office.

I followed him through the darkened waiting room and past the receptionist's cubicle. On Saturdays, office hours didn't begin until ten. As I moved down a hall lined with shelves for toys and magazine racks filled with AIDS literature, I wondered if Hal had been in the office all night.

"When was the last time you ate?" I asked finally.

"I'm on a diet," he snapped.

"Of what, bourbon?"

"Oh, now I suppose I've got a *drinking* problem. In addition to all my other fucking faults."

"Hal—"

"I'm thirty-seven years old, for Chrissake. And I'm really making a big effort here to act like a grown-up. How come nobody's willing to give me any credit?" He stomped into his office, slammed the container of coffee down onto the desk, threw himself into his desk chair, and glared at me. "And I hate this office. Jesus, she complains about the high cost of medicine, she fucking *rants* about how her middle-class patients are losing their medical insurance when they get sick and can't work anymore—the government should pay for *this,* the government should pay for *that*— but look what she spends redecorating the office! It looks like a goddamn courthouse in here!"

The "she" of all these rantings was, of course, Denny Aubuchon. On days when Hal didn't mind the decor he grudgingly called the style "Vermont"; on the days he hated it, it metamorphosed into "a goddamn courthouse." I personally found the office suite light and airy, and the style simple and uplifting. It consisted of old-fashioned oakwood bookcases and file cabinets, antique library tables to serve as desks, Victorian lamps to augment the recessed ceiling lighting, and straight-back chairs. But to Hal it was stark and unwelcoming. In his own office, he had added as many softening touches as possible. The walls were decorated with the usual medical school diplomas hung at adult eye level, but at kid eye level Hal had hung pictures children might like to look at, including photos of Dr. Murkland "being silly." In one photo Hal appeared to waltz with one of the Ninja Turtles; in another he posed in an elf costume next to Santa Claus; in a third, he waved at the camera with Mickey Mouse. For a while Hal had had cartoon pictures of the Mighty Morphin Power Rangers, but there were complaints from some quarters about five-year-olds karate-chopping one another, and he'd taken them down again.

I set the breakfast bag on Hal's desk and sat on one of the straight-back chairs, moving a large Paddington Bear to the floor, where some other bears were already ensconced with a pair of dolls, monitoring a large fleet of small Mack trucks.

"Besides which, the woman needs a fucking psychiatrist," Hal continued, on a roll now. "I know her father the Great Santini beat her, and her son was killed in that auto accident, but this overprotectiveness she has for her patients is psychotic—"

"Neurotic," I said. I assumed Hal was ranting about Denny to displace his grief and anger over Lisa's death, and braced myself. When Hal got on a topic, he shook it like a terrier, and there was no getting it away from him.

"Excuse me, *neurotic*. I forget who I'm talking to here, the shrink's girlfriend. But am I right, or am I right?" He threw his arms up in the air, like a fan demanding an umpire's agreement. "She doesn't like straight men because of her family history. Then that nursery-school teacher told her that her son had homosexual tendencies—"

I sighed. It was true; Dr. Denise Aubuchon had a terrible history with men. She grew up in one of those military families like the ones you see in a bad grade-B movie about drill sergeants who curse, drink, spout patriotic bullshit, wax sentimental about Old Glory, Mom, and apple pie—and who abuse their wives and children. Her dad was connected to the United States Military Academy at West Point in some capacity that was never precisely clear to me—although I gathered that he held a position of some rank—and was apparently a profoundly unhappy man who terrorized his wife and two daughters. Denny's mother began drinking heavily when Denny was about nine years old and spent most of Denny's adolescence passed out on the kitchen floor. Then there was the Prom Date From Hell . . .

"—and the next thing you know the kid is dead, so now Denny's built an *entire medical practice* out of taking care of men who have 'homosexual tendencies' and a disease that's going to make damn fucking sure that the next thing you know about them is, they're *dead*—"

"Hal," I said.

"*What?*" He glared at me. "Am I supposed to accept this as

normal? Am I supposed to *approve* of this? Am I supposed to pat her on the head and—"

"You had a very unhappy childhood yourself, and now you're a pediatrician," I said. "Why is that any different?"

"Oh, God," said Hal, blanching. An expression of sheer terror crossed his face, a dark storm cloud passing in front of the sun, then was gone. "Don't say things like that, Ev," he pleaded, suddenly very still.

I blinked. Had I missed something here?

His hand shaking, Hal reached for his coffee. "Please," he said, removing the lid and sipping the hot liquid, "can you just help me with the computer?" He pulled the bag from Sami's across the table and stuck his nose in it, like Pooh Bear sniffing at his honey pot. "These mozzarella and basil?"

"One is mozzarella and basil. The other is goat cheese and olives," I said. I had no idea what to make of his sudden transformation. One minute he was ranting; and the next he seemed cowed and subdued. "Take your pick."

"Which do you think has the higher fat count? I want to eat the one that's worse for me."

"Mad at your wife, too, huh?" I said. "The goat cheese is French; it might be richer."

"Good. If I'm lucky, I'll have an MI right here and now." He unwrapped the sandwich and bit into it. "Don't resuscitate me."

I opened my container of caffè latte and inhaled the fragrant steam, watching him. I had never seen Hal beside himself like this. He was not an emotionally labile person. In all the years I'd known him, he had suffered upsets and setbacks with patience and strength of character. When his mother died, he wept with uninhibited grief through the wake and funeral, then pulled himself together and went back to the hospital to look in on patients. When he applied for a partnership in a prestigious pediatrics practice and they failed to choose him, he cut his losses and accepted Denny's invitation to join her in practice on her grant to study maternal-childhood AIDS infections. Although subdued for a couple of weeks, he soon regained his pleasant, plodding disposition. Of course, the death of his mother—an elderly woman suffering from Alzheimer's in a nursing home who hadn't recognized Hal for years—and a missed business opportunity hardly fell into the same category of catastrophe as the stabbing death of a young woman Hal professed to have been in love with. Add to that the stress of being hauled off to the police station house for questioning.

Still. . . .

I watched Hal wolf down the sandwich in three bites and reach for his coffee. "Denny thinks the fucking government should wipe the people's goddamn asses for them," he sneered, gulping from the container. "Everybody's a victim. Everybody deserves their lives handed to them on a silver platter. Except she leaves the truly disadvantaged out of the equation. She's only for the *working* class, the *middle* class. She despises the underclass. It's a wonder she took me into the practice with all my Medicaid patients—she *hates* Medicaid patients. So much for her fucking ideology."

"Is it Denny who thinks you're not behaving like an adult?" I asked.

Hal blew a raspberry. "Ha," he said. Then, achingly, his voice barely a whisper, "My wife." Pause. "And Lisa."

Suddenly, in a rush of words that rivaled the speed of a used-car salesman, Hal launched a dozen apologies and explanations simultaneously, in such a jumble I couldn't sort through what he was saying. The gist of it seemed to be something about character growth. Self-examination. How he could learn to relate better to people, be more adaptive. Act like a grown-up. And for God's sake stop wimping out with women; his entire life women have been telling him what to do and he's been doing it. "No offense, Ev," and—quoting me in a mincing voice—" 'Hal, have you ever thought of going over to Brooks Brothers and buying yourself a couple of really decent shirts?' Christ, Ev, between you and my wife, I'm up to my fucking ears in Brooks Brothers shirts!" From the shirts he segued to haircuts and my brother's barber—whom

I had recommended, so naturally Hal had gone—which somehow got him onto the topic of Denny and her insistence that they computerize their office records, when he should have stood up for himself and said *No!* Like he should say to his wife: *"No,* I hate muesli; I'm not going to eat any more fucking muesli!" Lisa was the one person he finally got up the gumption to say *No* to— actually, it was a form of saying *No,* although what he was really saying was *Yes*—

"What?" I said, finally breaking in. Before I could stop myself, one of Phil's timeworn shrink phrases popped out of my mouth: "Can you say more about that?"

But like a rider finally getting hold of a runaway horse, Hal pulled himself to a halt. He blew his nose in a large pink handkerchief. "No," he said. "She's dead and it's private." He kicked back in his wheeled chair, rolling away from the desk and swiveling around to his computer console. "Phil Carchiollo uses this same software, doesn't he?" he asked, his voice vibrating with emotion. "Do you know how it works?"

I got up and went over to stand behind him. The floor under his chair was littered with computer manuals and instruction books. On the screen, Hal was still at C-prompt. I realized he didn't even know how to bring up the program.

I pulled up a chair.

" 'The coming changes in the health-care landscape,' " Hal pronounced bitterly, scooting over so I could sit in front of the screen. I typed in the command, and the credits for the program began to roll. While the computer was warming up, I got a yellow pad to take notes and rummaged among the books on the floor until I found the one I wanted.

"Okay, you understand the principle here," I began, trying to match the kind and nonpatronizing tone of voice Hal had used with me in medical school, when he tutored me in the finer aspects of cardiac physiology. "You want to make the office less dependent on paper. You can schedule the patient visit, document the visit, and seek remuneration for that visit . . . It's set up so you yourself schedule the patient's next appointment. Your calendar is on here, the patient's billing is on here, everything. There are no forms to fill out, you don't need to check with your reception-ist." I found the section in the book that paraphrased what I was saying, showed it to him, and marked it. "You call up the chart in the examining room and add your notes. With hard-copy charts there's always the question when the patient arrives where the chart is—with this, you don't have to spend twenty minutes look-ing for it. It's very convenient, and once you learn it you won't know what you did without it. Everything's archived on disc in the bank, so it's safe. You do know how to type, right?"

"No," said Hal.

"All right, you go to the store and get a typing manual. It's easy, you can teach yourself. Trust me, I had to learn in graduate school. I can't touch-type and I have to look at the keys, but I can type thirty-five words a minute. That's enough."

"Why is she doing this to me?" he groaned, his face crum-pling. "I've been sitting here, and sitting here—"

I took his hand and held it. "Remember when I couldn't start an IV on that little kid? The kid was screaming and I was crying, and you talked me through it and I got the needle in?"

Hal nodded, blew his nose again. Even smiled a little.

"You can learn this, okay?" I said. "You're not stupid. You're a doctor."

He laughed. "Can you show me how to pull up a chart?"

"Sure. What's the patient's name?"

"Joshua Waterman."

I sighed. I wasn't about to get into another argument with him about former patients of his who were now under Denny's care. I showed Hal the commands, then typed "WATERMAN JOSHUA." "No comma," I pointed out. "Last name first."

Waterman's chart came up.

"Can I print this?" Hal asked.

"Yes, but I don't know how. Phil only has the one computer

and the one printer. You have to queue for your printer and I don't know the commands for that."

"How do I read the next page?"

I showed him. I wrote the commands for the entire process of chart viewing on the yellow legal pad. Then I showed him how to close the file, and watched him as he called it up again by himself. I waited while he opened another file, practiced scrolling through it, closed it, and pulled up a third. After a moment, he became so thoroughly engrossed he forgot I was there.

Well, at least he had calmed down. Maybe now I could ask the questions I'd come to ask. "Hal," I said.

"Yeah."

"Did you tell the police you were sleeping with Lisa?"

Deep sigh. "Yeah." Then, "Christ. LaTonya Wilson's entire chart is in here, with my own notes, completely up-to-date! Who's been entering all this data, Joshua?"

I looked at him. Even I knew that one of Lisa's major responsibilities while working for Denny and Hal had been tackling the huge backlog of patient records that had to go on computer, and that Lisa had trained Joshua to take over from her at the end of spring semester.

"He's even got LaTonya's doll's name in here!" Hal exclaimed in wonderment. "Princess Fez!"

I looked at the entry: "Princess Fez, Afro-Amer, 12 in, Arabian Nights harem outfit."

"Hal," I said. "Did you tell the cops that you and Lisa had wild sex the night she died?"

"Yeah." Still looking at the screen.

"And you fell off the bed onto the champagne glass and that's how you cut your face?"

He nodded.

"The same story you told Denny when you came down the fire escape with your face bleeding."

"Yeah."

"Why?"

"Wait," said Hal. He scrolled through a chart, blinking at the data. "Son of a *bitch*."

"What's wrong?" I asked.

"*Shit.*" But he exited the file when I leaned over him to look. Then, wild-eyed and panicked, he put a hand over his mouth and tried to focus on me, blinking rapidly.

There was a long pause while we stared at each other.

"What are you saying?" Hal asked, clearing his throat.

"I want to know why you've been saying you were sleeping with Lisa when you weren't," I said, deciding to let the other matter pass.

"Excuse me?"

"And why you've been saying you had wild sex and fell off the bed onto the wineglass. When you didn't have sex and you didn't fall off the bed onto the glass."

His hand still over his mouth, Hal sat frozen in his chair. He regarded me with something akin to fear.

Bingo. I'd been right. "Hal. Listen. Last night Tony Firenze and Phil Carchiollo and I went into Lisa's apartment to see if we could find Jeff's cat. I got down on my hands and knees and smelled the carpet in the bedroom. You did not spill any wine in the bedroom. I got down on my hands and knees in the study—"

"I know," he said.

"There was wine on the rug in the study but not the bedroom. So what happened in the study that you spilled wine and cut your face?"

Hal winced. There was a small yellow matchbook car on the desk, and Hal drove it around a box of computer discs over to the phone, where he parked it. Then he picked up a pencil and let it slip through his fingers so that the eraser bounced on the tabletop.

"I tried to kiss her," he said finally in a small voice.

"Aw, c'mon," I said. "Are we going back to this story again? You kissed her and she slapped you? Hal, women don't hit men for a kiss."

"She said she wanted to be perfectly clear that that kind of behavior was unacceptable," Hal said softly, not looking at me, bouncing the pencil. "So that there would be no ambiguity, no ambivalence, no misunderstanding."

"Lisa said that?"

"It wasn't like I was Justice Thomas talking about penises and pubic hairs," he went on, almost whispering now. "I don't know what the problem was. Christ, I was just trying to talk about my *feelings*. I didn't say anything lewd—how can that be sexual harassment? How can I achieve character growth and self-examination if I don't talk honestly about my feelings? I thought it was *very* grown-up behavior. She's not being fair. Wasn't," he corrected himself miserably. "So I got a little upset. All I need to hear is 'sexual harassment'—unfounded sexual harassment charges are my worst nightmare! What mother would bring her daughter to me after that? God, she might as well charge me with child abuse—"

"Lisa was threatening you with *sexual harassment* charges?" I gasped.

"No!" Hal slammed both palms down on the desktop. "*No.* That's why she hit me. To get my attention. So the situation between us wouldn't deteriorate to the point where she would have to file charges to get my attention."

"She said that?"

"Well, not right away. Later. She was busy mopping up the blood with her shirt—"

"Mopping up the blood with her *shirt?*"

"She had a scrub shirt on and she took it off."

I put my forehead down on the tabletop, then sat up again. "Let me get this straight. After telling you your behavior was inappropriate, Lisa took off her shirt? Hal—"

"She had a tank top under it. What was she supposed to do, ruin one of Jeff Cantor's towels? The scrub shirt she can just throw in the hospital laundry."

I tried to take this all in. "Do the cops have this shirt? With your blood on it?"

"I don't know," said Hal. "I guess."

"You guess? Did they ask you about it?"

"Yeah. I said she used it to mop up the blood after I cut my face."

Something was skewed. "Let's rewind a minute," I said. "You told Denny and the cops you had wild sex with Lisa because the truth was too complicated?"

"Yeah," said Hal.

"But actually Lisa hit you because you tried to kiss her."

"Right."

"And when she swung at you, you raised your arm, so she hit the glass in your hand, and it broke and cut your face."

"Right."

"What was Lisa doing in your office before that, while you and your wife were entertaining Denny in your apartment for dinner?" I asked then.

"Lisa went over to download something onto disc. From the computer. Notes for a paper she was writing." Hal crossed his arms over his chest defiantly.

"I see," I said, although the only thing I saw was the abrupt change in atmosphere. "She wasn't in your office going through your records?"

Hal bristled as if I had flashed a stiletto. "I don't know what you're talking about, Ev."

"Lisa comes out of your office, you get out of the elevator, she says, 'I forgot to download all my notes,' and you start yelling, 'Oh, sure, you think that'll fly? You're in there going through the office records.' Sound familiar?"

"No."

"Two people heard you, Hal."

"Oh, is my office bugged?"

"Mick Healy—"

"Is confused," Hal said.

"Tony Firenze—"

"They misheard."

"How about, 'My ass is fucking cooked if she finds out'?"

"*That* I did say. You think I want Carol suing me for divorce and charging me with adultery?"

"Yes," I said. "I think that's exactly what you want."

"You're wrong. I want my wife to go for counseling with me."

He uncrossed his arms now, reached for his cup of coffee.

"I see." I again noted the change in atmosphere. Mr. Sulu, you may lower the deflector shields. "You're proclaiming your undying love to Lisa Chiu, and you want your wife to go to marriage counseling with you?"

"I'm getting in touch with my feelings," Hal said, not impervious to the irony. His mouth twisted briefly. "I have feelings for Lisa, and I have feelings for my wife. I've thought about why I was attracted to Lisa, and I know now what is missing in my marriage, and I want to work things out with my wife."

"And besides, Lisa was sleeping with Guy Shehadeh—"

Hal's head jerked up, and he started so violently, coffee sloshed out of his cup onto the desktop. His face flushed as he struggled with his emotions. "Son of a bitch," he muttered as he mopped up the spilled coffee with his handkerchief, which he distractedly stuffed back into his pocket. "That bastard. I'll break his fucking face."

"I think Brian Linhardt's already done that for you," I said. So Hal hadn't known. She'd kept it from all of us. But I moved on. "What happened with the police?"

For a moment I thought he wasn't going to answer. He closed his eyes and appeared to sink into a deep sleep. But then he roused himself. "I filled out a very long form," he said dully, as if nothing mattered anymore. "They wanted to know my name, address, age, education, hair color, height, weight, names of relatives, a description of my clothing, and about a hundred other things, I forget. Some detective whose name I can't remember made an extremely long, rambling speech about how the cops wanted to make sure I had a chance to tell my story. I told my story. The cops went out of the room and left me in there by myself for a while. Then they came back and said, 'Thank you very much, someone will drive you home.' " He smiled wryly. "I even let Denny buy me a drink, to celebrate not getting arrested."

"What *is* your story?" I asked.

Hal snorted. "God, Ev, doggedness always was one of your more endearing personality traits. My story. You want this with or without the *approximately*'s and *allegedly*'s?" He took a deep breath. "On Thursday, August third, I got up at my usual time, around six A.M., ate my usual fucking muesli, got dressed in my usual fucking clothes, and, since it was Thursday, as fucking usual I went to the hospital. Where I stayed all day, until about eight P.M., when I ran home to eat."

"And Denny was there for dinner," I said.

"Denny was there for dinner. Carol, me, and Denny. You want to know what we ate? Grilled scallops, pasta, zucchini, mesclun salad—"

"Hal," I said.

"—especially now that Carol's got that grill out on the fire escape, so we can have *deliciously grilled food*—my wife, Martha Stewart." He glared at me. His anger was mounting. "After dinner, I went to the office to catch up on my journals, when I wouldn't have to listen to jackhammers and buzz saws for once— and I bumped into Lisa coming out. She needed something she had stored on our computer, she'd forgotten to download it to disc when she'd downloaded all her other stuff at the end of spring semester. I thought, this is all I need, for Carol to find out Lisa still keeps a key to the office—"

"Why?"

"Because Carol thinks I'm having an affair with her, why do you think? So then I went with Lisa back to her place—"

"Were you drunk?"

"Yes. Because I had a few things to say to Lisa that I wanted to get off my chest, and I didn't feel like discussing them in the corridor outside my office, where your fucking friends Mick Healy and Tony Firenze had obviously installed all kinds of state-of-the-art listening devices—"

"They had the door to Mick's office open," I said.

"So I'm supposed to stand in the corridor and pour my heart out to Lisa with them listening? I went with her to her apartment. Where I tried to kiss her. And she slapped me. The glass broke and cut my face. I came back down the fire escape to the office because I was bleeding and I didn't want to explain to Security why. Denny was there catching up on charts and she'll tell you what time I came in. I can't remember."

"About two A.M."

"Is that what she says? Okay, fine. About two A.M."

"Then what? I mean after you sutured your face."

"I fell asleep on the couch in the waiting room."

"You didn't go back *up* the fire escape to Lisa's?"

"No. Christ, Ev, you taking the civil service exam to get into the police department, or what?"

"There was nothing else you wanted to discuss with her?"

"No." He crossed his arms over his chest.

What is it? I wondered. What is he hiding? And what's the point, now, when Lisa's dead? "Why didn't you go home?"

"Because I didn't know what to tell Carol had happened to my face."

"Oh." I'd run out of questions, and I hesitated, leaning back in my chair and crossing one leg over the other. I kicked over a stuffed animal, and looked down to see what my foot had hit.

Which is how my gaze came to rest on the bears and dolls.

Two babydolls, the plain-rubber kind. One dressed in a little blue dress, the other in a Pampers.

Then it sank in: Hal's office was full of dolls—babydolls.

CHAPTER
14

HAVING spent more time with Hal Murkland than I'd planned, I was running a little late for my 10 A.M. with Windy Sisk. I dashed out the doctors' residence on the Amsterdam Avenue side, set myself on automatic pilot for the subway, zipped through the walkway under the construction-site scaffolding and around the corner of 113th, and exited into daylight.

Hal had those rubber babydolls in his office.

Hal's computer files contained information on dolls belonging to patients.

Ergo—

I ran smack into a small claque of fervent people, a number of whom were clutching rubber babydolls.

Hamlet could not have been more shocked to see his father's ghost traipsing the castle ramparts than I was to confront these people with their dolls. My heart stopped. For a long, freeze-frame moment, I stared. They stared back.

Lisa Chiu's *They*.

They didn't know she was dead.

Since I had come around the corner under the scaffolding, not out the main door of the doctors' residence, they weren't immediately sure who I was. But they figured it out soon enough, and advanced upon me all the more resolutely for their moment's hesitation. "Did you know your neighbor kills babies?" yelled one woman. "Abortion kills children!" yelled another. There were about a dozen of them, men and women, their faces aglow with zealotry, their mouths agape and oddly orgasmic. They closed in on me, thrusting their dolls into my face. Dimly I registered that the dolls were wearing Pampers, as if they were real-life babies— in somebody's mind, I guessed they were. I put my arms up in front of me like a boxer, knocking the dolls aside with my elbows. Avoiding eye contact and saying nothing, I pivoted sideways, trying to use my shoulder as a battering ram to escape from the middle of the throng.

These people were not strangers. I knew them, and they knew me. They knew I was Lisa's friend; they had seen us together often enough—hell, they had *photographed* us. In fact, Lisa had photographed them photographing us, and the pictures were tacked up on a bulletin board at Westside Women's, where clinic workers posted photos of every anti-abortionist who had picketed WW since it opened four years ago. Along with each photo was a clinic-picketing rap sheet: name, address, ID number, a list of the subject's known church and organizational affiliations, and a précis of the subject's anti-abortion activities. The anti-abortionists probably had a bulletin board somewhere with my picture on it, and like information as well. "Evelyn, Evelyn," they now clamored, trying to get me to look at their gory photos of botched abortions, with crushed baby skulls and tiny mangled hands and feet. "Do you think Jesus approves of abortion?"

At first, I wasn't afraid. Strangely enough, most of them actually observe certain rules of body contact, so as to avoid assault-and-battery charges; they don't grab at you, they just thrust themselves in front of you. I concentrated on controlling my rage—my God, she's dead, this is *sacrilege*—and pushing my way through the crowd. But when an arm came around my shoulders and I couldn't see whose, my anger turned to real fear—someone not observing the rules, someone willing to step over the line, *someone pulling me against his chest—*

My arms, which I had been holding up in front of me, were suddenly pinned against him. My feet went out from under me. One of my shoes came off. He was dragging me, his hand in the small of my back, holding me up by my belt to keep me from falling—

"Stand back," Brian Linhardt said firmly. "She has nothing to do with abortion, she's an emergency-room physician."

"She consorts with—"

"No. Move back."

Amazingly, the crowd dispersed. They took their signs and their babydolls across the street, where they stood in front of the firehouse and regrouped in a desultory manner.

Linhardt let his arm fall from my shoulders.

Of all the men in the world, I had never expected to find myself in the arms of Brian Linhardt, magnificently sculpted muscles or not. He was anti everything I stood for: anti-feminist, anti-choice, anti-intellectual, anti–gay rights, anti–you name it, the list went on. Much as I appreciated his having delivered me from that claque of religious nuts, it infuriated me to have to acknowledge him, even for five seconds, as my rescuer.

"Is that your shoe?" Brian asked, as I hopped up and down on one foot. He knelt on one knee so I could steady myself with a hand on his shoulder—of course, he had the trapezius muscle of a linebacker. He held out my Cole Haan loafer. Well, at least it wasn't glass. I slipped my foot into it, swallowing my embarrassment, and made myself say, "Thank you, Brian," without gritting my teeth.

He stood and dusted himself off. Watching him smooth his hand over his short blond hair, I was struck by how economical his movements were. He was a remarkably self-contained person when he wasn't punching people out. Unfortunately, this made him difficult to read. And his flinty blue eyes revealed nothing. "You okay?" he asked.

I turned my arm over and looked at the clean dressing I'd put on my injured elbow after my shower; no blood. Good. It wouldn't do to show up for an appointment with Windy Sisk with my arm oozing blood. "Yeah," I said. "Thanks."

Linhardt bent down to retrieve the bag he had dropped in the melee. It was an old army cartridge bag in which he kept his paramedic's gear in case he happened to come upon someone who needed medical assistance. He fished his cigarettes out of it now. "You'd think they'd know she was dead," he said, glancing across the street at the demonstrators as he lit up. Sucking in a full third of his cigarette in one drag, he exhaled slowly and squinted through the smoke.

"You were in the crowd when they jumped me," I said.

He shook his head. "You're making assumptions."

"Am I?" I turned toward the subway, and he fell into step beside me.

"You think I'm in collusion with fanatics," he said.

"Well, if you're not in collusion with them, what are you doing standing around on the sidewalk shmoozing them?"

Unexpectedly, Linhardt laughed, a short, bitter bark. "Put up your dukes," he said. "Let's have it out. Right here. You and me. Settle this fucking abortion issue once and for all." He took a last drag of his cigarette and flicked it away. "Ev, they're assholes. For*get* about it."

"Excuse me," I snapped, "but I can't forget about it."

We had reached the subway entrance. "I gotta go," he said. "Brunching in the Village."

"Brunching or punching?"

"Oo, she's mad." He started down the stairs, reached the landing, and paused, looking up to see if I would follow.

"This the way you baited Lisa?" I asked cruelly.

The corner of his mouth twisted. "You don't know what you're talking about."

"I think I do."

"Yeah? Well, that's *two* strikes. Three and you're out." He turned on his heels and continued down the stairs, disappearing from view at the bottom.

I could have gone after him and apologized, taken the subway down to midtown with him.

But I didn't. I crossed the street and hailed a cab.

I wanted to do some thinking before I talked to Brian Linhardt again.

And if the truth be told, I was a little afraid of him.

What I needed, I told myself as my cab whizzed down Broadway, was a diversion. Something to get my mind off my troubles for five minutes. Bright lights, movie stars.

Hollywood.

Actually, there were plenty of bright lights and movie stars in Manhattan. As a New Yorker, I had traversed my share of streets turned into movie sets, tripped across sidewalks overlaid with generator cables, and peered through the windshields of Winnebago vans to see the production schedules displayed on the dashboards: what the movie was, who was directing, who was in it. Recently, Spike Lee had filmed several scenes on my block; another time I'd dawdled long enough on Broadway to watch Tom Hanks throw himself in the path of an oncoming taxi cab five or six times before someone yelled, "That's a wrap!" Once, when I wasn't looking where I was going, I ran into Roy Scheider on West Seventy-fourth Street; our shoulders brushed, he kept going, and I discovered I was taller than he was. The list goes on. You live in New York long enough, you see lots of famous people.

Meeting Windy Sisk wasn't going to be that big a deal.

Yeah, *right*, Sutcliffe.

I suddenly realized how nervous I was. I began to fantasize. Windy Sisk greets me, introduces me to some of his people, and we all sit down around a large table. No Windy Sisk movie was complete without a cream-cheese-and-bagel scene, so of course there are bagels with cream cheese served at this meeting, tea and coffee, maybe a little Nova . . . Suddenly, Windy Sisk, his hands to his throat, bucks over the table, then lurches to his feet. His chair crashes over backward. He is visibly distressed, but cannot make a sound. "Excuse me," I say. "Mr. Sisk, I'm going to bend you forward." I stand behind him, slide one arm around his waist, pound three times on his back, then slide the other arm around and execute the Heimlich maneuver. A piece of bagel shoots out of Sisk's mouth. In fact, a piece of bagel shoots out of Sisk's mouth, flies across the room, and beans his head assistant right between his or her eyes. Everyone is deliriously grateful, Sisk makes a speech thanking me profusely for having saved his life, and adds a little joke about how we can now start the meeting.

Actually, I'd done the Heimlich maneuver once on a big fat guy in a tony East Side bistro. The piece of veal did fly out of his mouth and hit his companion right between the eyes. Then he vomited all over himself, his companion, the waiter, and a woman sitting at the next table.

Bleah. I saw enough vomit at the hospital.

How about Windy Sisk greets me, then suddenly pitches forward, clutching his chest—

"Lady," said the cabbie, "you gonna pay and get out, or what?"

I paid and got out, and found myself standing on the sidewalk in front of Colony Music and a computer and video store. I checked the slip of paper on which I'd scrawled Jennifer Garland's careful instructions, then looked again.

Sandwiched between the two slightly seedy Times Square stores was a New York City wonder, the kind of thing you stumble on when you least expect it, and that takes your breath away. Gleaming brass doors flanked by speckled marble rose up to a spectacular Art Deco capitol, including the bust of somebody, all in burnished brass. I went through the doors into the lobby and found myself in Hollywood. Patterned marble floor, mirrored walls, brass trim, brass doors, brass chandeliers. The light from the chandeliers reflected off every surface. I was dazzled. I half-expected to see Marlene Dietrich leaning languorously against the wall, one arm flung over her head, exhaling "dahling" through a cloud of cigarette smoke.

Around the corner near the elevators I found the list of tenants, which included graphics, entertainment, and production companies, recording studios, edit rooms, and something called the Film-to-Tape Library. And, along with Wendell Sisk Productions, I noted, Paul Simon Music.

I got in the elevator and pushed the button for my floor. Then, out of habit, I sank into my thoughts. (They train you to do this in medical school; I had one book that had a section called "Elevator Thoughts" after each diagnosis: what you were supposed to be thinking about on your way to the emergency room, taking into consideration what the nurse had told you on the phone when he or she rudely awakened you from your hard-earned slumber.)

So immersed was I in my thoughts, I didn't immediately realize I wasn't exiting the elevator onto the ninth floor of the hospital. When the doors opened, I reflexively stepped over a long pair of legs, looked around for a path through the roiling masses camped out on the floor, and absentmindedly did a quick scan of the upturned faces in case someone with a life-threatening condition had failed to attract the attention of the triage nurse. I began to pat myself, a Pavlovian response to make sure I had everything I needed in the pockets of my white coat—except I wasn't wearing my white coat. I wasn't even at the hospital.

I was at Wendell Sisk Productions.

"Do I put him on the payroll or not?" someone was yelling. "You're not *answering* me—DO I PUT HIM ON THE PAYROLL OR NOT?"

I glanced around for a secretary or receptionist. Who were all these people? More than two dozen bodies were crowded into the tiny waiting room—huddled four to a couch, stretched out across the floor, leaning against the walls—all of them clutching pages like a bunch of anxious students waiting to turn in term papers.

Every one of them looked up hopefully, as if I might want them for something; when I returned their gazes blankly, they went back to their reading. Moved their lips when they read, too.

"YOU THINK I'M MADE OF MONEY? YOU THINK MONEY GROWS ON TREES?"

"Dr. Sutcliffe, so glad you could come," said a voice at my elbow. "Please come this way."

I recognized the honey tones of Jennifer Garland, Wendell Sisk's assistant, and turned to see a young woman with auburn hair who was already shaking my hand firmly and pulling me in the direction she wanted me to go. She wore a simple blue T-shirt, jeans, and a red velvet headband in her hair; a pair of tortoiseshell glasses perched on top of the headband. Her gaze was direct and penetrating, her manner poised. Ivy League. It was written all over her.

"Bit of a row going on this morning, I'm afraid," she murmured.

"SO I SHOULDN'T PUT HIM ON THE PAYROLL? I SHOULD JUST THROW MONEY AT HIM WITHOUT PUTTING HIM ON THE PAYROLL? WHAT, ARE YOU FUCKING NUTS?"

"Sounds just like my emergency room," I said. "Who are all those people in the waiting room? Actors?"

"Yes, we're doing readings this morning. We're still casting the smaller parts." She steered me into a tiny cluttered office and shut the door behind us, damping the shouts of the money man somewhat. "May I get you anything? Coffee? Tea? Bagel?" (What did I tell you?) She gathered a pile of scripts into her arms, clearing a chair for me to sit on. "Pastry? Fruit? I'm afraid Mr. Sisk's meeting is running over. It may be a half hour before he's ready for you."

"No, thank you," I said. *I'd* probably choke, and he'd have to do the Heimlich on *me*. "Well, maybe a cup of tea would be nice."

"Milk? Sugar?"

"Plain would be fine."

She went over to a wall unit, got down a tin, spooned real tea into a porcelain teapot, poured hot water from a Russell Hobbes kettle, and set an egg timer for three minutes. When she saw me watching her with astonished delight, she laughed. "I went to school in England for a bit," she explained. "Got into the tea habit."

"Me, too," I said. "Spent a semester in Oxford. You Oxbridge?"

"No, London." Her phone rang, and she excused herself to take the call.

I looked around. The place seemed just like any other busy New York office: file cabinet, desk, phone, computer, typewriter, fax machine, two chairs. No movie-making paraphernalia whatsoever, although what movie-making paraphernalia I had in mind I really couldn't tell you. Maybe a camera lens here and there, a director's chair . . .

Garland's tea-timer went off. She was still on the phone, busily writing on a large chart whiteboard that took up the entire wall behind her desk. "Yes, I'm marking the board," she said. "No, we don't require him until Tuesday. Yes, he *is* in that scene. That's scene twenty-three." I poured the tea into two mugs and set one on her desk. The mugs were splashed with big letters that said NEW YAWK MEMORIES. I recognized the purple, green, and yellow logo of Sisk's previous movie.

Which I had seen and thought brilliant. In fact, I'd seen all of Sisk's movies and thought every one brilliant.

My God, I thought. I'm actually going to meet Windy Sisk.

Garland hung up the phone. Immediately her intercom buzzed. "Yes, Mr. Sisk," she said. Then: "They're ready for you, Dr. Sutcliffe."

Wendell Sisk was not at all what I had expected, despite my having seen countless pictures of him in magazines. My immediate impression was that he was very, very square. Square jaw, broad shoulders, barrel chest—he seemed like a box on wheels, and as he came forward in greeting it was as if someone had tipped him onto a dolly and were rolling him toward me. The hands he extended were square as well—with thick, short fingers—and he used both to grab me in a bizarre sort of whole-arm handshake, hanging on to my hand and biceps throughout introductions, greetings, and his brief opening speech, which consisted of the usual "Thank you for coming, we value your input," et cetera. Despite this outward show of effusiveness, however, Sisk spoke in a soft voice, almost shyly, and I had to lean close to hear him.

Sisk introduced me to several people, explaining what each one did and why he or she was present at this meeting. They went by me in a blur: tall man with salt-and-pepper hair and Yankees cap; short, buxom woman with lots of jewelry and makeup, her eyebrows up in a permanent expression of droll incredulity, just like my great-aunt Sarah Chaya; movie-starrish woman in a mauve silk dress; plump man of mixed race with bright-green eyes. I promptly forgot their names, and was enormously grateful when Garland pressed into my hand a small card on which she had written *James Walker Hunt, co-writer; Linda Schapiro, set decorator; Gabrielle Wintertur, co-producer; Bob Fletcher, props.* Garland also carried into the meeting room my half-empty mug of tea and set it on the table, signaling me where I was meant to sit. I sat. They sat. Garland sat next to me and opened a notebook in her lap.

Without preamble, the tall man with the salt-and-pepper hair and Yankees cap said, "We're doing a metaphor for the alienation of patients in hospitals. We'd like lots of blood, and the doctors shrinking back from helping the patient. Flying-around blood, like shooting out of an artery—something along those lines."

I nodded. Sisk often went for the wide gesture of boffo. "Blood shooting out of an artery. Is the patient going to survive?"

This question somehow seemed to surprise everyone. "Oh, yes," said Yankees Cap with a puzzled look. "He makes a heroic recovery and triumphs over the doctors."

"An individual with severe blood loss, who—"

"—triumphs over the medical profession. Like Tom Hanks triumphs over the legal profession in *Philadelphia*, but with more irony. We want to go for irony rather than straight laughs.''

"I see," I said slowly. "Um. I didn't see *Philadelphia* . . . Tom Hanks got AIDS, so his partners fired him and he sued and won—that's the basic premise?''

"Right, triumphing over the legal profession," said Yankees Cap. I decided this must be James Walker Hunt, Sisk's co-writer. Sisk himself sat impassively at the end of the table, his body language suggesting that he was an observer at this meeting, rather than a participant. He made a note on a small pad in front of him and sipped a Perrier water. I turned back to Hunt. "Is your patient going to sue the doctors because they're negligent? What is the reason you're offering for why the doctors won't treat him?''

This time, they stared at me. If the lowliest of medical students had put a particularly naive and simpleminded question to the most eminent of neurosurgeons, the look could not have been more patronizing: *you wouldn't understand.* I stifled a sigh by coughing awkwardly into my fist. "Because I'm just trying to grasp the metaphor," I explained. Was I not supposed to ask questions? "How your patient triumphs over the medical profession.''

"I think we can move on," Sisk said mildly.

Immediately they all looked relieved.

"Let's go back to blood shooting out of the artery," Hunt suggested, as if I had missed the point. "The doctors shrinking back. Perhaps you could help us with that.''

"This is New York?" I asked. "An emergency room in a hospital in New York City?''

"Right. An emergency room in New York City.''

"Because you won't get doctors shrinking back from a patient in New York City, even with blood pouring out all his orifices. We would just suit up—gloves, goggles. The usual precautions.''

Hunt turned toward Sisk and lifted an eyebrow. Sisk looked at me attentively.

Feeling more and more that I had stumbled into a foreign country where I misunderstood local custom, I now directed myself to Sisk. "This is New York City. Many patients have AIDS," I explained. "We can't tell who does and who doesn't, so we suit up for everyone."

"Go on," said Sisk.

"How about this," I suggested. "Your patient has endocarditis and needs a valve replacement in his heart, but the doctors don't want to operate."

"No, no surgery," said Hunt. "The patient can't be unconscious. He needs to be able to make witty commentary."

"So you want a patient with blood shooting out of his arteries—Mr. Sisk, I'm afraid anyone who is bleeding out like that is not going to be getting enough oxygen to the brain to make witty commentary. Someone with blood shooting out of his arteries will probably be confused and lethargic, if not unconscious and in an advanced state of shock. What about an accident with flying glass? The patient could be quite bloody, without losing a life-threatening amount of blood—and still capable of making witty comments."

"Your point is, New York City doctors are not freaked out by flying-around blood," Sisk said, looking meaningfully at his co-writer.

"Right." I looked around the table. I could have sworn they were all holding their breaths. I began to get irritated.

When Sisk said, "Clearly the question is, What did he know and when did he know it?" and they all burst out laughing, I almost lost my temper. These people are *rude*, I thought. Can't they even show me the simple courtesy of explaining what's so funny?

When the laughter finally died down, Sisk and Hunt gathered their papers and headed for the door, smiling. The movie-starrish woman in the silk dress also stood. "Thank you, Dr. Sutcliffe, for coming," Sisk said. "Your assistance has been invaluable. We have another commitment, so please excuse us. Linda and Bob would like to ask you a few questions now, if you don't mind."

I decided a little grace was required here. They were paying me for my services, after all. "It's been a pleasure, Mr. Sisk," I said. "I've seen all your movies."

"The pleasure is mine," he replied with a flirtatious twist of his lips. "Jennifer has spoken with you about advising us on the set?"

"Not yet," said Garland, turning to me. "But I'll go over the schedule with you before you leave, if that's all right."

"That's fine," I said, wondering what I was agreeing to.

Sisk, Hunt, and the movie-starrish woman—finally paired in my mind with the name Wintertur—left the room, closing the door behind them. I turned to Linda Schapiro, who was passing me a typewritten list. I suppressed a wolfish grin of bemusement. Wait until I tell Lisa about this, I thought.

I almost got through the entire meeting without remembering.

Lisa was dead.

So much for Hollywood diversions.

CHAPTER
15

OUTSIDE on the sidewalk, the rain was coming down in sheets. Of course I hadn't brought an umbrella. I trotted across the street to the subway, thinking, Look, Lisa, I'm jogging, but got wet anyway. It was so humid it probably didn't make much difference whether I was dry or wet, but getting rained on seemed to add just one more indignity to the day. Fight with Phil. Worry about Hal. Get jumped by anti-abortionists and rescued by Brian Linhardt. Be insulted by Windy Sisk and his hangers-on.

Remember Lisa was dead.

The day couldn't get much worse.

Wrong. I stopped by the hospital.

"May I see Kennedy Bartlett's chart, please?" I asked the nurse on duty.

"No, Doctor, you may not," she said.

She was a large black woman with a Caribbean accent, and such enormous personal authority that I had the feeling she'd have me shot at dawn if I did not withdraw the question, immediately. But she noticed my dumbfounded expression and softened slightly. "Dr. Aubuchon has left strict orders that no physician other than herself may see Mr. Bartlett's chart," she explained, "excepting residents directly involved with patient care."

"I see," I said, although I didn't. I waited, hoping she might say more. But giving me one of those nurse looks that said All-doctors-are-crazy-and-I-just-do-as-I'm-told, she turned away and went back to her own work. After a moment, I slunk down the hall like a thief to Ken's room.

He was sleeping, his head thrown back and his mouth open, but he started awake when I touched his shoulder. "Did you bring the cheesecake?" he asked.

"No, but I can bring you some later, if you like," I said, puzzled. Ken hated cheesecake. Then I noticed the morphine drip.

Oh, God, I thought. You know it's coming but you keep yourself in denial, you tell yourself *not yet*. IV morphine in a continuous drip is generally not prescribed to someone who isn't dying; it slows down all the bodily functions and speeds death. Denny's having prescribed it at all meant that *not yet* was over. IV morphine said *soon*.

I felt my throat clog. "How are you feeling?"

For a moment he looked at me with obvious confusion, but then his gaze cleared. "I have this recurring hallucination," he said, his voice slurred drunkenly. "The bed is tipping up and I'm going to slide off the bottom." He flung his hand toward the foot of the bed. "Whoops! The food's terrible. I have a blood infection. They don't understand cuisine here."

I leaned over and read the pharmacy sticker on the IV, then the drip rate on the pump, pausing a moment to do the necessary calculations in my head. Denny was giving Ken a whopping dose of morphine. *Soon* was even sooner than I thought. "What blood infection is that, Ken?"

"Septic tank," he said. "You know." Suddenly, he gripped the guardrails of his bed as if his roller coaster had taken a sudden dip. "Whoa!" he shouted.

I saw real fear in his eyes.

"Is the bed tipping up?" I asked. "Are you having the hallucination? Here, let me hold you." I leaned over him, my arm across his chest. His skin was hot and dry to the touch.

After a moment, Ken said, "Okay, it stopped. I asked for seat belts but they didn't have any. What kind of hospital you work in, no seat belts?" He laughed gleefully like a late-night bar patron, enjoying the joke. "What if we all fall out of bed?"

"Then the doctor has to come."

"Really?"

"Yup. Hospital rules. Patient falls out of bed, nurse has to notify the resident on call."

"Keep it in mind," said Ken. He laid his head back against his pillow. "Did you bring my bills? Where's that Chinese kid with my Blue Cross, Waterman? All fucked up. They're billing *this*, they're billing *that*—I only had *this*, you know. I don't know where they're getting *that* from."

His speech was so slurred from the morphine that I could hardly understand him. Even when I understood, I still had to figure out what he meant. He seemed to be confusing Lisa Chiu and Joshua Waterman. Something about his Blue Cross bill . . . I remembered that Ken had complained the day before of a problem with it, and had said that Waterman had been by to help straighten out the paperwork. "I'll remind Denny that you're concerned about your Blue Cross bill."

"Where are my bills?" he asked again distractedly.

"I'll bring them next time, I promise."

"Write 'em a check," said Ken. He dozed off briefly, but roused himself. "Checkbook." He rummaged in a pile of papers he had on his night table. "Here somewhere."

He handed me his daybook.

"This is your daybook," I said, opening the small loose-leaf notebook he used to keep track of his appointments, obligations, thoughts, and wishes. "You want me to read something in here?"

"Write," he said.

"Write what?"

"Paid phone bill and electric bill."

I considered humoring him, but thought better of it. "We didn't pay the bills," I said patiently. "We'll pay the bills next time. Anything else?"

"You're here."

I wrote down that I had visited, and the time. As I shut the notebook and handed it back to him, I had a depressing thought: This is how he's going to spend the rest of his life, gorked out on morphine, obsessing about the phone and electric bills, making me write it all down.

"They're going to let me go, you know," Ken said.

"Home?"

"No."

He watched me as this sank in.

"Oh, Ken, I'm so sorry," I said.

"They think about two weeks." By *they* he meant Denise Aubuchon and his oncologist. "Gotta go sometime," he said airily, grinning like a loon. Then, as suddenly as a junkie nodding out, he was snoring.

I waited, but when he didn't wake again after five or ten minutes, I quietly slid my hand from his and left the room.

In the corridor outside Ken's room, my head emptied of all thought and I paused, uncertain where to go or what to do now. When I next noticed my surroundings, I was standing in front of the elevator banks. Some doors opened, and I got in and rode up and down for a while. Two weeks, then no more Kennedy Bartlett. How could somebody be here one moment, and not the next? I was a doctor. I'd seen people die. But this question never ceased to plague me. Here one minute, gone the next—how was it possible? Good-bye forever. I wondered whether to call the gay couple upstate who were to take the dog when Ken died. For a moment, panicked, I couldn't remember where I'd put the guest list for Ken's "going-away" party. In the file you and he started last winter, I reminded myself. When he started telling you things.

I got out of the elevator finally when it stopped on the ground floor. I thought about looking in on Joshua Waterman, but decided against it; I didn't have the heart, not after visiting Bartlett. Choosing instead to go see how Jock Lamartine was doing, I got back in the elevator. On the fifth floor I could walk across the skyway to the old hospital complex, where the Cardiac Care Unit was located. As I entered the skyway, a young Asian woman walked toward me from the far side. She wore a medical student's coat and rushed along in the harassed manner common to all medical students, her head down and brow furrowed. The light was behind her, and when she tossed her head, my heart leaped. Her lovely black hair, cut shoulder-length just like Lisa's, fanned out around her . . .

I held my breath until she passed me.

Then I burst into tears.

When I stepped out of the stairwell into the corridor outside the Cardiac Care Unit, mopping my face and blowing my nose, I found two uniformed officers in modified riot gear guarding the swinging doors to the CCU. Surprised, I stopped in my tracks.

"You have business here, Doc?" one of the officers asked gruffly, taking in my damp hair and sodden clothes and dubiously eyeing my hospital ID, which I had clipped to the breast pocket of my shirt. The cop stood with his feet apart, one hand on the handle of his nightstick, the other on the butt of his gun. What did he think I was going to do, whack him with my stethoscope? Attack him with my wadded-up Kleenex? Then I remembered why Lamartine was there, and felt a sudden rush of gratitude for the police protection. I explained that I had cared for Lamartine in the emergency room and wanted to confer with Dr. Alexander McCabe, Lamartine's surgeon. The cops let me by, and I pushed through the swinging doors into the CCU.

I found Alex sitting at the long counter that served as doctors' desks just inside the CCU doors. He was wearing tennis whites, his loosely curled Afro glistened, and his hazelnut-brown face was flushed with exercise and good health. When I leaned over to kiss him on the cheek, his cologne wafted up at me, Chanel for Men, mixed with sweat. I was beginning to think everyone in the world but me exercised and led a healthy life.

"How's Jock?" I asked, stepping over McCabe's racket bag and pulling up a chair.

"You missed all the excitement," Alex said, without glancing up. If he noticed I'd been crying, or that I was soaking wet, he was kind enough not to say. "He's stable now, but he suffered major bleeding. We eventually had to infuse him thirty units."

I whistled. The doctors had replaced more than half of Jock Lamartine's entire blood volume.

"But he's doing very well, all things considered," McCabe went on, still writing. "Luckily the twenty-two is relatively small and generally does less tissue damage than the larger calibers. The bullet entered his chest below the left armpit, as you saw, traveled slightly downward, then struck the seventh rib and was deflected backward into the lower left lobe."

"Huh," I said. "That really is just like President Reagan."

"Yeah, everybody's saying. We had a really hard time finding the goddamn bullet—we wound up taking five or six films. But we got it out, and the sucker didn't blow."

"Thank God," I said. "You wean him?" I meant off the respirator. I wanted to know whether Jock could talk yet.

"Yeah, three A.M. IIc's doing okay. This morning he took some soup and gelatin. Complaining about the pain, though. That's his wife with him now."

I looked across the CCU, where I could see a tall, slender brown-skinned woman bending over Lamartine's bed. She too wore tennis whites.

"I made her play a couple of sets with me this morning," Alex said. "I thought she needed to work off the stress. You know, you look like you could use a couple of sets of tennis to work off the stress, too. Or maybe you should take up—"

I held up a hand. "Don't say it."

"Jogging," McCabe said anyway.

"I know," I said. "Alex, did you tell Jock about Lisa Chiu?"

McCabe sighed and nodded, twirling his pen unhappily. "I would have preferred to wait, but the cops insisted," he said. "They needed to ask him about her."

"How did he take it?"

"C'mon, Ev, how do you think he took it? He was extremely upset. Of course."

"I was kind of hoping I could ask Jock a few questions myself," I said.

"Absolutely not," said McCabe. "I'll say the same thing to you that I said to Denise Aubuchon this morning, and to Brian Linhardt and every other damn person who's phoned me or stuck their head in here nosing around. N-o, no. Jesus, give Jock a break. What do you need to know that's not in the newspaper?"

"Whether Jock thinks an anti-abortionist could have killed Lisa," I said. "Whether Jock thinks the Babydoll Killer is an anti-abortionist. Yes, no, why, why not?" I crossed my arms over my chest. "Whether Lisa said anything to Jock about the guy who was following Theresa Kahr."

"What guy who was following Theresa Kahr?" McCabe asked.

I grinned like the cat who ate the canary, shaking my head. "Uh-uh. Trade you."

McCabe made a face and went back to writing in Lamartine's chart. A nurse came by and handed him a sheaf of lab results, which he read, slowly and methodically. Then he signed some pharmacy slips.

I waited.

" 'You wanna cut babies outta people, we'll cut one *into* you,' " he said after a while.

"Precisely," I said.

"No. Jock said he could see how someone might think an anti-abortion terrorist would do something like that, but Jock personally didn't think it was anyone in the Goon File."

"Goon File?"

"That's what WW calls their collection of photographs of anti-abortionists. Did you know they have a full-time photographer who does nothing but take still photographs and videotapes of the pro-life demonstrators? He sits in a room on the first floor of the clinic called the 'duck blind' and shoots through a special window; one side is mirrored." McCabe shook his head.

I knew about the Goon File; I hadn't known about the duck blind. Jesus. Imagine a pediatrician having to install a duck blind in order to provide routine medical services to his patients— would anybody stand for that? "Why did Jock not think it was anyone from the Goon File?"

"Too convoluted. The guy who killed Lisa had a complicated agenda, and Jock is strongly of the opinion that anti-abortionists are fairly simple people with a simple and direct message: 'Stop killing babies.' "

"Well, I guess he has a point," I said. "What about the Babydoll Killer?"

"Again, too convoluted. Maybe he killed Lisa, but he's probably not in the Goon File. As Jock pointed out, if a guy uses raping and killing women as an emotional release, why would he need to stand outside an abortion clinic and vent rage?"

"Huh," I said. "Jock certainly has a unique view of the world."

"You would, too, if you had to deal with terrorists and fanatics every single day of your life."

"Did Jock have any idea who might have killed Lisa?"

"You mean, other than the Babydoll Killer?" McCabe shook his head. "Not a clue." Alex must have seen the disappointment and frustration in my face, because he reached out and patted my hand. "Ev, let the cops solve it," he said gently.

"What about the people who were harassing Lisa personally?" I persisted.

Alex withdrew his hand and gave me a long look. But he answered the question. "Jock said Lisa was subject to the usual harassment. Hate mail, threatening phone calls until she got an unlisted phone number, people following her to the clinic and home again. She kept meticulous records of who was outside the doctors' residence with placards when she came out in the morning. You know she carried that little camera with her at all times, and if anyone bothered her or followed her, she took their picture. Everything went into the Goon File at WW. So the cops have all that."

"Did she keep copies of the photos?"

"I dunno, Ev." He was losing patience, and buried his face in Lamartine's chart. I'd run out of questions anyway. So, taking the hint, I looked at my watch, pretended I had somewhere I had to be, and said good-bye. I asked McCabe to convey my wishes to Lamartine for a speedy recovery. As I walked the half-block of hospital corridors to the Amsterdam Avenue side of the hospital, I began to wish that I really did have somewhere to be; I needed the distraction.

Outside it was still raining, but more softly now. The odor of hot, wet city sidewalks and the wet-basement smell of the construction site filled my nose. I was emotionally and physically drained, but too restless to go back to my apartment.

It's now or never, I thought. Hell, I was already wet anyway. Without further ado, I proceeded to jog around the block.

I turned the corner on my final lap, knock-kneed and gasping for breath. As I dodged around the red minicontainers that said "Demolition With Discretion" and the huge Vicon crane that took up half the block at the new Storrs Pavilion construction site, I imagined I could hear Lisa laughing.

CHAPTER 16

I sat down at my kitchen table, but decided I needed a pen and pad of paper.

Got the pen and pad of paper, sat down again, and decided I needed lunch. Made myself a nice big Greek salad with plenty of fresh feta cheese, mint, dill, and a gorgeous tomato I'd picked up a couple of days before at the Union Square greenmarket. Sat down again. Jumped up immediately to get a glass of cold Assam tea from the fridge. Sat down for the fourth time, and ate while looking out the window and watching the rain come down. It was raining heavily again, and the wind had picked up.

I did not relish the thought of reading the newspapers. The bombing at the OB-GYNs I could deal with; the shooting of Lamartine I could deal with; the tabloidization of Theresa Kahr's and Lisa Chiu's deaths I could do without. The tabloids trashed the dead and insulted the bereaved.

Bracing myself, I pulled the newspapers over. The *Times* was still folded to the page with the article on Drs. Guderian and Reichert that had so gripped Phil and his colleague Gina; the memory of my argument with him that morning stabbed me as I turned to the front page. I glanced at my watch and saw that it was only two-thirty. Briefly, I considered hopping the next train to Long Island. If I left now, I could still arrive in time for Phil's stepmother Sylvia's three-day-lasagna dinner.

Except I had to feed and walk the dog.

I sat down with the newspapers.

The headlines, spread across four columns, leaped out at me:

**BOMB EXPLODES BUS STOP,
HURTING AT LEAST TWENTY**

**FRENZIED PEDESTRIANS FLEE
SIDEWALK EXPLOSION**

**GUNMAN SHOOTS DOCTOR AT
ABORTION CLINIC**

**GUNSHOTS BRING CHAOS TO MANHATTAN'S
UPPER WEST SIDE**

The bomb, made of a gas canister for camping packed with heavy metal parts, exploded shortly after 7 A.M. in a crowded bus stop, in front of the offices on West Seventy-ninth Street of Dr. Jace Maraldo-Stern, an obstetrician-gynecologist participating in clinic trials of the abortion pill, mifepristone—known abroad as RU-486, after Roussel Uclaf, the French company that developed it. According to witnesses, the bomb had been hidden in a bag person's shopping cart filled with bottles and newspapers, and parked next to the bus stop. Police had a suspect in the bombing: 23-year-old Matthew Rushkin, an unemployed cook, who has himself suffered injuries from flying glass and metal. He was taken to New York Hospital Cornell Medical Center in Manhattan, where he was being questioned by detectives.

* * *

Somehow I didn't think Matthew Rushkin had killed Lisa Chiu.

The articles on Lamartine's shooting didn't tell me anything I didn't already know, but I read them carefully anyway. Turning to the jump on page 17, I found sidebars on the bombing and shooting, and a speculative profile of the Babydoll Killer: AN ODDBALL WHO BECOMES A MURDERER: THE PATTERNS OF A SERIAL KILLER. The usual rehash of stuff everybody knows by now: the "typical" serial killer has had a "painful childhood"; he has "limited social skills"; during his school years other children found him strange, and people who know him as an adult consider him "eccentric"; he "becomes locked in an inner world of violent fantasy that eventually drives him to kill." Plus the by now familiar recap of the crimes of Son of Sam, Ted Bundy, and Jeffrey Dahmer.

I read on. A forensic psychologist quoted in the article noted that "the killer enjoys thrills and risk-taking, is calculating, and has the ability to stay calm under pressure and focus on details, which enables him to plan and carry out his deeds in such a way as to elude detection."

Hell, that description fit every cop I'd ever known.

I sighed. It was probably safe to say that the Babydoll Killer had raped and killed Theresa Kahr.

But had he killed Lisa?

Next I read A YEAR ABROAD ENDS IN VIOLENT DEATH FOR GERMAN STUDENT, which feverishly lamented Theresa Kahr's death. Someone had eulogized her as a "terrific kid," an "ardent feminist" and "passionate environmentalist," and informed readers that Theresa "enjoyed American jokes, and radishes with her beer—"

Oh God. I put the paper down and looked out the window. Eight stories below, on a rainy Amsterdam Avenue, a few cars passed slowly up and down, their headlights on, even though it was mid-afternoon. Going to a funeral, maybe.

The reporter had interviewed Lisa. Whose own tragic death was covered right next to Theresa's:

IN SEPARATE DEATH, POLICE ARE PUZZLED

A medical student who had worked as a volunteer orderly at Westside Women's Health Center was found stabbed and unconscious in her apartment early yesterday morning, and died in the emergency room at University Hospital before doctors could revive her, police officials said last night.

The young woman, whose name is being withheld pending notification of the family, was discovered lying across the threshold of her apartment in the University Hospital doctors' residence, where she was living while assigned to the emergency room there as part of her clinical education. Police said she had been stabbed repeatedly in the abdomen sometime during the early morning, and appeared to have crawled to the door and opened it before losing consciousness.

She was found and aided by physician neighbors and emergency room personnel, who transported her to the hospital but were unable to save her.

The police did not know how long the 24-year-old student lay half-in, half-out of the door to her apartment before being discovered, or exactly when she had been assaulted. The apartment showed no signs of forced entry, but a bedroom window was open onto the fire escape, leading to speculation that the assailant arrived or departed via the window.

The student was last seen alive by a colleague with whom she had been reviewing medical records at about 2 A.M.

Despite the shooting of Dr. Jean-Jacques Lamartine at Westside Women's Health Center, and the bombing of the offices of Dr. Jace Maraldo-Stern, who was participating in clinical trials of the abortion pill, RU-486, investigators downplayed any connection between the student's activities at the clinic and her slaying.

"We have no evidence, forensic or otherwise, to connect the three cases at this time, although we are pursuing all leads," said Captain Raymond English of Manhattan North Detectives. "Department investigators have not determined a motive in this slaying."

Captain English also said officials did not believe the recent series of killings by the so-called Babydoll Killer were related to the attack on Dr. Jean-Jacques Lamartine or the killing of the medical student.

But eyewitnesses in the emergency room disagreed with police statements. "You have to make a connection immediately between the Babydoll Killer and the anti-abortion activists," said a senior physician on duty in the University Hospital emergency room when the student was brought in. "She had several stab wounds, but one in particular resembled a cesarean section. And the first thing that popped into my mind was, 'You wanna cut babies out of people? We'll cut one *into* you.' That could be the theme of both the Babydoll Killer and anti-abortion activists, who after all want to punish the woman and get Jezebel under control." The physician spoke on condition of anonymity.

So far only the student's colleague who reviewed medical records with her the night before she was killed is being questioned. But Captain English said the police did not consider the colleague a suspect at this time, and that the investigation was continuing.

Oh, God, I thought. Dispiritedly, I scanned an article on the weather, HEAT EBBS BUT 11 ARE DEAD IN NEW YORK CITY.

The good news was, Hal Murkland was not a suspect. The bad news was, Denise Aubuchon—glorious, opinionated, Joan-of-Arc Denny—was shooting off her mouth and muddying the waters as usual.

I got up from the table and padded in my bare feet into the living room, where I opened the front of my grandmother's old Queen Anne desk and took out a pile of greeting cards—I kept a collection on hand in case it was anybody's birthday, or someone got sick. Or died. Selecting a blank card with a picture of mist rising from a woodland stream, I went back into the kitchen and sat

down again at the table, sighed several times, and picked up my
pen.

> Dear Mr. and Mrs. Chiu,
>
>   *I am writing to express my condolences on the death of your
> daughter Lisa. I was part of the medical team that brought her
> to the emergency room and worked on her until she died. We all
> knew her and loved her and we did everything within our ca-
> pabilities to save her. I cannot express in words my loss and grief
> that she was taken from us like this.*
>   *Lisa was assigned to me during her emergency room rotation.
> She was my favorite medical student. It was a delight to teach
> her and work with her. She would have made a kind, competent,
> and caring physician. The profession loses one of the flowers of
> its youth.*
>   *My heart and mind are very much with you, and I wish you
> Godspeed.*
>
>   *Evelyn Sutcliffe, M.D.*

I started bawling midway through and had to hold the card at
arm's length so I wouldn't drip tears on it. I couldn't see what I
was writing and my handwriting snaked and spiked this way and
that, and I didn't even half manage to express my thoughts and
feelings. It was as if someone else had written the letter, just to
be polite—someone who hadn't known Lisa, hadn't worked with
her, hadn't loved her, hadn't wished from time to time that she
were her own daughter, and hadn't been stricken to the core of
her soul by her death.

It was the best I could do. I licked the flap of the envelope and
sealed it, and vowed to write again the following week and every
week thereafter until I got it right.

Even if that was never.

*   *   *

The first thing I noticed when I let myself into Kennedy Bartlett's apartment was that the dog seemed confused. On the one hand he was glad to see me, stretching his rickety forelegs out in front of himself, dipping his front shoulders a little, and barking a couple of times. But while I put down my dripping umbrella and picked up Bartlett's mail from the floor, stuffing it into my bag to take to him in the hospital, Maxie tottered into the dining room. He returned looking very worried, for a dog.

"I know, I know," I said soothingly. "I'm not Ken. I know you miss him. Why don't we go for our walk and then I'll feed you?" I leaned down and put my hand out for him to smell, but he wasn't interested, instead casting meaningful doggy looks toward the kitchen.

"Walk first, eat later," I said firmly.

If I had really been paying attention, I would have realized that Maxie always raised his ears hopefully when he thought about food, and that this was not the food look.

If I had been paying attention, I might have stopped to think about the dog's watchful posture, shoulders hunched and head down.

But I wasn't paying attention. It was still raining out, which I assumed Maxie could tell perfectly well from my dripping umbrella and raincoat. I knew he didn't like rain, and I assumed he was trying to tell me he would just as soon skip his walk and get right down to serious business—food. I picked him up, carried him out the house and down the front steps, and put him down on the wet pavement between two cars, where he unhappily but dutifully pooped. Then he pissed on a nearby tree, and I picked him up again and we went back into the house.

"Just let me hang up my wet coat," I said. "Then I'll get your food."

Maxie put his head down and slunk into the dining room, where I found him a moment later apprehensively smelling the closed bathroom door.

But no worry on earth could distract Maxie from his food for long. When I went into the kitchen, he followed, and stood patiently while I read Ken's detailed dog-care instructions, typed and Scotch-taped to the cabinet over the sink. I knew the drill, but I also knew Ken would ask me the next time I saw him if I had read the instructions, and I would like to say yes honestly. First, half a cup of steamed green beans. Steamed beans in freezer, each serving individually packed in a Ziploc bag. Only after Maxie ate the beans could he have half a can of his special dog food—which Ken ordered by the case from a vet who claimed he used only organic ingredients. Then two all-natural treats from Vermont Animal Cookies, a bakery specializing in snacks for dogs, cats and horses.

Afterward, I imagined Maxie casting one last worried look over his shoulder before I opened the refrigerator.

But actually, I'm not sure what exactly happened right before I opened the fridge.

I don't even remember opening it.

And I have no memory at all of having been hit on the head and knocked unconscious.

I was in a dark room with an animal and I couldn't see.

Why couldn't I wake up? I didn't like this dream. I was pinned by the hips, I was underwater, I couldn't breathe, the floor was hard—and Jesus Christ, *what was this fucking animal?* I hit the dog and he fell down on top of me, then scrambled to get up, yelping and scaring me out of my wits.

I was conscious. Finally I knew the animal was Maxie and I knew I was at Kennedy Bartlett's apartment.

But it was pitch-dark and I couldn't see. "Ken?" I said, "Ken? What's happening? Is there a blackout?" My voice sounded slurred. Maybe I was still asleep after all, maybe I only thought I was awake. I *willed* myself awake. "Wake up," I said out loud.

I remembered that Ken was in the hospital, and I'd come over to walk and feed the dog.

Christ, it was *really dark*.

I was lying on my side on the floor, sort of facedown and scrunched up under the open refrigerator door. I could hear the refrigerator groaning because the door was open. But the light in the refrigerator was off.

Wait a minute.

If the light in the refrigerator was off because there was a blackout, why was the refrigerator still *on*?

Oh my God.

I was blind.

Fighting panic, I put my hands up to my eyes. They were open. I blinked a couple of times, feeling my eyelashes bat against my fingertips; I gingerly touched my eyeballs and reassured myself they were still in their sockets, the vitreous humor hadn't leaked out. My face was wet and I licked my fingers to see if I tasted blood, but I didn't. Saliva. I had saliva all over my face.

Big lump on my left eyebrow.

My heart became a caged quail beating its wings against my ribs. Someone had hit me. I was blind. The someone might still be in the room with me, for all I knew it was high noon and he was standing over me in radiant sunlight pointing a pistol at my head. No. Wait. Maybe the refrigerator light had burned out from the door being open so long, and maybe it *was* dark out.

How long had I been unconscious?

It was very difficult to think with my mind screaming *I'm blind I'm blind* and *Jesus, what if he's still in the apartment?* With my heart filling my throat and my mouth and my ears, I couldn't hear properly—was my assailant gone? If not, would he kill me if I moved? Should I play dead? I heard the dog's toenails clicking on the wooden parquet floors in the living room and dining room, then on the tile of the kitchen. When he nosed me, I jerked. Then I lay still, rigid with fear, as he began smelling me from head to foot, painstakingly arriving at his own diagnosis—maybe that should be dog-gnosis—of my condition. Hoping with all my being that the dog's rapt attention meant that the intruder was no longer in the apartment, I slowly pulled myself into a sitting position, my back against the kitchen counters. I stretched and wiggled all my extremities, and carefully palpated my scalp. Tender swelling on the back of my head, small bump over my left eye. Nothing seemed broken.

But I still couldn't see.

Or maybe it really was dark outside.

Slowly getting to my feet, I tried to remember what I knew about head-bonk and temporary blindness—oh God, please let it be temporary. A girl in my biology class in college had been blinded in a car accident—she suffered head injuries, although I never really knew the details—and her blindness was permanent. I took a ragged breath and felt my way around the counter to the kitchen door, then felt for the light switch. I flicked it on and off a couple of times, imagining the lights going on and off and willing myself to see. Nothing. On the other hand, there was that patient I had a couple of months ago, the one who got head-bonked during a robbery; he was moaning he couldn't see when they brought him into the ER, but a half hour later he could see fine. Please let that be me. I wondered if God made deals with people who normally didn't spend much time talking to him—what if I said I'd go to synagogue once a month? Hell, what if I said I'd join one and go once a week? I got down on my hands and knees and began to crawl toward the phone in the living room, sweeping with one hand in front of me, then the other. But God probably knew I wouldn't go to synagogue once a week no matter what I promised; how could I negotiate with someone who knew the future and whether or not I would hold up my end of a bargain? "No offense, God," I said, "but talking to you is too much for me." Silently I pleaded, *Please* make me see again. What would I do for a living if I couldn't see? Were there any blind doctors? I found the phone and had to puzzle out, by feeling and counting the buttons, how to dial 911.

At long last I heard the gruff and jaded "Where's the emergency?" of the police operator.

I told him.

I said I had been hit on the head by a burglar, had been briefly unconscious, and I needed an ambulance. No, I couldn't give a description of my assailant; I hadn't seen him. I had no idea whether anything was missing; it wasn't my apartment. I was in the apartment to feed the dog while the owner was in the hospital. I did not know whether anyone else had keys to the apartment; I could ask the owner when I saw him, but he was sedated and his answer might not be worth much.

Clever cop. He was helping me calm down by asking me all these questions, and keeping me on the line until the ambulance arrived. As I talked, I could hear the tremolo of fear in my voice lessening.

But I still couldn't make myself say that I couldn't see.

There were two cops: one with a raspy smoker's voice asking gentle questions; a second whose voice had a youthful quality and a touch of bravado. Both voices vibrated with the nasal honk a' da Bronx. Still another voice wanted to know my name, who the President was and if I knew where I was—this voice I took for the EMT. He sounded like Brian. Or maybe I just mixed them up, since I'd heard Brian ask these questions so many times.

We went around in circles a little bit with "Who's the President?" I said, "Bubba." They said, "Bubba who?" "Aw, c'mon," I said. "You know—*Bubba*." There was a small silence. I had flunked the President question; I wasn't fully oriented. I said, "You didn't give me any meds so far, did you?" Shit, I'd already flunked "Ma'am—can you see us?" I heard the rip of Velcro and felt the C-spine collar come around my neck; next they stood a longboard up behind me, trussed me to it, and took me down, laying me and the board on the floor while they continued to immobilize me with complicated straps. Velcro makes a lot of noise—never noticed that before. "My speech slurred?" I asked anxiously.

"No, ma'am."

"Talk loud?"

"Can we talk louder, you mean? Are you having difficulty hearing?"

"No. Am I?"

"She wantsa know, is *she* talkin' loud—right, ma'am?" This from Officer Bravado, the young one.

"Yeah," I said. I thought, Christ, *what's the matter with me?*

"You talkin' kinda loud, yeah," said the cop.

Their voices faded in and out. I became convinced Brian Linhardt was in the room, although somewhere in my mind—some part of my mind that had remained intact while the rest of my brain was still ricocheting off the insides of my skull—I knew Brian was nowhere near here; Brian was brunching in the Village, brunching when he wasn't punching, punch-drunk—that's it, I was punch-drunk.

"Let me tell you about Lisa Chiu," I heard Brian's voice in my punch-drunk head, mixing with the voices of the EMTs and cops, who now seemed to be murmuring in the distance. "Lisa Chiu's got the situation sussed. She walks in, she takes one look, she figures it out. Like with Dr. Cabot, sized him up like *that.* Cabot's giving his friendly little talk to the new clinical clerks, the usual it's-not-as-bad-as-it-seems, we've-all-gone-through-this, rah-rah-you-can-do-it, and he says what he always says, from *Alice in Wonderland,* 'Here, we are able to believe six impossible things before breakfast.' And Lisa says, 'Is that before or after we see the test results, Dr. Cabot?' So, for a minute, no one says anything. The other medical students are cringing—I mean, that's brave, the new clerk teasing the fucking director of the department—and the preceptor is turning red. We're in OR One, and I'm unpacking boxes of IV tubing and stashing 'em in the cabinet, which is how I hear this. So Cabot finally says, 'Perhaps, Dr. Chiu, you'll tell *me,* after your time here.' And later on I hear Cabot telling Dr. Madding, 'That Chiu woman certainly has a lively mind.' That's Cabot's highest praise, 'Has a lively mind.' "

"Ma'am? Don't go out on us, Ma'am."

"I'm here," I said, speaking into the haze. Or from the haze, hard to tell. "I work at University Hospital. I want to go there."

"Okay, we can do that."

"Dr. Cabot."

"You want to be seen by Dr. Cabot?"

"Please. President Clinton."

"Ma'am?"

"The President is Bill Clinton."

"Atta girl," said Officer Raspy.

"Taking you out, now, ma'am," said the EMT.

"Thank you." I opened my eyes. "Oh, thank God," I breathed.

"Ma'am?"

"I can see you. But why is it so dark in here? Didn't you turn on the lights?"

"It's daylight out," said Officer Raspy, bending over me. I could make out the outline of his head and hat, and tell that he was a big, beefy sort. I saw him as if backlit from a streetlight outside the house.

"What time is it?" I asked.

"Four P.M."

We were rolling toward the front door, then out of the house onto the stoop. The EMTs collapsed the gurney to take me down the front steps. "This is daylight?" I said. "It's dark out."

"Sometimes your sight comes back in stages," one of the EMTs explained. He turned his head, and I made out his profile. He was black or Hispanic. "It may seem dark for a while." They hoisted me into the back of the ambulance.

My head began to clear, and my heart filled suddenly. With love for my rescuers, with relief at being able to see again even if I thought it was night—and with the sickening realization that I had had a brush with death.

CHAPTER
17

THE great thing about working in an emergency room is that, if you need care yourself, they roll out the red carpet. The only problem is that you know all the doctors personally. You know exactly how good their medical skills are—or are not—and exactly what quality of care—or lack thereof—you are likely to receive at their hands.

Despite my supreme relief and thanksgiving for my restored vision—which by now had completely cleared—I was not happy to see Guy Shehadeh's battered face looming over mine as the EMTs catapulted my gurney through the doors of the ambulance bay and into the emergency room. I had completely forgotten his encounter with Brian Linhardt after Lisa Chiu's death, and was startled to see the red and purple contusions under his long-lashed eyes and the strip of surgical tape across the bridge of his swollen nose. My first selfish thought was, Christ, I hope he isn't medicated.

"Ev, what happened?" he asked worriedly, his voice clogged like someone with a severe head cold.

I was trying to remember how well he did with neuro evaluations. Fuck, that patient with bacterial meningitis—Shehadeh thought he was stroking out. "Head bonk," I said tenuously.

"You fell, something hit you—what?"

"I think someone hit me."

"Burglar, looks like," said Officer Bravado. Since I was, in police parlance, an "aided case" as well as a victim of a crime, Officer Bravado—whose name tag read "Hughes"—would stay with me until I was either released or admitted to the hospital. Officer Raspy had disappeared after feeding the dog and locking up Ken Bartlett's apartment.

The gurney came to a halt in the middle of the ER's OR One, under the big domed light. Nurses appeared and counted aloud for the heave-ho, transferring me, backboard and all, to a stretcher. Immediately Shehadeh slipped his hands between the longboard straps and palpated what he could reach of my scalp, while the head EMT gave his report. Whipping out his penlight, Shehadeh checked my pupils, spending a lot of time going back and forth, from one to the other. Frowning, he showed me two fingers and asked, "How many fingers am I holding up?"

"Two," I said.

"Show me your teeth," he ordered, baring his own.

I knew the drill. I bared my teeth. "I went over to a friend's house to feed his dog. Someone came up behind me in the kitchen and must've whacked me with something, I don't remember. Woke up on the floor."

"You lost consciousness."

"Yes."

"How long were you out?"

"Don't know. Guy, I couldn't see when I came to. I mean, not a thing—I was completely blind for about half an hour." I shuddered. "And I wasn't fully oriented. They asked me who the President was, and all I could remember was 'Bubba.' "

This gave him pause, and he stared at me. "Christ," he said. "That would've scared me to death. You see okay now?"

"Yeah, think so. I thought it was night out for a while—I was seeing the way you see when you're in a dark room, just silhouettes—but I think I'm seeing okay now."

"Look at my finger. Follow my finger without moving your head." He sketched a large *H* in the air.

I looked.

"Move your feet?"

I moved.

"Hands?"

Moved those, too.

Shehadeh checked my ears, nose and throat while Margaret O'Hearn, the charge nurse, took my vitals and shooed out of the room the residents and interns crowding in. Word had gone out that a staff member had come in, and everyone wanted to know what had happened and how I was and whether they could help. "Out," said Margaret. She was an old-style, no-nonsense matron, strict as a boot-camp commandant, with graying russet hair and a large bosom that never jiggled—it was rumored that she wore an armor-plated corset. With my head immobilized, all I could see of her out of the corner of my eye was her nursing-school cap. (Margaret was the only nurse I knew who still wore a nursing-school cap, and I had no doubt she would be buried in it.) She threw Officer Hughes out of the room as well, and a few minutes later I heard his booming voice explaining to all the interns and residents how I had gone to feed my friend's dog and surprised a burglar hiding in the bathroom. So much for police confidentiality—I guessed cops liked gossip as much as doctors did.

"What's the last thing you remember?" Guy asked.

"The dog. I remember looking at the dog."

"That's it?"

"That's it."

"So you never saw who hit you."

"Never saw him."

"So how do you know he was in the bathroom?" Guy asked, canting his head toward the door to OR One as Officer Hughes's voice rebounded off the tile walls. Hughes was now explaining how I got hit so hard I couldn't see or remember anything afterward. "That cop has a loud voice, huh?"

"Big mouth, too," I said, wincing. "The door to the bathroom was closed, and the dog was nosing around the door acting worried."

"And when you regained consciousness, you couldn't see anything."

"Right."

"I'm ordering you a CAT scan," said Guy, bellowing for Julio. He started barking orders to Margaret. "CBC, 'lytes, type and cross, hang a bag of D5W—"

For the first time I noticed how anxious he was. Sweat beaded on his swollen upper lip, and his eyes shifted back and forth under their blackened lids.

"And I want Dr. Healy in here," Shehadeh said. *"Right now."*

By the time Mick Healy showed up, Denise Aubuchon was on the scene, having materialized out of nowhere to appoint herself my personal physician and take over my case. When Healy rushed in the door of OR One, Denny was pacing back and forth next to my stretcher, doing her best Sigourney Weaver/Lieutenant Ripley imitation from *Alien* and scaring the interns and residents. She had one med student thoroughly cowed in the corner because he hadn't taken me to X Ray and brought me back again in what Denny considered a timely manner. After snarling at the needle-sticker who hadn't hit my vein on the first try, and having pronounced my spinal films clear, she supervised Guy Shehadeh as he took me out of my C-spine collar and released me from my longboard restraints. Guy was looking more and more like a wounded refugee, his head hunched down onto his shoulders.

"This is your idea of 'on call'?" Aubuchon snapped at Healy, scornfully appraising his sweat-drenched T-shirt and jogging shorts. "Forty-five minutes, and you arrive smelling like a locker room?"

Healy barely acknowledged Denny as he strode to my stretcher, brushed past Shehadeh, and, leaning over, peered into my face. "Christ, darling—what in hell is going on? Was it the same man?" He anxiously fluttered his fingers against my cheek, my throat, his touch that of an uncertain lover rather than an accomplished neurosurgeon. Denny, behind him, blinked, and Guy's head came up. I had already put my own hand up to Healy's sweaty face, without thinking. Too late. By the following morning the entire hospital would know with fixed certainty that Healy and I were an item.

I was becoming used to the fact that Mick's sudden appearances caused me to burst into tears. I could feel my throat clutching and my face crumpling, but being conscious of Denny's hovering, attentive presence, and Guy's rapt stare, I controlled myself. "I didn't see him," I said, my voice wavering. I filled Mick in on the details of my head bonk in Ken's apartment. As I spoke, Mick helped me sit up on the stretcher and put me through the same cursory paces Guy had already put me through—bare your teeth, follow my finger, et cetera—proceeding to a more thorough evaluation of the twelve cranial nerves. Dutifully, I read the newspaper at twelve inches with alternating eyes, identified the smell of alcohol, clenched my teeth while Mick palpated the base of my jaw, shrugged my shoulders, put my finger on my nose, and demonstrated heel-to-shin coordination by walking up and down the way you do when the state trooper wants to see if you're drunk. Meanwhile, Mick metamorphosed into his neurosurgeon self, coolly professional and intellectual—and impervious to Denny's bullying tactics. As she barked questions at him he smiled, as if she were posing particularly astute rhetorical queries for the sheer enlightenment of the intern and medical student, and addressed his answers to them.

Finally, after tapping me with his reflex hammer and sticking me with pins, Mick seemed satisfied and proclaimed me neurologically intact. He straightened up.

Denny, standing next to him, immediately whacked him

across the chest with the envelope containing my X rays. Just in case Mick might have forgotten that *she* was the personal physician, and *he* was the consult, I supposed.

"These the spine films?" Healy asked politely, removing them from their envelope and holding them up to the ceiling light.

"They're clear," said Denny.

"Yes, I see," said Mick. "Thank you." He gave them back. Turning to me, he said, "Seen yourself in a mirror yet, darling?"

I wished he would stop calling me "darling." "Not yet."

"Wee bit of periorbital ecchymosis on the left side, I'm afraid," he said. Great. I had a black eye. "Otherwise, I'm happy to sign you out."

"Mick, what are you talking about?" Denny cut in. "She's got anisocoria a mile wide!" One pupil larger than the other. "Discharge is really unwise without a CAT scan."

Again, Healy sidestepped Aubuchon's provocation. "Anisocoria is a sign of brain herniation that would never be present in a perfectly alert patient," he explained to the medical student and Guy Shehadeh. "She's alert, and the exam is otherwise normal. She's had some trauma to her left orbit and the pupil is constricted on that side, rather than dilated on the opposite side. A CAT scan is not indicated." To me, he said, "Have you someone at home to wake you every couple of hours if you nod off? If not, I can—"

"I'll take her home with me," Denny said firmly.

Amazing, I thought. Denny, who believed Mick to be my lover, was challenging him for the right to take care of me. I began to understand Hal Murkland's rage at her unrelenting possessiveness vis-à-vis their shared patients.

"What about the blindness?" the med student wanted to know. "She was temporarily unconscious, disoriented and blind for thirty minutes—"

"Loss of autoregulation of the cerebral circulation in a contrecoup area," Healy explained. "The occipital lobes, if she is hit from behind, and falls and strikes her forehead."

"Oh," said the student. He looked at me uncertainly.

"Of course," Mick continued, "we have to keep in mind the possibility of what?"

"Delayed intracranial clot?"

"Right. Manifestations?"

"Progressively severe headache, weakness of one side, visual disturbance, undue drowsiness?" The medical student, whom I recognized but whose name I had forgotten, had an irritating, Valley-girl manner of speaking; all his statements were punctuated with question marks. Denny Aubuchon began to grind her teeth, and Guy Shehadeh's eyes glazed over.

"And you tell whom?" Healy asked.

"The family members?"

"And what's the most important consideration?"

"General condition of the patient? And changes—"

"Christ," muttered Denny. "I called you in for a consult, not teaching rounds."

A small smile briefly played about the corners of Mick's mouth, then was gone. I realized he was baiting her.

"That's enough," I said. I slid down from the stretcher, where I'd been sitting to have my knees and elbows whacked. I was still dressed in my jeans and madras camp shirt, having refused to disrobe. (Take off my clothes in front of Guy Shehadeh and Mick Healy? You gotta be kidding.) "I'm all right. I'm going home," I announced.

"You're going home to my apartment," said Denny. "I'm putting you on neuro watch."

"You really shouldn't be alone, Ev," Mick said. "Why don't I come sit with you?"

"You're on call," said Denny to Mick. "I'll take her home with me."

"I'm not on call," Healy shot back. "I came in to see Ev. As a professional courtesy."

"What about you?" I asked Guy. "Going, once, twice . . ."

"Oh, yeah," said Denny. "*Professional*. Uh-huh." She slid her arm through mine companionably. But her grip was like iron. "If we get in touch with *Phil*"—she glanced pointedly at Mick, who flushed—"and he's able to come back and stay with you, I'll let you go. Otherwise, you're on my couch until six A.M. tomorrow morning."

CHAPTER
18

"HOW long has this been going on?" Denny demanded, throwing open the fire door to the tunnel to the doctors' residence: *Bam*!

The banging of the door against the wall reverberated in my head, pulsing behind my eye sockets. I winced. Denny was still in her Lieutenant Ripley mode, eyes flashing and nostrils flaring, her expression aggressive and bullish.

"How long has what been going on?" I asked distractedly. The last time Denny and I had been together in the tunnel we'd been propelling Lisa Chiu's stretcher pell-mell to the ER. In my mind I saw Lisa's head thrown back, her mouth guppylike around the plastic airway, Brian Linhardt's fine, strong hands pumping the ambubag to ventilate her.

Strange how, when I thought of Lisa, I saw him.

"This *harassment*." Denny spat the word.

I blinked. "What harassment? What are you talking about?"

"I mean Mick Healy, with his hands all over you!"

Oy vay. Air-raid sirens began going off in my internal ears, *Androphobia Alert, wa-WOO, wa-WOO.*

Not the anti-men diatribe again.

"Denny," I said, as mildly as possible, "that wasn't harassment."

She snorted. "He was unprofessional."

"You were both unprofessional, standing there in the middle of the ER arguing over who was going to go home with me and take care of me."

"Mick comes home with you, he'll take advantage, not care—"

"That's not true," I said. "He's completely trustworthy."

"—unless you're already sleeping with him. Are you?" she demanded.

I had half a mind to tell her yes; Denny would believe what she wanted to believe, regardless of what I said. My mind flashed to Hal Murkland, who had confessed to her that he was sleeping with Lisa Chiu rather than argue with her. "No," I sighed. "It's tempting—I mean, I have those feelings for him, and he's made all the . . . ah . . . appropriate advances—"

"Oh, spare me," said Denny, rolling her eyes. "Phil's not enough, you have to have two of them?"

Two of them. She made them sound like house pets. Perhaps that really was the way she thought of straight men; perhaps only gay men were worthy of motherly care. I thought of how much love and attentiveness she had lavished on her patients the day before, calling around to make sure everyone understood that the FBI had closed their pharmacy because of a Medicaid scam. Murkland's analysis of Denny was beginning to sound downright watertight to me—that because she had lost her son, she had built an entire practice out of taking care of gay men who would die, allowing her to re-experience the loss of her son.

Well, I felt sorry for her, but I did not have the energy, bodily or mentally, to indulge one of Denny's harangues. Not tonight. Tonight I needed to concentrate all my energies on myself, on resting up, on recuperating from my injuries. My head hurt and my thoughts were fuzzy.

To say nothing of the fact that someone had tried to kill me.

Or, it dawned on me, had tried *not* to kill me.

What if he had knocked me out so I wouldn't see him? Like the guy who had knocked me down on the street, and pulled my shirt over my head?

But we're talking about a murderer here. Someone who killed Theresa Kahr and two other women—and possibly Lisa Chiu—or, if Lisa *wasn't* killed by Babydoll, but was killed by someone she knew and I knew—

The gears of my befuddled brain groaned as I labored up the incline of these implications, trying to put it all together. Why would someone capable of killing Lisa Chiu have reservations about killing *me*? Why knock me down on the street and pull my shirt over my head, why head-bonk me in Kennedy Bartlett's apartment?

"Ev, I'm sorry," Denny said, sliding her arm through mine. "It's none of my business who you sleep with. Mick's a very appealing guy, talented, ambitious, on the fast track—"

Mick asking, *Was it the same man?*

Of course, that was the question in my own mind. But everyone else thought I'd been hit by a burglar. Why would Mick jump to the conclusion that the guy who knocked me down on the street was somehow lurking in wait for me in Kennedy Bartlett's apartment?

"—and he's clearly devoted to you. I can see it in the way he looks at you. Really. I'm sorry I said those mean things about him. I was overreacting. You know me and men." She laughed self-consciously. "You'd think I'd feel a little more in common with him since a drunk driver killed his sons and a drunk driver killed my son . . ."

The man who knocked me down and pulled my shirt over my head—and the man in the Superman shirt scoping me out as I walked Kennedy Bartlett's dog—had that been Mick after all? He had certainly reacted to my asking him about the Superman shirt.

An assistant chief of neurosurgery would know everything

there was to know about the art of landing the well-placed blow—had that been Mick lying in wait for me in Ken's bathroom?

Denny and I reached the end of the tunnel, and she opened the fire door to the doctors' residence. "And, um, it's hard for me," she said. "You know I don't deal with personal loss very well . . . because of Gray and all . . . and what with Lisa, the thought of losing you, too . . ." She trailed off.

I turned my head to look at her, and the tunnel dipped to the left, like a plane coming in for a landing. I grabbed her arm to keep from falling. Immediately her free hand was in my armpit, holding me up as she peered into my face. Her big brown eyes were wide with concern. "What?" she said. "You dizzy?"

"No." I refrained from shaking my head. "Maybe a little traumatic labyrinthitis." What I meant was, the balance mechanism in my ears might be slightly out of whack from the head bonk. *Get a grip, Sutcliffe—why would Mick Healy kill Lisa Chiu?*

"Feel nauseous?"

"No."

"Want a wheelchair?"

"No, let's go on. Den, listen—did you ever see Mick and Lisa together? I mean, not in the ER—"

"Mick was the last person I saw her alive with," Denny said.

I scrutinized the floor, then the cinder-block walls of the basement corridor of the doctors' residence. If I concentrated, my world might not turn upside down. Hanging on to Denny's arm, and with her other arm around my shoulders to support me, I took a tentative step forward. When I tried to put my foot down, the floor dropped six inches out from under it, then undulated up again. *"Shit,"* I said. I took another step and the floor held firm. All right, that was progress. I advanced a third step; again the floor didn't move. One step at a time. "When was this?" I asked.

"On my way to Hal and Carol's for dinner," Denny said. "The evening before Lisa was killed. You sure you don't want a wheelchair?"

"I'm fine." I proceeded down the corridor at a ponderous

pace, like a ship of state. The floor remained its solid self. "Where were they together?"

"Right here. On their way to the tunnel."

"And?"

"Walking together toward the hospital," Denny said. We had reached the elevator banks and she pressed the button for the elevator.

I leaned against the wall and closed my eyes. The cinder blocks were cool to the touch. I had the impression Denny was talking louder, slower, and more concretely than usual, but my mental faculties seemed in such an altered state, I couldn't tell whether she was actually talking that way, or whether my head-bonked brain merely perceived it as such. A feeling of acute disorientation swept over me. "Just hang in a few minutes more," Denny said. I felt her palm against my cheek and on my neck, her mother's soft, tender touch, fleeting yet poignantly, comfortingly present. I was transported vividly to the sickbed of childhood, with Mom bending over me. I opened my eyes.

"Elevator's here," she said. We got in, and Denny punched the button for the tenth floor.

"You were talking about Mick and Lisa," I reminded her, marveling at the sense of comfort I had imbibed from her. No wonder her patients called her Doctor Mom.

"They got out of the elevator having a *very* serious conversation," Denny said.

"About what?"

"I don't know. They were talking quietly, and they shut up when they saw me. But he was as white as a sheet. Whatever it was, it was very bad news."

"How about Lisa? How did she look?"

"Grim," said Denny. "Listen, I was serious earlier about your staying with me. I really do think you should be on neuro watch. We can send out for some food and have a quiet evening together, and you can rest." She touched my hand, smiled.

I almost said, Thanks, Mom. Instead, I smiled back and nodded. "I'd like that. So you think Lisa was telling Mick something that upset him?"

"I don't know what to make of it," said Denny. "It could have been a conversation of a personal nature, or it could have been about a patient—Theresa Kahr had died, after all. But it stuck in my mind, because that was the last time I saw her alive, and you always think back on that. Like Gray trying to climb out the truck window after his father put him in and shut the door. That was the last I saw of him. It's stuck in my mind right behind my eyeballs forever."

I didn't like the analogy; Gray's father had killed *him*. "You're sure you didn't hear anything they said."

"Zip," said Denny. The elevator doors opened on the tenth floor and we got out. "All I can tell you is, Mick was very, very upset."

The unspoken hung for a moment in the air between us, scented with Denny's expensive French cologne:

And Lisa Chiu was still very, very alive.

Denise Aubuchon's apartment was cool and inviting. A haven of Old World ambience and comfort, it nestled like a secret garden within the overworked and underpaid realm of the New-York-City–resident rat race. As we stepped into her foyer—lined floor-to-ceiling with built-in directoire bookcases, and softly illuminated by recessed lighting—I reflected as I always did on the great deal of money and effort Denny had invested in decorating her doctors'-residence apartment, especially compared to the comparatively little I had invested in decorating mine. While I still sat on the ancient sofa that had graced my grandmother Bubbeh Hazel's Newark apartment, and walked on her threadbare oriental rug of dubious origin, Denny perched on a kilim-upholstered chair from Somebody Smith in SoHo, and sank her toes into luxurious wall-to-wall carpeting. While I made do with mismatched end tables from Gimbel's fire sale when the store went out of business, and a coffee table that had had a previous incarnation as a battered plywood toy box, Denny surrounded herself with gorgeous one-of-a-kind pieces picked up on her weekend jaunts to New England antiques fairs. I couldn't have a cleaning lady come in—even if I could afford one, which I couldn't with my medical school loans—because my apartment was so cluttered, a cleaning lady would have to dig a path before she could clean; Denny had a twice-a-week housekeeper who did everything a housewife might have done (cleaning, laundry, grocery shopping and cooking, dry-cleaner runs) *and* a once-a-week plant person who cared for her big potted palms and ficus trees.

Then again, Denny probably needed a nice home more than I did, to make up for the brutality of the home she'd grown up in. And a nice housekeeper to cook her meals, to make up for all the meals her mother had never cooked her because she had passed out in an alcoholic stupor on the kitchen floor. And maybe she liked the plants because they were alive and they flourished in ways Denny had not felt alive and had not flourished as a young girl.

Denny plumped up a couple of Victorian-era velvet pillows on the couch and pointed in a firm but motherly fashion, and I lay down as commanded. The pillows were filled with goose down. So was the couch.

"Excuse me while I swoon," I said.

"Go right ahead." She set a tile-topped occasional table from Spain next to the couch. "What can I get you? An Evian water? Iced tea? Fruit juice? Want me to run down to your apartment and get you one of your favorite teas?"

"Whatever you have will be fine," I said. I wondered if stimulants would help unfog my head. Of course not; silly thought. I wondered, even as I luxuriated against the goose-down-filled pillows, how long I would have to submit to Denny's motherly doctorly fervor before I could rise, stretch, and announce that I thought I'd just go downstairs now to my own apartment. If Denny insisted on neuro watch, I could leave instructions with the ER charge nurse to call me every two hours to make sure I wasn't slipping into a coma. I didn't need Denny to wake me—and herself—at two-hourly intervals throughout the night. Besides, I needed to call Phil. And Brian Linhardt. And Guy Shehadeh, for that matter—after all, Guy was the one who'd beaten his head on the floor of the ER, weeping and wailing, "I killed her, I killed her." And Jesus, I'd never called my boss, Chris Cabot. Chris had asked that I talk to him before Monday morning, and here it was already Saturday evening—

"Here," said Denny. She handed me her telephone, looping the wire over the arm of the couch, and set a glass down on the Spanish tiled table. "I made you some of that Casablanca tea you got me the last time you went to your tea store, and poured it over ice. You probably need to rehydrate a little."

"Den, you're a gem," I said.

Chris Cabot wasn't home; we were playing telephone tag. Phil had taken his nieces out for ice cream; his father, alternately roaringly indignant at what had happened to me and gruffly sympathetic, assured me he would have Phil call me—as soon as he returned. Then he said, "Sweetheart, you need any muscle or protection, you let me know—you understand me?" I thanked him and said I'd be sure to call him if I needed help. Just what I needed in life, a potential father-in-law who was *connected*. Either that, or Mick's Dad, my only other possible candidate for the position, the police captain who had been stripped of his command. Oy vay. And people wanted to know why I hesitated to marry.

I phoned the ER and asked for Guy Shehadeh; he came on the line breathless and anxious, probably sure I was about to die from some cerebral event he would be blamed for. "What?" he cried. *"What?"*

"I need to talk to you," I said. "About Lisa Chiu. Can you meet me for breakfast at Sami's tomorrow?"

"Oh my God, are they *sanctioning* us?" Shehadeh yelped. "Is this an incident death? Is this going to go in my tracking-and-trending file?"

I let him think that was what I wanted to discuss. "Calm down.

Chris Cabot doesn't think there will be a problem."

"Me neither," said Denny, returning from the bedroom. She had changed out of her silk blouse and linen trousers into a pair of madras walking shorts and a sea-green Lacoste shirt; she looked cool and country-club. She plopped down onto her kilim-covered club chair and crossed her legs. Her toenails were red. "Tell Shehadeh to stop shitting his pants. There was an adverse patient outcome, but the standard of care was met. Besides, if anybody's ass is in a sling, it's mine."

I said, "I'm with Denny Aubuchon and she says not to worry. Meet me at nine, okay?"

There was a short silence, then a wary "If there's no need to worry, why do you want to see me? No, listen. I'm going away as soon as I get out of here tonight. I'll be back Monday morning. I'll meet you before I go over to the hospital." He hung up the phone before I could protest.

"Very clever," said Denny. "Sherlock Ev, I presume?"

"It's eating me up," I admitted.

"Mm," she said. "You could let it eat up the cops."

"Isn't it eating *you* up?" I asked.

"Yes, of course. But I know how to delegate, and to whom. We have very smart cops in this city. Besides which, it could be dangerous for you. Who hit you today?"

"I knew you were leading up to that," I said.

"Hey. Every Sherlock needs a Watson."

"Did Sherlock ever ask Watson any questions?"

Denny smiled. "I am at your service." She reached for her drink, bourbon on the rocks with a sprig of mint, in a cut-crystal glass.

"What about these medical records Hal was reviewing with Lisa the night she was killed?" I asked. "You know anything about that?"

There was a long pause during which Denny contemplated her drink without drinking it, opened her mouth a couple of times without speaking, and shifted in her chair as if about to get up, but didn't rise.

Finally she leaned forward, her elbows on her knees, her crystal glass of bourbon cradled in both hands. Her big brown eyes were steady and somber, and a little sad.

"I wouldn't say the word was *reviewing*, exactly," Denny sighed. "For a while now I've suspected Hal of defrauding Medicaid. I hired Lisa to catch him at it, and maybe she did."

CHAPTER
19

"*HAL?* Defraud *Medicaid*?" I cried. "But he's a Republican!"

"He has debts," Denny said flatly. "He was up to the ceiling of his Mastercard and Visa, and Carol charged her Saks and Bloomingdale's cards to the max. Twice now I've had to go into his office to get him to pipe down—he's in there shouting at Carol on the phone loudly enough to be heard in the waiting room."

"But he's such a Goody Two-shoes," I protested.

"Not Goody Two-shoes enough. What's he going to do? He's got a wife, he cuts up all her credit cards with scissors, and she just calls up mail-order catalogs and charges everything to his American Express card. He's practically bankrupt. I advised him to get one of those loans to consolidate his debts and cancel all his cards—which he finally did—but what he really needs is a divorce. That woman's taking him for all he's worth."

"I didn't realize things were that bad," I said.

"They're bad."

"I thought he inherited a pile from his aunt who died last year."

Denny shook her head. "Hal told me she left most of her money to charities. He received a small token, and his cousin got the rest."

"So you think he's defrauding Medicaid to pay his debts? I dunno, Denny, I still find it pretty hard to believe . . . Do you have any concrete evidence?"

"Uh-uh," she said. "Just a suspicion. Josh Waterman picked up on it, actually. You know I hired Josh and Lisa last summer to help us go on-line. Then Lisa went back to school in the fall, and Josh continued entering the backlog while she was away. So Josh comes to me one day about a month ago and says, 'Dr. Aubuchon, there are some discrepancies here, I think you should have a look.' What it looked like was double-billing. The appointment book and the billing records didn't tally. One appointment, but billing for two, that kind of thing."

"But you know Hal's such a sloppy record keeper," I said. "Who keeps the appointment book?"

"Josh. That's the point. Hal wasn't keeping any of these records, he was handing the details to Josh. Bill Medicaid for such-and-such, order these tests for this patient, enter those charges in that patient's chart, et cetera et cetera. Last summer, when Josh first started, he just did as he was told. But he's a smart cookie and a fast learner, and now that he knows all the ropes, he can identify a discrepancy when he sees one."

"So you hired Lisa Chiu again this summer, to investigate?"

Denny nodded and knocked back some of her drink. "I hired Lisa to investigate. Josh isn't well, as you know, and he has all the work he can handle as it is. So I hired Lisa. She had troubles of her own, and needed money for her med-school tuition in the fall. Her father had taken a big hit in the real estate market and told her he couldn't pay her tuition this year. So she was scrambling. I said I'd pay her under the table, cash, and I'd pay her the going rate for a computer consultant. But that she wasn't to tell Hal what she was doing. Then I told Hal I'd hired Lisa to help Josh because Josh's health was deteriorating. As far as I know, Hal believed me."

"Well, did Lisa find out anything?"

"I don't know. I asked her to review Hal's charts for the last calendar year, to keep tabs on her hours, and to give me a bill and a written report at the end of the summer. I bought her computer software—a Fastback program—so she could download all the office records onto disc and work on her own computer at home. That way, the time she spent in the office she would actually be doing Josh's work and helping Josh, as I'd told Hal."

A feeling of heaviness began to drift over me, like a low-lying fog. I had no trouble assimilating the idea of Lisa Chiu as a white-collar crime investigator; it was the image of Hal Murkland as a white-collar criminal, an embezzler of sorts, that I was having trouble with. Maybe I was confused, but somewhere in the back of my mind I remembered Hal saying it was Denny who thought the government should pay for everything—

The next thing I knew, someone was shaking me. "What?" I cried, bolting upright in a darkened room.

"Shh," said Denny, cradling me in her arms. She was sitting on the couch next to me. "Know where you are?"

"Your apartment," I said, immediately calmed. Again I marveled at her sure motherly touch, which transported me to the safety and security of childhood as reliably as the aroma of madeleines transported Proust. "What time is it?"

"Ten. Cover your eyes." She switched on the lamp. "What day is it?"

"Jesus Christ, is the rest of my life going to be one endless fucking neuro evaluation? Saturday." She had covered me with a soft cotton throw. I threw it aside. "The President is Bubba Clinton."

"You're doing fine so far," Denny said. "Just talk to me a little." All business now, her doctor persona. Every doctor is a two-faced Janus; the off-duty self and the doctorly *persona*. "Then

I'll let you go back to sleep. Count backward from one hundred by sevens.''

I sighed. "Ninety-three, eighty-six, um, let's see, six take away seven . . . seventy-nine, seventy-two—has Phil called?"

"Yes, he'll be on the ten-oh-three from Huntington. So he should be here by eleven-thirty."

"I have to feed the dog," I said. "Where are my shoes?"

"The dog's right here," Denny said. "While you were asleep I went and got him."

As if on cue, Maxie appeared and nosed me with his moist snout. He seemed worried and guilty, twitching his expressive brows as he looked from me to Denny and back again. I scratched his head. "Hey," I said. "Not your fault I got head-bonked. You tried to tell me someone was in the bathroom, and I didn't listen."

"I think he's disappointed Ken's not here," Denny said. "I have half a mind to smuggle him into the hospital for a visit. Listen, ah . . . I'm afraid Ken's apartment has been burgled. His medications are gone from the fridge, and his toe shoes, the ones he wore when he danced with Nureyev. There may be other items missing as well."

"Aw, shit," I said. "I'll go down there tomorrow and have a look. Did you tell the police?"

"No, I thought you should have a look, see what's missing. Listen, if you're going there, take someone with you," she warned. "Brian Linhardt, maybe. He probably even has a gun."

"Mm," I said. My mind had jumped. "Den, do you think Lisa would confront Hal with what she knew? I mean, if she found out he'd been defrauding Medicaid in a really big way—"

"You mean, do I think she threatened him and he killed her?" She chortled. "No way. Hal's not that desperate. Besides, he was in love with her."

"Yeah, I guess." Something was jogging my memory, but I couldn't put my finger on what. Brian Linhardt again. The guy was becoming a refrain in my unconscious. "Listen, I think I need to go downstairs to my own apartment. Sleep in my own bed. Phil will be here soon."

"Well . . ." said Denny dubiously.

But in the end, she gave in. Packing several frozen dinners prepared by her housekeeper into a boat tote and bringing the dog, Denny came downstairs with me and I gave her my spare keys, just in case Phil failed to show up—Denny always had a contingency plan, no matter what. She insisted on checking my apartment for intruders, opening all the closet doors, making sure no one was in the kitchen or bathroom. Maxie, instinctively recognizing a search-and-seizure mission, chipped in and smelled everything, signaling the all-clear by turning around a few times in a circle, lying down in the middle of my living-room rug, and yawning. Denny insisted that we do follow-my-finger, bare-your-teeth, et cetera. She pronounced me neurologically intact, at least for the moment and, stuffing my freezer with the frozen dinners, left strict orders for Phil to call her as soon as he arrived.

"Always talk to the relative, not the head-bonkee." I grinned.

"Damn straight," she said.

"You calm now?" I asked, as we stood on my threshold saying good night.

"I am never calm, I am ever vigilant," she joked. But then she threw her arms around me, crushing me against her in an intense bear hug. "I lost Lisa, Josh Waterman's getting sicker—you think I'm going to be calm about almost losing you?"

Then she was gone.

I waited until I heard the faint closing of the elevator door.

Checking my watch—it was now ten-thirty—I shut my front door, wrote a quick note to Phil, patted the dog, grabbed my foul-weather jacket, made my way into my bedroom in the dark, opened the window onto the fire escape, and climbed out into the cool night air.

I had a lot to do.

*　　*　　*

I went up the fire escape in a half-crouch, mindful of my footing on the wet metal treads. If I'd had half a wit Friday night, I would have asked Tony Firenze to let me keep Lisa's apartment keys.

The rain was coming down in torrents, whipped by a strong wind, pinging off the air conditioners that whirred perpetually in the urban nightscape. People in my building ran their air conditioners all summer long, regardless of the weather, to drown out the racket of our exuberant neighbors to the north—from across the yard blared the sound track of a small Latino village compressed into a moldering red brick apartment building: salsa music, a hundred TVs, clanking dishes, electric fans, extended families yelling at one another over the dinner table, dogs barking, lovers carousing. *They* all had their windows wide open despite the downpour. Ah, New Yawk, New Yawk—its a helluva town.

No wonder no one had seen or heard Dr. Harold Murkland—drunk, clumsy, lumbering, and bleeding—negotiate his way down the fire escape the night Lisa Chiu was stabbed to death in the comparative quiet of her doctors' residence apartment.

And no wonder no one saw or heard me now.

I pulled my foul-weather jacket up around my neck. On the ninth floor I carefully made my way around Carol Murkland's clutter of state-of-the-art grilling equipment, wondering if Hal was home now, wondering how Carol was taking Hal's grief over Lisa's death. The lights were on but the shades were down. I passed the tenth and eleventh floors; both apartments were dark, and it occurred to me that they were possibly unoccupied. Interns and residents came and went from year to year, and we'd just had the annual first-of-July transition. The doctors' residence was really nothing more than an overrated college dorm, and I didn't always know all my neighbors.

On the twelfth floor, where I had to step over Rita Firenze's tomato plants and thrash my way through the foliage of several large potted trees—which I guessed Rita had put outside for the benefit of a drenching summer shower—I suddenly lost my footing. Scrambling not to pitch over the railing, I crashed against the window of Lisa's apartment and fell painfully to my knees, crying out. The altimeter in my ears swooped and dived; I squeezed my eyes shut until it leveled out.

Christ. I hoped I didn't have post-concussive syndrome or some damn thing. That son of a bitch . . .

Well, I thought, testing my equilibrium and finding myself able to stand without teetering, *nobody* knows where I am now, so I should be safe from attack *here*.

From my mouth to God's ears. Easing the window up, I slid into the dark apartment, listening to my heart resound like a Chinese gong, hearing my breath whistle down my throat like a hurricane down a chimney. At least the smell wasn't so bad as it had been the day before.

Once inside, I waited, dripping in the darkness, for my eyes to adjust. The floor plan was exactly the same as my own apartment, and I tried to convince myself that feeling my way from the bedroom into the hall, without turning on the lights, and from there into the study, would be a piece of cake. Yeah, right, Sutcliffe. *But screw your courage to the sticking-place.* I put out a hand, took a tentative step toward the dresser and—

I heard movement.

Somebody threw something at me, hitting me against my legs, something large and—

Furry.

"Fat Face!" I said softly, bending down to the large mass of wriggling, purring fur on my foot. "God! You almost gave me a heart attack! Where did you come from?"

The cat stood up on his hind legs, stretching his front paws almost to the tops of my thighs, happily sinking his claws into my legs. Painstakingly, I disconnected him, crossed the room and shut the window so he wouldn't escape again. If, indeed, he'd escaped in the first place. I had no idea whether he'd been in the apartment the entire time, hiding from all the people traipsing in and out, or whether he'd been out visiting friends with open windows up and down the fire escape. If he'd been in the apartment all this time, he was probably famished. I should feed him.

The need for the cat to be fed made my exaggerated sense of stealth and subterfuge seem foolish. It was hard to play James Bond when such a warm, fuzzy being was so delighted to see me. I gave up and switched on the bedside lamp.

The room was as I had last seen it, the night before with Phil and Tony Firenze. Queen-sized futon bed, two simple night tables, a dresser. Clothes, books, papers, and medical journals strewn about the room. I took off my wet jacket and hung it over the back of a chair, bent to pick up the little crocheted pillow that said, "Is There a Doctor in the House?!?" I placed it gently on the bed and headed for the kitchen. There I found a small can of something called Ocean Fish Feast, which delighted Fat Face no end. "If you're still hungry after this, I'll find something else for you," I told him as he dived in, purring louder than the hospital's emergency generator. Jeff Cantor hadn't named him Fat Face for nothing.

I went back to the bedroom and wondered where to start.

And what, precisely, I was looking for. If Lisa knew who the Babydoll Killer was, and was killed because she knew, then I was looking for information.

If Hal Murkland killed Lisa because she knew he was scamming Medicaid—a possibility I found highly unlikely, but which I was forced to consider—again, I was looking for information.

If Mick Healy killed Lisa—but why would Mick kill Lisa? Because she told him something upsetting in the elevator? Maybe; if the information she conveyed was enough to make him turn as white as a sheet, as Denny described it, perhaps that information was worth killing for, if Mick didn't want anyone else to know whatever it was that Lisa knew.

Lisa was systematic, I thought. If she had information to hide, she'd hide it somewhere logical.

But where was logical?

By now my gonging heart and hurricane breathing had decreased to a comfortable level of anxiety—perhaps that of two cups of espresso, no milk.

I went into the study and turned on the light.

*　　*　　*

From the threshold, I surveyed the mess in the room. An aura of malevolent force still hung in the air.

A small rectangular area along one end of the room had been cleared, however, and papers and books were stacked neatly into piles along the bottom of the bookcase. Funny that I hadn't noticed that the night before. Did the cops start one of their systematic searches, breaking off after they'd found something important?

Lisa, I thought, if you want me to find whatever it is, you gotta help me.

I recalled Brian Linhardt's remark again, as I had while the paramedics prepared me for transport to the hospital: "Let me tell you about Lisa Chiu. Lisa's got the situation sussed. She walks in, she takes one look, she figures it out."

I don't think so, Brian, I argued halfheartedly in my head. She was bold and self-confident, and not intimidated by anything— but so what? That's what got her into trouble.

That's what got her killed.

No, wait, maybe there's a message here . . . I walk in, I take one look, I figure it out . . .

My eye fell on a book on the shelves, *The Compleat Yoga Reader*. My heart bled a little; Lisa was always urging me to take up yoga and jogging. Even with her busy schedule, she managed to go to yoga class at a nearby students' gym two and sometimes three times a week. If jogging didn't work out, maybe I should take up yoga. As I pulled the book down, an envelope fell out of the bookcase where the yoga book had been, and tumbled to the floor. I bent to retrieve it, my heart rate escalating. Photos.

I slid the small stack out of the envelope. On top, a slightly out-of-focus picture of a man looking over his shoulder at the camera, grinning sardonically. Behind him, a blur of faces in a crowd, the ubiquitous "Your Neighbor Kills Preborns" signs carried by Lisa's "They," the anti-abortion protesters.

The man was Brian Linhardt.

I sank heavily into Lisa's utilitarian desk chair and stared at the photo, sorting through the implications. Why had Lisa snapped this picture? To portray Brian Linhardt in his role as abortion protester? For the Goon File down at Westside Women's, to add Linhardt's picture to those of others who had harassed Lisa in her capacity as abortion-provider-to-be?

The cat had returned and jumped into my lap as soon as I sat; I put him down again. He jumped right back up. I let him stay. I flipped to the next photo: Lisa, tanned and beautiful, in a simple black cocktail dress, drink in hand. Grinning at the camera, she stood behind a table full of liquor bottles and platters of food. A party somewhere. Lisa was standing between two men, her arms slung around their shoulders. Mick Healy and a slightly younger, more robust version of himself: one of Mick's brothers. Probably Jimmy, the Mafia maven, or, as Mick called him, the "silk-socks expert." Or maybe it was Matthew, from the Dirty Thirty—no, wait, was that Simon who worked out of the Dirty Thirty? The only one I really had straight was Donal, whose avulsed leg I had examined in the ER. Then again, Donal made a pretty penetrating impression, even without the damning *Daily News* headlines . . .

In any case, Lisa must have returned to the city after Bobbi and James Strathearn's wedding in time to make Mick's house-warming party, the one Phil and I had missed because we'd lingered at the reception.

Huh.

I flipped through more pictures from the party. Guy Shehadeh, grinning soppily over his wineglass, as he and several other interns and medical students raised their glasses in a toast. All the Healys together: Mick, Simon, Matthew, Jimmy, and Donal, their sister Bernadette, and their father, the cops holding up their badges to the camera, Mick waving his stethoscope. Everyone laughing, having a good time. The Healys in different combinations: Mick with his sister; Mick with his father.

Finally I flipped to the last picture: an extremely fuzzy, out-of-focus photo of Mick walking on the park side of Riverside

Drive, wearing jogging clothes, his head down, wiping his neck with a small towel.

I looked closer.

There was a red-and-yellow insignia on the front of his blue T-shirt.

Superman.

So Mick *did* own a Superman shirt, and that *had* been Mick, following me yesterday to Kennedy Bartlett's and downtown to SoHo . . .

I flipped back to the photo of Brian Linhardt. Brian was certainly capable of killing people. We all suspected him of CIA activity during his Ranger days in Latin America.

Then it struck me, a thunderbolt from Thor: *Lisa had selected these photos to take to show to Theresa Kahr.*

Is this the man who's been coming in the shop, asking you out for a date? No? How about this man, the one in the Superman shirt?

My mind skidded off in five or six different directions at once and I stood up abruptly, dumping the cat to the floor. My head reacted to the too-sudden movement and I suffered the sensation of a plane banking and coming in for a landing, as I had in the tunnel earlier with Denny. Staggering back, I put my hand on the computer to steady myself.

It was warm.

Checking, I saw that the screen was dark, but the hard drive was on. I felt the flesh draw taut along the edges of my scalp.

When I turned around, Brian Linhardt was standing on the threshold of the room.

CHAPTER
20

HE stood with his hands on his hips, wearing combat fatigue pants with many pockets and a tan tank top with none. I noticed a number of things about him that I had never noticed before. His wide, sensuous mouth. His utter stillness when he willed it. The suggestion of strength and threat. A scar on the back of his left wrist standing out white against his tan—an old stab wound? Across my inner eye flashed a clip from an old movie: stealth commandos moving through a jungle backlit by the moon; their faces blackened, leaves woven through the webbing of their helmets, making them barely distinguishable from the foliage.

Doesn't it bother you? I heard Guy Shehadeh's voice inside my head, insistent, whispering. *God only knows what he did down in Central America with the Rangers, all that clandestine stuff he can't talk about. He was probably down there shooting people for the CIA.*

My eyes went to the belt of Linhardt's fatigues. Was he armed? Did he have a knife?

You think I'm gonna kill one of the patients, you should worry about him killing one of the staff.

"Find anything interesting?" he asked.

I couldn't read his face. Was he laughing at me? About to kill me? Quickly, I considered my options. He stood on the threshold, baring exit. The window in this room did not open onto the fire escape, although, with care, nerves of steel and the balancing skills of a gymnast, it was not unreachable. I had long legs; I could manage it. But I needed to open the window. Could I distract him? Knock him out? With what?

A lightbulb-going-on expression suddenly spread across Linhardt's face and widened into a grin. He burst out laughing. "Christ, Ev—you really think I killed her, don't you?" he chortled, shaking his head. He raised his arms and hands, as if under arrest. "You ninny. Come over here and pat me down if you like, I'm not carrying."

"No," I said. "Show me what's in your pockets."

"Not sure of yourself in the frisking department, huh?" Snapping open the metal clasp of his canvas belt and unzipping his fly, he dropped his drawers and stepped out of them, using one foot to toss them across the room to me. Then he whipped off his tank top and tossed that over as well. He stood before me in all his glory, wearing nothing but a pair of baby-blue French briefs and his old Army dog tags, flaunting his flat stomach and hardened, muscular arms and legs. Grinning, he clasped his hands on top of his head and began to mime body-builder poses, flexing this, stretching that. "Whaddya think?"

I considered him more dangerous than ever; I had no doubt he could kill me with his bare hands.

"Lie facedown on the floor and put your hands on your head," I said.

"Oo, been watchin' *cop* movies," he taunted. But he did as I asked.

Keeping my eyes on him, I retrieved his pants from the floor and began to search the many pockets. Keys, wallet, Swiss Army knife, cigarettes, matches, EMT scissors, individual packages of scalpel blades, stainless-steel scalpel handle, hemostat, wire cutters, pliers, two wrenches, a small flashlight, tweezers, and an optician's repair kit.

"I hope you realize I'm humoring you," Linhardt said.

I didn't answer. The wallet was alligator, well-palmed to a fine patina. I looked inside and found the usual: Visa card, condoms, driver's license, bank ATM, Blockbuster video. I also found the unusual, or at least the unexpected: a strip of photos from one of those take-your-own-picture booths.

Brian Linhardt and Lisa Chiu. One photo serious, one laughing, one smirking.

And one kissing.

"She sleeping with Shehadeh, too, or just you?" I asked.

He snorted. "Use your head, Ev—Shehadeh has zip between the ears and no personality anyone's aware of. What's he got that a smart girl like Lisa'd want? And she was working three jobs, seven days a week. Think she had time for more than one guy?"

"I'm glad to hear that your liaison with her was of such an affectionate nature," I said dryly.

"Whaddya want me to tell you—that I was in love with her? I wasn't. I liked her a lot. *A lot*. She was smart, she was brave, she had guts. Not that I agreed with her causes. But she had guts."

I looked again at the picture of Brian and Lisa kissing. Actually, the camera caught them just as they were about to kiss. Their expressions were playful and mutually seductive. Even staring at the evidence, however, I had a hard time imagining them together. Lisa? With a right-to-lifer?

Brian took his hands off his head and propped himself up on his elbows. "So my credentials check out, or what?"

"Where's your bag?"

"I came without it."

I hesitated. I had never known Brian to go anywhere without that bag, but I couldn't expect him to lie passively on the floor while I made a tour of the apartment looking for it. Besides, I was running out of bluster. Against my better intuition, I tossed him his pants back. I pocketed the scalpel blades and the Swiss Army knife. "What are you doing here, Brian?"

"Same as you, Ev. Looking for clues who killed her." In a fluid motion, he pushed up and leaped to his feet, snatching his pants and stepping into them. He zipped up, put his arms through his shirt, and pulled it over his head. "So who gave you the shiner? That's not from this morning, is it?"

This morning was so long ago, I blanked for a minute. Oh, right—the melee with the abortion protesters. "No," I said. "It's a long story. I don't want to get into that right now."

He fumbled for his cigarettes, stuck one in his mouth and lit it. "You're still wondering how she could sleep with me, aren't you?" he snorted, shaking his head. "Damn."

I eyed his cigarettes; I hadn't had a smoke in a very long time. But this was no time to start up again. "Well, you have to admit, it's, ah, a little surprising—"

"Gimme a break, Ev. You think everyone takes their idealism to bed? We agreed to disagree. She was gung-ho abortion rights. I'm against abortion, except in cases of rape or incest or the mother's gonna die. But abortion is legal in this country, and I don't have the time or energy to harass people exercising their legal rights. As far as I'm concerned, it's a political issue. You gonna tell me you never went to bed with a Republican?"

I coughed.

"Am I making my point, or the smoke getting to you? Never mind." He cocked his head toward the computer. "You know how this fucking thing works?"

If he was capable of killing Lisa, there was no telling what he was capable of. Bravura, sleight-of-hand, self-assurance—for all I knew, Brian Linhardt had been cronies with Oliver North. Wasn't Iran-Contra going down about the same time Linhardt was doing God only knew what in Central America? Oliver North could lie through his teeth and weep with sentiment while he did it. Maybe Brian Linhardt could, too.

Then again, I wouldn't be surprised if melodrama was among the sequelae of head bonk.

"Pull up a chair," I said.

It took me about fifteen minutes to ascertain that all Lisa's computer files had been deleted.

"Was the computer on or off when you came in?" I asked Brian.

"Off. I turned it on."

"They're gone, then," I sighed. "If someone erased the files and the machine was still on, continuously, a computer hacker might be able to restore the deleted files. But if the computer's turned off, they're gone."

Linhardt chewed the inside of his cheek. "You got any idea what files we're talking about here?"

I shook my head, hoping that I was a convincing liar. "But I have a hunch she knew who the Babydoll Killer was," I said carefully, turning my head to watch him. "You know anything about that?"

Linhardt looked from my eyes to my mouth and back to my eyes. "Why don't you tell me what game we're playing here?" he demanded. "Chess? Cat and mouse? Just so I can line up my men."

"Do you know anything about that?" I repeated.

"I know the same thing you know, which is what Hal Murkland knows, which is her saying to Theresa, 'Let me see if it's who I think it is.' That's the first I heard of it." He looked around for an ashtray, didn't find one, and settled for a coffee mug full of pens and pencils; he dumped the pens and pencils out onto the desktop. "So I'm thinking, one of the anti-abortion protesters. But that doesn't add up."

I showed him the pictures from Mick Healy's party.

"These are your candidates for *Babydoll*?" he snorted. "Mick Healy's party guests, and me? You serious?"

I laid the pictures out on the table in front of him, as if I were dealing him a solitaire hand. "You're Theresa Kahr. I'm Lisa. I show you these pictures. I say, 'Anybody here you recognize? Anybody here the guy who's been coming in the shop, asking you out?' "

"Why would Babydoll go to a party at Mick Healy's?"

I put two fingers on one photograph and pushed it away from the others, singling it out.

"Hm," said Brian. "Maybe you're on to something."

"You saw the newspaper articles."

"Sure as hell did."

"Okay, so you're Theresa, I'm Lisa. I show you this picture, you say, 'That's him.' Next thing we know, you're raped and dead, and I'm stabbed and dead."

"Go on."

I took away the photo I had singled out, turning it over in my lap. Then I collected all the remaining photos but one.

"Damn," said Linhardt. "You tell the cops?"

"Not yet," I said, tucking the photos into the breast pocket of my camp shirt. "But I will. First thing tomorrow morning." I reached over and turned off the computer.

"Not so fast," Linhardt said. "What's your second theory?"

"My second theory?"

" 'My second theory,' " he mimicked in a mincing voice. "You just handed me your photo theory. Now I wanna hear your computer theory. Spit it out."

"Nuh-uh." I crossed my arms over my chest. "You tell me *your* theory. *Then* I'll tell you my second theory. Maybe."

Linhardt sucked hard on his cigarette, assessing me. "She was blackmailing him," he said.

For a moment I thought I was having another head-bonk symptom; my world seemed to revolve ninety degrees without my revolving with it; I scrambled to catch up. When I did, Linhardt had me by both upper arms and was peering into my face, his cigarette clamped between his teeth. "Doc? You with me?"

"Blackmailing *whom?*" I cried.

Brian took a last drag of his cigarette and stubbed it out in the coffee mug. "I'd have someone give you a neuro exam, if I was you," he advised. "Whoever gave you that black eye knocked a few bolts loose. Who do you think? Murkland."

Inhaling his smoke, I resisted the urge for a cigarette. "How could she be blackmailing Murkland? He doesn't have any money. He's in debt up to his ears."

"He has money. He inherited a pile from his aunt."

"No, he was *expecting* to inherit a pile from his aunt. But she left the bulk of her estate to charities and to her daughter, Hal's cousin. Hal only got a token. Or at least that's my understanding," I said.

Linhardt was grinning and shaking his head slowly from side to side. "That's what he wanted his wife to think. She spends his money faster than he can make it. She's run up enormous debts. So he tells her there's no money from the aunt, and makes up this cock-and-bull story that they're so poor he's taking out loans to consolidate his debts. Meanwhile he's got a cool million socked away in the bank and in investments."

I blinked. "Hal Murkland inherited a million dollars? Are you kidding me?"

"Auntie must've loved her sonny boy," Linhardt said. "He's rolling in it. But it's a big fat secret. He's also worried his wife will divorce him if she finds out about the money. Right now he's got her thinking he can't afford a divorce."

My mind ran around in circles, trying to line up what Brian was telling me with what Denny Aubuchon had told me earlier in the evening. Either Hal was debt-ridden and desperate and defrauding Medicaid, or he was rolling in dough—which? "How do you know all this, Brian?"

"He told Lisa. He and Lisa were great pals. He apparently told her everything."

"And she told you?"

"Well, not much. But once in a while he would call while I

was here, and I'd overhear her half of the conversation. She didn't usually say much about him, but she did explain his money situation to me."

"Why? If she wasn't in the habit of talking about him to you, why would she tell you his money situation?"

Brian lifted his shoulders. "Hospital gossip, gossip about the boss—this is what people talk about, isn't it?"

"Yeah, but you're telling me Hal Murkland was confiding in Lisa—who was *blackmailing* him—"

"There are a few things that don't exactly add up," Linhardt conceded.

"And how do you know she was blackmailing him? How do you know Hal wasn't just giving her money?"

He shook his head. "No, there was something off about it, something covert. He was passing her envelopes with large sums in cash several times a week."

"He's married. He doesn't want his wife to know he's got money. If he's giving money to a medical student he's smitten with, don't you think he'd be secretive?"

"Ev, I'm talkin' about a thousand dollars a pop. Her bank statement came in the mail today. Over the last four weeks she deposited sixteen thousand dollars into her account. That's a lot of money, and I don't think he was just 'giving' it to her, even with his one-point-four million stash from his aunt. Besides which, I heard her say to him on the phone one time, 'Hal, stop fucking around. Are you going to give me the envelope, or do I have to come over there myself and get it?' You don't talk that way to someone who's 'giving' you sixteen thousand dollars because he's infatuated with you and dumb enough to throw money around like a sugar daddy."

But what could Lisa know about Hal that she could blackmail him with? I wondered. That he was defrauding Medicaid? But why would Hal be nickel-and-dime-ing Medicaid when he had a cool million in the bank?

"But the real question is," Linhardt said, lighting up another cigarette, "why would he kill her if she wasn't blackmailing him?"

This gave me pause; then I realized Linhardt was being provocative, tossing out sketchy ideas as if they were well-worked-through theories. He wanted my reaction. "Because he was in love with her and she rebuffed him for another?" I suggested.

"You don't really think that."

I thought back to my one-night stand with Hal my last year in medical school. I'd rebuffed him for another, but he hadn't killed me. "No," I said. "But you're not really sure she was blackmailing him, are you?"

Linhardt hesitated. "I don't know," he said. "I don't have enough information."

"She ever say anything about Hal's being in love with her?"

"She said, 'Here's a guy who falls in love with strong women and then gets mad at them for being strong.' "

"That's prescient. Anything else?"

Linhardt smoked and thought. "She thought Murkland was a pressure cooker about to blow his top," he said, picking a stray piece of tobacco off his tongue. "Let's face it—Murkland's one sorry son of a bitch. He's got Denise Aubuchon, who's hell on wheels, bossing him around at the office, and he's got that wife of his, who's like the executive secretary of a bank president, running his life at home. Everywhere he turns, he's wimping out to some broad. I've seen guys like that wake up in the morning and take an Uzi to a McDonald's full of moms and kids."

"Is that what you think happened?" I asked. "Hal snapped and killed her?"

"Somebody snapped and killed her," he said. "Nine knife wounds—that's not killing in cold blood."

Brian stuck his cigarette between his teeth and stretched his hands in front of himself, interlacing the fingers and cracking his knuckles.

"I'd say that was killing in hot blood," he mused, squinting at me through the smoke. "Wouldn't you?"

CHAPTER
21

AT 6 A.M. Monday morning the front door to Sami's Café banged open, and Guy Shehadeh came in. Dressed in a form-fitting purple polo shirt with the collar up, retro black-framed sunglasses, cream-colored linen slacks, and loafers but no socks, he looked like a movie star or a drug dealer. The drug-dealer effect was heightened by the battered nose and, when he took his glasses off, the blackened eyes. But damn—he was still gorgeous.

If I hadn't been so groggy and headachy from an entire Sunday spent asleep except for the two-hourly neuro checks, I might actually have taken a moment to admire him.

I held my caffè latte under my nose and inhaled the chocolate-scented steam, hoping I'd feel better any minute now. On Saturday night, I'd stayed up too late talking to Linhardt and breathing the smoke from his cigarettes, after which I'd gone downstairs to find Phil frantically phoning people—Denise Aubuchon, Mick Healy, the ER night charge nurse, and anyone else he could think of to find out where I was—he'd failed to find the note I'd left him. A rather testy interaction ensued, augmented by the even more testy interaction between Jeff Cantor's cat, Fat Face—whom I'd brought down from Lisa's apartment—and Maxie, the dog. By the time I'd calmed everyone down, it was after 2 A.M. Sunday morning.

That was about when my adrenaline had run out. I vaguely remembered Phil's waking me throughout Sunday for the neuro checks, and I had a hazy recollection of consuming two bowls of avgolemono soup and a number of cups of herb tea. Mick Healy had stopped by at some point, ultra-formal, careful to give the impression that any feelings he harbored for me were strictly within the realm of professional concern. Denise Aubuchon came twice, to walk the dog; my brother Craig phoned, full of opinionated advice for Hal Murkland should Hal be up to considering a legal strategy (Phil doubted Hal was up to anything of the kind); Shehadeh dutifully called from Shelter Island to inquire after my condition, but, ascertaining that I wasn't dead yet, hardly waited for the answer before hanging up; and Linhardt dropped off a Chinese herbal remedy that allegedly stimulated the central nervous system to healing and recovery. (Who would have thought Brian Linhardt knew about such things?)

Except for these strange and disjointed highlights, however, a day of my life had passed essentially without my participation. Now it was Monday morning, and I was struggling nobly to wake up and get with it. I felt as if I were rising from the dead.

Guy pulled out his chair, sat down without saying hello, and gripped the sides of the marble café table. He radiated nerves and false bluster. "Just give it to me straight," he said. "Are they going to sanction me?"

"No," I said. Nerves, false bluster, and *anger*. "There was an attending there, and a third-year resident—"

"But Lisa died. I intubated the esophagus, and she died," he countered belligerently.

I looked out the plate-glass windows of the café. Already the heat shimmered in the haze; it was going to be another scorcher. An ambulance zoomed by on Amsterdam Avenue, zipping into the ER ambulance bay across the street. It was still too early for the full-court siren, but the driver bleeped to let the ER staff know he'd arrived. A half hour from now, I'd probably be briefing Shehadeh on what to do for that patient, and watching him screw up, as usual.

Nonetheless, I decided that I might as well be kind. I'd been an intern too, once, fumbling and bumbling and tormenting myself with hindsight and second-guessing—and all the while brazenly showing a self-confident, if not downright arrogant, face to the world. Shehadeh was probably eating himself alive because of the guilt he felt over having "killed" Lisa. "She would have died anyway, Guy," I said. "She was in refractory shock. Have your coffee. We'll talk." I waved Sami over.

Sami, a portly gentleman in his late sixties with thinning black hair, was a man of Middle-Eastern sensibilities. Passionate outbursts and battered visages didn't faze him for a moment. If he wondered why I had a black eye and a bandaged elbow and Guy had two black eyes, or why Guy looked as if he might be about to suffer an acute psychotic break, it didn't show in his face. "Yes, please," he said politely. Guy ordered a double espresso and an egg-and-bacon sandwich, and Sami bowed and disappeared into the kitchen. I had already eaten my basil-and-mozzarella roll.

"Let go of the table," I suggested.

Shehadeh nodded, but did not let go. Still gripping the marble, he looked around the café. "I've never been in here," he said in a strained voice. "It's nice. Like that café in Paris Hemingway used to hang out in."

I didn't want to be diverted into a discussion about the marble-topped tables, rattan chairs and wall sconces with tiny shades that Sami had painstakingly ordered from French manufacturers. "Now listen to me," I said firmly. "When you go before the committee this afternoon, keep in mind that the standard of care is to have the anesthesiologist intubate, but no anesthesiologist was available because of the bombing victims. The situation was emergent, so the decision was made to intubate without the anesthesiologist. Secondly, you had to pass the ACLS test, so you know perfectly well how to intubate."

"But—"

"Thirdly, while you intubated the esophagus, she died not because of that, but because we as a team were unable to restore hemodynamic stability."

"But—"

"And you have to go in there with a demeanor of humbleness tempered with self-confidence, and you absolutely must control yourself and behave in a professional, dignified manner."

"I'll try," he said.

" 'No try,' " I said, miming Yoda from *Star Wars*. " 'Do.' Finally, expect the committee to ask you what you learned from this experience. They're very big on learning. You learned to auscultate after intubating, to make sure there are breath sounds. Think up some things about hemodynamic instability that you learned, too."

He smiled wanly.

Seeing the smile, I changed the subject to what *I* wanted to talk about. "I need you to tell me about Lisa," I said. "Not how she died. How she lived. How well you knew her and what you knew about her."

Shehadeh snorted.

Sami came with Guy's order, then retreated back into the kitchen. A small claque of construction workers from the new hospital wing came in, commandeered a table on the far side of the room, and carried on boisterously among themselves until a second claque came through the door: the suits from the project-managers office, the on-site construction bosses. The managers, two men and a woman, sat on our side of the room. A couple of family-practice residents arrived and waved, and lined up at the pastry counter for takeout. The café was beginning to bustle, as it did at this time every morning.

Picking up his espresso and blowing on it, Guy said sourly, "You should have told me that's what you wanted to talk about,

Ev. I could have saved you from wasting your time."

"Meaning?"

"Meaning I didn't know her at all."

"That's not what Tony Firenze says," I countered. "He says you were over at Lisa's apartment quite a bit when you first started your internship."

"Who's Tony Firenze?"

"Lisa's next-door neighbor."

"Who, that little bald guy who kept opening his door to see who I was every time I went in or out of her apartment? I'll tell you why he thinks I was over there so much—he was jealous. He had the hots for her himself."

"I see," I said, assessing Guy's bitter, angry tone. Hell hath no fury like a suitor scorned. I wondered if he knew about Brian Linhardt's relationship with Lisa, but decided I didn't want to ask. "You weren't lovers?"

"That's none of your business," he snapped.

I took that to mean *no*. Although Guy was not the boastful type when it came to women, he was vain, and I didn't think he'd deny having been lovers with a woman if asked. "She tossed you over for someone else?" I ventured.

"Yeah, for Hal Murkland! What she saw in him, I'll never know."

I sighed. Pretty soon I'd have to start keeping score: who thought Lisa was sleeping with Hal Murkland, and who thought she *wasn't* sleeping with Hal. Or who thought she was sleeping with Guy Shehadeh. Or Brian Linhardt, for that matter. How had there come to swirl around the topic of Lisa's sex life so much innuendo, speculation, and rumor? "Why do you think that, Guy?"

"Why do I think what?"

"Why do you think Lisa tossed you over for Hal Murkland?"

He made no effort to conceal his scorn and impatience. "C'mon, Ev. He was in a position to advance her career, write good recommendations for her, pull strings . . . Plus, he's a wimp. She could have her way with him."

"I see," I said. What I saw was, Guy Shehadeh thought Lisa was ambitious and arbitrary. "But what makes you think they were sleeping together?"

"He was in her apartment *at night*. She was in his office *at night*. What does that sound like to you?"

"But how do you know that?" I persisted, puzzled.

"Because I clean my apartment when I can't sleep, and I take out the garbage," Guy explained, as if I were too dumb to put two and two together, "and I used to see them going up and down the fire escape."

"Used to? More than once?"

"Twice a week. At least."

I blinked. Who in New York City would use the fire escape as a routine stairwell? "Are you sure?"

"No, Ev, I'm making it all up," groused Guy. "He's married, too. I have half a mind to stick it to his wife, just to get back at him."

I put my coffee cup down.

"That's a *joke*," he said, seeing my expression.

"I guess women don't say no to you very often," I mused, setting the fire-escape escapade aside for a moment.

"No. They don't."

"Can you tell me what happened, or are you incapacitated by this egregious blow to your vanity?"

For a minute I thought I'd gone too far; Guy's eyes flashed and his mouth set in a thin-lipped line, corners curled into a sneer. Then I realized that these facial contortions served as an unintended overture to the aria that would follow. Lights. Camera. *Action*.

"She invited me over for supper," he began, in a tone of voice that suggested aggravated assault rather than a dinner date. "She made a nice soup with all kinds of fresh vegetables in it, and a hot French bread with cheese. I brought a nice bottle of wine. We had a nice evening—or *I* thought we had a nice evening. We talked about medical school and the hospital, who the doctors were, which ones were the hard-asses, which ones might actually teach us something. She was friendly and flirtatious, but I never make a move on the first date."

"Of course not," I said.

"So after we ate, I took her out for ice cream," Shehadeh went on, nostrils flaring, "and we came back to the doctors' residence, and I said good night. I let a week go by and then I called her and suggested a movie. She said she'd rather have dinner in the neighborhood and talk. So I took her to the Italian place on Broadway and we had dinner and talked. About the hospital again. I invited her back to my place for a drink, but she said no, some other time."

I pondered this. Clearly, according to some code that existed only in Shehadeh's mind, "Some other time" violated a statute of the highest order. Which presented me with my least-favorite cocktail-party dilemma: Should I, or should I not, pretend that I know what the other person is talking about? I decided not. "Was she being sarcastic?" I asked.

"She was being *duplicitous*," hissed Guy, leaning forward, thrusting his face into mine so that I inhaled the spray of his venom. "I found out from Kessie Savarkar, the other intern, that Lisa'd had her over to supper, too. Same soup, same French bread. Same talk about the hospital. Then I heard Lisa had the other medical students over—more bread and soup. Then she went to dinner at Murkland's apartment with him and his wife and Denny Aubuchon."

Lisa's "crime" came into focus, slowly.

"She was just *shmoozing* me," Guy said. He spat the word. "She was schmoozing all of us!"

"She was networking," I suggested. I, too, had been invited to Lisa's for an evening of collegiality and bread and soup. A cold mushroom bisque, if I recalled—perfect for a hot summer night.

But my gentle disagreement only served to ignite rocket fuel under my breakfast companion. "She was leading me on," he snarled, slapping the table for emphasis.

Then, as I looked on, astonished, a man known to me only as a bumbling intern and a thwarted lover blasted into temper. Launching himself to his feet, he swept his dishes in a clatter to the tile floor—where they shattered—threw his chair against the marble table, and stormed out of the café. My face burned from the heat of his ignition as I watched him dash across the street, dodging traffic, spinning off into the stratosphere of rage, betrayal, entitlement, and self-righteousness.

The café went deathly quiet. Sami, brought out of the kitchen by dishes crashing, refused to let me pick up the broken pieces, and waved away the two construction workers who were hovering, pained by my embarrassment. Nor would Sami allow me to pay for the breakfast or the dishes. "No, no, Doctor," he said, flipping his hand at Shehadeh's retreating back in a Middle-Eastern gesture I'd never seen before. "You go. On the house."

I wondered what kind of man felt cheated on by a woman he'd never slept with when she broke bread and shared soup with her colleagues.

Sami wiped his hands on his apron and cupped a hand under my good elbow. With his pitch-black eyes he gazed pointedly at my purple orbit. "A violent man," he said. "You are better you stay away from him."

"I'm beginning to think so," I said.

But staying away from Guy Shehadeh was a luxury I couldn't afford. "Stand by for a gunshot wound," the clerk announced as I came into the emergency room through the ambulance bay. "Cardiac arrest."

I swore under my breath and made a mad dash for the doctors' locker room, yanking open my locker and grabbing my white coat. "Get your head out of the sink, cardiac arrest incoming," I yelled at the bathroom, where I assumed Guy was soaking his head after our stimulating breakfast. I put my arms through the sleeves of my white coat—

Wait. The coat was too small. And too short.

It wasn't my coat, it was a med student's coat.

Confused, I looked at my locker and checked the number, a silly exercise—of course it was my locker, I'd opened it with my combination.

"Where's a fucking towel?" yelled Guy Shehadeh, running out of the bathroom, his hair dripping. He banged the hair dryer on the wall and stuck his head under the hot air, running his fingers through his hair. "Goddamn Housekeeping, can't they fucking keep us in towels?"

It was Lisa Chiu's coat.

I'd given her the combination to my locker the morning before she died.

Brian Linhardt threw open the door of the locker room. "We've got a multiple GSW, ETA *now!*" he yelled. The door banged shut again.

I heard the blip of the ambulance as it pulled into the bay. Ripping off Lisa's coat and tossing it back into my locker, I grabbed my own coat and, just as I slammed the locker shut, caught a glimpse of Lisa's Filofax on the top shelf. I groaned and twirled the dial of the combination lock, bolting for the ER, skidding to a stop just as the stretcher shot through the double swinging doors. Damn, damn, damn, of all times to find that Filofax. "OR One," I yelled, grabbing one side of the stretcher as Dr. Alexander McCabe materialized and grabbed the other, with Linhardt pulling from in front.

Then I took a look at the patient. A surly young black man with his hands crossed over his belly.

Wearing handcuffs.

Wide awake.

In fact, staring me balefully in the face.

"Wait a minute," I said. "This guy's not in arrest."

"I am too under arrest," the patient objected. "She-yit, just ask *them* if I ain't under arrest." He tossed his head toward a phalanx of police officers who were following his stretcher into the ER like a promenade of the gendarmerie.

"Linhardt," I said, "we need to keep OR One open for the gunshot wound in arrest."

"Where's the doctor here?" one of the officers demanded, pushing forward. He was wearing SWAT gear and held a very large shotgun across his chest. Or maybe it was an assault rifle; I really couldn't tell. McCabe and I exchanged a look. Even in the 1990s, white male cops still had a tendency to assume that female house staff (me) were nurses and black male house staff (McCabe) were orderlies. The cop's eyes alighted on the white-male medic (Linhardt). "You the doctor here?" he demanded, scrutinizing Linhardt's ID, clipped to the front of his scrub shirt. He didn't bother to read my ID or McCabe's.

Behind this exemplary specimen of New York's Finest, more officers armed to the teeth were crowding into the ER. This presented a logistical problem, because they were all going to be in the way when the gunshot wound in cardiac arrest was brought in.

"Gentlemen," I said, "can you hold on a minute while we figure out where to put this guy? JULIO!" I yelled out to the clerk, "What happened to the multiple gunshot wound in arrest?"

"That's me!" the patient yelled just as loudly. "I am shot and under arrest!"

"You shut up when the nurse is talking, you dumb shit!" the head cop yelled, even more loudly.

Julio stuck his head around the corner of the nurses' station. "I'm sorry, I'm sorry," he said. "They took the multiple gunshot wound to Harlem Hospital."

"Well, next time tell us, why don't you?" I said. "We're holding OR One for that patient."

"Sorry. Mercury's in retrograde." He disappeared around the corner again.

"What?"

"Astrology," explained McCabe. "Julio's been saying that since he came in this morning, 'Mercury's in retrograde.' " He turned to the kid on the stretcher. "So, where you shot?"

"My leg."

"Okay, my man, we'll let your honor guard here disrobe you, and then we'll have a look." McCabe stood aside as the cops took their charge into OR One. Patients deemed violent by the police were disrobed by the police, not by hospital staff. That way the cops could confiscate any concealed weapons.

"I'll take this kid," said McCabe. "What happened to your eye?"

"I got mugged," I said. "Tell you later."

"You got *mugged?*"

Eager to get back to my locker and Lisa Chiu's tantalizing Filofax, I was already moving off down the corridor. "See you at rounds," I tossed off over my shoulder. Not looking where I was going, I ran smack into—

Jesus Christ, the hospital's chairwoman of the board of directors.

"Who are you?" she snapped, and, before I could answer, "Do you know who *I* am?"

I clenched my teeth, stifling a groan. I knew exactly who she was. A bad impersonator of Joan Rivers, loudmouthed, insinuating, and hell on wheels, permanently coiffed with a bouffant hairdo so lacquered it might withstand U.S. Armed Forces testing for infantry helmets. She was also a terrific fund-raiser, and as co-chair of the hospital's last gala ball was rumored to have brought in millions. "Mrs. Wilensky," I said cordially, "what can I do for you?"

Her penciled eyebrows shot up to her lacquered hairline in mock disbelief. "Oh, good, good," she said. "Someone finally who knows who I am." Her voice rose an octave. "*My husband,*" she said, as if pronouncing the name of the highest official in the land, "is having a heart attack, and *no one will look at him.*"

Pulling on gloves, I went with her immediately into OR Three, where Ivan Wilensky lay on a stretcher parked between two other stretchers, one with a patient calmly snoring, and the other containing a junkie I recognized. He was one of the ER's prime ROs—"repeat offenders," persons who "overutilized available medical resources" in the jargon of the current mayor. The junkie, splotched with the purple lesions of Kaposi's sarcoma, was busy pulling out all his IVs and spraying the room with HIV-infected blood.

"Linhardt!" I yelled, and, "I need a nurse!"

Mrs. Wilensky, to her credit, moved her well-dressed self out of range without comment.

"Mr. Wilensky, I'm Dr. Sutcliffe," I said. "We've met, at the gala ball. You don't look so good."

"Trouble," he said, "breathing." A barrel-chested seventy-year-old dressed in yachting clothes—faded red pants, a cloth belt decorated with signal flags, and a white golf shirt emblazoned with a yacht-club burgee—he looked uncomfortable and tired. When I had last seen him, dancing at the spring fund-raiser ball, he had been in exuberant health, enjoying his golden years. To see him now having difficulty breathing touched my daughterly heart.

"I see that," I said. I reached for his wrist and took his pulse, then counted his breaths. Pulse 110, respiratory rate 30 and shallow. "Has anyone seen you?"

"No," said Mrs. Wilensky.

"Nurse been in?"

"No."

"How long have you been here?"

"About fifteen minutes. Is he having a heart attack?"

"We'll see." Many cardiac problems did present in the ER as difficulty-breathings. "We'll run some tests to rule out heart attack. Sit up for me now, please, Mr. Wilensky." I put my stethoscope in my ears and auscultated. "Deep breath"—he winced—"another"—he winced again. Diminished breathing on left side, heart sounds normal.

"Mr. Wilensky, you having any chest pain?"

"Only when I take these deep breaths you're so fond of."

I smiled. "Any pain in your arms, neck, teeth?"

"No."

I palpated his abdomen, shone my penlight in his eyes. "What do *you* think is the matter with you?"

"Well," said Wilensky, "I think it's my lung."

"I think you're right," I said. "I'd say you probably have a tension pneumothorax—that's when there's a little leak some-where in the lung, and air gets trapped between the outside of the lung and the lining. But we'll get you an EKG to help rule out heart attack."

The junkie on the next stretcher—in the throes of acute al-cohol withdrawal or heroin-induced delirium tremens or cocaine psychosis or God only knew what—chose that moment to make his escape, and began to climb down from his stretcher. He had an open hospital gown on backward, and he flagrantly mooned Mrs. Wilensky, his balls swinging in the breeze. "WHOA," he said loudly. "WHOAAA."

His diagnosis became suddenly clear. He was drunk. He crashed to the floor.

"LINHARDT!" I bellowed.

The snoring patient on the other stretcher gave a snort and sat up. "NURSE!" he yelled. Without further ado, he leaned over and vomited onto the floor. Luckily he was considerate enough to spew over the opposite side, thus sparing Mrs. Wilensky the spray.

Linhardt came in. "Restrain that guy," I said, pointing at the junkie. A nurse came in. I pointed at the vomiting patient."Excuse me," I said to the Wilenskys. "Did you come by ambulance?"

"No, the police brought us," said Mrs. Wilensky, unfazed by the junkie and vomit. My respect for her rose. "There were no cabs."

"Okay, I'll need to track down your chart and find a nurse, so we can get you on oxygen, for starters." I excused myself and went out to look at the nurses' board to see who had been assigned to Wilensky. He wasn't on the board. Nor was there a chart for him in the chart rack. I wondered if the cops had brought him in, plunked him down on a vacant stretcher, pushed him into OR Three, and left him there without telling anyone. That would be very unusual, but not unknown. "Christ," I muttered under my breath. All I needed was a grand fuckup involving the husband of the chairwoman of the hospital's board of directors. Well, I would give him the EKG and wheel him to X Ray myself, if necessary. I scooped up the charts for the three other patients whose names were scrawled under mine on the nurses' board, delegated the ward clerk to see to a chart for Wilensky—"VIP, chop-chop STAT"—and page me thoracic, fortuitously nailed a nurse and med student to set up a chest-tube tray and organize vitals, bloods, and an EKG for Wilensky—again "VIP, chop-chop STAT"—alerted the attending physician and the ER director, and . . .

I was suddenly ambushed by thoughts of Lisa Chiu. My heart burned in my chest, an unexpected firestorm. Then the ache fanned out. God, I thought, will it always be like this? Sinking into a chair at the doctors' desk in the nurses' station, I put my head in my hands. I imagined Lisa standing next to me, placing a hand on my shoulder, solicitously asking, "You okay?" then making some crack to get me to snap out of myself. No, I'm not okay, I said to her spirit. I miss you.

Her Filofax called to me with an insistent inner voice, but I didn't have time for it now. I got up again and went out of the nurses' station, flipping through my charts. Let's see, I had a "weak and dizzy all over" and a "difficulty swallowing and throat pain." Contrary to popular opinion, shaped by too many TV programs where all patients seemed to enter the ER propelled at fifty miles an hour on their stretchers, with medics shouting out vitals and signs and symptoms, life in an inner-city emergency room could be boring and repetitive. It was not unusual to have a day where you saw ten little old ladies who were weak and dizzy, and ten guys who were complaining of chest pain or difficulty breathing, and you ordered the exact same tests on everybody and the results came back more or less the same. Hours could go by without the arrival of a patient in extremis.

I reminded myself that normally I liked this work and normally I liked saving lives. Then my mind flew to Detective Ost. I'd meant to call Detective Ost, but had forgotten during my Lost Sunday of Sleep Cure.

Shehadeh wandered by, and I grabbed him. Still smarting from his bad behavior at Sami's café, I snapped out exactly what I wanted done for Wilensky, taking care to scare Shehadeh with threats of yet another Quality Assurance Committee convocation if he fucked up Wilensky's treatment. I reminded him that the previous month a patient with Wilensky's signs and symptoms had died of a tension pneumothorax because hospital budget cuts had delayed his STAT X rays, because too few X-ray technicians were available to ensure prompt response to STAT X-ray requests. "Take him to X Ray yourself, if you have to," I said. Meanly I added, "And if they don't X-ray him VIP chop-chop STAT, have a temper tantrum. Unless you spent yourself earlier."

Shehadeh gave me a bald stare, then went off.

Then I plunked myself down in the farthest corner of the doctors' desks in the nursing station, fished Ost's card out of my wallet, and dialed the Twenty-sixth Precinct to leave him a message.

I wasn't expecting to get him on the phone—it was only twenty after seven. So when he picked up and I heard his voice, I was momentarily thrown. By speaking to Ost, I was about to hurt someone I cared for deeply. I felt my heart stir with a sudden slosh of anxiety.

"I think I know who killed Theresa Kahr," I said.

CHAPTER
22

DETECTIVE Ost stood against the counters in the doctors' lounge, his arms crossed over his chest, and listened without expression while I explained.

"He has a history of abusing women and other acts of violence," I said, perched on a corner of the table. "You already know about that. He's a bad egg. You know that, too. Theresa Kahr was raped in a pile of glass, and he has cuts on his knees—he says he broke a glass bowl in the kitchen. You guys put out a bulletin to emergency rooms saying you wanted to talk to anyone who came in to have glass removed from his knees. But this patient didn't have to come in. Conveniently, he was able to have the glass removed from his knees at home."

"Go on," said Ost.

"Theresa Kahr told Lisa Chiu that she'd been flirting with a guy who'd been coming into the Good Earth. Theresa telephoned Lisa one evening while Lisa was working in Hal Murkland's office, and Hal overheard Lisa's half of the conversation. Apparently Theresa called to say she thought the guy was following her, and that she was nervous about his intentions. Lisa said, 'Don't do anything—let me find out if it's who I think it is.' But for whatever reason, Lisa did not get back to Theresa. At least not in time to prevent her assault. And then it turns out that Theresa was assaulted by the Babydoll Killer.

"You can imagine how racked with guilt Lisa was," I continued. "I tried to draw her out on Thursday evening as we walked over to the Good Earth together, but she was short-tempered and I didn't press it. Then sometime after she left me, Lisa had a conversation with Mick Healy in the tunnel walking from the doctors' residence to the hospital. Denise Aubuchon passed them going in the opposite direction and did not overhear what they were saying. Denny did say that Mick looked as white as a sheet. He was clearly upset by what Lisa was telling him.

"Then early the next morning, Lisa was stabbed in her apartment and died. I didn't know that she had spoken to Mick Healy the evening before. Meanwhile, I was mulling over in my mind the fact that Mick fit the description of the man who knocked me down and pulled my shirt over my head—"

Ost blinked.

"—and that I'd run into him late Thursday evening. He was out jogging, which is what he does when he wants to think and clear his head and come to a decision about a matter which may be troubling him. Then late Friday afternoon, when I was walking the dog for a friend who lives on Eighty-ninth Street, I thought I saw Mick Healy—again, jogging by. An hour and a half later, I ran into Mick again, down in SoHo. I was really beginning to think the man was following me."

Ost cleared his throat. "Where in SoHo?" he asked.

I told him. "So I confronted Mick—asked was he following me, asked whether he had a Superman shirt—he'd been wearing a Superman shirt when he jogged by Eighty-ninth Street earlier, and a pair of green scrub pants. Or at least that's what I thought I saw—I wasn't wearing my glasses. Mick was nervous and evasive. He denied up and down owning a Superman shirt. He made me recount to him exactly when it was I thought he'd been following me. It was all very strange."

"Mm," said Ost noncommittally.

I told Ost about finding photos of the Healy family among Lisa Chiu's papers—and of Brian Linhardt, who bore a passing resemblance to the Healy clan if only due to his similar coloring and vague air of military training. I believed that Chiu had assembled the pictures I'd found as a kind of photo lineup to show Theresa Kahr, but that Theresa had been assaulted before Lisa got around to doing it.

Fishing in the breast pocket of my shirt, I handed Ost the out-of-focus photo of what looked like Mick Healy wearing a Superman shirt and jogging shorts.

Ost took the picture, glanced at it, and returned his eyes to my face.

"On Saturday afternoon I got knocked unconscious," I said, taking off my glasses and showing Ost my shiner. I explained how that had happened. "Clearly someone wanted me to know I was asking too many questions. But here's the strange thing—first, on Thursday, the guy knocks me down and pulls my shirt over my head, so I don't see him —but then he runs on. Then he hits me over the head. What's keeping him from killing me? He killed Theresa Kahr. It looks like he may have killed Lisa Chiu—so why not kill me?"

"Good question," said Ost.

"You might as well know," I said, "that, ah, Mick Healy and I are having . . . *un petit contretemps,* and that, um, seemed like a good reason not to kill me. Or at least that's what came to mind."

Ost's eyes appeared to go in and out of focus, and I imagined that the corner of his mouth twitched. Whatever he was thinking, he was trying very hard not to give it away. For the most part, he was succeeding.

"When Theresa Kahr saw Mick Healy in the ER, she screamed," I pointed out.

"Yeah," said Ost.

"And when Mick came to see me in the ER after I'd been knocked unconscious, the first thing he asked was, 'Was it the same man?' Everybody else thought it was a burglar, but he wanted to know if the guy who hit me over the head was the same man who had knocked me down on the street."

Ost's eyes began to gleam.

"This is not news to you," I said.

He looked at his watch. "Doc, forgive me, but I can't say."

I fished a second photo out of the pocket of my shirt and handed it over.

I did not feel it was necessary to mention the fact that Theresa Kahr's killer had shown up in the ER, daring me to recognize him. Or that what, in the end, finally put me on to him was the feeling that he undressed me with his eyes as if he had already undressed me in reality, which I was bound to remember if I just put my mind to it. Well, I did put my mind to it. And I remembered. He undressed me on the sidewalk.

He didn't kill me, on the sidewalk or in Kennedy Bartlett's apartment, because he knew Mick was in love with me.

"There's your man," I said. "Donal Healy. Mick Healy's brother. That's not Mick in the out-of-focus picture of the guy wearing the Superman shirt. It's Donal. In the second photo, you can see the strong resemblance between Mick and Donal, and understand how people might mix them up. Like Theresa Kahr did, when Mick bent over her in the ER, and like I did, when I saw Donal at the end of Eighty-ninth Street, while I was out walking the dog." I drew a deep breath. "I think Donal's the Babydoll Killer."

"Son of a bitch," said Ost, shaking his head. "Doc, you really take the fucking cake."

His beeper went off, and he put a hand on my shoulder as he rose to go. "You get any more ideas, you call me. I mean it." His gaze was steady and intense. "You understand I can't say anything."

"I know, Ozzie."

"Good. Buy you a beer after it all goes down."

Watching Ost's back disappear around the corner into the utility room, I felt my heart plummet. Who was going to buy Mick Healy a beer after it all went down? Me?

I pulled the scroll of Ivan Wilensky's EKG tape through my fingers; there was no evidence of a heart attack.

"Let's see the films," I said.

Guy Shehadeh clipped the X ray into the light board and pointed. Just as Wilensky himself had suspected, the problem was with his lung; he had a tension pneumothorax. We should listen to the patients more often.

"What else?" I asked.

Shehadeh made a sweeping gesture that took in the cardiac silhouette. "Slight midline shift."

"Okay," I said, "now what?"

"Dr. McCabe's coming back down. He took that kid who got shot upstairs."

"Good. Labs reveal anything?"

"No."

"Show me."

He slapped the sheaf of computer printouts into my hand. I glanced down the columns of results. "You emphasized to McCabe that the films show midline shift?" I asked.

Shehadeh set his jaw. "You're riding me because you're pissed about the scene in the restaurant," he complained.

I counted to five. "Yeah," I said, barely controlling myself, "I am. That was the most unbelievable asshole behavior I've ever seen, throwing those dishes on the floor like that. It made a piss-poor impression. But this patient is the husband of the hospital's chairman of the board of directors, Guy, and if you stopped thinking about yourself for five minutes, you might realize I have a very valid reason to be concerned about his care." I threw the lab results back at him. "Don't forget to brief the attending. *And* Dr. Cabot."

I stomped off, broiling. Don't let him get to you like this, Sutcliffe, I told myself, glancing at my watch for the umpteenth time within the hour. The day was progressing incredibly slowly. My entire being itched to barricade myself in the doctors' locker-room bathroom with Lisa's Filofax, and stay in there until I had read every single word, twice. Heaving the kind of deep, audible sigh my grandmother, Bubbeh Hazel, used to call a *krechtz*, I wrenched my mind back to my patients. I had seen my weak-and-dizzy-all-over, but I still needed to get to the difficulty-swallowing-and-throat-pain, and check on Mr. Wilensky. What I needed was an hour of peace and quiet so I could think. God. A quiet moment alone with my thoughts. It seemed like a long-forgotten luxury.

A little old lady in a housedress and bedroom slippers shuffled by, pushing an IV pole with one hand and carrying a urine bag in the other. "*What* heat?" she demanded of an unseen companion. "Everybody's gotta die sometime, I'm an old lady! My daughter calls, she says, 'Ma, you gotta drink more water.' You know what hard work it is for the heart, the kidneys, to push all that water around? I drink enough so I shouldn't get dehydrated, that's enough."

"Ma'am?" I said. "Ma'am?"

"Last week a young man, fifty years old, he just went to the doctor and all the tests were okay. He played tennis every morning—and he drops dead in synagogue! I have no control over when I'm going to die. Just so long as there's no World Trade Center explosion to overexcite me, I'm okay. I *like* the heat."

"I'm glad to hear that," I said, taking her elbow. I waved Julio over. "Can you tell me your name?"

Ignoring me, she shuffled in place as I held her arm. "There's no news from Bosnia, so they tell us about the *weather*," she said. "It's not so hot. Those weathermen, they just need something to talk about."

I turned her over to Julio.

"This is Mrs. Gelb, Dr. Savarkar's patient," he said, gripping the wayward patient firmly but gently by the biceps. "Mrs. Gelb gets a little confused since her last stroke. Dr. Sutcliffe, did you see Dr. Carchiollo? He was looking for you. Mrs. Gelb? How about if we stay in bed and wait for the doctor?"

"No," I said. "Where is he?"

"He was zooming around here just a minute ago. Try Psych." Julio led the patient away. "My husband was in Burma during the war," she said. "Now *there*, it's *hot*."

I went around to Psych; Phil had been and gone. Next: the difficulty-swallowing-and-throat-pain patient. I stopped at the nurses' station to collect the chart.

"Dr. Sutcliffe?"

"Yes, Julio."

"Dr. Aubuchon for you on three." He handed me the phone.

"Sutcliffe," I said into the receiver.

"Hi. You've got Edward Zoller over there, and I want him admitted." Zoller was the architect who built airports and municipal buildings in South America, and took Denny out to dinner at fancy restaurants when he was home in New York. She filled me in on the patient's history: seropositive for HIV for six years but without a defining illness, two-week history of pruritus, jaundice, and loss of energy. The list went on: night sweats, intermittent fever, sinusitis, gastrointestinal intolerance of one drug, switch to another—"Oh, and anorexia and intermittent nausea without vomiting. No abdominal pain, no diarrhea," Denny concluded.

"What do you want, a liver workup?" I asked.

"Exactly," she said. "I'm wall-to-wall patients and I just can't get over there right now, can you tell him that? Tell him I'll come as soon as I can."

"Gotcha," I said. I hung up. "Julio, do you know where Edward Zoller is?"

"Closet Two." Names stuck in the ER. Before extensive renovations three years ago, a three-stretcher patient examination area had been a cloakroom for the nurses; it was now Closet One, Two, or Three, depending on the slot the patient's stretcher was parked in.

"You request Zoller's chart from Records?" I asked.

"Just sent Luis two minutes ago."

Now, if I could just palm off the difficulty-swallowing-and-throat-pain patient on Kessie Savarkar—

"Hi," said Phil, at my elbow. "Did you hear the news?"

I turned. "No, what news?"

He put his arm around me, steering me away from the nurses' station and into the utility room, where one of the orderlies was busy flushing the contents of a bedpan down the bedpan toilet. A sound not unlike that of Niagara Falls filled the air.

"This has to be some news, to require the privacy of the utilities room," I said, raising my voice slightly to be heard.

Phil's face was suffused with the glow of good gossip. "*Major* police activity this morning on my way over here," he confided in what would have been a stage whisper had he not had to raise his voice so much over the bedpan toilet. "At Mick Healy's. I go by, and they're carting off one of his brothers, *in handcuffs.*"

My heart fluttered, then took off. "When?" I asked.

"On my way over. About seven-thirty. Mick was there, the sister was there—what's-her-name, the detective—and a lot of cops with heavy-duty weapons and state-of-the-art bulletproof gear, you should've seen this shit, it was like the ATF raids Waco, Part Two. Unbelievable!"

Relief filled me, then sorrow, then pride. At seven-thirty I'd been talking to Detective Ost. I was talking to him right while the thing was going down. No wonder Ost's face was twitching.

"Mick canceled all his operations. He's taking a personal day," Phil went on excitedly. "I've been trying to find out which of the brothers it was, but nobody knows anything."

"It's Donal," I said. "The one from the midtown anti-crime team, the one who got busted for beating up prostitutes and their pimps. When did Mick cancel his operations?"

"What, you mean did Mick know ahead of time?"

"Yeah," I said. What I really wanted to know was: Did Mick turn his brother in, or not?

"You know something about this," Phil said accusingly. "What?"

"I don't *know* it, I *think* it. I think Donal Healy's the Babydoll Killer," I said.

"Thanks a lot for telling me," said Phil.

The report of Donal Healy's arrest spread through the emergency room like news of a multiple-casualty incident. A housekeeping custodian with a Sony Walkman was hovered over by doctors and nurses, and begged to tune in one of the all-news stations; jobs for the custodian were trumped up throughout the ER to keep him busy swabbing the decks so he could make periodic announcements when he heard anything. "Okay, the mayor and the police commissioner are calling a press conference at noon," the custodian called out around 11 A.M., mopping up vomit in OR Two. "They're saying it's Babydoll!" Later, sweeping up debris after a code, "He confessed!" and "It's definitely Dr. Healy's brother Donal!" Admissions suddenly became popular; taking an admission upstairs from the emergency room afforded the chance to scour the halls for patients who had rented TVs and were willing to switch for a few minutes to CNN. Julio's grandmother, a little old lady with chronic obstructive pulmonary disease parked in front of her TV at home, was put on Red Alert and instructed to glue herself to New York One, the city's local station, and phone Julio with the latest. Dr. Savarkar volunteered to visit the old lady at home for her next scheduled doctor's appointment, "professional courtesy" (in other words, free).

"What in God's name is going on?" asked Edward Zoller from his stretcher in Closet Two, a vantage that allowed a view of doctors and nurses running pell-mell this way and that, talking excitedly. "Is this some kind of drill?"

"The cops arrested the Babydoll Killer," I said, squinting at Zoller's chart, which was about the size of two volumes of the *Unabridged Oxford English Dictionary* and required an optician-grade magnifying glass to read it. I'd have to have a word with that Senegalese medical student, the one with the high-tech pen that allowed such eensy-teensy handwriting. "His brother is a doctor who works here. Have you been immunized against hepatitis B?"

"I don't think so."

"Exposed to anyone with tuberculosis?"

"Yes, my lover. He died in June."

I looked up. "I'm sorry," I said.

He nodded, accepting the sentiment but clearly not wishing to dwell on it. I pushed on. "Have you had a recent skin test?"

"In the spring. It was negative. Dr. Aubuchon thought it was too early for me to be anergic." What Edward meant was, his HIV infection had not yet progressed to the point where his body would fail to respond to the PPD test for tuberculosis if he had the disease. Like most of Denny's patients, he was well-informed and articulate.

"I'm sure she's right," said Hal Murkland cheerfully, blowing suddenly into Closet Two like a leaf on a storm. "Mr. Zoller, how are you?" He stuck out his hand. "Hal Murkland. We've met. I share offices with Dr. Aubuchon. She's chock-a-block patients and says to tell you she'll be over as soon as possible." Still pumping Zoller's hand, Hal turned to me and said, "Mick Healy's office is going berserk. His receptionist is charging around hyperventilating, the phones are ringing off the wall—utterly berserk."

Then, as casually as if he were somehow assigned to oversee my work, Hal set his reading glasses on his nose with an authoritative air and began flipping through Zoller's chart. Addressing the patient, he said, "I saw in *Architectural Digest* that your new airport in Bogotá received a prestigious award for design excellence. Congratulations."

Zoller smiled. "Thank you for mentioning it. We're very proud. I think I could have done without having to spend so much time in South America, though."

"Yes, I'm sure," said Hal. "But then Denny wouldn't have such a wonderful collection of postcards, or so many funny stories to repeat at dinner parties. Tell me again about this experimental compound you were taking.''

''The PCM4?''

''Yes.''

Tell me *again?* I wasn't so sure *Hal* wasn't going berserk. Zoller, a man in his late forties with graying hair and the confident mien of a highly successful businessman, was hardly young enough to have been one of Hal's patients before ''graduating'' to Denny's practice. What was Hal doing going through Zoller's chart and meddling in his case?

''Dr. Aubuchon said it was whacking out my liver-function values, and I'd better stop taking it, so I did,'' Zoller told Murkland.

''And when was this?'' Hal asked.

''About two months ago.''

''And for three months you've been off the AZT and DDI?''

''Right.''

''Dr. Murkland, perhaps I could speak to you in the corridor for a moment,'' I said.

''Denny and I have a new agreement,'' Hal protested, when I had steered him around the corner into the utilities room. With his four day beard and sutures, he was beginning to look a little like the madman of Chaillot. ''We're going to share all the patients. This way we can cut down on the competition.''

''That is utter bullshit,'' I countered.

Hal smiled brightly. ''Well, you won't know until you take it up with her, will you?''

''I'll take it up with Dr. Cabot right now, if you don't get out of here and go back to Peds where you belong.''

''Fine,'' he said, ''fine. Cheers.''

And, much to my surprise, off he went.

''Dr. Sutcliffe?''

''Yes, Julio.''

''Dr. Healy called. He asked you to beep him when you get a moment.''

I got a moment immediately. ''Mick, I'm so sorry,'' I said

when he came on the line after an interminable wait of two minutes. "This is terrible for you and your family."

"I wanted you to be the first to know," said Mick, skipping the sentiment. He was probably in shock. "I gave Bernadette the job of calling my father and brothers. Ever since we got here, I've been trying to formulate in my mind what I would say to you. Holy Mother of God, Ev—Donal was indignant because I wouldn't give him credit for not killing you when he knocked you down on the street. He was yelling at me because I wasn't *grateful* enough—"

"Where are you?"

"At the Twenty-fourth Precinct. Donal's confessing to everything, Ev. Killing those girls." His voice caught. "Oh, God. I believed him about the glass, that he fell in glass when he was jogging. It didn't even go through my mind that Theresa Kahr'd been raped in glass, but when Lisa—I should have gone to Bernadette sooner, I don't know why I waited. I should have gone home and called Bernie as soon as Lisa told me she suspected him."

"In the tunnel," I said.

"In the tunnel. Lisa knew it was Donal. She'd seen Donal once or twice on her way to the Good Earth, and it was just a hunch at first, but then I bumped into her and I had the suture kit with me because Donal'd called and said he'd fallen in the glass—"

I found myself struggling to breathe. I knew all this; I'd figured it out. The date Mick was keeping when I bumped into him in SoHo was with his sister. To discuss turning Donal in. Still, I groped for a stool and sank onto it.

"Did Lisa confront Donal?" I asked in a small voice. I had a flash of Donal Healy climbing the fire escape of the doctors' residence as dawn broke over the hospital. With certainty I saw how it had happened: Lisa confronted Donal sometime during the evening on Thursday; he waited a few hours, then walked the two blocks from Mick's building to—

Mick's voice came to me from far away. "No. I urged her not

to, and I'm quite sure she did not. I was with Donal all evening, except for when I went out to run and bumped into you. And I know he didn't go out in the night because he sleeps in the same room with me—that's where the one air conditioner is. Besides, he'd really tied one on—drank half a bottle of Scotch—and he was still sleeping it off when I got up to go to the hospital Friday morning."

"What?" I said.

"Donal did not kill Lisa Chiu. And he wasn't following you; when you saw him on Eighty-ninth Street he was just out jogging and he saw you and stopped. Donal didn't head bonk you, either," Mick said. "I'm sure of it."

CHAPTER
23

It was like a difficult diagnosis. You started with the patient's chief complaint, then ran down a long list of signs and symptoms, ordering tests to confirm one suspicion and rule out another. Eventually you accumulated evidence that the patient suffered from, say, ulcers, and not heart disease.

But sometimes you found out the patient had both ulcers and heart disease.

Or neither.

I wanted to discover that Donal Healy had killed Lisa Chiu, and had attacked me in Kennedy Bartlett's apartment.

No such luck. Under ordinary circumstances, if I ran down a blind alley and reached a brick wall, I'd have another chat with the patient, and see if I couldn't order a different series of tests. If that came up blank, I'd stew.

In this case, the patient was dead and there were no more tests to order.

That left stewing.

And, I reminded myself, the Filofax.

At least seven hours to go before I could reasonably expect to get out of the ER and sit down with Lisa's Filofax.

In the meantime, the ambulance-bay doors were beginning to bang open with increasing frequency as the sun rose on the horizon of the day. Hot blasts of air blew in like gusts from the Sahara, along with stretchers bearing the tired, the poor, the yearning to breathe free, and other assorted refuse from the teeming shore.

First came fourteen teenagers who had disturbed a nest of yellow-jacket wasps in Central Park; then seven people from a five-car pileup on the Westside Highway; then, as the temperature soared into the high nineties and the humidity reached record-breaking levels, the difficulty-breathings, sick-to-my-stomachs, chest pains, heat strokes, and hyperthermias.

In the midst of the commotion Denise Aubuchon blew in to admit Edward Zoller, only to find that volume two of his OED-sized chart had gone missing in the melee. Moreover, the results of Zoller's liver series were unavailable.

"Maybe we should stop the day and start over," said Denny, surveying the chaos, as I tried to impress upon some lackey upstairs in Pharmacy the importance of an immediate resupply of bee-sting kits. "Are all of these kids old enough to be in the adult ER? Maybe you could turf some to Peds."

That's all I needed, I thought—Denny turfing patients to Hal. Although it would be a welcome change from their usual tug-of-war over patients. I watched as Denny moved over to Closet Two and pulled the curtain aside. Zoller's face creased into rapture when he saw her. He looked as if he were greeting the Goddess Athena, descending from heaven armed with sword and buckler to champion his cause personally. Denny moved to the side of the stretcher and took Zoller's hands in hers. Neither spoke. I saw Zoller's eyes well with tears, then Denny reached up and pulled the curtain closed again.

"Dr. Sutcliffe?"

"Yes, Julio."

"The MVA with the fractured femur?"

"In OR Two."

"Right. We figured out what language he speaks. It's Tagalog."

"Thank you," I said. "An interpreter coming down?"

"Yeah, Nuncie from the ICU. Oh, and here's Edward Zoller's chart you were looking for—it wound up in Peds by mistake. The clerk just brought it back over."

"Give it to Dr. Aubuchon. Who's on for Ortho?"

"Dr. Hernandez. Um, Dr. Sutcliffe?"

"Yes, Julio."

"My grandmother's taping the news conference with the mayor and the police commissioner, about Dr. Healy's brother, and my uncle's coming down with the tape right after."

Despite myself, I laughed. The way things were going, none of us in the ER would see the noon news conference otherwise. "What would we do without you, Julio?"

"And Dr. Cabot says not to forget the Quality Assurance Committee meeting at two," Julio said. "And not to worry. The committee is pro-forma reviewing all the cases that came through the ER at the time of the bombing, not just yours."

"Good to know," I said.

But my stomach lurched anyway.

By 2 P.M. I had seen and treated ten bee-stung kids, three with eyes swollen up like balloons, until they couldn't see. I'd seen the motor-vehicle-accident who only spoke Tagalog; he turned out to be a felon on the lam and threatened the interpreter and me with a .22 pistol the medics had failed to notice and confiscate. While we were waiting for the cops to disarm the patient, arrest him, and handcuff him to his stretcher railing, an elderly hyperthermia went into convulsions and died. The mayor and the police commissioner held their news conference and did not announce anything we did not already know, a disappointment to staff and patients in the ER alike. Hal Murkland and Denny Aubuchon got into an argument I couldn't overhear about Edward Zoller. I suggested to Hal that he speak to Phil Carchiollo about the stress he was under. This did not make me popular with Hal. He stomped back to the Peds ER after telling me to mind my own business.

"I already tried to get him to talk to Phil," Denny gasped, as we ran up three flights to the conference room where the Q&A was convening. "I even considered putting Prozac in his food. Ev, he's so frayed I wouldn't be surprised if he suffered an acute psychotic break."

"God forbid," I said, as we slipped through the doors to the conference room, five minutes late.

My eyes went first to a young woman seated at the end of the large mahogany table who lifted her gaze from her notebook to meet mine. I registered steady blue eyes and a frosted, large hairstyle—the kind that suggested an intimate relationship with her blow-dryer.

Next I spotted Dr. Christopher Randolph Cabot III, the director of the Emergency Department. Six feet six and angular, he was still arranging himself in his chair, crossing his legs this way and that, folding and unfolding his long, bony hands in front of him, fussing with his water glass, yellow pad, and pen. Cabot was always in motion. He jumped to his feet when Denny and I came in, so of course the others jumped to their feet as well.

There was Dr. Wystan Hugh Auden Madding, the chief of Neurosurgery, well-known as the hospital's odd duck. A thin, middle-aged man with the bedside manner of a rocket scientist and the type of English accent John Cleese made a career out of lampooning, he was the highly acclaimed author of *Computerized Tomographic Scanning and the Sequelae of Traumatic Subdural Hematoma* and *Clinical Implications of Recent Studies of Superoxide Production in Experimental Brain Injury*. Uh-oh, I thought, trouble.

On Madding's right, Dr. Robert Geller, a medium-echelon hospital bureaucrat, chairman of something, I forgot what exactly. Short, pudgy, and blandly nondescript, Geller faded into the background in the company of the two stellar personalities of Cabot and Manning. Tricky to predict what he might do; it depended on whether he chose to side with Madding, who was clearly the adversary, or with Cabot, our defender and protector.

Last but not least, Dr. Guy Shehadeh slumped at the end of the table, bravado and terror alternately playing across his face like the oscillating colors of a police-cruiser roof light.

Denny made our apologies, and we sat. Guy, Denny, then me. My nerves began to dance. I calmed myself by exchanging a glance with Cabot and taking in the familiar specter of him: slate-gray hair flopping in his eyes like a schoolboy's—he probably hadn't changed the cut of it since graduating from boarding school forty years ago—and his bow tie, as always hand-tied and slightly askew.

Madding was staring confusedly from me to Shehadeh and back again. Geller averted his sleepy eyes. "Perhaps I'm confused," said Madding, coughing his silly little cough and shuffling perplexedly through his documentation. "I thought the fist-fight was between Dr. Shehadeh and the ER medic?"

"Yes, that's right," said Chris Cabot.

"You'll forgive my asking, Dr. Sutcliffe"—Madding coughed—"but who hit *you*?"

I wished I knew. "A burglar," I said. "Not a work-related injury."

Madding lifted an eyebrow, suggesting—at least to me—that he secretly believed Guy Shehadeh and I were involved in some sort of sado-masochistic relationship, in the throes of which we achieved unheard-of ecstasy by socking one another and inducing periorbital ecchymosis. Disdain was an art form with Madding. But he moved on. "Dr. Aubuchon?" he prompted.

Denny's hand fluttered against my thigh under the table for reassurance as she opened Lisa's chart in front of her. Then, with her usual aplomb, she launched herself into her authoritative doctor persona. "This was a twenty-four-year-old female of mixed Hawaiian and Chinese parentage," she began. A moment later, she was expertly cataloging the details of Lisa's case and the salient particulars of our treatment of her, without excuse or apology.

Her voice betrayed not a single hesitation; no sentiment hung in the air. About the intubation fuckup, she said merely, "After intubating, we found we had intubated the esophagus. We discovered our mistake within the minute, and corrected it." Moving quickly to the point—Lisa's death—Denny continued, "Because we were unable to obtain early and aggressive operative treatment, we were unable to control internal hemorrhage. We found it impossible to generate an adequate blood pressure and perfusion level. The patient deteriorated and expired. Appropriate notifications were made."

Madding digested Denny's speech. "You are aware," he said, "that hypovolemic shock in a young, healthy adult generally carries a mortality rate of less than twenty percent?"

"I am," said Denny.

"And that overzealous correction of acidosis with bicarbonate may, through the Bohr effect on Hb affinity for O_2, actually reduce O_2 delivery to the tissues?"

"With all due respect, Dr. Madding, I do not think our administration of bicarbonate was 'overzealous,' " Denny disagreed warily.

To my surprise, Madding conceded the point with a sly smile. Turning to Guy Shehadeh, he said, "Doctor, I find your behavior deplorable. What have you to say in your favor?"

I jumped in my chair. While Denny had been speaking, my anxiety level had decreased; now, as Madding directed the glare of his headlights onto Guy, it shot through the roof. *You'd better acquit yourself*, I thought menacingly at Guy. *Rise to the fucking occasion for once.*

"Hugh, please, less provocation," said Cabot. "This is not a trial. Dr. Shehadeh, I'm sure you've had ample time since this tragedy to consider your actions. Please share your reflections with us."

For a moment, a shrill silence reigned. Shehadeh gripped the arms of his chair as if preparing to eject from the Batmobile. I found myself gripping the arms of *my* chair, and holding my breath, too. I willed myself to breathe.

He opened his mouth. "The standard of care is to have an anesthesiologist intubate, but none were available because of the bombing," he said in a rush, "so the situation was emergent—"

Good, I thought. He remembers what I told him this morning.

"—and the decision was made to intubate without the anesthesiologist, but I was distraught because I was in love with her and I failed to auscultate, and, and, and—"

Next to me, I felt Denny stiffen.

"—to the esophagus, and, and, she was my lover and I was in love with her AND I KILLED HER," he finished with a dramatic sob.

Christ. He was playing the sympathy card.

"I learned a lot about hemodynamic instability, too," Guy added hysterically.

Oh, he had their number. If Madding could have fled the room, he would have. Geller, acutely embarrassed, averted his eyes. Even Cabot, normally on even keel no matter what, was reduced to a perfect nonplus.

Denny shot me a sidelong glance: Do you believe this?

Weeping now, Guy raised his gaze to the ceiling, as if imploring forgiveness from on high, then shot his eyes around the room, conveying lacerating distress to the point of distraction. I had no idea he was such an accomplished actor. "I was with her the evening before she . . . before she . . ."—he stumbled over the words—"*was attacked*. If I had only stayed with her the night, I would have been there to protect her when . . . when . . . *he* came in through the window . . ."

I must have made some move as if to hush him. Suddenly, Denny's fingers were digging into my thigh.

"Dr. Shehadeh," said Cabot, "are you saying you know who killed her?"

"He was in love with her, too," Shehadeh went on, barely audible now. His anguish struck just the right note; he was playing himself like a violin, adagio. "He killed her out of jealous rage, out of his jealousy because I was with her and he wasn't—"

"Oh, Guy, don't do this," I said.

"It was Dr. Murkland," said Shehadeh. "If I'd stayed the night with her, I could have protected her from him. It's my fault she's dead."

CHAPTER 24

"YOU'RE not serious," said Phil for the third time, as I followed him into the kitchen.

"I *am* serious," I fumed. "How could Shehadeh do that to Hal like that—claim that Hal had committed *murder*, for God's sake, for the sole purpose of deflecting attention away from himself!"

"Was he successful?"

"Immediately, yes. Madding and Geller and Cabot were so appalled by this outrageous display of emotion, they ended the meeting. 'Thank you very much, Doctors, this committee finds no gross negligence, blah-blah, good-bye.' They practically pushed us out the door. What the long-term effect will be on Shehadeh's sorry career, I couldn't tell you. Although Cabot did suggest to me, in his discreet patrician way, that I was to let him know if Guy suffered any further 'episodes of distress.' "

"Maybe there won't be any further episodes of distress," Phil mused. "You can get away with anything, once. And you can really intimidate people with that kind of emotional display, especially a bunch of traditional, set-in-their-ways guys over the age of fifty. Although I'd worry what the cops are going to make of this sudden impassioned declaration. Did anyone take what he had to say seriously?"

"I doubt it. I mean, they heard the part that Shehadeh was her lover—that's a laugh, I'm sure he wasn't—but I'd bet they discounted the rest. Laid it down to grief and hysteria."

Phil opened the oven and slid out a pan of osso buco and garlic potatoes, setting it on the stovetop. "If Guy engineered that entire scenario, and it worked the way he expected, we're underestimating his talents," he pointed out. "He's cleverer by far than we think. But he's not acting in his own best interests. What did Denise Aubuchon have to say?"

"She was utterly fascinated." I opened the fridge and got out a lemon. "She said, 'I didn't know Shehadeh could do that—did you?' Later she said, 'He's much too high-strung for the ER. He should take up dermatology or something more low-key.'"

"Yeah, I don't think he's cut out for the ER either," Phil said. "Unless he's planning on being the emergency himself. You want a glass of wine?"

"Thanks, no. I think I'll just have lemon water."

It was 7 P.M., and we were at Phil's apartment, in his elegant kitchen with the French bicentennial wallpaper, which, against my will, I was really beginning to like. Phil had all the air conditioners running, and the apartment was cool and quiet—except for the fact that I was yelling about Shehadeh. Okay, I told myself, time to calm down. Think like Lisa. Think yoga.

"This smells fantastic," Phil said. "Denny make it herself?"

"Denny doesn't cook. Denny decorates. Her housekeeper cooks her dinners and freezes them." I squeezed a quarter lemon into a glass, dropped it in, and filled the glass up with ice cubes and water.

"You should get hit over the head more often. How many meals she give you?"

"About four. You'd better appreciate them, too—I went through a lot for those dinners."

"I'm appreciating them already. *Favoloso.*"

We carried our plates into the living room, now furnished with Phil's futon couches, oriental rugs, little Tibetan coffee tables, and brass torchère lamps. Phil liked to eat off the coffee tables while watching TV, usually the evening news hour on PBS. But tonight he switched to CNN, to hear the latest on Donal Healy.

Several ominous and dramatic bars of music issued from the set just as we turned it on, and a picture of Donal Healy looking even more ominous and dramatic flashed on the screen, with a graphic that said KILLER CAUGHT. Then the frowning-serious face of the anchorperson, a woman with frightful hair and a glaringly bright outfit.

"A woman detective in New York faced an agonizing decision," intoned the anchorperson, "after realizing her brother fit descriptions of the Babydoll Killer. The brother of Bernadette Healy is now being held on manslaughter charges."

"Manslaughter?" snorted Phil. "Are you kidding me? He fucking murdered those women."

"But first," continued the anchorwoman, "a story about a very tough choice for any family. Do you turn in someone who's a close relative but who is accused of a terrible crime? CNN's Tracy Levitas reports on the dilemma."

With the magic of TV, we were instantly transported to the Upper East Side, where a perky Tracy Levitas stood in front of the Twenty-fifth Police Precinct. "Imagine you hear the description of a man wanted for rape and murder, but it's not just any man. You think it's your brother. Authorities say Donal Healy's sister was already suspicious of her brother. When she heard the description, she agonized and talked it over with another brother, neurosurgeon Michael Healy, then went to her boss, Detective Lieutenant Vincent Cassatt—"

A clip of police at work, presumably at the Twenty-fifth Precinct.

"This sound familiar at all to you?" Phil asked.

"Not exactly," I said. I cut a piece of osso buco, slathered it with garlic potatoes, and forked it into my mouth. Heaven. Suddenly, I was ravenous.

"She knew it was the right thing to do," said Lieutenant Cassatt, "and she knew that her loyalties lie with justice."

"I love it," said Phil. " 'Her loyalties lie with justice.' God, who writes this stuff?"

"Shh," I said.

We were glued to the set. With fascination, we heard a slightly off-kilter version of the story told to me by Mick on the phone that morning. No mention of Lisa Chiu. Emphasis on Detective First Grade Bernadette Healy, who appeared briefly on camera looking wan but dignified. She sported her sandy Healy hair in a new do since I'd last seen her, short and bouncy, and wore an elegant lime linen suit with a yellow blouse and understated silk scarf.

"Think Bernie had a makeover?" asked Phil.

"Maybe," I said. Bernadette was Homicide, and you couldn't possibly wear a suit like that to a crime scene; you'd never get the smell out of it.

"He said he broke a glass bowl and cut himself while he was cleaning it up, but we knew the third victim was raped in a pile of glass," said Bernie. "And he fit the description."

"What description?" Phil wanted to know. "Who gave a description?"

"I did," I said. "The guy who knocked me down on the sidewalk."

"Oh, God, that was him after all? Christ, Ev!"

We were seeing footage now of Donal Healy and the other "rogue cops," former members of "an elite plainclothes anticrime squad in the Times Square area," as the six men made their way down the courthouse steps after "the grand jury failed to indict," according to Levitas. "Their mandate provided ample opportunity to use and abuse the area's denizens of the night," she intoned, "but the jury must have seen things their way."

"I always wondered about that," said Phil. "The jury failing to indict. How do you think they finessed that?"

I shook my head. Scarfing down the meat and potatoes and guzzling my glass of lemon water, I wiped my hands on my napkin and picked up Lisa's Filofax. Levitas wound down her report. Donal Healy's arraignment was set for the following morning.

"By eleven they'll have the analysis and psychoanalysis ready," Phil said. "How his mother told him he should have been aborted, or his grandfather threatened to cut off his wiener with scissors if he ever dared wet the bed again."

"When it comes to relatives," said Levitas, "blood may be thicker than water. But not when it comes to cold-blooded murder. Tracy Levitas, CNN, New York."

Barely taking a breath, CNN switched to Christiane Amanpour in Sarajevo. With outrageously sexy indignation, Amanpour began to relate the atrocities of the day. Screaming mothers carting wounded children off to the hospital appeared on the screen. Normally I watched these reports, following the heroic escapades of Doctors Without Borders, hoping to catch a glimpse of Dr. Jeffrey Cantor (or hoping not to hear that he had been killed). But tonight I lay back on the couch and turned my attention to Lisa's Filofax.

An expensive burgundy model from Coach Leather—a gift from Lisa's father several years earlier, before he went belly-up in the real estate market—it was fat and full. Lisa used the Dayrunner system and seemed to have all the inserts: datebook, checkbook, addressbook, and a section for expenses. Where to start?

Hoping against hope, I turned to Thursday, August 3, the day before Lisa's death. A business card dropped out; Detective Ost's. With my heart quickening, I scanned Lisa's notations for the day, jotted in her rounded, schoolgirl hand:

Theresa Kahr assaulted A.M.
Call Detective Richard Ost NYPD
at hospital 0630–1830
Good Earth with EFS
M. Healy agrees to take matter up with sister
cancel BTL

That didn't tell me anything I didn't already know, except that she had apparently canceled a date with Brian Linhardt. I paged through the Dayrunner pages after Lisa's death; they were all blank. The pages before her death were haphazardly full, some containing lists of activities; some blank except for notations, "to D.C.," "Return to NYC," and the like. The pages from her medical school semester listed times and classes.

It was not a conventional daybook where you wrote down what you planned to do, cataloging appointments you didn't want to forget. It was like the one Ken Bartlett kept, where you wrote down what had happened and what you did on a particular day, so you could remember in the future where your life went and what you did with your time.

Huh.

Too bad Lisa hadn't written as fulsomely as Ken did.

I flipped from January through May, when Lisa had been in school, then began carefully reading the days since. On May 24 she moved into Jeff Cantor's apartment. The following morning, Jeff left for Bosnia. On May 26 I found the notation "Murkland/ Aubuchon, 0900–1700" and "dinner Aubuchon, summer vegetable;" on May 28, "Murkland/Aubuchon" and "dinner Hal & Carol Murkland, gazpacho." Thereafter "M/A" appeared most days, along with hours worked, interspersed with "WW"—Westside Women's—and hours worked. One or two nights a week, Lisa noted dinner guests, and what kind of meal she had served them. On the first of July Lisa started her summer clerkship, and thereafter there were notations "at hosp" and the hours.

There were no mystery notations—at least not as far as I could tell—that would indicate when Lisa had done the computer work that Denny had spoken of, investigating Hal Murkland's alleged defrauding of Medicaid. In fact, there were no mystery notations whatsoever—everything seemed straightforward and clear. Perhaps not trusting her own memory to decipher cryptic notes at a later date, Lisa wrote most things out rather than using obscure abbreviations. There was even a list in the front of the section with the full names of persons referred to by their initials.

I read through June, July, and the first week of August again, to see how many evenings were unaccounted for. Most of them, I noted. "At hosp" or "M/A" or "WW" during the day, but no entries for the evening hours, except dinner guests and meals served here and there.

So she had logged the hours she worked for Denny elsewhere?

I flipped to the "expenses" section. It worked like a checkbook register, and I had to turn the Filofax sideways to read it. I ran my eye down entries for groceries, CDs (not too many of those), books (mostly medical; a novel here and there), computer discs, stationery supplies, three pairs of chinos from the GAP, two shirts from Tommy Hilfiger, a pair of the popular white boating shoes favored by nurses and med students. Whenever she bought anything with her American Express card, she stapled the receipt to the page and wrote on it what it was for. God, you'd think she had a degree in accounting.

Phil turned off the TV. "Find anything?" he asked, stretching. He started collecting the dirty dinner plates and glasses.

"She kept meticulous records of how she spent her day and how she spent her money," I said. "It's as if she planned to have someone other than herself read it; it's all perfectly clear."

"No clues?"

"Not so far."

"Rats," said Phil. He took the dishes off to the kitchen.

When he came back, I said, "What do you think of Mick Healy?"

Phil flopped on the other couch. "Well, as the oldest brother he's looking after the younger ones. His job is to take care of people and protect them. But ultimately, he fails."

"In what way?"

"He couldn't keep his wife and kids alive. That's a husband's and father's primary responsibility, to protect the wife and kids. Now I'm sure he's going to feel responsible for these terrible crimes Donal's committed.

"He's different from his siblings," Phil went on. "Most cops don't do gray. Developmentally, they never get to gray; gray's a developmental accomplishment. But Mick lives with gray; he's a clinician. At the same time, he faced the ultimate black and white. His family was killed."

I pondered this. "How about Lisa?" I asked.

"*Very* seductive," said Phil.

"Really?"

"Oh, yes, very. With men it was vaguely sexual, with women it was intellectual. She invited admiration and lured you in with it. But I'd bet intimacy was too much for her. And that interesting little quirk of feeding everyone, accommodating everyone—I'd wonder what it was she expected to get back."

"You think she seduced me?" I asked.

"I'd say you and Denise Aubuchon were two of her prime targets," Phil said. "You both liked her and admired her. Then, of course, there was Hal Murkland. Her tactic backfired with him."

I hadn't told Phil about Brian Linhardt and Lisa. "If she was busy seducing everyone," I said, "how would she single out someone she actually wanted to sleep with?"

Phil smiled. "He'd probably single her out. And he'd be a strong character, very individual. She would respect him for that, even if he differed from her. But I would expect him to be a little black and white. Lisa was like Mick Healy's brothers and sister. She didn't exactly do gray."

"Brian Linhardt," I said.

Phil did a double take. "You're kidding. The guy everyone thinks was CIA?"

"Apparently."

"Damn," said Phil. "Well, I can see it. Now that you mention it."

"Hal Murkland's pretty black and white, too," I said. I began going through Lisa's address list, backward from Z, just for a change.

"Hal could use a little therapy," Phil said. "He has a lot of shadow material he's not owning up to. It kind of hovers over his head like the mushroom cloud from the Hiroshima bomb." He lay back on the couch and opened the novel he was reading, a Judith Krantz with a steamy cover showing lots of cleavage. He liked Tom Clancy, too—go figure.

Under *Y* (for *Yoga*, I guessed) I found a card for a place called Bodyworks on 106th Street. Lisa's gym. I imagined Lisa walking through the door of Phil's apartment like that actor in *Ghost*, what's-his-name, from *Dirty Dancing*. I imagined her standing next to the couch, saying, "Ev, when are you going to take up some form of exercise?" or "Your back's been bothering you? Yoga would help, you know."

"Lisa thought I should take up yoga," I told Phil.

He was immersed in his book. "Probably help your back," he said absently.

I clicked open the Filofax and removed the card. On second thought, I decided to leave the card in the Filofax for the cops; I planned to call Detective Ost in the morning and hand it over. You never knew, the cops might like to go down to Bodyworks and interview the staff and other yoga enthusiasts. I clicked the Filofax shut again, and stared off into space for a while.

I probably dozed off for a few minutes.

When I woke, something prompted me to look at the back of the Bodyworks card.

There I found two six-digit numbers.

The first I didn't recognize.

The second was the combination to my locker in the doctors' locker room at the hospital.

CHAPTER
25

It was a little before 9 P.M. when I arrived at Lisa Chiu's gym, a walk-up on the corner of 106th and Broadway, over a stationery store and jewelry shop. I pushed a bell and was buzzed into a narrow stairwell with a bicycle chained to its railing. Making my way to the next landing, I found a door that said "Check In Here."

"Hi," called a friendly woman behind a desk when I walked in. She looked like one of those young women you see Roller-blading in what seems to be their underwear and knee-pads. Her blond hair was in a ponytail high on her head, toppling over a striped terry-cloth headband, and she wore neon-colored spandex. "You're new?"

My eye was briefly caught by a young god pumping iron on the other side of a plate-glass wall. The faint throb of disco music penetrated the room. I remembered Lisa's saying that the gym was open late, after midnight, and I wondered what the neighbors did to cope with the pounding.

"I'm a friend of Lisa Chiu's," I said.

Her face fell immediately. "Oh, I'm sorry," she said. "God, we just couldn't believe it when we saw it in the papers. How terrible."

I sighed and nodded. "We still don't know who did it," I said, bracing myself for the inevitable New York chat about the latest horrible happening. "Of course, you never expect—"

I carried the conversation on for a while in this vein, until I felt I had the young woman's total and absolute sympathy. Then I said, as if sorry to change the subject by bringing up a regrettable necessity, "Her mother asked me to clean out her locker."

"Oh," she said apologetically, "they're combination locks. And you bring your own. We don't have the combination. I'd have to get the manager's permission to cut it off for you, and she won't be in until after ten tomorrow morning."

"That's okay," I said. "I have the combination."

"Oh, good. Let me just find out which is her locker."

After consulting a ledger, she led me down a corridor and through two sets of curtains made out of Indian cotton bedspreads. Following her, I was able to admire her firm buttocks, muscular legs and arms, and ramrod posture. I wondered if you got to look like that doing yoga, or if you had to take up aerobics or—God forbid—Rollerblading in your underwear and knee-pads.

We came into a small room furnished with mirrors, lockers along one wall, a shower, and a bench. Notices about exercise and nutrition plastered the walls that weren't mirrored, along with tear-off sheets of phone numbers to call for information. On a counter under one mirror I saw several piles of flyers, one a schedule of yoga classes. As a salute to Lisa, I took one and slipped it into my bag.

"Here," said the woman. "This one."

"Thanks." I had brought a canvas tote with me, and I dropped it on the floor, then fumbled in my wallet for the combination. I was hoping the receptionist would leave, but she had clearly decided I might need moral support, and as she wasn't doing anything else important, she might as well hover. I was relieved to hear the phone ring. Looking disappointed, she excused herself and jogged out.

Alone at last. I held my breath and dialed the combination lock.

The lock clicked open on the first try, sparing my nerves. I swung open the door.

At first I thought the locker contained only Lisa's leotard, tights, a towel and hairbrush, and I clicked my tongue with frustration. But when I removed all these, dumping them into my bag, I found a large manila inter-office envelope and a box of computer discs. With a surge of tachycardia, I tucked the envelope and box into my bag, stood up on the bench to look into the locker to make sure I had everything, zipped out to the check-in counter, where I said good-bye to the girl with the ponytail, and practically danced down the stairs. I refrained from jogging the seven blocks home to 113th Street, reminding myself that I was a recuperating head-bonkee.

But I swore I'd take up yoga yet.

Back at my apartment, I spent a few minutes patting the dog and stroking the cat, poured myself a large glass of ice water with a slice of lemon, and finally sat down at the kitchen table with the envelope and box of computer discs.

The box, which said "3M High Density DS,HD," seemed to be the original packaging, although the cellophane wrapping had already been removed. When I opened it, all I found was what looked like ten brand-new computer discs with no labels. I put the discs aside; I'd need Phil's computer to tell what was on them, if anything.

I undid the string tie on the envelope and carefully lifted out the sheaf of papers inside.

The top sheet was a tally sheet of dates and hours, written in Lisa's hand in neat columns on a piece of lined notebook paper. Beginning with "July 1, 8–12p, 4hrs," it continued up through August 2, the day before Theresa Kahr's assault and two days before Lisa's own murder. Glancing down the list, I saw that most entries were for "8–12p" and guessed these to be the evening hours Lisa had worked for Denise Aubuchon.

I turned the page.

It took me a moment to figure out what I was looking at. The paper was good-quality watermark, but old. The handwriting was fountain pen and odd: Germanic, I realized. I took off two rubber bands holding together the inch-thick pile, scanning the first page. Some sort of psychiatric documentation—

A stillness descended on me.

I read it once. Then twice. Then reached for the phone and dialed. While I waited for Phil to answer, I read it a third time, still hardly believing my eyes.

"Dr. Carchiollo," Phil said in my ear.

"You'll never guess what I have here," I said. "Did you know Hal Murkland was a patient of Dr. Guderian's when he was nine years old?"

"No!" said Phil, his interest piqued immediately. "Really?"

"Got his records right here. Anton Reichert must have mailed them to Hal when Reichert was busy mailing all Guderian's patient records to former clients. And guess where they were?"

"Don't tell me," Phil said. "In Lisa Chiu's gym locker?"

"Yup. Put on some water for tea. I need you to help me read them."

"Hot dog," said Phil, and hung up.

For a moment I remained sitting, feeling suddenly heavy-headed. I read Dr. Guderian's spidery hand yet a fourth time:

Harold Murkland "Hal" 9 years 7 months of age. Mother states Hal attempted to force neighbor girl Sally (6 years old) to fellate him.

Girl refused and told parents. Parents confronted Mrs. Murkland = how Mother found out. Other problems according to Mother: Hal does poorly in school despite high intellectual ability; suffers from feelings of inadequacy; fears injury; is withdrawn; emotional situations induce anxiety; outbursts.

I remembered Hal saying to me, "Sexual-harassment charges are my worst nightmare! What mother would bring her daughter to me after that? God, she might as well charge me with child abuse—"

Perhaps Lisa *had* charged Hal with child abuse. Attempting to force the girl next door to fellate you was certainly child abuse, even if you were nine years old and had been abused yourself. Because what mother of any of Hal's young patients would believe that Hal had been cured?

I carefully rubber-banded the sheaf of papers and put them back in the manila envelope, then slipped the envelope along with the box of computer discs into my overnight bag, along with a clean shirt and underwear.

I parked the bag next to my front door and collected Maxie for his nightly excursion. I had to carry him in the elevator—his ability to balance himself was not quite up to the staccato stops and starts of the ancient doctors'-residence elevator—but once outside, he showed some vim and vigor, at least as far as the activity of smelling went. While the dog reconnoitered the portal of the doctors' residence and the plywood barricades of the Schiff construction-site scaffolding, a pile of steel girders, two trees, a couple of curbside garbage cans, and a nearby fire hydrant, I reconnoitered my thoughts.

All I could think was, *So Lisa was blackmailing Hal Murkland after all.*

And not just with her knowledge of his Medicaid fraud.

Which would give Hal a perfect motive to kill her.

Maxie, having investigated all the possible sites within a twenty-yard radius that might or might not be suitable spots to poop and piss, selected a curbside location between two parked cars and squatted, then pissed on one of the two trees. Having dutifully performed, he looked up and wagged his tail.

"If I could solve my problems as fast as you solved yours, my life would be a whole hell of a lot simpler," I said.

*   *   *

"Well, let's see," said Phil.

He lay back against the colorful Tibetan pillows with which he had decorated his futon couch and began turning the pages of Dr. Guderian's report over on his chest. "Rorschach, HTP, TAT . . . probably Hal's mother took him first to see a psychologist who ordered a battery of tests, then referred him to Dr. Guderian for analysis. At the first session with Guderian Hal arrived 'neither disheveled nor clean/neat.' " Phil looked up. "Sounds like the Hal we know and love, huh? Neither disheveled nor clean/neat." He went back to reading. "Says when she asked him why he was coming, he said it was because he had 'pushed' the girl next door. Of course, what you want to find out in cases like this is: Who abused the abuser? That's what Guderian's going to be looking for."

I plumped up the pillows on the other futon and lay down myself, cradling my mug of weak Darjeeling tea on my sternum. Phil had gone off one afternoon with Denny Aubuchon and the two had raided the pillows department at ABC Carpets, Denny returning with a few Victorian needlepoints and Phil with an armload of Tibetan pillow covers, which later required an entire afternoon at Bloomingdale's hunting down the pillows that would fit inside the oddly shaped covers.

But they were nice, and I liked them. Once again I had to resist being seduced by Phil's magnificent apartment. Aren't these nice pillows? These could be your pillows, too!

"Ah, the telltale Dairy Queen," said Phil. "In session six Hal acted out going to the Dairy Queen, where he bought a vanilla ice-cream cone that was 'gurgling.' These are play sessions— you're familiar with that, right? The therapist 'plays' with the kid and they act stuff out together. So Hal wants Guderian to eat the ice-cream cone and throw up. Doesn't take too much imagination to figure out what *that* means." He sipped some tea. "In another session, Hal's acting out a scenario with a stuffed horse and camel . . . Horse and camel go to the lake for a picnic; the camel wants ice cream; the horse sits down and the camel lies with its head in the horse's lap . . . So Guderian says, 'Boy or girl camel?' and Hal asks to go to the bathroom. Kids always want to go to the bathroom when their anxiety becomes unbearable; they want to discharge it.''

"Did he answer the question?" I asked.

"No, but a lot of the time they don't. They skirt the issue. That's how you know you're hitting pay dirt. Okay, here we go. Session twelve Hal draws a girl with large sharp teeth like a crocodile, no neck, blank eyes, breasts outside her clothing . . . He says this is 'Cousin Debbie,' and when Guderian asks him to talk about her, he says she is twelve years old, *she likes horses and has her own horse*, and *'she likes ice cream but she threw up.'* Bingo. Debbie fellated him.''

I made a face. "That's a hell of a leap, isn't it?"

"Well, no, not really. Kids play out the events metaphorically, and it's our job to figure out what the real story's about." He flipped a few pages. "Let's see, Guderian requests a meeting with Hal's mother, and—oh, get this. Mrs. Murkland shows up with her sister-in-law, Debbie's *mother*. 'Surprising T,' Guderian says. "T" is Guderian, she's the therapist. I'd be surprised too. So Guderian suggests that she and Mrs. Murkland confer in private, but she says she tells the sister-in-law 'everything . . . ' Guderian has no choice. She gets right to the point: she believes Hal and Debbie have engaged in sexual play together and Hal is distressed. Oh, God—Mrs. Murkland turns to Debbie's mother and says, 'No wonder you offered to pay for the treatment—what kind of perverts are you raising? Who taught her to do that to him?' Hal's aunt breaks down and confesses she divorced her second husband because he was diddling with Debbie. Guderian notes, 'Highly cathartic session for both sister-in-law and Mother.' Wow. I bet.''

"Is there a conclusion here somewhere?" I asked. Already my mind was moving to the next question: *What was this stuff doing in Lisa Chiu's gym locker?* If Anton Reichert mailed it to Hal, what was Lisa doing with it?

"Yeah, here we go," said Phil, sitting up and reaching for his tea. "Termination considerations. Apparently, just when Guderian had high hopes for the progression of Hal's therapy, Mrs. Murkland announced they were moving to another state. She withdrew Hal from Guderian's care." He scanned what I could see was a typewritten sheet, then handed it over. "Why not read this yourself."

Termination Considerations: Unfortunate that we have to terminate just when H is making good progress in bringing repressed material to sessions. Recommended to Mother that she place H in ongoing therapy in new city. T offered 2 names of colleagues.

H will need to monitor impulse control as he grows older & will need to learn to sublimate effectively. How will he do in 30 years when faced with some of the same—when his children get to be the age he was at time of these events? Will he be swamped with anxieties if overstimulated as adult? How will he react when faced with powerful aggressive women?

Hal's inner world, as demonstrated in projective drawings on HTP and the kinetic family drawing, reveal aspects of betrayal and stigmatization, powerlessness, traumatic sexualization, and aggressiveness. In addition there appears to be an inhibition of his self-caring functions, an estrangement from feelings, and a difficulty in mastering his considerable anxiety and rage. Hal's self-drawings especially offer useful metaphors for his damaged sense of self: his head was separated from his body without connection. There were no hands on his body and no mouth through which he could scream, but there were daggers emanating from his orbits. An extremely phallic tree appears to be weeping from a cut in the top. This is a sad and angry and confused youngster who is struggling to master his experiences.

In addition, his Rorschach and TAT provide fantasy material that corroborates his sense of isolation, violation, and sadness. His defenses appear fragile and immature and his superego functions seem punitive and punishing. The key will be whether or not Hal can control his aggressive impulses with which he is so desperately wrestling.

"Christ," I said.

CHAPTER
26

"**Dr.** Sutcliffe?"

I picked my head up from the chart on which I had laid it briefly. Or maybe it had been more than briefly. I had that telltale sandy feeling in my mouth.

"I haven't been asleep, have I?" I asked Julio suspiciously.

"Oh, I don't think so, Doctor. I think you were only resting. You've been standing up the whole time." He handed me the phone over the counter of the nurses' station. "Dr. Carchiollo for you."

I looked at my watch, which didn't help, because I couldn't remember what time I had put my head down. In fact, there were a number of things this morning that I couldn't seem to remember. Like what day it was. "Tuesday" sounded familiar, but I couldn't be sure, and I was embarrassed to ask, in case I'd asked already and forgotten that, too. I looked at my watch again, even though I'd only just looked at it. Noon. Maybe food would help.

Brian Linhardt came around the corner of the nurses' station as I put the phone to my ear. "Hang on," I said. I stuck my arm out and grabbed Linhardt by the sleeve. Then I couldn't remember what I'd grabbed him for, and had to think about it for a minute. "Brian, can you vital me that patient in Closet Three so I can call the ENT consult?" I asked finally.

"You got it," said Brian.

"I didn't ask you already, did I?"

"No, no, that's fine."

"How many times have I asked you?"

"This is the third," he admitted.

I took a stab at humor. "Well, why haven't you done it already?" I barked gruffly, and handed him the chart. He opened it, loitering.

He'd been loitering within earshot all morning. I figured he'd noticed I was having some symptoms of mild concussion (confusion, foggy thinking) because he'd asked rather solicitously once or twice if I felt okay, or if my head hurt. Then again, he could also be loitering in case I said anything that would allow him to deduce my "computer theory" regarding Lisa's death, which I had avoided telling him Saturday night. Linhardt had that casual air about him that he got when he was eavesdropping. I was sure his ears had pricked when Julio said Phil was on the phone.

"Ev, are you all right?" Phil's voice floated out of the receiver.

I put it to my ear. "No. I'm having foggy thinking and confusion."

"Have you talked to Mick Healy?"

"Phil, his brother's being arraigned this morning. I don't want to bother him. I don't even think he's in the hospital yet."

"Well, for God's sake—put in a page for him to see you as soon as he's in. How can you possibly treat patients if you're foggy and confused?"

"It comes and goes. I'll be okay." I didn't add, *And I've got Linhardt watching me like the holy hound of heaven, I don't need you to fuss over me, too*. "Which patient is this you're calling about, Phil?"

He knew that I knew perfectly well that he was at home, and

that he wasn't calling about a patient. He was calling about the computer discs Lisa had in her locker. "Linhardt stalking you, huh?" he said, and then, "Hon, you sure you want to hear this now?"

"Could we get on with it, please?"

There was a pause. Irritability was also among the sequelae of head bonk. I knew this and everybody I worked with knew it, too. Which was very exasperating. But I couldn't be exasperated, in case they thought I might be irritable. Which, frankly, was pretty irritating.

"The irritation is helping me focus," I said, sticking out my tongue at the phone. I did actually feel as if the fog was lifting. It was the damnedest thing—it rolled in, it rolled out. "But I'll call Mick Healy if you're concerned. Now talk."

"Promise?"

"Promise."

"Okay," said Phil. He took a deep breath. "The discs are Hal Murkland's patient records, just as we thought. I've been through about thirty patients' worth, and there are definitely irregularities. To put it mildly. Creative billing at the very least."

"Like what?"

"Duplicate billing, redundant testing, phantom charges . . ."

I sighed. Because of its size, fiendish complexity, and lax management practices, the Medicaid program was a sitting duck for scam artists and thieves every which way including loose. Medicaid fraud was routinely perpetrated by billing companies, health-care providers, medical-equipment suppliers, and even organized crime and drug dealers. Gouging the government's principal health-care programs has become so easy and lucrative, in fact, that I'd recently heard that some of Florida's cocaine importers were dropping out of the drug trade to take up the less dangerous enterprise of scamming Medicare and Medicaid. Even honest doctors perpetrated minor Medicaid deception. Everybody knew that, when dealing with tight-fisted third-party insurers who balked at paying for recommended treatment, you had to follow the guidelines: one symptom from Column A and two physical findings from Column B, with supporting notes in the chart. But duplicate billing, redundant testing, and phantom charges were carrying things too far. Seriously too far.

"You determined this how?" I asked, picking up another chart, bracing the phone between my ear and shoulder, and pretending to scan the triage notes. Brian Linhardt was still hovering. I caught his eye. *Stat,* I mouthed, and he moved off.

"It's not hard," Phil said. "You read the chart notes for a patient visit and see what Hal did for the patient. Then you look up the CPT billing codes in the trusty Physician's Current Procedural Terminology Manual, and see what Hal's billing for. You compare the two and see if they jibe. For every chart I've looked at so far, what Hal did for the patient is not what he billed for."

I watched Linhardt disappear behind the curtain of Closet Three. Turning my back, I said quietly, "Hal didn't back his charges up in the chart notes?" Then it dawned on me. "Just a minute—he's charting on the *computer?*"

"Yeah, the program has a word processor built in for chart notes. I don't use it because I'm a shrink; if my patient records are ever subpoenaed, I want them on paper—you give them a disc and the next thing you know they're doing an Ollie North search on it. But the point is, it's easy to use; you hit F-nine and you can write up the notes. Hal's got very good chart notes for all his patients. Comprehensive and diligent. Very bad idea, though, if you're going to snooker Medicaid. The first thing any investigator is going to say after he subpoenas your records is, 'You billed for an injection, but we can't find the documentation for it.' "

I wondered if Hal's alleged computer illiteracy and his begging me for help could have been some kind of act, just in case he got caught: "Not me, officer, I don't even know how the damn thing works—how could I enter all these false codes? Must be the billing clerk's fault." But if Hal were that clever, he would be clever enough to make his chart notes agree with the billing codes.

Unless Hal had been concerned he wouldn't remember which

chart notes were true and which he'd finessed, so he'd maintained correct chart notes regardless of what he billed in order to know exactly what he had and had not done for the patients . . . But could Hal be that stupid? If he was going to scam Medicaid, and if he was dependent on Joshua Waterman and Lisa Chiu to computerize his records, he'd have to anticipate that they would notice the discrepancies. Which is exactly what Denny Aubuchon said had happened. According to Denny, Josh had been entering the backlog of office records while Lisa was away at med school, and had approached Denny with discrepancies.

"Oh, and by the way," Phil added, "you know that doll, the Raggedy Ann, that Lisa had? It belonged to a little patient named Ruthie Day who died at the beginning of the summer. Lisa was with Ruthie and her family when she died, and Ruthie's mother gave Lisa the doll to remember her by."

"This was in Hal's chart notes?"

"Yeah, I told you—he keeps meticulous chart notes."

"Just a minute. Hal includes in his chart notes all this information about how the patient's mother gave Lisa a doll, but he doesn't back up his billing charges? Phil, it doesn't make sense."

"Sure it does. Hal screws up as a kid and gets caught—very humiliating—and even though he finally gets a good mother in Dr. Guderian, with whom he can begin to expiate some of his guilt, that gets cut short when his real mother yanks him out of treatment to move to another city. This Medicaid scam is probably some kind of massive repetition compulsion. Let's face it, his impulse control sucked then—excuse the pun—and apparently it sucks now—scamming Medicaid is poor impulse control. Hal's still looking for the good mommy and waiting to get spanked."

The rest of the day went downhill from there. In the ER, we got creamed. First there was the screaming Hispanic woman in an advanced stage of labor—already cresting—with the seventeen hyperventilating male relatives who refused to decamp to the waiting room. One had a knife and stabbed the security guard. A

melee ensued, the cops arrived and arrested the seventeen relatives, and the woman gave birth to twin boys. "As if she didn't
already have enough male relatives," a nurse commented sourly.

Next came the homeless man with the maggot-infested leg
ulcers and God only knew what else. Still mad at Shehadeh for
his outrageous behavior the day before, and knowing full well
that Shehadeh harbored a pathological horror of maggots, I assigned him the patient and told him to keep me informed.

After that, the woman suffering from postpartum depression
who tried to drown her baby in the bathtub. Luckily the child's
father was at home and intervened. The baby was in respiratory
arrest when the medics arrived, but they got her intubated and
rushed her into the pediatric ER. (The last I heard, the baby was
in guarded condition but expected to survive.) Meanwhile, we
had to deal with the mother. She slit her wrists after trying to
drown the baby. The cops were still trying to figure out how to
handcuff someone with bandaged wrists to the stretcher rail as
they wheeled her off to Psych.

Plus the usual weak-and-dizzy-all-overs, chest-pains, dehy-
drateds, difficulty-breathings, emphysemas, asthmas, sore-
throats, fractured-wrists, sprains and torn-ligaments—the
Rollerblade and bicycle-messenger contingent—

Oh, and another pileup on the Westside Highway shortly after
3 P.M., including the dispute about whose fault it was and the
resultant gunfire. The two guys who got into the argument at the
scene were DOA; they shot each other dead. Everyone else came
into the ER, where *they* got into a dispute about who was going
to be seen first by the doctors. "Nobody else is armed, are they?"
I asked, and paged Security to find out. Security confiscated three
box-cutters, one .22 pistol, a switchblade, and a hunting knife. "I
don't want any of their relatives coming into the ER proper," I
decreed. "I don't care who they are. They wait outside."

The really big event of the afternoon was Tony Firenze's impaled construction worker. "He fell from the scaffolding and
landed on those half-inch rods that reinforce concrete," Tony

breathlessly regaled any and all possible listeners afterward. "A big fat fellow, young guy, Irish as Paddy's pig, wide awake and *freaking*. All retrospinal, did not enter the abdominal or chest cavities." Firenze pantomimed his horror and astonishment, and laughed at his own adrenaline high. "What do I do? Jesus, what do I do? Cut down over it, flayed him, and took it out." Netted Firenze a spot on the evening news, too.

Meanwhile, I chewed over in my mind what I knew about Hal Murkland and Lisa Chiu. Hal Murkland was defrauding Medicaid. Lisa Chiu was dead. Lisa had had Hal's patient records on disc in her gym locker, along with Dr. Guderian's damning notes. She'd deposited sixteen thousand dollars into her bank account in the four weeks before she died.

By the time I sat down with a pile of charts at about 5 P.M. to write my notes, my mind was buzzing with the details of what happened the evening before Lisa was so brutally stabbed to death.

In particular, I was beginning to appreciate a personality trait of Hal Murkland's that I had never noticed before.

Turkey Murky, the guy we all made fun of in medical school for his shy and bumbling nerdiness, and for never seeming to have his wits entirely about him, it turned out was an inspired and pathological liar.

He cut himself shaving.

No, a guy fell on him at a bachelor's party.

No, he and Lisa were having wild sex, and he fell off the bed onto the glass.

No, he tried to kiss Lisa and she slapped him, and the glass broke against his face.

Suppose none of these explanations was true. Suppose Lisa hit Hal not because he was trying to kiss her, but because he was attacking her. Suppose she broke the glass herself, wielding it like a dashed beer bottle in a barroom brawl—and when that didn't work, suppose she then ran to the kitchen for a knife, Hal hot on her heels—

Suppose he wrestled the knife from her—

Of course, afterward he would be appalled at what he had done. But he was an emergency-room physician. He was used to functioning under the influence of adrenaline, he was trained to calm himself and think clearly no matter what the circumstances. I could almost hear him telling himself what to do: Put out another glass in the dining room, pour some champagne in it, say it must have been someone who came after you left. The Babydoll Killer, blame it on him. Need a doll. Didn't Lisa have that Raggedy Ann, the doll What's-her-name's mother gave Lisa when the little girl died?

Oh, Hal, I thought. What pushed you over the brink? You calmly let her blackmail you for four weeks, gave her the sixteen thousand dollars for her medical school tuition. Kissed her outside your office. Went with her to her apartment, opened a bottle of champagne to celebrate—celebrate what, Hal? Did you really think she would run off with you if you left Carol? Love you, if you paid her tuition? What is it with you and women's tuition, anyway? You were already paying for Carol's, and continuing to pay even though you knew Carol didn't love you—why repeat the same old ploy with Lisa? If it didn't work with Carol, what made you think it would work with Lisa?

The clerk's voice broke my reverie. "Dr. Sutcliffe?"

"Yes, Julio."

"Dr. Quinn's on the phone. Did you want to talk to him?"

"No, have Shehadeh talk to him."

I thought about Shehadeh's anger toward Lisa, and how Guy had complained bitterly about her "duplicity," as he called it.

Did the scales fall from Hal's eyes? Did he, like Guy Shehadeh, come to the conclusion that Lisa was shmoozing him, leading him on? Hal went to Lisa's apartment with expectations that there was something worth celebrating with champagne, but instead there were raised voices, according to Tony Firenze.

Had Lisa become one strong woman too many for Hal to have to deal with? Lisa thought Hal was a pressure cooker about to blow his top. Denny said she was fantasizing about putting Prozac in Hal's food. Even I had suggested to Hal that he speak to Phil about the stress he was under . . . Of course, that was after Lisa had been murdered.

"Dr. Sutcliffe?"

"Yes, Julio."

"We've got a pair of domestics coming in." By "domestics" he meant people involved in a domestic dispute resulting in injury. "Apparently, he beat her and she stabbed him a couple of times, then he cold-cocked her with a cast-iron frying pan."

I looked at my watch. It wasn't anywhere near time for night-float sign-out. I resigned myself to two more patients. "In the head?"

"Yeah."

"She conscious?"

"A-plus-oh-times-one, lapsing in and out."

"We'll need a neurosurgeon. Stabbed where?"

"Chest, abdomen."

"Probably need thoracic, too, but let's have a look when he gets here. Coming in with cops, right?"

Julio nodded and reached for the phone. I shut the chart I'd had open in front of me for the last ten minutes, tossed it back in the chart rack with a mental note to record my orders later. Got a pair of gloves and went to stand by the doors to the ambulance bay.

It happened all the time. Husband beat wife. Wife stabbed husband. Afterward, everybody weeping with contrition. I'd seen couples trying to kiss and make up as we wheeled them both off to surgery.

"What have we got?" asked Dr. Kessie Savarkar in her bell-like, lilting voice. Like a third of the doctors at University Hospital, she was foreign-born and still spoke with her native accent—in her case, the clipped tones of British Colonial India. She lined up beside me in front of the ambulance bay doors. As usual, she was immaculately made up: eye shadow and mascara, blush, lipstick that matched her fingernail polish—all contrasting startlingly with the tikka on her forehead. She had short black hair and customarily wore boys' clothes, today tailored trousers and a plain white shirt buttoned to the neck. I found her extremely exotic.

"Domestic." I filled her in on the details as she pulled on gloves. Then Guy Shehadeh sidled up.

Savarkar, Shehadeh, and I were known as the "S Squad." I was the resident; they were the two interns on my team. All we needed were a couple of med students with last names beginning with *S* and we could start a secret society.

"I've been meaning to ask you, Guy," I said, "whether there was any truth whatsoever to all that bullshit you spouted about Hal Murkland at the Quality Assurance Committee yesterday."

He bristled. "Fuck you, Ev."

Savarkar shot us a sidelong look.

"Because I was just wondering where you were," I said, "between two and six A.M. Friday morning after you got done—"

He brought up his forearm and slammed me against the wall.

"—taking out the garbage and cleaning your apartment," I persisted, even though my vision clouded with millions of little sparkly stars from the blow. For a minute I couldn't see anything. Oh, shit, I thought.

But the stars went away. And when I opened my eyes I saw the emergency-room director, Chris Cabot, peering at me. His large bony hand, fingers splayed, rested on Guy Shehadeh's chest. Kessie Savarkar gazed at me openmouthed from over Cabot's shoulder.

"Dr. Sutcliffe, are you all right?" Cabot was asking.

"Yes," I said, although I wasn't. I blinked a few times and steadied myself against the wall.

"I think you should sit down," said Cabot.

"I'm okay," I insisted. By now I was working hard not to slide down the wall to the floor.

He wasn't convinced but, gracious as ever, deferred to my

judgment. "I'll see you in my office now, Dr. Shehadeh," he said, turning on his heel and moving briskly off.

Guy glared at me, then turned and followed Cabot. The small crowd of nurses and orderlies who had been watching the entertainment dispersed. By concentrating, I found I could stand on my own. But I was careful not to move my head too suddenly.

Brian Linhardt appeared. "What are we waiting for?" he asked.

I told him about the two domestics. I didn't think he'd seen the commotion with Guy, which was probably just as well.

Brian snorted. "She stabbed him, and he cold-cocked her with a cast-iron skillet? Anybody dead?"

"Not yet," said Kessie Savarkar.

Only Lisa, I thought.

CHAPTER
27

KENNEDY Bartlett roused himself from his morphine-induced stupor. "Bills," he said.

"How about a kiss first?" I asked.

"Okay. Kiss." He turned his cheek and I planted a noisy buss on it. I pulled up a chair and sat down.

"Dance wi' Merce again lass night," Ken slurred. "Wait'll he hears *that*." He cackled merrily, then became serious. "Howsa dog?"

I explained that I thought it might be better if Maxie came to stay with me for a while, so he wouldn't be lonely. To my relief, Ken nodded, and didn't find it necessary to engage me in conversation about the dog's elaborate food routine or his bathroom habits. "Fun inna elevator," Ken said.

"He's adjusting superbly to the elevator," I agreed. "And he's very proud of himself. But he misses you."

Ken smiled. "Give'm a kiss."

He looked about the same as he had when I saw him on Saturday; no better, no worse. But he looked *old*. For several years now he had been losing weight steadily but not precipitously, and suddenly it seemed to have caught up with him. I remembered the time my grandparents had come to the airport to pick me up— I forget where I'd been—and they suddenly looked *old*. I was fifteen at the time. I felt fifteen now, going on six: vulnerable, vulnerable, and more vulnerable. I realized I was afraid. Afraid of losing Ken and afraid of getting old and afraid of getting sick and afraid of dying. "How are you feeling?" I asked with forced cheerfulness.

Ken blew a raspberry and waved his hand in flamboyant dismissal. "Whassa matter wi' your eye?" he demanded. "God, listena me, I can' even talk." He reformulated himself, speaking with exaggerated articulation as if to a deaf person forced to read his lips. "What's the matter with your eye?"

I debated whether to tell him. Finally I said, "I got mugged." That was a mistake; he wanted to hear all about it. I'd forgotten that Ken was even more of a gossip hound than Phil. I made the same raspberry Ken had made when I asked how he was feeling, and waved my hand in the same gesture of flamboyant dismissal.

We shared a good laugh.

"Atta girl," said Ken. "Knew you could handle it."

"Would you like to go over your bills?" I asked, taking the rubber-banded wad out of my bag. After work I'd dutifully gone home and walked the dog, then traveled by subway down to Ken's apartment and back so I could bring him his bills.

But the conversation had tired him. He lay back against his pillow and shut his eyes. " 'Lectric high causa air-conditioning," he said, his voice once again slurred. "Joshua Waterman tryin' straigh'n out medical bills." He snored for a little, maybe a minute or so, then woke with a start. "Phone all fucked up, callsa Dominican Republic." Then, more clearly again: "You pay the bills. You take care of it."

"Okay," I said. Since he'd arranged for me to have power of attorney at the beginning of the summer, I could sign his checks. "Where's your checkbook?"

He fumbled under the covers, handed me his daybook.

"Checkbook," I said. "This is your daybook."

"Take it. Lista calls I made."

"Do I have to talk to the phone company, or you talked to them already?"

"You talk. Happened before. They know I don't call Dominican." He pointed weakly at the table next to the bed. I saw his checkbook, and reached over and took it.

"Okay, I have your checkbook and your daybook. Anything else?"

He tried to sit up, didn't quite succeed, and slung an arm over the bedside rail at the night table, knocking a pile of papers and file folders onto the floor. Out of one folder fell his résumé, and press clippings from his fifty-year career in dance.

"Yeah," he said as I bent down to gather the papers. "Take that file." He lay back and closed his eyes.

"Countin' on you t'write my obituary," he said.

I had to brace myself before entering Joshua Waterman's room. The last thing I wanted to do was walk in, say hello, and burst into tears because Ken Bartlett looked *old* and I felt fifteen going on six and vulnerable and afraid of losing Ken and afraid of getting old and afraid of getting sick and afraid of dying. Josh Waterman had all he could handle facing his own illness and mortality—why should he have to deal with my wimping and whining when here I was healthy?

"You have to be strong for the patients," my Dad liked to say, "because you're a mythological figure to them, the high priest or priestess of the health god." Dad was a pediatric neurologist affiliated with a hospital in New Jersey. He'd had two heart attacks, coronary bypass surgery, and a couple of angioplasties, but he still practiced and kept a full schedule. Presumably he was still being strong for the patients, too.

I expelled a lungful of air like an old plow horse, and walked into Joshua Waterman's room.

I found him playing cards with Carol Murkland.

"Hi!" they chorused, looking up from their game. "Wanna play?"

I felt a smile of relief crease my face. Josh looked wan but cheerful. "Pull up a chair," he said, grinning up at me and running a hand through his floppy brown hair to get it out of his eyes. "We'll deal you a hand."

"You can help me beat him, Ev," Carol chimed in. "He's been beating me all afternoon."

"Thanks, but I can't stay. I just wanted to look in. You look much better, Josh." I glanced up at the IV pole to see what antibiotic Denny was prescribing: cefuroxine. Behind the bed, the Pleur-Evac machine bubbled. "How you doing with the chest tube?"

"Okay, right now," Waterman said. "It kind of moves around. Yesterday it was really bothering me, but right now it's in a relatively painless position."

Carol Murkland mouthed something at me and shook her head.

"The main problem is the chills and fevers," Josh went on.

I nodded. I was standing on the left side of the bed and Carol was sitting on the right side, so while Josh was talking to me he had his head turned away from her. "That might be a side effect of the Bactrim."

"That's what Denny said."

Carol held up one hand in the deaf sign for *L* and I understood suddenly that she was mouthing "Lisa." She tapped her head and pointed at Josh, then crossed her forearms back and forth like a football umpire, shaking her head.

He doesn't know about Lisa. Don't tell him.

"But I feel much better," Josh said bravely. "And Carol's been bringing me power juice to boost my immune system, and echinacea tea."

"Power juice?"

"You know, power juicing," said Carol. "Hal gave me that

Braun juicer for Christmas last year. I make one juice out of carrots, beets, ginger root, and apples—''

''It's really good,'' said Josh.

''—and there's also spinach, kale, and parsley with carrots and
beets—''

I tuned out briefly while Carol recited recipes for her various
power juices. How could they not tell Josh that Lisa was dead?
He'd worked with her, for Chrissake. He seemed to be doing
well—it wasn't as if he were about to undergo emergency pleu-
rectomy, or lying in the Intensive Care Unit battling for his life—
why coddle him like this? Why not tell him?

''Carol takes good care of me,'' Josh said. He put down his
cards and reached for her hand, which she took, smiling.

I looked at the two tousled heads. Carol and Josh both affected
the same floppy, in-your-eyes hairstyle. With their similar coloring—dark brown hair, warm chestnut eyes—they looked almost
like brother and sister. It occurred to me that Denny Aubuchon
and Hal and Carol Murkland were all the ''family'' Josh Waterman had. His own family had disowned him two years ago when
he announced he was gay and infected with the AIDS virus.

If they hadn't told Josh about Lisa's death, I couldn't talk to
him about the computer discs I'd found in her locker.

It was a dumb idea, anyway, I supposed. Josh probably
wouldn't have told me anything, and I would have put him in an
extremely awkward position asking him to talk behind Denny's
and Hal's backs.

It was just as well I'd found Carol Murkland with him.

Jeff Cantor's cat Fat Face sat square in the middle of my chest,
one paw stretched to either side of my neck, and purred and
purred. Out of curiosity that morning I had weighed him on my
bathroom scale—he weighed *twenty-four pounds*—and I could
hardly breathe from the weight of him. But I was grateful. The
cat was not in love with me like Mick Healy was, nor was he
scamming Medicaid like Hal, nor had he possibly murdered some-

one . . . I had had enough of complicated relationships, complicated thoughts, complicated conversations, and complicated maneuvers. It was nice to lie on the couch and commune with a fuzzy being whose idea of a pleasant interaction was to sit on you and snore.

It was just after 9 P.M. Tuesday evening, and Phil and I were in my apartment. I was lying on the couch enjoying the cat and Phil was clearing away the dinner plates. We had dined fabulously on veal goulash prepared by Denny Aubuchon's housekeeper, and a green salad with avocado dressing whipped up by Phil in the Cuisinart.

Every time he went into the kitchen Maxie the dog staggered after him, and every time he came back the dog staggered back.

"I feel like a new parent," said Phil, gazing down at Maxie, who wagged his tail hopefully and tried to look worthy of dinner scraps. "Guilty and incompetent, but wary of being manipulated." Phil went back into the kitchen. I heard him put the dinner dishes down on the floor so the dog could lap up the gravy.

"What did Mick Healy say?" Phil asked when he returned with two cups of mint tea.

So much for communing with the cat. I reluctantly put him down on the floor and sat up.

I had seen Mick right after night-float sign-out. I dutifully went over to his office on Schiff Two, filled out the form all first-time patients had to fill out, and schmoozed the receptionist, a kindly-looking middle-aged woman with frosted hair. I allowed myself to be escorted to the examination room, took off my clothes and put on the cotton patient bathrobe, got weighed and had my height measured by the physician's aide—a young man who looked very much like Joshua Waterman had before Josh developed full-blown AIDS—and had my blood pressure taken. After that I fidgeted for five minutes until Mick came in.

He looked terrible. His cornflower-blue eyes were bloodshot and sunk in shadow. His face was slack, as if all the muscles had collapsed from exhaustion. Even his clothes seemed lifeless. Although he wore a crisp business shirt with a colorful rep tie tucked into it, and pressed linen slacks, they hung on him like limp sheeting.

"Oh, Mick, I'm so sorry about Donal," I said. "How was the arraignment?"

He shook his head. "Bad. There was talk about him 'doing the right thing,' and I was worried they might just leave him in a room with a loaded pistol. And that after Bernie and I bent over backward to go in and take him fast—when he was arrested—so he couldn't get his own gun and go out in a blaze of glory." He turned on the water in the sink and reached for the Betasept dispenser.

I looked at his big, broad back sagging in defeat. "Talk by whom?"

"Cops. He's an ex-cop. It looks bad, an ex-cop is a serial killer. They'd all love it if he just shot himself. One guy came up to me afterward and said, 'He spit on the shield that I hold dear and that my friends died for.'" Mick pulled down a towel and dried his hands.

"How awful."

"I can't take much more," he said. "Now tell me again about this foggy thinking."

I wanted more than ever to take him in my arms and banish his sorrows. In the split second before he touched me, it would have been possible had I had the gumption to make the first move. But he seemed so vulnerable, I would have felt as if I were taking advantage of him. And as soon as he touched me—he put his fingertips lightly on either side of my jaw—I'm sure he would have felt that he was taking advantage of me had he in any way behaved in a sexual manner. Because now he was my doctor and I was his patient. I was under his care. A door closed between us. There was not a hint of sexuality in anything he did or said, not even a flicker of it in his eyes. His bedside manner was impeccable.

Afterward, when I was dressed again and saw him in his office, he was visibly tense. Instead of sitting at his desk, he leaned on a bookcase behind it and spoke to me with his arms crossed over his chest.

"I don't know what causes foggy thinking and I don't know anyone who does," he said. "It's probably due to traumatic labyrinthitis or some inner-ear disturbance. Of course, there's always the concern that there's a subdural brewing . . . We could get you a CAT scan, or I could recommend an ENT or a neuro-otologist if the symptoms persist. Up to you."

I nodded.

We looked at each other.

"I wish I could make as eloquent a speech about comforting you in your time of trouble as you made the other day at T Salon about comforting me in mine," I said finally.

He recoiled as if I had slapped him. "Oh, Ev, don't," he pleaded. "Unless you're willing to tell me your mind."

I thought about saying I didn't know my mind, but I did know it: I knew in the long run I couldn't leave Phil for Mick. And in the short run I couldn't sleep with Mick without having left Phil. The physical pull was so strong, however, I could barely make myself stay in my chair. If he had asked me my body instead of my mind, the answer would have been simpler.

"Let's talk in a few days," I suggested.

That seemed to hurt him more. Fearful of saying anything else—if I wounded him further I knew my control would go right out the window, and I'd be all over him just like that night on the street—I did the only thing I could think to do. I left.

"He said the symptoms might continue," I told Phil, "or they might not. It's not uncommon to have attention and memory problems for six weeks to six months after the injury. The pattern is that most people get gradually better. I don't have any neurological deficit that he can see." Even talking about Mick stirred me. I reached for my mint tea, carefully. I didn't want Phil to detect any defensiveness on my part concerning Mick Healy. "He also said to avoid stress. That's a laugh."

Fat Face jumped up again, and I put him down again. He

looked confused. Surely I hadn't meant it. He jumped back up. I put him back down. He crawled under the couch, which was where he liked to sit if he wasn't sitting on me. The dog couldn't pester him there.

"I was just going to ask you what you wanted to do about Hal Murkland's patient records," Phil said. He blew on his tea, then set it on the table to cool. "Maybe I shouldn't."

"If, and, yes, no, and but," I sighed. "I don't know what to do. I have a real ethical problem here. I don't know whether to tell Denny we have the discs, or to tell Hal we have them. I'm disinclined to hand them over to the cops."

"No, let's not."

"What do you want to do about Guderian's files?"

"Well, rightfully they belong to Hal," Phil said. "But if we hand them over, he'll know we read them."

Neither one of us voiced what was uppermost in both our minds: if Hal had killed Lisa the files were evidence.

"How about Lisa's Filofax?" I asked.

"That was in *your* locker. Why don't you put it back and 'find' it tomorrow, and call Detective Ost?"

"I can't bear any more subterfuge," I said. "I think I'll call Ost and confess I kept it overnight."

"Then you have to confess you went to her gym. Because eventually *he'll* get to the gym, and they'll tell him you cleaned out her locker."

I pushed away my tea. "There's no way to do this except to come clean with Hal and the cops, Phil."

He considered this. "Tell Hal first, then the cops."

"Right. Give Hal the opportunity to explain."

"That's only fair. And he probably needs a lawyer. Maybe your brother could help with that?"

I snorted. "It would certainly make us feel less guilty, wouldn't it—if we helped Hal get a lawyer after we accused him of defrauding Medicaid?" I didn't add, *and of murdering Lisa Chiu.* I was still hoping it wasn't possible.

"You want to call, or should I?" Phil asked.

I sighed and reached for the phone. Dialed Hal's number. Reminded myself that there was a difference between melodrama and tragedy, and between fate and destiny.

"I don't know where he is!" Carol Murkland shrieked into the phone without saying "hello."

Jesus. I pantomimed to Phil that he should go into the bedroom and get on the extension. "Carol, it's Ev Sutcliffe."

"The cops told him not to go anywhere without telling them and I don't know where he is! He didn't tell Denny, he didn't leave me a note, he canceled all his patients for tomorrow and he called the ER and said he was taking a personal day Thursday—"

I heard Phil pick up the extension. "Did Hal go down to D.C. for Lisa's funeral?" he asked in that reasonable tone of voice only shrinks possess. "Could he have done that?"

"The funeral's private." Carol got a grip on herself immediately; Phil's magic touch. "Nothing in the church, just something at the graveside. Family only. Besides which, do you think the Chius want him at her funeral when the police think he's the one who killed her?"

"But could he have gone to D.C.?" Phil persisted.

His skin was thicker than mine. I was shocked that Carol would come right out and say that her husband might have murdered Lisa.

"I guess," Carol conceded. "The funeral's tomorrow morning."

"Have the cops been looking for him?" I asked.

Carol groaned. "The cops, Denny, the ER—one of his patients came in. He's going to get himself in such a big mess, disappearing like this. Now the cops will probably arrest him. Why does Hal always have to be so provocative?"

"Anyone else Hal might tell where he's gone?" I asked.

A frosty silence greeted this question.

"Carol?" Phil asked after a moment. "Would you like some

company? Should we come up, or would you like to come down?''

"No," said Carol bitterly. "No, I don't want some company. I want people to stop calling me. I want to unplug the phone, take a shower and cool off, and get in bed with a drink and a book. Good night." She hung up.

"Oh, boy," I said when Phil returned to the living room. "This is too much for me. What was it Scarlett O'Hara said, 'I'll think about it tomorrow'?"

"Something like that." Phil came around the coffee table, sitting down next to me on the couch. "How's your head?"

"Fine right now. Except for all the thoughts in it."

"Not foggy?" He slid his arm behind my shoulders.

"Nuh-uh."

"Or confused?"

Fleetingly I thought of Mick, but firmly put him out of my mind. Phil feathered his fingers against my throat, which always gave me shivers. I shivered deliciously.

"About what?" I murmured.

"Oh, I dunno," he said. He unbuttoned one button of my shirt. Phil was always very good about doing one thing at a time, until you couldn't stand it anymore, and finding four or five things to do before he even got around to kissing you. I pulled his shirt out of his pants and trailed my hand over his belly.

"Let's get out of our brains for a while," he groaned, his breath coming hard.

CHAPTER
28

MY emotions and the aftereffects of head-bonk conspired against me. For three days I went to the hospital, worked all day, came home in the evening, ate dinner, went to bed directly after dinner, fell asleep immediately, and slept all night. I awoke feeling exhausted amidst pieces of dreams. Hal's cousin Debbie with her crocodile teeth, no neck, blank eyes, and breasts outside her clothing. Hal yelling and throwing naked babydolls and small cars and trucks at me, while I asked about Medicaid fraud, unable to hear my own voice. Mick Healy bending over me, Guy Shehadeh behind him. Brian Linhardt offering me Chinese nerve tea, asking, "Are you feeling all right?" Lisa Chiu, her hair lifting on the wind, turning toward me very very slowly, speaking without sound.

It became extremely difficult to get up in the morning. I relied on Phil to haul me out of bed and throw me into a cold shower. I relied on Phil to make my tea and breakfast. I relied on Phil to push me out the door when it was time to go to the hospital, and to pull me back in when I arrived home at night.

I overheard him speaking in low tones on the telephone. "I

don't know whether this is a biologically based problem that needs a biological follow-up, or a psychological problem." Pause. "She says she doesn't have nausea." Pause. "Depression related to the loss of her friend." Pause. "Foggy thinking, some headache, dizziness if she stands up too fast—that's post-concussive. But the oversleeping I think is depression."

Tell me about it, I thought. I made a big pot of Linhardt's herb tea, cooled it, poured it into an empty Evian bottle, and took it to the hospital with me.

I met with Chris Cabot because I thought he should be aware of the problems I was having, and why I thought I should continue working despite them. He pointed out rather kindly that I was recuperating from a serious injury, that I was recently bereaved, and that these things took time. I had just enumerated for him in exquisite detail exactly what I had forgotten, he said, which showed I wasn't forgetting as much as I thought I was. He suggested that I take off a few days, and when I refused insisted that I take breaks from time to time throughout my shift. He offered to "put a word in the ear" of the attending. I said I would appreciate it.

Detective Ost, normally willing to engage in elusive and elliptical discussion of the matter at hand without actually telling me anything, rebuffed me entirely. "Doc, I can't talk to you," he said early Friday morning. He was in the ER on a robbery case, but I shanghaied him and dragged him into the utilities room for an impromptu tête-à-tête.

"Just tell me if you know where Hal Murkland is," I said.

Ost settled the features of his face into that blank, bland impassivity so favored by police.

"I'm not asking you where he is, I'm just asking you if you *know* where he is."

A nurses' aide came in with a bedpan. Ost watched with a mixture of fascination and revulsion as she stepped on the foot pedal for the bedpan toilet, slid the bedpan between the clamps, and took her foot off the pedal. The bedpan toilet shut and did its Niagara Falls imitation.

"You think *you* know where he is?" Ost asked.

"He might have gone down to Washington, D.C., to Lisa Chiu's funeral."

"Yeah? So why you askin' me?"

I gave up on Ost and called Denise Aubuchon. "I'm waiting for the other shoe to drop," she said gloomily. "Pretty soon they're going to find out that Hal's blood is all over that shirt she had on."

I called Dr. Rebecca Bayard down at the Medical Examiner's Office. "Got anything on Lisa Chiu?"

"Lisa Chiu, Lisa Chiu," Bayard mused. I heard papers rustling. "Death due to multiple penetrating instrument wounds . . . no indication of rape or sexual assault . . . tox shows scopolamine—"

"What? *Scopolamine?*"

"Oh, yeah," said Beck. "*Burundanguiado.*"

"Excuse me?"

"That's Spanish for 'victimized by scopolamine,' " Beck explained.

My mind leaped as if from electroshock therapy. I tried to remember what I knew about scopolamine. Combined with morphine, it's a popular premedicant before cardiac surgery; it's used in surgery for bad trauma cases, when conventional anesthesia will probably kill the patient; it's the main ingredient in some motion-sickness pills and seasickness patches. An anticholinergic, it acts against acetylcholine, a substance in the brain that "greases" the nerve endings and allows a thought to jump from one synapse to the next. People who OD'd on anticholinergics couldn't think. They arrived in the emergency room groggy, confused, and thoroughly disoriented, usually with no memory of what had happened to bring them there.

Beck was saying, "Burundanga is a kind of Colombian voodoo powder made from plants from the nightshade family. You know, belladonna alkaloids. Indians used to use it in religious ceremonies. When you refine it you get scopolamine. Very popular among bad guys in Bogotá. You mix it with sedatives and slip it into somebody's drink, then the person does anything you want: takes all his money out of the ATM and gives it to you; has sex with you and six of your friends; gives you jewelry, the house, the car—and afterward doesn't remember a damn thing. It's like chemical hypnotism. You lose your will entirely and submit to any suggestion whatsoever."

"I've never heard of this," I said.

"You don't remember the crazed executives?"

"The what?"

"Businessmen were turning up *burundanguiado* in emergency rooms all over New York City. Dr. Goldfrank at Bellevue finally decided the bad guys were Mickey-ing their drinks with scopolamine eyedrops. I think Goldfrank talks about it in his book *Toxicologic Emergencies*."

"I'll look it up. But the bottom line is: I Mickey your drink, you do what I want, and you have no memory of what happened when you wake up."

"Right."

"The ATM withdrawals, sex with six people—"

"I'm clueless. *Nada*."

"I could tell you to—let's say—turn on your computer and erase all your files?"

"I'd do anything you want, babe. *Anything*."

"*What* is going *on* here?" Denny Aubuchon groaned when I called her back and told her about the scopolamine. "Hal was such a sweet guy—how did he turn into a ruthless killer when we weren't looking?" Hardly pausing for a breath, she went on, "Hal didn't harden himself enough. I had a bad childhood, too—worse than Hal had. My father beat my *mother*, he beat my *sister*, I got pregnant by a guy who beat *me*—"

Her emotions swept over me like a tidal wave. "I know," I said.

"—who killed my *son*—"

"I *know*."

"But I hardened myself," she concluded.

I almost gasped for air. How did we get from *ruthless killer* to Hal's not having hardened himself enough? Hal didn't *harden* himself enough, so he flipped out and killed Lisa? I realized Denny was talking from a place deep within herself where Lisa's death had touched her in ways she didn't want to be touched, and that the tidal wave from Denny's deep place was rolling directly into a corresponding place within me—where Lisa's death had touched me in ways I didn't want to be touched, either.

I fought through my anxiety to ask Denny the question I had called to ask. "What are you going to do about the Medicaid fraud?"

"That's a problem," Denny admitted. But she seemed relieved to refocus on the concrete and practical. "Either I make the chart notes agree with the billing charges, which distorts the record of what's been done for these patients, or I change the billing codes and hope no one notices—I don't know. My accountant employs shady characters called 'diary writers' who come over and clean up your records so they all tally, but I'm not really sure I want to go that route. I have to think about it."

"Why don't you let me talk to Hal?" I offered.

"About what? Killing Lisa?"

"No, about the fraud. Just to let him know someone's on his side—"

"You're on his side? What do you mean, you're on his side?"

I could feel myself going under, swamped in the sea of Denny's emotion.

"Ev, do you know what you're saying? How on-his-side are you going to be if they arrest him for murder? You can't be on his side now, you have to be on my side."

Desperately, I struggled to keep my head above water. "Your side?"

"If he sinks this practice, I go down with the ship. The bottom

line, Ev: Are you going to help him sink my ship, or are you going
to help me keep it afloat?"

"You're absolutely right, Denny," I said loudly. "I have no
business meddling in your practice."

"Thank you."

When she hung up on me, I was relieved.

Lisa Chiu was buried in a private ceremony in a cemetery
outside Washington, D.C. I spoke to her cousin, the Episcopal
priest, who told me that the ceremony had combined elements
from the Christian and Buddhist traditions, and that only blood
relatives were present. I found "blood relatives" a jarring choice
of words. A memorial service in New York City would take place
at St. Michael's Church in late September, the cousin said.

I tried to think of some delicate way of wording it: Was there
anyone, ah, *lurking?* Observing the funeral from a distance?

But I suddenly remembered reading somewhere that murder-
ers often went to funerals and hovered on the periphery.

And that the cops always went and watched the mourners,
looking for the murderer.

I decided not to ask.

"If I can help you in any way, please let me know," I said.

I found Brian Linhardt stocking the crash cart and told him
about the arrangements for a memorial service for Lisa. He nodded and passed a hand over his eyes and through his hair. "You
drinking that nerve tea I gave you?" he wanted to know. I said
yes, I'd drunk a quart of it that very morning. And that I actually
thought it was helping.

"Drink a little more for me," he said.

I went to see Kennedy Bartlett, who seemed no longer able
or willing to rouse himself from his morphine stupor. I held his
hand while he slept. I told him the dog was trying to make friends
with the cat, but the cat was having none of it, and that Maxie

had met the dalmatian who lived across the street at the firehouse, who liked him better than the cat did. I said he was eating his green beans every night, which Denny Aubuchon's housekeeper was now preparing for him in little plastic packets, and dropping off along with the amazing dinners she was bringing me and Phil each evening. I didn't explain that Phil had hired Denny's housekeeper to fix extra dinners because I'd been headbonked. My voice caught with the realization that I would probably never explain to Ken about the dinners and the head bonk.

Ken smiled, so I hoped he was listening.

And I hoped he couldn't hear in my voice that I was crying.

I called Mick Healy. He was distraught over a tabloid newspaper article that blamed his brother Donal's psychopathic personality on an acute psychotic break suffered by their mother shortly after Donal was born; the article said that their mother had burned Donal with cigarettes all over his body.

"That's just *not true*," Mick said. "She never burned him with cigarettes."

The way he said it chilled me and made me wonder what she *had* done. "I'm really sorry," I said.

But I could feel myself distancing from him. I wasn't quite sure why. Something seemed to be beckoning me away.

All the while, I took care of my patients. I relied a little more than usual on the attending physician, an extremely smart and competent individual who reminded everyone of Colin Powell. And I sensed Brian Linhardt hovering on the periphery, ready to step in if needed.

Friday morning I helped the medics transport a twelve-year-old who had been struck by a car to the Peds ER, and was flabbergasted to find Hal Murkland back at work.

"Where have you been?" I demanded as soon as the medics had recited their report.

"D.C.," he said, his mind on the patient. "CBC, check the

urine for blood, and let's get X Ray in here, full spine."

A nurse pushed past me. "Is he oriented?"

"He's got tire tracks on his belly—we'll need a crit," one of the residents said.

"Bowel sounds hyperactive."

"Okay, we've got a possible intra-abdominal hemorrhage, let's set up for lavage."

I stood back and watched the swirl of activity around the patient, and marveled at the change in Hal. The barbed-wire sutures were gone from his cheek. He'd shaved and had his hair cut. He wore a freshly laundered pink shirt, the sleeves rolled up, showcasing his big, beefy arms. His glasses perched jauntily on the end of his nose. An air of doloroso still hung about him, but there was also a determined quietude.

He looked up at me and smiled. "We'll talk," he promised.

I went back to the adult ER, torn between Hal and Denny.

Again.

Friday afternoon there was another pair of domestics. He beat her with his fists because he didn't like what she was preparing for dinner; she stabbed him a couple of times with her paring knife. By the time they arrived in the ER, they considered themselves even. He refused to press charges. She yelled at the police.

I took him; Kessie Savarkar took her.

"You'll live," I told him, after determining that his "stab" wounds were not stab wounds after all. She had slashed him a couple of times, and fairly ineffectively. "These wounds are not penetrating."

Afterward, I found my words echoed and spoke to me directly.

You'll live.

These wounds are not penetrating.

I went home and made love to Phil, very gently and sweetly and with enormous relief.

I drank a little more of Linhardt's tea, the tea that allegedly stimulated the nervous system to healing and recovery.

I felt a little better.

The fog began to lift.

CHAPTER
29

ON Saturday morning I awoke clear-headed for the first time in what seemed like months.

Phil was sleeping quietly, his back to me. I turned and snuggled up against him. The light was just creeping in under the shutters. I didn't have to go to the hospital.

But I did have to face Hal.

Then I remembered I had promised to go to Windy Sisk's movie set.

Oh, Jesus. I sat up and looked at the clock. It was five-thirty, and I was supposed to be there by seven. I threw back the covers and leaped out of bed.

"What?" asked Phil sleepily. Then, coming awake, "What's the matter? Are you all right?"

"I'm fine. I'm getting in the shower. Gotta go to the movie set today."

I was standing under the water before I realized that I had jumped up without losing my equilibrium. My headache was gone, too. *Yes.*

*   *   *

For the hospital scenes, the location scout for Wendell Sisk Productions had rented the emergency room of an old, now defunct hospital on the Upper East Side. It was nowhere near any subway line I knew of, and in all the time I'd lived in New York City, I'd never managed to figure out which buses go crosstown where. So I took a cab. Naturally, at 6:45 A.M. on a Saturday morning, the only cabdrivers on the road were bleary-eyed Robert De Niro impersonators; mine made me so nervous I made him put me out at Mount Sinai Hospital, from where I proceeded on foot. Consequently, as 7 A.M. approached, I found myself trotting briskly east from Fifth Avenue to make my destination on time, cursing all cabdrivers and especially those from foreign countries where driving was the national homicidal sport. The day was already uncomfortably warm. The last thing I wanted was to arrive breathless and sweaty.

Movie people take over the world, with the connivance of the New York Police Department and Hizzoner the Mayor. A full two blocks from the defunct hospital, cardboard "No Parking" signs hooded the parking meters and blue police sawhorses marched helter-skelter across the sidewalks. Even at this early hour the Winnebago dressing rooms and huge gaffer trucks were already on site, the backs of the trucks open and disgorging electrical equipment. Thick generator cables snaked everywhere. Production people—all of whom looked to me like members of Generation X—ran around in their gaffer uniforms: sleeveless T-shirts, shorts, and high-top black basketball sneakers. I passed one guy with wild tresses cascading to his shoulders. High on his left arm he sported an enormous tattoo of a woman whose face was half obliterated by blue hair and a large pink flower. "I have the tennis racket?" he shouted into his walkie-talkie. "*I* have the tennis racket?"

The outside of the hospital was draped in huge plastic sheeting. More people in sleeveless T-shirts, shorts, and basketball shoes positioned eight-foot-tall klieg lights, the lights trained to shine through the plastic-draped hospital windows into the interior. I passed a guy whose job seemed to be tape; reels and reels of brightly colored electrical tape hung from his waist and from a string around his neck. I asked him where to go, and he pointed at a large sign that said "Set."

Skirting a huge table with doughnuts, fruit, and coffee urns large enough to caffeinate a party of three hundred, I entered the ER through the ambulance bay. Just like home.

Inside, the uniform of the production crew changed: same shoes and shorts, but T-shirts with sleeves and the multicolored logo of the Wendell Sisk Production Company. Here there were fewer walkie-talkies; many people wore headsets like telephone operators, wired to radio packs on their waists. I began to sense a hierarchy among the ranks. After wandering around for a while I spotted Jennifer Garland's headband with the glasses on top. She turned, saw me, and lifted her chin to come over. Her arms were full of pink, blue, and yellow pages.

"Great," she said, by way of greeting. She handed me my allotment of pages, pulled her glasses down from the top of her head onto her nose, and said, "O.K., we're doing three scenes with medical talk and action, and five scenes with medical talk only. We need you to choreograph the scenes where there's action. Your job basically is to say, 'Doctor One, you stand there and put this tube down her throat, and Doctor Two, you shine the light in her eye,' that kind of thing. You don't really have to do much for Scene three-fifty-four, the medics are bringing in the patient. But we want you to look it over and see if anything occurs to you. O.K., first the medical technical stuff."

I nodded and read:

MEDICAL TECHNICAL PRODUCTION NOTES
Based on Draft of August 2

SCENE 354

ACTION: Paramedics bring in Forrester

PROPS: Paramedic gurney, backboard, EKG monitor, oxygen tank, 2 IVs

WARDROBE: shirt precut up the middle, pants up each leg

HAIR/MKUP: Gunshot wound to head of Forrester, bloody Kerlix, gray matter in hair

ATMO: 3 doctors, 4 nurses, 2 paramedics

"Looks O.K.," I said.

"Good." She handed me the next page. "Here's the script."

DOCTOR #1: Let's get her into Trauma One, chop-chop!

MEDIC: Stephanie Forrester, 24 years old, Gunshot wound to the head, pulse 60, BP 80 palp, Glasgow 5. ID says she's a film student at NYU.

Oh, God, I thought, as my heart paused.

"You're not happy," Garland suggested. "Have some thoughts?"

"No, fine." I erased the mental image of Lisa's soul drifting out of her body, floating up toward the ceiling, and turning for a last look before traveling on to the beyond. "What happened to the guy with blood shooting out his arteries, who was supposed to make witty commentary and triumph over the medical profession?"

"Well, you said they couldn't do that. So they're doing this. That is, if it looks all right to you."

The jump in logic escaped me. They went from a guy who wasn't getting enough oxygen to the brain to make witty commentary to a gunshot wound to the head with a reading of five on the Glasgow Coma Scale?

Garland smiled at my expression. "Okay, here's Scene three-fifty-six," she said, handing me more pages and flipping through her own. "Doctor One intubates while Doctor Two orders the drugs, and, let's see, brains in the hair, sinus bradycardia. Doctor One says, 'I need a six-point-five endotrach tube.' Doctor Two—that's the attending—says, 'Mannitol, seventy-five grams, and let's piggyback the ancef IV, one gram.' Then Doctor One says,

'Better hyperventilate' and 'CBC, Chem-seven, cross-match two units'—well, you see it all here.''

"Boy, that medical jargon rolls right off your tongue," I said, impressed.

"I try to keep up," said Garland modestly. But I could see she was pleased. An ambitious young woman. "So then the pupils are blown," she went on, "and there's no reflexes, and they start talking about a donor ID card in her wallet and notifying her next of kin."

"The patient dies?" God, I thought, all I needed right now was a re-enactment of Lisa's death. They would have to make it a 24-year-old student.

"Uh-huh. In Scene three-fifty-nine she goes to the morgue. But there's no dialogue in that scene, we just see her being loaded into the elevator. Now, in the next scene—"

"Who wrote this stuff for you?" I asked, trying to distract myself. "It must have been a doctor."

"Yes, the consultant adviser. He's an emergency-medicine doctor, like yourself."

"Um, forgive me for asking, but if you have someone who can write this kind of thing, why isn't that person here advising you?"

"You mean, why do we need you?" She grinned broadly. "Believe me, it's a *very* long story. Windy paranoia. Basically, the consultant adviser works with the writers, and the technical adviser—that's you—works with the actors on the set. Oh, here are your doctors." She shifted the papers to one arm and put the other up in the air and waved.

The actors came over, and there were introductions all around, although I got their names mixed up immediately. Doctor One was a young Hispanic man with a supercilious air and a pouty mouth; Doctor Two a balding, paunchy gent with a kindly air, who looked to be in his mid-sixties; and Doctor Three a woman about my age with frizzy orange hair and sassy eyes. Doctors One and Three were dressed exactly as residents at my own hospital dressed: white coats over casual street clothes and running shoes. Doctor Two, clearly the avuncular attending physician, wore his white coat over a yellow button-down with colorful tie and matching braces, suit pants, and dress shoes, leading me to wonder briefly if he had raided Chris Cabot's wardrobe. All sported the usual accoutrements: hospital ID with photo, pens, and penlights peeking out of the breast pockets of the white coats, stethoscopes slung around necks. If they had walked into my own ER I wouldn't have been able to tell them from the real ER staff.

"Good, you didn't shave," said Garland approvingly to the men.

"Told not to," said Doctor Two, pumping my hand up and down. His voice boomed out from his diaphragm like that of a singing coach. To Garland he said, "What the hell happened to the witty commentary?"

"Yeah, I look at the new pages and find out they killed the bastard, too," said Doctor Three, lifting an eyebrow the same orange as her hair. "After castrating him. I mean, it was a guy last week and now it's a woman, right?"

"I must say I was surprised myself," I admitted.

"You'd probably be the last person they'd tell," joked Doctor Two. "You're only the on-set technical adviser."

"What did she know and when did she know it?" chimed in the other two doctor-actors in unison.

They all laughed. "That's a running joke on the set," Garland explained. "You know, Senator Baker at the Watergate hearings?"

"I've done six movies with Windy," Doctor Two elaborated. "It's always, 'Did you know this?' 'No, this is the first I'm hearing it, did *you* know this?' Every time you turn around, he's making some change, and we're all scrambling to catch up."

"He shoots so many pickups I don't know how he stays in budget," Doctor Three chuckled.

But their voices began to fade. A dim vision of Senator Baker floated across the balcony of my mind, asking, "What did he know and when did he know it?" I looked down again on Lisa Chiu as I'd come upon her the morning she died: sprawled on the floor outside her apartment, naked except for the bikini briefs that had once been baby blue but were now soaked red, her bloodied scrub shirt flung aside . . .

It was at that moment that I knew, with sickening certainty, who had killed her.

A minute later I wasn't so sure. My mind fanned out like braying foxhounds in all directions, panting after the scent: *Why*? I knew who the murderer was but not why the murderer had done it. As I instructed Doctors One, Two, and Three on the delicate art of intubation of a patient—or, in their case, on the delicate art of *faking* intubation of a patient—I ran through everything I knew about Lisa's death. What I knew factually, what I had assumed, what I had deduced. Who had said what, who had agreed, who had disagreed.

Why kill Lisa?

And why make it look as if Hal Murkland had done it?

With my mind braying after Lisa's murderer and my adrenaline rising, I watched myself guide Doctor One's hands through the procedure, demonstrating on the hapless actor who was to play the dying film student. She had blond hair and a voluptuous, surgically enhanced bosom. I watched myself think, Not Lisa. Not anything like Lisa. I watched my mind leave the room and travel to that other room, the room where Guy Shehadeh and Brian Linhardt had intubated Lisa Chiu right before she died. *Yes, exactly like Lisa*. Except that this Lisa would get up after her dying was done, would wash the brains out of her hair and the blood off her face and arms, and would go home. *Not Lisa*. I watched myself watch Doctor One as he fumbled through the procedure on his own.

I excused myself five times to call Hal's various answering machines to leave messages for him. His office machine. His home machine. *Hal, we must talk. Immediately. Right now. As soon as possible.* With growing desperation, I searched for him in both ERs, leaving word with the Peds ER charge nurse, the Peds ER chief resident, the adult ER charge nurse, and the adult ER chief resident. I left messages on my own answering machine for Phil and on Phil's home and office machines. *I think I know who killed Lisa Chiu. We must talk. Leave word where you are.*

I called Detective Ost and was told he was "on meal"—dinner break. By then I had realized I needed to check one last detail before I could actually point a finger and say with conviction "J'accuse," and I was unwilling to confide my suspicions to the gruff, world-weary sounding person at the Twenty-sixth Precinct who'd answered the phone. I left my name and said I'd call back.

Four actor-nurses arrived on Windy Sisk's make-believe, fantasy-land ER set, and with a growing sense of disconnectedness I showed them how to shoulder their way between the doctors. "You have to ram yourselves between them even if they won't get out of the way," I listened to myself tell them. "You have *your* work to do." I entertained everyone by explaining the old intern joke, "See one, do one, teach one." We discussed sinus bradycardia, hyperventilation, and what it means when the pupils are blown and there are no reflexes. I answered questions about my life as an emergency-medicine resident. Doctor One wanted to know if doctors were arrogant. I laughed. My laughter was a cackle of desperation in my ears. You have *your* work to do—what are you doing wasting time on a movie set when on the real set of real life you know who killed Lisa Chiu?

Windy Sisk arrived and watched as we rehearsed the scene. Watching him watch us—*the watcher watches the watched*—I was struck with a sudden bolt of realization.

Next the murderer would kill Hal Murkland.

If I was right in my suspicions.

I had to find Hal.

* * *

When I arrived back uptown at my apartment in the doctors' residence, it was dark and well after 9 P.M. The cat threw himself lovingly on my feet, then rolled into the air and hit the floor running as I tripped over him and cursed. The dog appeared, took one look at me, and disappeared. Talking to myself and yelling messages into the phone at people's answering machines—Christ, where *was* everyone?—I changed out of my clothes, which were spattered with something called "reel" blood, and pulled on a pair of dark-colored sweat pants and a black T-shirt from the Miró exhibition at the Modern. Rummaging in the closet, I unearthed a large fanny pack and belted it around my waist. Into the pack went Kennedy Bartlett's bills and daybook, and Brian Linhardt's Swiss Army knife and scalpel blades. In a drawer in the kitchen where I threw all my hospital junk when I emptied my pockets at night I found a stainless-steel scalpel holder, and one of those little flashlights from L.L. Bean. I tried the flashlight. The beam seemed dull, so I replaced the batteries. Tried it again. Brighter.

I made myself drink a bottle of Gatorade to hone my electrolyte balance while I listened to my answering-machine messages.

No message from Hal.

A message from Phil, logged in at 8 P.M., saying that he had a suicidal patient and didn't know when he'd be home.

A message from Linhardt, asking me if I needed help.

Yeah, I needed help—*I needed help finding Hal.*

I was reaching for the phone to start one last round of phone calls before I went out when it rang beneath my hand.

"Hello," I heard my voice say.

"Ev?"

"This is Dr. Sutcliffe."

"Ev, it's Carol Murkland. Can you come up here? I think Hal's dead."

CHAPTER
30

I bolted out of the apartment. Through the door leading to the stairs, taking the stairs two at a time. Not Hal. Oh God, please not Hal. Yanking open the door on the ninth floor, I leaped into the hall, colliding with Carol Murkland.

She was covered head to foot with blood.

Her white camp shirt was soaked and smeared; her yellow cotton slacks red from the knees down, thighs streaked where she had wiped her hands. She was still wiping her hands: over her breasts, up and down her upper arms, back and forth across her belly. Blood clots clung to her thick sienna hair like leeches. A high-pitched mewling sound emitted from her as, twitching, she paced this way and that.

She walked into me a second time as if I weren't even there. "Carol," I said. "*Carol*."

"Eeewweeoo," she whimpered.

The door to the Murklands' apartment was ajar. Seeing blood on the doorknob, I shouldered through, my arms instinctively up and in, hands under my chin as if going through the swinging doors into surgery. The lights in the living room were off. Blood on the floor and a light around the corner led me left toward the bedroom and study.

I saw him immediately, sprawled across the tile floor of the bathroom. Lying on his back, his head turned aside, one knee up in the air like a misplaced flagpole.

His throat was cut and his wrists were slashed.

The blood had geysered everywhere—in my mind I could see the pulsing arches of it—as long as his heart beat. It was not beating now. Even standing a good twelve feet away, I knew it with certainty.

With an almost audible scrape of metal, the steel trapdoor between my head and my emotions slid into place. I felt only physical sensations: a quickening heart and fanning heat across the chest, then the grand-slam cardiac explosion of adrenaline, anxiety, and fear. For a moment I looked at him. He was barefoot and bare-chested, dressed only in an old pair of chambray shorts, his favorites. His legs seemed bulkier than I remembered. The fingers of his hands curled gently. He lay in his own red-black lake, seeming to float farther and farther away from me as I watched, beyond my grasp or the grasp of any other living being. I was flooded with images of him: Hal laughing; Hal dancing down the corridor of the hospital with a baby over his shoulder and a two-year-old under his arm, singing "all-fall-*down*"; Hal in the neonatal unit, bending over a tiny, doll-like infant who had stopped breathing.

Hal taking me ferociously into his arms when he realized I was saying *yes,* that one time we'd gone to bed.

I turned away, my hand over my mouth, knuckles against my teeth.

By now I was breathing deeply and rhythmically, stoking oxygen for my increased heart rate, sucking the air down my constricted throat as if I'd never get enough. My chest ached from the sorrow and adrenaline. Nudging the front door open with my foot, I pulled a small table in front of it to hold it open. I found Carol in the hall. Carol was still pacing, still frantically wiping her hands on herself, her soft mewling heightening to a pitched keening. Lady Macbeth came to mind: *Out, damned spot! Out, I say!*

"Carol," I said loudly, "Did you call the police?"

No response. I wondered how she had managed to call me. And talk so calmly, too.

I banged on 9B, 9C, and 9D. "We need some help here!" I yelled. Christ, where was everybody? Saturday night, nobody home. A dusky-complexioned woman in a cotton robe appeared from around the corner: Kessie Savarkar. Seeing Carol bloodied and staggering toward her, Savarkar froze.

"Hal Murkland's been murdered," I called to her. "Call the cops and get dressed." When she didn't move, I spoke more urgently. "His throat's cut. He's dead. His wife found him. Call the cops. Then go downstairs and open the door for them. *Right now.*"

"Right-o," she said finally. She ran off down the hall.

Carol flailed her arms at me. I tried to get her to sit down in a corner of the hall, without much success; she sat, but got up again immediately and resumed her frenzied pacing. "Oh God, oh God, oh God," she was saying now, which I considered an improvement over the keening.

I left her and went back into the apartment, moving quickly down the hall past the bathroom, past Hal floating in his gory black lake.

In the bedroom I found the window open onto the fire escape, and the air conditioner running. A soft light burned on the night table. Carol had the place decorated in ersatz Caribbean, including mosquito netting, which moved gently in the breeze, billowing like eerie clouds around the mahogany four-poster bed. I remembered Hal shrugging when he showed it to me a year earlier; "Why not?" he'd said, leaving all his *why nots* unspoken. It gave me the willies.

I moved quickly across the room toward the window, stuck my head out. Looked up, then down. Nobody. Amazingly, the night was quiet; not a peep out of our noisy neighbors to the north. Somewhere jazz played softly. A truck went by on Amsterdam.

Just as I was pulling back, I saw out of the corner of my eye a light-colored something on the fire escape below.

A rubber babydoll.

Naked.

One flight below, outside my own bedroom window.

I stared. Then I pulled back in, moving swiftly into the study without a reason to go there. Hal's keys lay on the desk; I scooped them up and pocketed them, thinking, the keys will make what I have to do next easier. I heard the short whoop of a police car pulling up in front of the building. I went out into the hall to look after Carol Murkland.

Initially there were two cops in uniform; then there were five, among them a sergeant. "The deceased is Dr. Harold Murkland; he's in the bathroom, appears to have his throat cut and wrists slashed," a very young officer explained to the sergeant. "That's Mrs. Murkland, the deceased's wife. She found him. She called Dr. Sutcliffe here on the phone in the bedroom."

"Dr. *Sutcliffe*," the sergeant repeated musingly. He fixed me with a long stare, as if trying to recall whether he'd ever seen me on a "Wanted" poster. He was thin and wiry, with a lined, hard face, yellow hair and mustache, and extremely pale eyes, so pale they seemed almost without color. "You the in-house rescue squad?"

"Excuse me?" I said.

"You the in-house rescue squad?"

I didn't know what he was asking. The tone that underlay the question seemed so provocative, belligerent, ironic, and sarcastic, it canceled out any sense the simple English might have carried. I read his name tag: Szulz. I guessed it was pronounced *Shultz*. "I'm not sure I understand," I said.

Szulz pulled a face that said, What am I dealing with here, *dummies?* Glancing at his watch with an enormous sigh, he waved over a second officer, this one appearing even younger than the first. "Get Ost in here," he said. "Tell him never mind who's catching, and make sure he knows Dr. *Sutcliffe* was *first on the set.*" To me he said, "Don't go anywhere. You been in the apartment?"

"Yes," I admitted.

Szulz pulled another face, this time managing to convey both extreme exasperation and saintlike patience.

"I didn't touch anything," I said defensively. "I didn't even touch the doorknob. I shouldered my way in. I didn't go into the bathroom; I only stood on the threshold."

"You get a medal, Doc," he said. He turned to look at Carol Murkland.

Carol was weeping and patting her blood-smeared face and neck in a repetitive way that suggested psychosis. Her teeth chattered and she shivered. Kessie Savarkar stood with one hand on Carol's back, and with the other offered a mug of tea; I caught a whiff of whiskey as the steam rose. Kessie spoke to Carol softly in her bell-like, lilting voice. After a moment Carol stopped patting and took a sip of tea. She wrapped both hands around the mug. The mug shook and tea sloshed on the floor.

"How'd she get all that blood on her?" Szulz asked the first officer, whose name tag read "Daley." He looked hardly old enough to shave. I examined him more closely. He didn't.

"She, ah, ran around in it when she found the deceased. I think she got down on the floor with him, maybe hugged him or lay down on top of him."

"Yeah? You ask her?"

Daley averted his eyes, eliciting another of Szulz's masterful facial expressions. It resembled a smile but wasn't. "Everybody's so fuckin' on the ball tonight," the sergeant observed. "Tell me, Officer Daley. Any of this blood *hers?*"

"I don't know, Sarge."

"How about a weapon? We got a *weapon?*"

"Not yet, Sarge," said Daley.

"Any signs of forced entry?"

"No. Window's open onto the fire escape, so that's a possible exit route—"

Szulz gave him a withering look.

Any thoughts I had about confiding my suspicions to Szulz evaporated. One huge hole remained in my argument, and until I filled that in, I was not going to convince someone as skeptical as this guy. Better to wait for Detective Ost, and to utilize the interim until he arrived to nail down the last outstanding piece of evidence I needed to make my accusation.

I began to edge down the hall toward the stairs.

Szulz rearranged his features into a facade of kindliness and concern. Going over to Carol, he said softly, "Ma'am, I'm Sergeant Barry Szulz. I'm sorry for your troubles. Do you know anyone with a grudge against your husband, or who might've wanted to do him harm?"

Carol shook her head vigorously. Her hands still shaking, she carefully brought the mug of tea to her chattering teeth and sipped.

After she drank, Szulz gently took the cup away from her and handed it to Kessie Savarkar. He grasped Carol's hands in his own and spoke to her in a low voice I could no longer overhear, massaging her hands, looking at her hands, almost making love to her hands with his—

I saw the gash across her right palm.

Still bleeding.

"Where's the knife, Mrs. Murkland?" Szulz asked.

CHAPTER
31

I stuck around long enough to hear Carol explain. How she'd put her arms around Hal, and the knife was under him. How she hadn't seen the knife, and she cut herself hugging him. How she threw the knife down the garbage chute because she panicked when she realized her fingerprints were now on it. This all came out between jagged sobs and gulps of tea from the cup that shook in her hands and rattled against her teeth. Tears streamed down her face. Her anguish filled the corridor like a humidity from hell.

The cops were having none of it.

"Mrs. Murkland, you'll feel better if you unburden yourself and tell us the truth," I heard Szulz say. "Let us help you. We can't help you if you don't tell us the truth."

But I was already slipping away, sliding down the stairs on the balls of my feet. The high pitch of Carol's voice and the low murmur of Szulz's receded into wordlessness as I let myself into my apartment two floors down. Grabbing my white coat, I stayed long enough only to button it over my mufti. Made my way downstairs. Went out the building and around the corner under the scaffolding to the Amsterdam entrance to the Schiff Medical Suites. Flashed my hospital ID at the security guard, who yawned and nodded and took little notice. Climbed the stairs to the second floor, opened the door a crack, and listened.

It was quiet.

Outside the door to Hal and Denny's office suite I listened again. Glanced to my right down the corridor, then to my left at the plywood temporary barricade the construction workers had put up when they made the tie-ins between Schiff and the new Storrs Pavilion. Plastic sheeting hung loosely over a doorway in the plywood, crinkling softly as it billowed in a sudden small breeze. My nose filled with construction dust.

I read Hal's and Denny's fancy nameplate: DENISE AUBUCHON M.D. / HAROLD MURKLAND M.D. Now or never, Sutcliffe. Let's go.

I let myself in with Hal's key.

By the light of my trusty little flashlight I made my way through the receptionist's area and down the hall, past the toys and magazine racks full of AIDS literature. The door to Hal's office was ajar. I went in and switched on the desk lamp low.

I turned on the computer, and as it whirred and hummed took off my white coat and my fanny pack and tossed them on the desk. Sat down. Looked at the pictures of Hal waltzing with the Ninja Turtle, and waving at the camera with Mickey Mouse. Remembered how Hal was the only person I'd ever quarreled with comfortably, and the only man I'd ever met who understood the female convention of apology: that women apologized so that men would apologize. I brought up the computer program. Typed in what I hoped was the password.

Bingo.

I hadn't sat through *Ferris Bueller's WarGames* for nothing.

I was just finishing up at midnight when I heard a key in the lock. The front door opened and closed. Footsteps padded down the hall, and Denise Aubuchon appeared in the doorway.

She was wearing her country-club outfit: soft-green Lacoste

shirt. Madras shorts. Pom-pommed tennis socks and canvas Tretorns with pink chevrons. No makeup. Her lovely auburn hair cascaded in waves to her shoulders. It was freshly washed and I could smell her shampoo as well as her delicate, expensive perfume. Her big brown eyes were wide open and clear, as if she were about to make an exciting and brilliant diagnosis.

"Hal's dead," Denny said.

"I know."

"Cops are looking for you."

"Yeah."

She sat down on one of her oak courthouse chairs. "They arrested Carol."

"Figures."

For a minute or two she watched me. Then: "I thought you might be here. But what's Sherlock without her Watson?"

"Which one of us is Sherlock?" I asked.

"Oh, you. Most definitely."

For the first time I realized how beautiful she was. Breathtakingly beautiful, even without makeup. And sexy. I imagined that the musk of her sex wafted to my nose along with the shampoo and perfume. Or perhaps it was the musk of her adrenaline. Except that I would have smelled that before, working with her at difficult codes and on patients who died.

"No," I said. "I think you're Sherlock and I'm Watson. I'm the plodding one. You've always been way ahead of me."

"Oh?" she said.

I smiled coldly and exited Hal's computer program, the one he never really mastered. "Look at the way you figured it out," I said. "With a little help from Joshua Waterman, who was entering all Hal's patient data for him: scheduling the patients, documenting the visits, all the patient charting, the billing codes. The whole thing is really a magnificent sleight of hand. You should congratulate yourself."

"I'm not much in the mood for congratulations," Denny said.

"Not with Hal lying dead on his bathroom floor. Would you like a drink?"

"I don't think so, thanks." I wasn't much in the mood for a drink.

Not with Hal lying dead on his bathroom floor.

"Mm." Denny examined her nails. She often wore colored polish, but today she sported a French manicure. "Josh is really the one who figured it out. He noticed the discrepancy between Hal's charting and what he was asking Josh to bill for. But I didn't want to proceed until I was one hundred percent convinced that Hal was really defrauding Medicaid. Which is why I hired Lisa Chiu to help Josh go through Hal's records. But life became so complicated."

"You didn't count on Hal's falling madly and passionately and wildly in love with Lisa—"

Denny laughed affectionately. "The way only a middle-aged man—"

"No," I said. "The way you *imagined* only a middle-aged *straight* man thinking with his gonads would be stupid enough to fall in love with a young medical student." I heard the edge of bitter emphasis in my voice.

Denny heard it, too, and looked up sharply. "Well," she said.

"And you certainly didn't anticipate Lisa's getting her hands on Hal's old shrink records."

Denny blinked. "What old shrink records?"

"Blackmail. Ring a bell with you?"

"Blackmail? What are you talking about? Hal had no money. That's why he was defrauding Medicaid. How could anyone black-mail him—for what?"

I shook my head. "Hal had money. He inherited that cool one-point-four million from his aunt."

"No, he didn't. His cousin inherited that money."

I explored the backs of my teeth with my tongue. "Then Lisa turned up dead," I said softly. "Someone Mickeyed her drink with

scopolamine and sedatives, and got her to erase all her computer records while she was *burundanguiado*."

"While she was what?"

"And stabbed her nine times. She was so gorked out she didn't even resist. But her attacker had it all worked out ahead of time. Even took the time to mime a Pfannenstiehl incision from the first cut"—I drew my hand horizontally above my mons pubis, just as Denny had done while describing Lisa's cesareanlike wound to me the afternoon she died—"to confuse the police and make them think it was the anti-abortionists, or the Babydoll Killer; a cesarean incision could point to anti-abortionists or Babydoll."

"Sure you don't want a drink?" Denny asked.

"No. The bit about the doll was good, too . . . Lisa had that doll that used to belong to one of Hal's little patients who died. It was a Raggedy Ann doll, not the same kind of doll that the Babydoll Killer was leaving at his scenes, but what the hell—Lisa's lying there bleeding to death on the floor in her scopolamine fugue state, why not toss the doll at her? And why not take her pants off to make it look like a guy was thinking about raping her even if he didn't get the chance? Then just leave her to die. Pressing the doll to her abdomen so she didn't eviscerate. Then that business with the phone cords—nice, slightly hysterical touch: Take all the phone cords. Logical message: Don't tell. Don't tell anyone I'm scamming . . . Medicaid, Blue Cross. Whomever."

"More probably don't tell about the shrink notes," said Denny. "Pretty damning—a famous shrink says Hal harbored suppressed violent tendencies and could snap at any minute, and moreover has harbored these tendencies for the last thirty years, to say nothing of the fact that he molested the girl next door—"

"Thought you didn't know about the shrink notes," I said.

"They came in the mail, addressed to me," Denny admitted. "Now he's dead, I guess it doesn't matter if I tell you. Since you knew anyway."

I clenched my hands in my lap, under the table. "Then the next thing we know, Hal turns up dead."

Denny was becoming impatient. "Carol killed Hal," she said, in a could-we-get-on-with-it tone of voice.

"Yeah?" I was beginning to have trouble controlling myself.

"She never loved him. She married him because she needed someone to support her and pay her tuition, and when he asked for a divorce, she killed him. To get his money."

That's two strikes, I thought. Three and you're out. "Think so, huh? Denny, Carol wouldn't let Hal eat pizza because it was bad for him."

She chortled. "You're in denial, Ev. The stress is getting to you. The case is closed. Hal killed Lisa because she was blackmailing him, and Carol killed Hal because he wanted a divorce."

"She had clots in her hair," I said. "By the time she discovered him, the blood had already congealed."

"Have it your way. It'll all come out at the trial." Denny stood and stretched languorously. "Look, I've got a really smooth single-malt whiskey in my office, why don't we pour ourselves that drink?"

"No," I said. "The case isn't closed. Because Hal Murkland wasn't defrauding Medicaid. And you didn't hire Lisa to go through his computer records. And she wasn't blackmailing him. And he didn't kill her."

Denny turned. Her face pulled into a grin that was not a grin. Slowly, slowly, as if in Hal Murkland's worst nightmare, she meta-morphosed into a demon with large sharp teeth, like a crocodile, and blank eyes. "What do you mean?" she said.

"*You're* the one doing the defrauding, Denny. Not Hal. You're defrauding Blue Cross, big-time. Josh Waterman didn't go to Hal about discrepancies in the billings, he came to you. About *your* billings. So you wouldn't trip yourself up. Unfortunately, Josh wasn't the only one who caught on. Lisa was there by this time, helping Josh with his work. And Lisa went to Hal. Who told her that *you* were blackmailing *him*. Not for his money, for his silence. So *he* wouldn't spill the beans about *your* Blue Cross scam. *Hal* hired Lisa to spy on *you* and get the goods on *you*.

"*You* killed Lisa, Denny," I went on. "You Mickeyed her drink and got her to erase her computer files or to tell you her password so you could erase them, whatever, and then you got her to put back on the scrub shirt she'd used to mop up Hal's blood—and you stabbed her nine fucking times and slashed her like a Pfannenstiehl and threw the doll at her and opened the window so we'd all think you went out the fire escape. And then you waltzed out the front door, leaving Lisa there pressing the doll to her abdomen so she wouldn't eviscerate, you bitch! *You* took all the phone cords. 'Don't tell anyone I'm scamming Blue Cross.' *You—*"

"You're overwrought, Ev, let me get you something—"

"You were the only one who knew *before Lisa died* that Hal's blood was on that shirt, Denny. Because Hal came down the fire escape after he cut his face on the champagne glass and told you a story. Not exactly an entirely true story, as it turned out—they didn't have wild sex and Hal didn't fall off the bed onto the glass—and he wasn't sleeping with her, he only told you that to explain why he was spending so much time with her in case you got suspicious. But a consistent element of the two stories was the shirt Lisa used to mop up the blood."

"Ev, you're making this up. Please! Let me get you a drink. Okay? We'll sit. We'll have a nice drink and calm down."

She went out. I heard drawers and cabinets opening and shutting. My blood began to run cold. I opened the window onto the fire escape.

She came back with a bottle and two shot glasses.

Did she seriously think I would drink anything from her hand?

"Would you sit down, please?" Denny said. She fussed with the whiskey bottle, a very expensive, very old Scotch, Glensomething. "I don't know how you've managed to get the story so upside-down. And you're basing the whole thing on this crazy idea that I'm defrauding Blue Cross. But you must know that all I have to do is make sure my chart notes agree with the billing codes—and if my chart notes agree, you have no evidence." She poured two drinks. I watched her hands very carefully to see how she hocus-pocused the scopolamine, but I didn't catch her at it.

"The hospital charts," I said. "You haven't doctored those. I've treated Edward Zoller and Joshua Waterman. I know what you've done for them in the ER and what you haven't done, and what they need and don't need. And Kennedy Bartlett's daybook. You never did get your hands on that. He wrote down every test you ordered, and every conversation you had with him, and every appointment, every procedure—and he read his Blue Cross bill when it arrived, unlike most patients who never bother. *He* knew the charges on his Blue Cross bill were wrong. He complained to you about it, he complained to Josh Waterman, and he even complained to Lisa. I'm not telling you anything new here, Denny. You knew about the daybook. You were looking for it in his apartment last Saturday when I came in and surprised you and you head-bonked me. I only hope to God that you've got Ken on whopping doses of morphine because it really is his time, and not because you want him out of the way like you wanted Lisa and Hal out of the way. Because you killed Hal, too, goddamn you."

Inside me everything began to rattle the way windows rattle in a strong wind. My voice came out like the thrashing of trees: "Hal and Lisa were going to hit you where it hurts worse than your father ever hit you, and probably even worse than Gray's father hit you when he killed Gray—because now the stakes are higher, it's not just one son, it's an entire practice of sons. Hal could wipe out your medical practice, your expensive car, your antiques, your housekeeper, all with one little phone call to the insurance-fraud people—"

She was holding out the glass of whiskey to me. Her eyes were steady and her lips were slightly parted, as if we were about to kiss.

I knocked the glass out of her hand just as I realized she was standing between me and my fanny pack.

And between me and the open fire-escape window.

"Et tu, Brutè?" she said.

CHAPTER 32

I didn't wait to see if Denny had a knife. She had gone to Lisa's apartment intending to kill Lisa and she had gone to Hal's apartment intending to kill Hal and my working diagnosis was that she intended to kill me, too.

I bolted out of Hal's office and down the hall toward the front door.

I hadn't gone ten paces before Denny turned off the light in Hal's office, plunging the suite into darkness. I put one hand on the wall and the other out in front of me and ran as fast as I dared blindly. I ran smack into the corner of the nurse-receptionist's cubicle, hitting the oak counter square with my lower left rib cage.

The pain was a fireball that tornadoed in my chest and spiraled up into my head, where it burst like the Fourth of July behind my eyes. A wind rushed and roared in my ears, mixed with my breath, panting, groaning. Dimly, I was aware of not wanting to get cornered in the cubicle and of pressing myself against the far wall, willing myself still, to breathe only very slowly in, very slowly out. It hurt to breathe. I wondered how many ribs I'd cracked.

I considered my options. I did not want to head for the door, only to have Denny come up behind me as she came up behind Hal in his bathroom. Hal's blood on the bathroom walls was vivid in my mind. But I did not want to face her head-on if she had a knife I couldn't see in the dark. Hell, I didn't want to face her head-on even if she had a knife I could *see*. She had stabbed the unresisting Lisa nine times in hot blood. She would come at me all the more ferociously because I was resisting.

The sole of her tennis shoe squeaked on the floor.

I realized I could just barely see the outline of her, backlit by the dim glow of the computer screen. About four feet away, inching toward me.

I wondered if she could see me.

Just as I realized that if I could see her, she could probably see me, she leaped into the air like a springing cat. Her arm arched. Something glinted. My left cheekbone stung sharply, then ran wet.

She had a knife.

Reflexively I snapped my knee up. The only kind of self-defense I'd ever learned was self-defense against a man; the techniques relied heavily upon the vulnerability of the male genitalia. I connected with Denny's pubic bone without much effect. Through some primordial instinct I managed to grab her by the wrist and yank down, throwing her off balance. I pivoted and felt her breast against my right shoulder. But I couldn't remember the one judo throw I'd learned back in high school and we got stuck: I in my attempt to throw her, she in her attempt to resist. She couldn't free her knife hand and flailed at the left side of my head with the other, while I threw her against the wall and tried to knock the wind out of her or get her to drop the knife. On my third throw I slammed her against the light switch and the lights came on. I didn't know whether lights were an improvement or not.

By now we were panting and grunting like two tennis combatants at Wimbledon; I grunted as I threw her; she grunted as she slammed against the wall. But I couldn't seem to make myself scream. Screaming would be giving in, showing fear. I didn't want to show fear to Denny. Not now. Not while she still held a knife in her hand and her blood lust rose hot hot hot the way I imagined it had risen when she killed Lisa Chiu.

While I was trying—SLAM—grunt—*grunt*—to figure out what in God's name I could do next—SLAM—grunt—*grunt*—I lost my footing under Denny's weight and misjudged where the wall was and lobbed her instead into the middle of the waiting room, where we fell down in a heap together. She finally let go of the fucking knife. But I didn't know that and rolled the other way and she recovered it and rolled over on me. I got my knee up between us and my foot into the softness of her belly, and I threw her. She connected with the receptionist's desk and dropped the knife again. But the knife was one way and the door the other. I chose the door. Fumbling with the locks, I managed to get out before she got up.

She came after me, of course.

I couldn't punch the button and wait for the elevator. But in the confusion of the moment I found myself running toward the elevator anyway and not toward the stairs—putting Denny between me and the stairs.

I couldn't go back. In front of me was the plastic sheeting over the plywood door to the Storrs Pavilion construction site. The sheeting billowed. The door was open.

Like Alice entering Wonderland, I went through it.

By now I was moving purely on instinct and adrenaline and not thinking much. My senses on alert and my heart swelling with fight or flight, I loped across the concrete floor, my knees flexed, my feet wide, and my body weight low. Overhead, bare lightbulbs in yellow plastic grilles cast an eerie light. I heard water dripping. My sneakered feet pah-pahed through the dust, kicking up small clouds into my eyes and nose. I sneezed.

I heard the crinkling of the plastic sheeting as Denny came through behind me.

Somewhere here there had to be a stairway, but finding it would be like finding it on the moon. Desperately, I scanned the landscape. Partitions for what would become walls were already framed out, and in every direction metal studs stretched from runners in the floor to runners in the ceiling, quickly dazzling the eye with reflected light. Looking at and through this forest of studs I lost my depth vision immediately. The studs seemed to move, like the trees of Birnam Wood toward Dunsinane. Blinking, I skirted a thicket of optical-orange netting haphazardly slung around a shaftway. I couldn't see where or how far to go.

I turned to face Denny. She advanced upon me, her knife held low against her thigh, pointing at the floor. It was a sizable kitchen knife, perhaps seven inches. Our eyes locked. We didn't speak. Reflexively, I put my fingers to my face where she had cut me earlier. My cheek and neck were slick. I wiped my hand across my shirt, and wondered if I could manage one of those judo kicks where you pivoted sideways on one foot and shot the other into your opponent's solar plexus. Grabbing one of the metal studs for balance, I tried it.

I missed.

Denny easily evaded my flying foot and lunged at me before I could get it back under me. I went crashing down, with her on top of me. I didn't know where the knife was. I didn't know whether she'd stabbed me or not. She had me by the hair and was trying to hold my head still. I got an arm free and socked her in the mouth, which was totally ineffective. I socked her again. Why had no one ever made sure that I learned how to hit like a boy? I realized I had Denny by the wrist of her knife hand and the knife wasn't in it. She had lost the knife. She began to pound my head on the floor.

"I need help here now!" I yelled. "POLICE!"

She punched me in the mouth, then up the side of the head.

Her fist came away red with my blood. As I struggled to get my feet back under me, crab out from under her, she struggled to get her feet back under her to stand. She was up on one knee, reaching out of my field of vision—

Where was the knife? I began to panic. I got my foot into her belly again as I had in her office—the one move I remembered from wrestling in the backyard with that kid next door who was on the freshman team—I got my foot into Denny's soft belly and I heaved with a cosmic explosion of adrenaline and fear and watched amazed as my past flashed before my eyes just as I had heard it would before death, my entire life in the twinkling of an eye, including my father standing aghast on the back porch as I wrestled with that boy, my father thinking God only knew what as we squirmed in the dirt together. I saw Denny fly through the air like the Wicked Witch of the West being sucked into oblivion. Over the optical-orange netting—

The thud when it came was terrible. Then a second, and a third. I was on my feet, shaking. I peered over the netting into the shaftway—someone would tell me later it was the shaftway for the HVAC ducts—and stared down into the well of my soul.

She lay at the bottom, her back arched far beyond any humanly possible position. Her head seemed to have moved laterally onto her left shoulder. Her hair fanned out on the concrete floor and blood fanned out around it.

I remember thinking with clinical detachment: She hit something on her way down.

My knees gave way, and I slid to the floor.

Brian Linhardt arrived. He had heard me yell from the street, and coming up the stairs he had seen me throw Denny down the shaft. He sank down next to me and said, "Christ, you would wear black—how am I supposed to see if you're stabbed?" and "You wet anywhere?" Pulling my shirt out of the waistband of my jogging pants, he ran his hands up under it, over my breasts and chest and abdomen, checking for blood. He did the same with my back, sliding both hands over my shoulder blades and rib cage, down around the sides into the small of my back. Dazed, I thought, Isn't this how the whole thing started? Somebody pulling my shirt out of my pants, over my head?

"Looks like all you're cut is on your face," Brian said. Rummaging in his old Army cartridge bag, he produced some tape and a package of four-by-fours and doctored my face.

I heard voices below, among them Detective Ost's.

"Anything you want to tell me before the cops get here?" he asked.

I shook my head.

"This justifiable? You feared for your life? Or we're going to do a song and dance?"

I looked at him.

"Just asking," he said.

The voices came closer.

I had no thought. No emotion. Just a void where the adrenaline had been. I was still tachycardic and sucking down air like a marathon runner after the finish line, aware of a sharp stabbing pain in my ribs where I'd run into the nurse-receptionist's counter in Denny's and Hal's office suite.

I was alive, alive, alive.

And Denny was dead, dead, dead.

"You okay?" Brian asked.

"I feel like Eve after she ate the apple in the Garden of Eden," I said. "I could do without knowing what it's like to kill someone."

"Yeah," he said. "I know."

CHAPTER
33

"**EVEN** before the Prom Date From Hell, Denny's life was not what you'd call good," Phil said. "Some of these dad-and-mom-drinking households are pretty chaotic."

"Yeah," said Brian. "Grew up in one myself."

"I'm sorry to hear that," said Phil.

Their voices ebbed and flowed like the tide. Lulled by the motion of the car and the Bloody Mary I'd drunk with my eggs Benedict at breakfast, I nodded in and out, lolling in my seat belt as if it were a hammock.

It was a little after ten Sunday morning. Brian was driving. I was in the front seat with him; Phil was in the back. The three of us were going out to Long Island to spend the day at the estate of a friend of a friend of Brian's.

To get out of ourselves for a bit.

Brian's idea.

I was already out of myself, wondering how to get back in.

But since no activity on earth seemed an appropriate follow-up to what had happened to me the night before, I tried to get in the spirit of things. I guessed I could go to Long Island. Sit by a pool, stare off into space. The idea of it seemed existential, straight out of Jean-Paul Sartre. I was looking for a mode, any mode, to replace the mode I was in. I could do existential. "What does that mean exactly, 'friend of a friend'?" I asked Brian. "Are you talking about a grande dame who supports the local boys' club, or a Doris Duke type buying helicopters for Iran-contra?"

Brian had smiled one of his maddening secret smiles.

But by now I wouldn't care who she was. I was glad to get out of the city. Away from Denny's dead body lying at the bottom of the heating-ventilation shaftway, away from the cops and their thousands of questions about how "the deceased" came to lie there, away from Hal's death and Lisa's death and Theresa Kahr's death. They were dead, dead, dead and I was alive, alive, alive and I wanted to get away, away, away.

"Denny's father beat her mother?" Brian wanted to know.

He and Phil had fallen into an ease of talking about Denny that was beyond me. Intellectual, divorced from emotion. I imagined their talk punctuated by the ululation of a hundred bereaved Arab women, or fanned by the white garments of rows upon rows of marching Hiroshima victims. Then again, perhaps restraint was the thing. I couldn't decide.

"Beat her black and blue, from what I understand," said Phil. "For kids who grow up in an environment like that, control becomes a paramount issue. Surprise is a problem, too—Denny didn't take surprise too well, or having the tables turned on her. My guess is, she was a woman who did very well with good external scaffolding; she relied on her job to give her external structure because she didn't have good internal structure."

"Yeah, me too," said Brian.

"You? Brian, I'd say you have very good internal structure."

"After the Army, sure. Why d'you think I joined up?"

My mind jumped from the Army to cops to Mick Healy. While the plastic surgeon had been suturing my fabulous new dueling scar—I felt like a Prussian with his *Schmiss*—I'd had to lie still under the drapes. Free-association time. I'd imagined Mick bursting into the ER's OR One and bending over me as he had bent over Theresa Kahr. Blanching when he saw her. Because he knew by looking at her that here was one more victim of the Babydoll Killer. And Mick had had his suspicions even then. Suspicions confirmed by the fact that Donal had broken glass in his knees, and Theresa had glass in her ass. Further confirmed by Lisa's confiding *her* suspicions to Mick that Donal was Babydoll.

All of which occurred before Mick and I shared our wild embrace in the well of the brownstone on 113th Street, two doors down from the Holy Sisters.

Yet Mick failed to warn me that I might be in danger, even after I saw Donal in his Superman shirt at the corner of Eighty-ninth Street. I now believed that Donal had just been passing by, out for an afternoon jog, when he saw me walking the dog and stopped. But that wasn't what it looked like then. At that early stage of the game, it looked as if Lisa had been killed by Babydoll. Who might come after me next.

Still, Mick failed to warn me. Even when I confronted him with my worry that a man in a Superman shirt might be following me. (He knew damn well that shirt was Donal's.) Even though Mick was in SoHo waiting on the corner outside T Salon to meet his sister Bernadette, the homicide detective, to confess his suspicions—and Lisa's—to *her*.

Maybe I was being too hard on Mick.

But I didn't think so.

"Conscience was not Denny's long suit," Phil was saying when I tuned back in.

I opened my eyes. "Yeah, she didn't think she was doing anything wrong scamming Blue Cross," I said. "If anything, the scam was the glue that gave her structure and definition in life. She got to say 'fuck you' to the establishment and get away with it. It doesn't make any difference whether it was the Army or Blue Cross, to her it was still the fucking establishment—and the establishment owed her for her miserable childhood and her miserable Army father and that miserable joyless fuck Whatever-his-name-was, the colonel's son who knocked her up. Hal and Lisa threatened her little world, and she fragmented. She just went to pieces."

"You see this kind of thing a lot with borderline organized personality disorder," Phil chimed in.

"She thought I betrayed her," I went on. "Like Hal betrayed her, and Lisa betrayed her. The last thing she said to me was, 'Et tu, Brutè?' "

"Yeah, she had quick splits," said Phil. "She went from love to hate immediately and instantaneously. That's what you see with these borderline types; they can't fuse good and bad in the same person—someone is pure good or they're pure evil. If someone very good becomes bad, that person has to be destroyed."

"Denny had no choice," I said. "She *had* to kill Lisa, and then she *had* to kill Hal. And that's the irony here: there was no gray for Denny even though she thought there was, and named her son Gray to prove it."

Brian laughed. "That's an *awful* lot of psychobabble you guys are turning out there," he said, throwing a look at me and another over his shoulder at Phil in the back seat. "The broad was damaged goods. Her paranoia got to her and she struck out at the enemy. So maybe she imagined the enemy—that's what you do when you're paranoid, right? Important thing is, she got what was coming to her. There is a God. Case closed. Or—excuse me—clo*sure.* That the right shrink word?"

"Indeed," said Phil. We laughed, too.

I felt myself suddenly enveloped in a haze of affection and well-being. It dawned on me that I *liked* psychobabbling with Phil. His psychobabble was the caviar of gossip, the champagne of concern for one's fellow being, the foie gras of efforts to understand what made people tick—so you could help them. Phil was never mean-spirited. His commentary became relentless at times, occasionally pedantic . . . But I was beginning to realize how interesting I found the people I knew, and how well Phil articulated the hows and wherefores of why they were interesting. How sharp his mind was, and yet how well he knew his own emotions and the emotions of those around him.

And how able a companion he was, now that I was faced with the task of mourning all these dead people. Because that was my real task at hand: mourning. Coming to grips with people who were dead, dead, dead, while I was alive, alive, alive. And coming to grips with myself coming to grips with them.

"Ev, you never did tell me your computer theory," Brian said. "About Lisa." He glanced sideways at me. "If you're awake."

"I'm awake." I sat up and explained how Denny had enlisted the aid of Joshua Waterman to "fix" Hal's computer records so that they showed Hal was scamming Medicaid, while she fixed her own records to show that she was *not* scamming Blue Cross. How Joshua, whose own mother had disowned him for being gay and having AIDS, loved Denny like a new replacement mother—just as Denny loved him like a replacement son. How Joshua was utterly dependent on her for his job and his health insurance. How Hal, who suddenly had a lot of money, hired Lisa, who suddenly needed a lot of money for her medical school bills, to help Hal put together the evidence against Denny that he would need to go to the authorities. How Denny received Dr. Guderian's session notes in the mail and held them over Hal's head. How Lisa encouraged Hal to rifle Denny's office for the envelope containing them and hand it over to Lisa for safekeeping. How Lisa stashed the computer discs and Guderian's notes in her locker at her gym. ("I *knew* there was a computer theory here somewhere!" Brian exclaimed.) And how Denny, seeing Lisa as the *agent provocateur* in this scenario, Mickeyed Lisa's drink with an ampule of scopolamine and a mixture of sedatives, got her to erase all her computer files—or to tell Denny her password so Denny could erase them, whichever.

How Denise Aubuchon, M.D., brutally stabbed Lisa Chiu nine times, miming a Pfannenstiehl incision. And then came up behind Hal Murkland in the bathroom and slit his throat.

"But how did you figure it out?" Brian wanted to know.

It all seemed so complicated. Yet at the same time, so *un*complicated: child's play, really.

"Well," I said slowly, "I was mulling over in my mind something Hal told me Lisa had said after an argument with Theresa Kahr, that Lisa had no patience with people who think the end justifies the means. That rang true with me. It really wasn't in character for Lisa to blackmail Hal. So that was one thing. The second thing was serendipitous: Someone quoted Senator Baker asking at the Watergate hearings, 'What did he know and when did he know it?' and a wake-up alarm went off in my head. I realized that Denny was the only person other than Hal who knew *before Lisa died* that Lisa used her scrub shirt to mop up the blood when Hal cut himself. Because Hal himself told Denny. Lisa was wearing that shirt when Rita Firenze found her. Obviously, Lisa didn't put the bloodied shirt back on herself; someone must have put it on her. So the question became, Why would Denny want to kill Lisa and make it look like Hal had done it?

"Meanwhile, Denny's telling me that Hal is scamming Medicaid. And it just doesn't ring true. Hal's like Lisa, he doesn't have any patience for people who think the end justifies the means.

"So I began to weigh all the things that Hal had said against all the things Denny had said. Hal said he had tried to kiss Lisa, and that Lisa had hit him to get his attention, and that he was holding a champagne glass and it smashed against his face, and that's how he cut himself. Denny told me that Hal had told her that he and Lisa were in bed together, and that he fell out of bed onto the glass. I decided I believed what Hal had told me, and that Hal was lying to Denny to hide something. The first thing Hal said to me after Lisa died was, 'I had a glass in my hand and she slapped me.' The second thing he said was, 'The cops are going to think I killed her.' The third thing he said was, 'Do me a favor—don't listen to Denny.' And the *fourth* thing he said was, 'What do you know about computers?'

"So I reviewed in my mind what Denny had said about the computer: that Hal couldn't learn it, that Josh was entering the data, that Lisa was helping Josh, and that Denny had hired Lisa to spy on Hal. And I thought, what's wrong with this picture? Maybe *Hal* hired Lisa to spy on *Denny*. Because if Hal wasn't sleeping with Lisa, what was he doing spending so much time with her? And why conceal that from Denny by saying he and Lisa were having wild sex? Which brings us back to the champagne glass. The champagne was not spilled in the bedroom, the champagne was spilled in the study. Which brings us back to the computer. What were they celebrating?

"I think Lisa had copied both Hal's and Denny's patient records onto disc earlier in the summer, when Denny's records still showed the evidence of insurance fraud. Lisa downloaded the discs into her own computer and stashed the discs with Hal's records in her locker at the gym. She probably had the discs with Denny's records in her apartment somewhere—maybe because she was still working with them—and Denny later took those when she trashed the place. But the evening before Lisa died, I think Lisa was showing Hal the extent of Denny's having altered Hal's patient records—which was when Tony Firenze overheard Hal shouting, 'Jesus fucking Christ, that bitch, I'll fucking kill her!' Then Lisa showed Hal *Denny's* records, which showed the evidence of insurance fraud and confirmed Hal's suspicions about Denny. And even if Denny had cleaned up her patient records on her computer in the office, Hal and Lisa still had the evidence of her original records. So they uncorked the champagne.

"Meanwhile Denny was downstairs, catching up on her chartwork. Denny, unlike Hal, had mastered the computer. Maybe she noticed that someone other than herself had opened certain files. Joshua Waterman hadn't been to work that week; he was out in New Jersey, recuperating from his PCP pneumonia, then in the hospital with a collapsed lung. Lisa must have known Denny's computer password, although it wasn't hard to figure out—Denny used her dead son's name, just like the guy in *Ferris Bueller's WarGames*. So there's Denny looking at her computer screen, having her suspicions confirmed: someone's been in her files, and in comes Hal, with a story about drinking champagne with Lisa. I think that maybe it was the champagne that tipped Denny off. The question with champagne is always, What are people celebrating? So Denny went upstairs to confront Lisa. But Denny liked to be in control, and she liked to hedge her bets, and she took along a little scopolamine. It's not hard to come by—you just slip into the anesthesia workroom and nick some—scopolamine's not a controlled substance. Denny Mickeyed Lisa's drink, and then, when she found out the extent to which Lisa had betrayed her, she killed Lisa *irato*."

"How do you think Denny duped Lisa into letting her in?" Brian wanted to know, looking in the rearview mirror.

"I think she called her on Hal's phone—the cops have phone records showing that a call was made from Hal's phone at four-thirty A.M. the day Lisa died. All Denny would have to say is, 'Hal's in a really bad way' or 'I'm worried about Hal—I need to talk to you.' Lisa was probably absolutely mortified that Hal's glass broke and cut his face when she hit him, and Denny could have played on that."

"I didn't think they used scopolamine anymore, except as an anti-emetic for chemotherapy," Phil said.

"It's good for a bad trauma, when the surgeons have to proceed but the blood pressure's tenuous and anesthesia would kill the patient," Brian said. "Scopolamine doesn't whack out the circulation so much. Ev's right—they keep it in the anesthesia workroom. I think they also keep it on hand in the CCU. It wouldn't be hard to nick some."

"Maybe Edward Zoller brought her some of the real stuff from Bogotá," I suggested. "What's it called, *burundanga?* He certainly could have heard about it on one of his architectural projects down in South America, and told Denny about it; he's a relentless raconteur."

"Maybe," said Brian. "But all you really need is the scopolamine mixed with sedatives."

We were well over the Triboro Bridge by the time I started

explaining, and by the time I finished we were off the expressway, driving through a small clapboard town of storybook Yankee America. The kind of town everyone seems to remember with great sentiment from his or her childhood—whether he or she grew up in any such town or not. We passed a hardware store that evoked my own childhood in New Jersey. And we passed a number of antique shops that would have evoked for Denny the childhood she never had.

We began to catch glimpses of grand houses behind tall shrubs. "A lot of Roosevelts still live out here," said Brian, turning onto a road that ran along the bay. "The Tiffany estate used to be around here somewhere, too. It's broken up now." He slowed and made a right turn into a driveway at the end of a fieldstone wall. "Here we are."

The driveway curved around a pond with ducks. On the left, a white house of many wings sprawled at odd angles, shaded by a willow and huge linden trees. On the right, a lawn sloped across several acres to two outbuildings joined by an archway. "That used to be a stables and carriage house," said Brian, following my gaze. "Some parts of the house go back to the seventeenth century. And that house over there is where the groundsman lives."

"Come here a lot, do you?" Phil commented from the back seat. "You sure this isn't Doris Duke's?"

Brian smiled and drove around a linden tree behind the main house, pulling into a parking area in front of a roofed-over patio with rooms on either side. "Pool house," he announced. "Ladies' dressing room on the left, gents' on the right."

I climbed out of the car. The day was bright and hot and dry. The pool house was modest and utilitarian, built in an era before pool houses qualified for *House Beautiful* stardom. I wavered between feeling guilty for being there, and feeling as if I deserved to be there after all I'd been through. I climbed the stairs, walked across the patio, and sat down in an old-fashioned wrought-iron chair with flowered plastic cushions. The men unloaded our picnic lunch into a refrigerator in the tiny kitchen and went into their dressing room to change into bathing suits.

I looked at the pool.

Very nice.

My face ached. I put a hand to my cheek, fluttering my fingers over the gauze dressing. I heard Denny's voice in my head, talking about mourning Gray: *I was in utter, total shock for about two months, but I had those injuries. I've often thought, looking back, that I was glad for the physical pain, because it gave me some kind of pain to have instead of the emotional pain.*

I wondered whether, if she'd faced the emotional pain at the time, later in life she'd have found it so necessary to kill two people.

I wondered how you faced emotional pain.

I was still waiting to *have* the pain. I felt stunned. Exhausted. Disenfranchised, floating between reality and unreality. Guilty that I was here and Lisa wasn't. I imagined her sitting across from me in her Lamy Jackie-O sunglasses, untying her Hermès scarf, tossing her hair free. I imagined Hal, wearing his favorite shorts, his love handles hanging over his waistband, doing something nerdy like looking in the bushes for crickets or catching ladybugs.

I recalled a quote from a seventeenth-century poet, *I know death hath ten thousand several doors / For men to take their exits.*

I remembered a friend, a rabbi, who had lost his wife. He started going to a self-help group for widows and widowers. People flocked around him, evidently in the hope that a rabbi who was bereaved might have special insights to impart. He said that being a rabbi had been of no help to him whatsoever in trying to rebuild his devastated inner self. Although being religious helped. "I'm just like you," he said.

I thought about C. S. Lewis's book on bereavement, and decided I would reread it.

In the long run, however, what everyone said was true: We all must face death alone.

Our own death and everyone else's.

EPILOGUE

HAL Murkland was buried with full Episcopal fanfare out of St. Michael's Church on a blindingly sunny but cool August morning. Carol Murkland sat in the front pew with Joshua Waterman, who was two days out of the hospital. Carol told Phil at the reception afterward that she was taking over Waterman's Blue Cross policy, and that they planned to rent a two-bedroom apartment together now that Carol had to move out of the doctors' residence. "It's what Hal would have wanted," she said. "Me too." Graciously, and with an inner strength that astonished everyone she knew, Carol also organized a Roman Catholic service for Denny Aubuchon. "It's what Hal would have wanted," she said again. "Me too." The service was not a funeral per se—the coffin was not present in the church, and certain parts of the service were different—because Denny had been a murderer. It was less well-attended than Hal's.

Kennedy Bartlett, after slipping into a coma, died at the end of the week. I wrote his obituary, which was published in the *New York Times*. I also hosted a fabulously catered "going-away" party, as he had wished. Among the big-name celebrities who attended was the anchorman of a network evening news. He had prepared an obituary videotape just like you might see on "Live at Five," and he set up Ken's small TV and showed it. Afterward, people got up and reminisced about Ken the way they do at some Quaker funerals. The stories got funnier and funnier as the guests became bolder and bolder in their willingness to recall Ken's wonderful and warm-hearted outrageousness. When people had laughed so hard that they could barely catch their breaths, I opened Ken's photo files—and he had many, many publicity photos, 8-by-10 glossies from his long, distinguished career—and invited everyone to take whatever photos they liked. The guests stayed long into the evening, drinking the wine and looking at the photos.

I liked Ken's "funeral" better than Hal's.

Jeff Cantor came back thin and tanned from Bosnia and his stint with Doctors Without Borders. He clutched Fat Face to his bosom as if the cat were his last living relative. Maxie, the dog, went to live upstate with the gay couple who had promised to take him when Ken died. I wondered whether to get a dog and cat of my own; the apartment seemed cavernous without them.

Phil, deciding that he and I could use a little mom-care, hired Denny Aubuchon's housekeeper to make us meals for four weeks.

Brian Linhardt finally gave up applying to medical schools. Instead, he sent in an application to the University's nursing school, where he was accepted with a full scholarship.

Guy Shehadeh—after a firm talking-to by Chris Cabot, and after receiving sanctions for unprofessional behavior—transferred into a family-practice residency. He also underwent evaluation by the psychiatric service and began a course of Prozac.

Mick Healy became bitter. His sister Bernadette, the homicide detective, decided she could do with a full course of Al-Anon and psychotherapy. Eventually Mick decided he could probably do with a full course of Al-Anon and psychotherapy, too. He became less bitter. I still thought sometimes about that extraordinary grope-fest we had together in the well of the brownstone. But my desire for him tapered off.

I called Rabbi Steven Reinish, my friend who had lost his wife, to see how he was. He said he was thinking about remarrying. A young widow in his congregation with two small sons, aged six and seven.

"Everything you've ever heard is true," he said. "Keep busy. Don't sit home alone. Time heals all wounds. Do something nice for someone who's worse off than you.

"None of it helps." He laughed wryly. "But it's all *true*. One day you wake up, and you realize you feel a little more hopeful than you felt yesterday."

I looked forward to that day.

ACKNOWLEDGMENTS

I acknowledge with gratitude the help of the following people: Bernadette Bernon; Elisabeth Abramowicz, M.D.; Jeffrey J. Arliss, M.D.; Lisa Baron, M.D.; Gordon Cotler; E.W. Count; Joanne Dobson; Sumner Gochberg, M.D.; James A. Hayes; Marilyn Henderson; Sharon M. Henry, M.D.; Jon Herbiter, EMT-D; Anthony Hume; Eleanor Hyde; Phil Kalmus; Susan Anderson Kline, M.D., Executive Vice Dean for Academic Affairs and Vice Provost for University Student Affairs, New York Medical College; Matthew Kreps; Sharon Lewin, M.D.; Detective Alfred J. Marini, Secretary, Detectives Endowment Association, Police Department, City of New York; Michael Morris, M.D.; Mary E. O'Brien, M.D.; Diane Ouding; Bernice Selden, Timothy Sheard, R.N., veteran critical care nurse and freelance writer; James Siy, M.D.; Richard K. Stone, M.D., Senior Associate Dean, New York Medical College; Theo Theoharus; Bill Vanderpool, Special Agent (retired), Federal Bureau of Investigation; and Diane Warren, R.N., M.S.N., critical care instructor and medical consultant, Fairfield, Connecticut. Any mistakes are mine, not theirs.